Praise for
The First Ladies

"This book will expand your perspective and keep you reading late into the night."

—Dolen Perkins-Valdez, *New York Times* bestselling author of *Take My Hand*

"It's an utter joy to watch civil rights activist Mary McLeod Bethune and First Lady Eleanor Roosevelt forge a partnership that changed America: plotting over teacups, negotiating tricky conversations about race and privilege, celebrating their triumphs, and never giving up. *The First Ladies* is a wonder!"

—Kate Quinn, *New York Times* bestselling author of *The Diamond Eye*

"This timely story encapsulates the unmovable power of when two strong minds come together in the name of justice and equality."

—Sadeqa Johnson, *New York Times* bestselling author of *The House of Eve*

"Explores the extraordinary legacies of these two historical figures, while also bringing us into their personal lives and their deep friendship. Benedict and Murray bring their knack for historical fiction to a story of the women's unlikely alliance and the ways their bond and efforts forged the beginnings of the modern civil rights movement."

—*Entertainment Weekly*

"A powerful and unforgettable story of female strength and the triumph of the human spirit."

—Pam Jenoff, *New York Times* bestselling author of *Code Name Sapphire*

"I've never read a more inspiring story about women raising up other women and working together to try to change the world. A tour de force."

—Natasha Lester, *New York Times* bestselling author of *The Paris Orphan*

"Marie Benedict and Victoria Christopher Murray herald the beauty and passion of a celebrated friendship across color lines and the complications of history."

—Vanessa Riley, award-winning author of *Queen of Exiles*

"This rich, compelling portrait of a friendship between two quiet revolutionaries overturns our ideas about class, race, and gender in the twentieth century. . . . A magnificently moving story, both intimate and monumental, that ultimately delivers a message of reconciliation and hope."

—Beatriz Williams, *New York Times* bestselling author of
The Beach at Summerly

"A compelling and captivating story. . . . I was moved by not only what they were able to accomplish together but the resilience displayed by both women. But more than anything, it was their friendship that kept me captivated until the very last page. I can't remember the last time I was so inspired by a novel!"

—ReShonda Tate Billingsley, author of *Miss Pearly's Girls*

"The novel really shines in the behind-the-scenes moments when the women support each other during personal struggles with marital infidelity, illness, and loss. This impeccably researched, relevant novel is a must-read and destined to be a book club favorite."

—*Booklist* (starred review)

"Benedict and Murray deliver a dazzling narrative. . . . A potent tale of two crusading women's accomplishments." —*Publishers Weekly*

Praise for
The Personal Librarian

"Historical fiction at its best. . . . *The Personal Librarian* spins a complex tale of deceit and allegiance as told through books."
—*Good Morning America*

"Benedict, who is white, and Murray, who is African American, do a good job of depicting the tightrope Belle walked, and her internal conflict from both sides—wanting to adhere to her mother's wishes and move through the world as white even as she longed to show her father she was proud of her race. Like Belle and her employer, Benedict and Murray had almost instant chemistry, and as a result, the book's narrative is seamless. . . . I became hooked."
—NPR

"A marvel of a story. This unflinching look at one woman's meteoric rise through New York's high society is enthralling, lyrical, and rife with danger. Belle's painful secret and her inspiring courage will capture—and break—your heart. Serious kudos to Benedict and Murray for bringing this true story to life."
—Fiona Davis, *New York Times* bestselling author of
The Lions of Fifth Avenue

"*The Personal Librarian* illuminates the extraordinary life of an exceptional, intelligent woman who had to make the impossible choice to live as an imposter or sacrifice everything she'd achieved and deserved. That Belle denied her true identity in order to protect herself and her family from racial persecution speaks not only to her time but also to ours, a hundred years later. All that glitters is not gold. This is a compelling and important story."
—Therese Anne Fowler, *New York Times* bestselling author of
A Good Neighborhood

"As richly depicted as the lush world of art and literature Belle da Costa Greene presided over . . . an immersive, sweeping delight as well as an intimate, moving, and powerful portrait of Belle's personal and professional life. An unforgettable, captivating read!"

—Chanel Cleeton, *New York Times* bestselling author of
Our Last Days in Barcelona

"Meticulously researched, heartbreaking, and inspiring . . . a fascinating look at a very public figure fighting a deep private battle, whose story still resonates with surprising power and immediacy today."

—Kristin Harmel, *New York Times* bestselling author of
The Book of Lost Names

"An intimate and extraordinary conversation with the past. . . . As Belle da Costa Greene achieves her dreams by forsaking an identity, we wonder if we would or could do the same to irrevocably alter the literary world and our family. A novel abundant with culture, art, literature, and romance—the beauty and recklessness of love are revealed with astonishing clarity."

—Patti Callahan, *New York Times* bestselling author of
Surviving Savannah

"Upon starting this novel, be prepared to do nothing else until you've reached its poignant, reflective end. Through brilliant pacing and with painstaking care, Benedict and Murray paint a vibrant portrait of a woman whose accomplishments, relationships, and secretive history were as complex and intriguing as the collections she helped curate. . . . A timely, provocative read perfect for book clubs. I loved it."

—Kristina McMorris, *New York Times* bestselling author of
Sold on a Monday

The

FIRST
LADIES

Titles by
Marie Benedict and Victoria Christopher Murray

The Personal Librarian
The First Ladies

The

FIRST
LADIES

❧

Marie Benedict
AND
Victoria Christopher Murray

BERKLEY
NEW YORK

BERKLEY
An imprint of Penguin Random House LLC
penguinrandomhouse.com

BERKLEY and the BERKLEY & B colophon are registered trademarks of
Penguin Random House LLC.

ISBN: 9780593440292

The Library of Congress has cataloged the Berkley Hardcover edition of this book as follows:

Names: Benedict, Marie, author. | Murray, Victoria Christopher, author.
Title: The first ladies / Marie Benedict and Victoria Christopher Murray.
Description: New York: Berkley, [2023]
Identifiers: LCCN 2022058264 (print) | LCCN 2022058265 (ebook) |
ISBN 9780593440285 (hardcover) | ISBN 9780593440308 (ebook)
Subjects: LCSH: Roosevelt, Eleanor, 1884-1962—Fiction. | Bethune, Mary McLeod,
1875-1955—Fiction. | Presidents' spouses—Fiction. |
Civil rights workers—Fiction. | African Americans—Fiction. |
LCGFT: Biographical fiction. | Historical fiction. | Novels.
Classification: LCC PS3620.E75 F57 2023 (print) | LCC PS3620.E75 (ebook) |
DDC 813/.6—dc23/eng/20221220
LC record available at https://lccn.loc.gov/2022058264
LC ebook record available at https://lccn.loc.gov/2022058265

Berkley hardcover edition / June 2023
Berkley trade paperback edition / June 2024

Printed in the United States of America
1st Printing

Book design by Nancy Resnick
Title page photograph by Mary Ann Madsen/Shutterstock.com

For Mary and Eleanor,
First Ladies and first friends . . .

The

FIRST
LADIES

CHAPTER 1

MARY

New York, New York
October 14, 1927

Nearly fifty blocks whir past my cab window as I ride through the upper reaches of Manhattan from the Hotel Olga in Harlem. Traveling toward the Upper East Side, I feel as though, somewhere, I've crossed an invisible line. The shades of complexions fade from colored to white. Not that it matters to me. I have never been hindered by the views and prejudices of others, not even the Ku Klux Klan.

My cab stops in front of a limestone town house amidst the expanse of brick facades on East 65th Street. I exit the cab, then pause before I mount the few steps to the front door. The number 47 is on the left of the wrought iron gate, while 49 is on the opposite side. Yet there is only a single entrance.

Odd, I think, *and a bit confusing to have one door for two residences.* I certainly hope Mrs. Roosevelt gets along with her neighbor.

The door is opened by a young woman wearing a white-collared black uniform. For a moment, she stands still, her eyebrows raised and her blue eyes wide with astonishment.

"I am Mrs. Mary McLeod Bethune, here for the luncheon," I say.

She recovers. "Yes, ma'am." As she gestures for me to enter, her face becomes, once again, the expressionless servant's mask.

Chatter and laughter float in from down the hall. "Ma'am?" she asks, reaching for my coat.

I shrug out of my black fur-collar wrap and pat my hat to make sure it hasn't tilted. The young lady leads me down a hallway darkened by mahogany panels. As we approach the sound of voices, I listen to the medley of tones, searching for the accents and intonations that will give me clues to who these women are and where they're from.

When I step into the drawing room, the gleaming chandeliers, the velvet burgundy drapes framing the large windows, the deep chintz sofas, and a crackling fire offer a warmer welcome than the women inside. Unfazed, I move to the walls covered with bookcases. Glorious leather-bound volumes line the shelves. How much my curious students at Bethune-Cookman College would enjoy and appreciate a library like this.

If I didn't know this was a luncheon for women leaders of national clubs and organizations—some of the most powerful women in America—I'd think I'd stepped into a fashion show. Each woman wears a different variation of the latest styles; there are skirts and sweater sets and drop-waist dresses, and all, of course, are wearing silk stockings. Quite the contrast with my ankle-length navy dress trimmed in velvet.

I peruse the bookshelves, noticing that the conversation dips to a whisper whenever I skirt close to a group. As I draw near women I recognize from my position as president of the National Association of Colored Women's Clubs, I smile and nod, but I only occasionally receive a nod in return. Most often, my acknowledgments are met with steel-cold glances. Funny how the same women who talk with me about the advancement of women in a formal meeting space open to whites and Negroes pretend not to even see me in this social setting. Instead of allowing this to smart, I read the titles as I survey the books: a biography here, a novel there, a historical study in between.

"Ah, Dr. Bethune. What a pleasure."

My smile widens as the officious-looking Mrs. Sara Delano Roosevelt approaches, surprisingly light on her feet for her seventy-something years. "It is good to see you again, Mrs. Roosevelt."

"You as well, Dr. Bethune."

I hesitate, then say, "I hope you'll pardon me for clarifying." I pause, and Mrs. Roosevelt's expression hardens; she's not used to correction. "I prefer to be called Mrs. Bethune. Although I am grateful for the recognition, my doctorate degree is an honorary one. I prefer that honorific be reserved for the men and women who worked hard to earn their doctorates."

"As you wish." Mrs. Roosevelt's voice softens at the benign nature of my clarification. "Please tell me—I understand you've just returned from Europe. How was your trip?"

"It was the most glorious eight weeks."

"Isn't Europe amazing? So full of history." Leaning closer, she whispers, "Did I hear you had an audience with the pope?" The astonishment in her tone matches the amazement I felt standing before Pope Pius XI and receiving his blessing. As we talk about the Vatican, I wonder how news of my travels spread so fast and so wide.

But of course I say nothing about that, and when Mrs. Roosevelt asks the purpose of my trip, I tell her I traveled to Europe with Dr. Wilberforce Williams, the noted public health care expert and writer. "He's a friend from Chicago who's been to Europe several times, and when he arranged a travel group, I knew it was time for me to get an understanding of life across the ocean."

We chat about our experiences in Europe, especially the beautiful gardens. "I love Kew Gardens in London in particular," Mrs. Roosevelt says. "They have the largest botanical collection in the world, you know."

"Ah, yes," I say. "I found it lovely as well, but I preferred the black roses in Switzerland."

"Black roses? Oh my," she says with a bit of surprise. "I don't think

I've ever seen such a rarity." A butler approaches and whispers to her. "It seems I am needed for a matter crucial to the luncheon. Will you excuse me?"

I am left alone once again and find myself facing a cluster of three women. I can imagine their thoughts, wondering what on earth I have in common with the society matron, mother to former assistant secretary of the Navy and failed vice presidential candidate Franklin Roosevelt. He'd been considered a promising politician on the rise until polio felled him six years ago. But I am not here because of him.

The women and I catch one another's gazes, and I smile. When I'm rewarded with cold shoulders once again, I resume my perambulation, letting my favorite walking stick lead the way.

I do wonder which of these women is Mrs. Roosevelt's daughter-in-law. Her name was on the invitation, and she is my host as well. I long to meet Mrs. Eleanor Roosevelt, who has become an advocate for the underrepresented and one of the most prominent women in politics, albeit for the Democratic Party. From what I've read, she, alone among the women in this room, shows promise.

CHAPTER 2

ELEANOR

New York, New York
October 14, 1927

Move, I tell myself. *Walk across the room and offer your hand in welcome.*
But as I watch Mary McLeod Bethune stroll around the drawing
room alone, I don't break away from the conversation I'm having with
the head of the American Association of University Women. The sight
of the only colored woman in the room unnerves me, and I wonder
about the wisdom of including the renowned educator in this national
luncheon of women's club heads. Were my mother-in-law and I naive
to invite her?

Dr. Bethune is a sturdy, rather short, smartly dressed colored
woman. She moves confidently, seemingly impervious to the women's
slights, like that of Mrs. Moreau, a leader of the Daughters of the
American Revolution, who stares at her with mouth agape. Oh, how I
wish my mother-in-law would return. No matter how easily she can
irritate me, this is the sort of situation she would handle with command and grace.

How does Dr. Bethune maintain her poise? Even in the face of this
inhospitable crowd, she doesn't cower. Not like I would have.

You look like a granny, the constant refrain of my mother's words to
me—an insult conveying the ugliness and joylessness she saw in me

as a child—comes back now. Those words haunt me from time to time, returning me momentarily to the darkness of my childhood. My long days were spent alone in the children's attic nursery with only a governess and my brother Hall for company, trotted out at mealtimes for my mother's inspection and inevitable criticism. It didn't matter that I'd been raised in wealthy homes or that I had the elite Dutch ancestry of the Roosevelt and Hall families. I grew up believing that I had to apologize for the unpleasantness of my existence, that somehow, someway, I must find a way to prove my worthiness.

That the hateful insult of "granny" came from the lovely, delicate lips of my beautiful, slender, fair-haired mother, Anna Hall Roosevelt— the leading debutante of her season—made it especially hurtful. I knew I was everything my stunning mother was not. Still, part of me wondered what society would think if they could hear a daughter and wife from two of the most esteemed families in America speak to her child in such a way. Not that I'd ever divulge it; I was better bred, and anyway, I was only eight years old when she spoke those words for the last time. Still, they remain.

Our house steward announces luncheon, snapping me back to the present and jolting me into action. I make my excuses to the woman to whom I've been speaking. I rush after Dr. Bethune, who has started toward the dining room, marching proudly with a walking stick in hand. It is then I feel a firm tug on my arm.

"Mrs. Roosevelt, what were you thinking?" It is Mrs. Moreau, with a gaggle of women in tow. "How can we sit down to lunch with her?"

I flinch. Mrs. Moreau is speaking loudly. It's as if she isn't aware that Dr. Bethune can hear her, or perhaps she just doesn't care.

A woman with a Southern drawl chimes in. "I am astonished that you and your mother-in-law thought it appropriate to include a colored woman."

The six women encircle me. "Ladies," I say, my voice sounding even more high-pitched than usual, "Dr. Bethune is one of the most respected women in her field—in the nation, even—and the head of a national club. Her presence here is perfectly appropriate."

"We know who she is. And she might be respected," that same woman says, her arms now crossed over her chest, "but she's still a Negro, and you cannot possibly expect us to sit down to lunch with her."

Embarrassed and ashamed, but also boiling mad, I cross my arms, too. No more apologizing or explaining. "My mother-in-law and I wanted to bring together women who run clubs across this nation. I expect us to find common ground so that we may bring change and opportunities for women and girls of all kinds."

My eyes take in these supposed leaders. They are a representation of America, old and young, some from the South, others from the North, and I'd assumed their altruism would extend to *all* people. "Ladies, Dr. Bethune is my guest, and we shall treat her as such, in keeping with our missions to support the women of America."

But my tone and intractability do not make them back away.

"Do you know what's not acceptable?" the woman with the Southern drawl practically yells. "Being labeled a woman who loves nig—"

I gasp before she can finish spewing out her venom.

"Dr. Bethune has as much, if not more of, a right as any of you to be here. And I will not allow you to speak about my guest this way." My heart is racing as I pivot away from them.

Following Dr. Bethune, I wonder if I am partly to blame for the behavior of these women. If I had rushed to her side as soon as she entered, would they have dared? Maybe I am as bad as they are for not greeting her upon arrival, for allowing her difference to make me hesitate. Every time I think I've made progress, think I've become more like my dear, forward-thinking friends Marion Dickerman and Nan Cook—the principal of the progressive Todhunter School for girls we recently acquired and the secretary of the Women's Division of the New York State Democratic Committee, respectively—I realize how much further I have to go.

When I enter the dining room, I see that Dr. Bethune sits by herself at the central table, around which the other tables stem like petals of a flower. It is a chair where she can see and be seen. As the other guests move into the room, many join the crowd forming at the periphery with Mrs. Moreau, who refuses to select a chair. With utter aplomb, Dr. Bethune accepts a bowl of soup from a maid. She dips her silver spoon into it as if all this strangeness is nothing. As if all is proceeding as normal, which perhaps it is for her.

I race to her side, sputtering, "It—it is nice to finally meet you, Dr. Bethune. I am Mrs. Franklin Roosevelt. When my mother-in-law mentioned that you'd accepted our invitation, I was thrilled I'd have the opportunity to meet the woman who serves not only as the president of the National Association of Colored Women's Clubs but also as the president of Bethune-Cookman College."

Dr. Bethune carefully places her spoon down next to her bowl and replies, "It's a pleasure, Mrs. Roosevelt, and please call me Mrs. Bethune. I thought you'd forgotten about me."

Her words, spoken bluntly but without acrimony, cut through me. How could I have allowed her to flounder in the face of this disrespect? What I've done is unforgivable, and my cheeks flush with heat.

"I cannot apologize enough for putting you in this awkward position, Mrs. Bethune. My mother-in-law and I did not anticipate that the ladies would behave in this way. After all, these women have pledged to lift up other women in their work," I say, feeling that I must give her a complete explanation for what she's had to endure.

She smiles and asks, "How did you think this luncheon would go?"

I am silent. *What can I say?*

"Mrs. Roosevelt," she continues, the smile never leaving her lips, "you need only to have asked me. While many will sit in a meeting or a conference with me, there aren't too many white folks in this country who care to break bread with colored people, no matter their station in life." She gives a rueful chuckle.

"Mrs. Bethune, I'm so sorry for what you may have heard."

"Oh, there is no *may*. I *definitely* heard them."

"I don't know what to say. I have never—"

"*You* may have never, but I have. Women and men like this pass through my life every day." Her voice holds no anger or even frustration.

"It's unacceptable, and I want to apologize."

"You must never apologize for a sin someone else has committed," she says with a shake of her head.

"I appreciate that, but still, I'm terribly sorry. May I join you for lunch?"

"I was hoping you would," she answers with a nod. "I have a feeling we've got lots to talk about." Then she smiles at me with such warmth that I feel at ease for the first time since the luncheon began.

"I agree," I say, lowering myself onto the chair next to her. "I have been following your impressive career for years, and I'm in awe of your accomplishments."

"And I yours." She tilts her head toward the ladies refusing to sit. "In the meantime, those ladies are missing out on some excellent soup."

CHAPTER 3

MARY

New York, New York
October 14, 1927

We sit for a few minutes in silence, both sipping our soups. I'm not usually one to hold back my thoughts. While I don't speak for the sake of speaking, I employ my words to do that to which I am called: *Open thy mouth, judge righteously, and plead the cause of the poor and needy*, as it says in the book of Proverbs.

But I stay quiet for Mrs. Roosevelt. I know she needs these moments. Confronting racism may be my daily cross to bear, but I suspect the highborn Mrs. Roosevelt has not faced many situations like this. Why would she? The color of her skin has never defined what *she* can and cannot do.

Imagine, I think, *to reach your middle years before you have to address prejudice.* I was only a young girl when I discovered that a happenstance of birth, nothing but skin color, could deem a person a blessing or a burden. It was racism that started me on my life's journey, although I wouldn't have called it racism when I first confronted it as a nine-year-old.

"Now, Mary Jane, I'm just going to drop off this wash," Mama said as we stood before the back door of the main plantation house. She switched the basket of folded clothes onto her other hip. "Then Pearlene and I are gonna sort through what I'm taking back, you hear me?"

"Okay, Mama," I said, shifting from side to side in excitement over entering the Big House.

She wagged her finger at me. "I don't want to have to call you twice the way I did last time."

"You won't have to, Mama," I promised as she gave me one last stern glance before knocking on the back door.

A moment later, Miss Pearlene appeared, dressed in the same black uniform with the overlay white apron that she always wore. Miss Pearlene was as tall as my daddy, and she swallowed Mama up into a hug.

"Come on in here, Patsy." Then she turned to me. "How you doing, Mary Jane?" Before I could answer, she pulled me into a hug, too.

Her arms were as thick as tree trunks, and when she embraced me, I inhaled the scent of the kind of pies she'd baked that morning. Huckleberry. I hoped Miss Pearlene would send a pie home with Mama today.

"Go on up and play with Margaret," Miss Pearlene said. "Just remember, when your Mama calls you—"

"Yes, Miss Pearlene," I interrupted her, already halfway up to Margaret's room. She was the only girl my age whom I knew, and I loved that our names began with the same letter—at least, that's what she told me. But what I adored even more was her playroom filled with toys. Every time I visited, Margaret had something new.

The door to her playroom was wide open, and Margaret sat in the middle surrounded by five or six dolls. She glanced up, smiling. "Mary Jane! I didn't know you were coming with Patsy today," she said, shocking me as she always did when she called Mama by her first name.

Bouncing up, she said, "I'm so glad you're here. Look what Papa brought me from his business trip to England."

I nodded, even though I didn't understand what she meant by "business trip" or "England." Then I froze. In front of me was one of the most beautiful things I'd ever seen.

"Look at my new rocking horse," Margaret announced, lifting her flowered cotton dress just enough to swing one leg over to sit astride the burnished wooden horse with a mane and tail made of silky hair.

"Your daddy got that for you?" I said, in awe.

"Yes, isn't it just grand? I would let you have a ride, but—" Her nose turned up a bit as she glanced at my bare ashen feet, covered with dust from the two-mile walk Mama and I had just taken. "You really must get some shoes, Mary Jane. Being barefoot is so unbecoming, even for children our age."

I froze. Of course I had a pair of shoes, and Margaret knew that. But I had to save them for church.

"You can play with something other than my rocking horse." She waved her hand in dismissal. "Like with my dolls over there."

She pointed to where the dolls were strewn about, but I decided to explore instead. Being in Margaret's room was like being on a treasure hunt.

Lingering in front of the bookshelf, I admired the dozens of volumes that lined the shelves. Except for our family Bible, I'd never held another book. Reaching for the one closest to me, I eased it from the shelf and studied the cover. Letters were printed on the front, although I could make out only a few.

I flipped open the pages. But before I could focus, Margaret hopped off the rocking horse and snatched the book from my hands. "What are you doing?" she shouted.

"I was just—"

"Don't you know you can't read! Only I can read, not you," she yelled, then slid the book back into its place, stomped across the room, and threw herself back on top of her horse. "Never touch my books again!"

She rocked, keeping her eyes straight ahead. In all the years we'd been playing together, Margaret had never spoken to me that way. Her rocking grew faster and harder, almost as if she was trying to gallop away from me.

I backed out of Margaret's room without a goodbye and headed downstairs. When I reached the bottom of the steps, Miss Pearlene said, "I have a surprise for you, Mary Jane." She handed me a pie wrapped in a red-and-white-checkered cloth. "Your favorite."

"Thank you," I whispered, keeping my eyes down so she couldn't see my hurt.

What did Margaret mean? Was she saying that I couldn't read because I had never learned, or was she saying I couldn't read because I was colored? Maybe *that* was the difference between white people and colored people. Maybe *that* was why Margaret had more shoes and more dresses and why she lived in the Big House while I lived in a three-room wooden cabin with Mama, Daddy, Grandma Sophie, and sometimes as many as ten of my sixteen brothers and sisters.

As we made our way down the road toward home, Mama asked, "What's wrong, Mary Jane? I didn't even have to call you down from Margaret's room today."

"Nothing, Mama."

She hummed, as if she didn't believe me. "What happened up there in Margaret's room?"

How did she know? "Nothing happened, Mama." I didn't want to fib, but I was still trying to make sense of Margaret's words. One thing I knew for certain: If seeing me with a book made Margaret that angry, then I needed to learn how to read. Within a year I was in school, because Margaret had taught me the importance of education for colored girls like me.

"Mrs. Bethune," Mrs. Roosevelt says, breaking our silence and pulling me out of my reverie about the day that changed my life.

"Mrs. Bethune," she says again. "I am truly taken aback by their behavior."

I study Mrs. Roosevelt. "Have you never come face-to-face with those views before today?"

"No." She shakes her head. "I have never heard anyone say what those women"—she gestures to them—"said today."

"Well, you learned something. And any day a lesson's learned is a good day."

"I suppose, although I am ashamed the lesson came at your expense." After a pause, she says, "Now, may I ask you something, Mrs. Bethune?"

I smile at the somewhat gangly woman with prominent front teeth, who has softened her appearance with a lovely hat decorated in pink silk flowers. "Of course."

"If you knew those women were going to behave this way, then why did you agree to attend this luncheon?"

Her expression is earnest, and in truth, I'm surprised by her frank question. "I was invited. And even though I anticipated their reaction, their racism isn't my problem. Racism belongs to the people who are racists."

I see a flicker of understanding in her blue eyes. More important to me than her actual ability to comprehend is her desire to try. It is refreshing and hopeful. "Let's talk instead about your reason for bringing us together. I'm guessing there is one?" I ask.

For the first time, Mrs. Roosevelt's face brightens. "Of course, I'm eager to get your thoughts on women's clubs and what we can do for our sex. But what I *really* want to hear about is your school."

Her words do not surprise me. I know she's recently taken over Todhunter, a girls' school with an ambitious curriculum, and teaches there as well. "I'm proud of what we've done at Bethune-Cookman College. We've come a long way from when it was a school for Negro girls. But for all that we've accomplished, there is more work to do."

"What you've done in the last twenty years has been impressive, especially considering how you founded it." She leans forward as if she wants to make sure she's not overheard. "Mrs. Bethune, is it true you started the school with just two dollars?" Her eyes twinkle when she asks, as if we are sharing a grand secret.

I keep my voice low as well. "It was less than that."

"Oh my." She presses her hand against her chest. "Well, that makes what you've done all the more amazing."

I laugh at her expression, a blend of admiration and horror. Then, seriously, I add, "While I've always had to be somewhat concerned about money, my main focus has been on my objectives. That's a lesson I teach my students, particularly the young ladies—to keep their eyes on their goals."

She nods. "So true. And *our* goals should be to educate girls in the practical matters of the world. To offer them something beyond the usual finishing schools that prepare young women to be wives, mothers, and society mavens. That's what we do at Todhunter: We instruct our girls in the arts and provide them with a solid foundation for college, should they want to pursue careers or higher education."

"Exactly. At our school, we offer an academic curriculum alongside the domestic science courses."

"That is the way to raise up young women." Mrs. Roosevelt beams. "I've discovered how much I love teaching." I smile in understanding.

As we enjoy our chicken and scalloped potatoes, we venture away from serious talk and chat about our families—in particular, my six-year-old grandson and her five children, all in different life stages. Our conversation shifts when she surprises me with her knowledge of Roland Hayes, one of my favorite singers.

"I regret I didn't return to New York soon enough to attend one of the concerts he was holding in the city," I say.

"What a coincidence!" she exclaims. "I'd hoped to attend as well but had a prior engagement. You know what this means, Mrs. Bethune?"

I put down my fork and frown. Have I missed something?

"This means the next time Mr. Hayes tours and it suits our schedules, we must go to his concert together."

She must be joking. I cannot think of a single venue where Roland

Hayes might play that would allow both colored and white attendees; he performs at either white-only or colored-only concert halls. But when Eleanor smiles back, I realize she is in earnest—whether out of ignorance or determination, I cannot say. Either way, I am game.

"Well, Mrs. Roosevelt, we must make a date."

CHAPTER 4

ELEANOR

New York, New York
October 14, 1927

I finally spot my mother-in-law. She's circulating around the room, stopping to talk with this club president and that association head, some of whom are settled at tables and some of whom still line the parlor, refusing to sit. In her element, she's dispensing advice with the rat-a-tat of a ticker tape machine and bristling with the sense of purpose that serves her well in this realm but causes so much friction in our family.

Finally, she makes her way to us. "May I join you?" she asks. As if we dare decline. As if there isn't ample space.

"Of course, Mama," I say, although I'm enjoying having this bright, plain-speaking woman to myself.

"I've long admired your success in the educational field, Mrs. Bethune," my mother-in-law says as a housemaid races over to fill her cup with tea.

"Thank you, Mrs. Roosevelt. Education is precisely what your daughter-in-law and I have been discussing. Specifically, the challenges in heading up a school."

"Have you, now?" My mother-in-law shoots me a glance.

I know that expression well. She doesn't hide her dislike of my projects that fall outside the usual roster of women's clubs and Franklin's political work. She found my acquisition of the Todhunter School for girls objectionable, but when I decided to teach history there as well, an unpleasant fracas ensued.

That, however, paled in comparison to the row we had when Marion, Nan, and I created Val-Kill Industries, a workshop dedicated to reproducing early American furniture and providing carpentry training and work for the unemployed. Yet even that was not as irksome to her as my work with the Women's Division of the New York Democratic Party alongside Nan. "Unladylike" was the word she used for my efforts to muster support among the ranks of newly voting women for Democratic candidates. Only Franklin's support of *all* these endeavors stopped her from attempting to outright forbid me.

Her opinions do create a fissure between us, and yet I am still loyal to her. After all, nine years ago, when it mattered most, she supported me, quite against the interest of her precious son.

"Eleanor, whatever is wrong. Are you ill?" she'd cried out in alarm when she discovered me curled up on my bed on that hot spring afternoon. I'd ignored all calls for afternoon tea, and she'd taken it upon herself to find me.

I didn't answer. The past few hours had been spent sobbing, and I was beyond words at that point. My despondency was so deep and profound, I might have even thought I was beyond living.

My typically standoffish mother-in-law lowered herself onto my bed, clearing a space among the scented letters scattered across my hand-embroidered rose bedspread. "What's all this?" she asked, gesturing at the missives scrawled on heavy ivory writing paper.

Again I didn't answer. Nor did I meet her gaze. I simply couldn't.

A rustling of papers was followed by a long period of silence and then the only profanity I'd ever heard her utter. "Damn him and damn these letters," she seethed. "My son is a bloody fool. An affair with Lucy Mercer? How dare he. I'll cut him off without a penny."

I winced at the sound of the name Lucy Mercer. To envision

Franklin in an amorous entanglement with Lucy, the lovely young woman who'd served as my social secretary for two years and whom I considered a friend, was a pain beyond imagining.

"I'm leaving him," I croaked.

My mother-in-law let out the deepest, most sorrowful sigh I'd ever heard. Then she wrapped her arms around my wrecked shell of a body and said, "I understand why you'd want to. I'd feel the same way if Franklin's father had behaved so despicably. And I will not stand in your way if you do. In fact, I'll make certain you and the children are well cared for."

Her ready acquiescence astonished me, because I knew what divorce would mean. Scandal for the family and the evisceration of Franklin's vast political ambitions, for which my mother-in-law would usually do anything. Anything but sanction this misbehavior, it seemed. Although she *must* have been horrified at the other ramifications of divorce—the gossip, the division of her family, the notion of her precious son ending up with this Lucy woman, a Catholic, of all things.

"But," she said, her tone subtly shifting. I knew then that the empathy she was offering me had strings. "What if there is another path?"

"What are you talking about?" I whispered. "There is no other path."

"What if you stayed husband and wife, but in name only? Keeping your family and children intact, but otherwise pursuing a life of your own choosing?"

It had taken more begging on her part and soul-searching on mine, but I stayed, of course. Even thinking of that time—those horrible long months in 1918—makes me feel sick. I'm not sure I'll ever get over Franklin's adultery. How could the man to whom I'd given my whole self—heart, mind, and spirit—be capable of such painful, blatant betrayal? A deception that took place under my very nose, with no regard for me at all. How could he have been so callous when he knew my difficult childhood—riddled with the illness and death of my parents, and my mother's disdain during her brief life? He knew that all I'd ever wanted was to create a family of my own.

So here we are, nearly a decade later, sleeping in separate bedrooms and leading separate lives, united for the eyes of the world and the children—but truly unified only in our beliefs. I am no longer the young woman he married. How different might things have been if Franklin had never committed adultery?

I hear Mrs. Bethune let out a low laugh in response to my mother-in-law's comment about my work at the Todhunter School, and I return to the present moment. "Oh, yes, we have been talking about education. The struggle to provide meaningful instruction for girls from all backgrounds is real, and critically important," she says.

"Eleanor and I feel much the same way," my mother-in-law echoes, and she speaks the truth. No matter her views on *my* focus, she does believe in supporting women. Within limits, of course.

"May I borrow you for a moment, Mrs. Roosevelt?"

We hear the voice over our shoulders, and both my mother-in-law and I turn. It is Mrs. Moreau, and from her refusal to make eye contact with me or Mrs. Bethune, it's obvious to which "Mrs. Roosevelt" she is referring. Having exhausted her efforts to convince me to eject Mrs. Bethune—or at least keep her out of the dining room—she clearly thinks my mother-in-law might be swayed.

"Excuse me, Mrs. Bethune," she says as she takes her leave. Her irritation at being interrupted is plain.

Mrs. Bethune and I are quiet for a moment, uncertain how to navigate back to the pleasant conversation we've been having.

"I see that your mother-in-law supports educational endeavors for women in theory, but perhaps a little less in practice," Mrs. Bethune observes.

A burst of laughter escapes from my mouth. *What an unexpected remark.* In the span of a few short minutes, Mrs. Bethune has seen into the very heart of the dynamic between me and my mother-in-law and captured it with polite astuteness. It's a feat that no other woman in this room could have managed. And not a single one of them would have tried.

If only Mrs. Bethune knew the whole story, I think. For example, my mother-in-law began the construction of these two connected red-brick and limestone home residences on East 65th Street in 1905 in secret and presented them to Franklin and me as a surprise "gift" soon after our marriage. One town house for her and one for us, with one entrance for us all. Having lost my parents at a young age, I had been looking forward to the maternal assistance of my mother-in-law and followed her every morsel of advice at first, until I realized that she planned on inserting herself into every facet of our married lives and that next-door town houses with a bevy of interconnecting doors was just the beginning.

"Indeed," I say with a smile that Mrs. Bethune returns. "She would like me to stay a little closer to hearth and home." Funny how my mother-in-law began to back away from her support of an "independent life" for me once I'd agreed to stay in my marriage. She pushed me to return to my old activities, nudging me away from teaching and politics—unless my political stumping and strategizing involved some benefit for Franklin. Perhaps a political role again, someday.

This will only happen if Franklin is sought out for a position and if he's willing to leave behind his full-time focus on recovery. Not that I want him to return to politics. Before polio—even before his infidelity—Franklin served in two political roles: New York State senator and assistant secretary of the Navy. I spent years at his side, barely surviving the constant rotation of calling on other politicians' wives, hosting teas, attending dinners, and entertaining politicians and naval officers alike. Now that I've fashioned a very pleasing life of service for myself, following the lead of my friends Marion and Nan—a life without the empty, exhausting demands of being married to a politician—I cannot imagine going back.

"She would not be alone in that sort of desire," Mrs. Bethune replies.

Returning the conversation to slightly safer ground, I say, "I'd love to hear more about how you started your school."

"Ah yes," she says. "Well, when I purchased the site for my school, it was the town garbage dump. I made the down payment with money I raised from selling sweet potato pies."

I try to keep my reaction even as she dabs at the corners of her mouth with a napkin before continuing. "But I didn't stop there. I knew I'd have to find some deeper pockets to cover the costs of constructing a building. And there were quite a few deep pockets in Daytona Beach. Many affluent people from the North become winter residents, and I met James Gamble—"

"One of the Procter and Gamble founders?" I ask, thinking that can't possibly be whom she means.

"One of Mr. Gamble's sons," she answers with a wry grin. "After I had a few conversations with him, the funds to pay off the land and build a four-story brick building soon followed. I find if I'm able to secure a meeting and get a potential benefactor to understand my goals and see my vision, the meeting usually goes the way I hope."

I doubt that even my mother-in-law would be so brash.

She continues, "Now, the money from Mr. Gamble gave us just the bare bones of the first school building. The girls and I were still using a dirt floor inside that brick exterior, but after a visit to one of the lavish oceanfront hotels where I gave a talk, one of the men in the audience came to visit our little campus. One look at the straw matting on the floors and the single broken-down Singer sewing machine the girls were using for their dressmaking lessons, and that man became one of our biggest donors."

"He was moved by the conditions?"

"In part, yes. But it didn't hurt that he was Thomas H. White, owner of White Sewing Machine Company, Singer Manufacturing Company's chief competitor. He later told me he couldn't stand to see my girls struggling over that broken Singer machine, not when he could do something to fix the situation. With his own machines, of course."

Mrs. Bethune smiles. This is clearly the part of her story where she invites prospective donors to help "fix" things on campus, as Mr. White has done. It is quite inventive and irresistible, and I realize that, in telling me the origins of her school, she is also sharing the method of her fundraising. How hard Mrs. Bethune has worked to build an entire institution from nothing. It almost makes me embarrassed how easily I helped purchase Todhunter School from the renowned educator Winifred Todhunter when she wanted to retire: the initial payment came from my own family funds.

"My goodness, Mrs. Bethune, I have much to learn from you— certainly with respect to fundraising. I suppose I've not yet mustered up such moxie on Todhunter's behalf. In that way, we are certainly different."

"Oh, I wouldn't say *that's* the difference between us, Mrs. Roosevelt."

Of course, I think. I hope she's not insulted by my choice of words. Of course there is a much bigger difference between us: the color of our skin. I wait for her to explain how she sees the differences between our races, bracing myself.

Her expression is stern and serious when she says, "I'm a Republican and you're a Democrat."

We both burst out laughing. Her statement is humorous, in part because it's unexpected and in part because it's true. As our laughter dies down to a chuckle, Mrs. Bethune's smile fades. "Mrs. Roosevelt, I believe you underestimate yourself in terms of moxie. You have courage in droves. After all, you invited me here today."

CHAPTER 5

MARY

Daytona Beach, Florida
February 2, 1928

Our car rolls past the iron gates, and Albert Sr. slows as he rounds the Gamble Estate governor's drive. My son releases a long whistle as he eyes the space crammed with Mercedes-Benzes and Vauxhalls and Lancia Lambdas. Albert selects a brand-new shiny red Pierce-Arrow behind which to park his Model T.

"Man." Albert hops out of his vehicle. As he comes around to my side, his eyes are fixed on the fancy automobiles. Could seeing these cars become a motivator for my twenty-nine-year-old son? I hoped he'd find some direction after speaking to the men at the event tonight. But if a car will do it, I'll take that, too.

Albert reaches for my hand as I ease from the passenger seat, careful to hold up the hem of my emerald-green silk gown. Stepping onto the cobblestone walkway, I let the dress flutter around my ankles and sigh. This is a gorgeous gown, but what was I thinking? These newfangled styles with their slim silhouettes are not flattering on my generous hips. I tug at the seams. *I should not have allowed Miss Esther to talk me into this.*

"You look great, Mother Dear."

I glance up at my son, so handsome in his brown three-piece suit.

Then I pause. My goodness, with his thick brows, full lips, and coppery complexion, my son looks just like his daddy. I clear my throat and thoughts of my deceased husband at the same time.

Albert leads me to the steps, then past the huge columns I've walked by more than a few times over the last twenty years.

"You ready?"

I squeeze Albert's arm. "I don't believe there's ever been a time in my life when I wasn't, son."

My son chortles, then knocks. A young lady, dressed in a full maid's uniform, welcomes us. She isn't the one who usually greets me when I visit Mr. Gamble, yet her eyes shine with recognition.

"Mrs. Bethune," she says with excitement, then catches herself. "Please come in." Her voice is steadier now.

The parlor to the right is the epitome of elegance with its three sparkling chandeliers, gleaming marble floor, and windowed wall offering an unobstructed view of the ocean. It's like a ballroom on the beach.

As my son and I move toward the parlor, the young woman whispers, "Mrs. Bethune, would you mind—m-may I get your autograph?"

"Of course," I say, keeping my voice low. Even though her employer is fond of me, I never assume that my good fortune extends to others. This interaction could be grounds for the young woman being fired. "We'll work it out."

She nods. "I hope one day to be a student at Bethune-Cookman."

Her eyes are bright with hope, an expression I've seen in so many of my students. "Well, maybe we'll work that out, too."

As we enter the parlor, we're greeted by three dozen or so stylishly dressed men and women. The women wear a rainbow of gowns similar to mine, and the men sport stiff-collar white shirts and black dinner jackets. Gold and diamonds glitter everywhere. There is a soft swing tune playing from a phonograph that I cannot see, and a black-coated waiter offers Albert and me flutes of iced tea.

Suddenly, Mr. Gamble's voice booms with surprising strength, given his ninety years. "Ah, here she is. The woman of the hour."

Everyone swivels toward me, and the room explodes in applause. I nod, looking into the blue and hazel and green eyes of the white wintertime society of Daytona Beach.

"Mrs. Bethune." Mr. Gamble bows. "It is so good to have you here."

"Well, it's good to be here, Mr. Gamble. This is quite a celebration for both of us."

"Ah yes," he says, "our twenty-year partnership."

Mr. Gamble, of Ivory soap fame, has been my biggest benefactor, and his generosity has impacted the lives of hundreds of my students. As he greets Albert, I stand back and study the son of the man who founded Procter & Gamble. He has certainly aged in the years I've known him; wrinkles crisscross his face, and the hair atop his head is sparse now. But he's maintained his height and his lean frame. His long white beard—reaching to his chest—remains as well.

"Everyone wants to have a word with the queen of Daytona Beach," he says, and I laugh. "But there is someone I'd like you to meet first."

"Really?" I say. "After all these years, is there anyone left for you to introduce me to?"

We laugh, but it's true. Because of him, my circle of white benefactors is extensive. I can count Mr. John D. Rockefeller, as well as dozens of other philanthropists, among my acquaintances.

"Well, this particular gentleman," he says to me and Albert as we move across the room, "usually resides in Fort Myers, but I convinced him to come into town for a few days."

We approach a gray-haired man several inches shorter than Mr. Gamble. "Mrs. McLeod Bethune and Mr. Bethune," Mr. Gamble says, "I'd like to introduce you to Mr. Thomas Edison."

My son's eyes are wide as I nod. "Mr. Edison, what an honor to meet the famous inventor."

"Mrs. Bethune, the pleasure and honor are mine. My friend here has talked about you for decades."

Turning to Mr. Gamble, I tease, "Have you been telling tales about me?"

"I have," he says, "and every tale is true."

Everyone laughs, and I ask Mr. Edison how he met Mr. Gamble. The two men entertain me with stories of Edison being hired as a young man to improve the communications between the departments at Procter & Gamble. After several minutes of chatting, Mr. Edward Armstrong steps into the circle.

"Mrs. Bethune," he greets me, and then nods at the others.

I say, "Mr. Mayor, it's good to see you."

"It's really good to see you outside of my office." Then, to the others, the mayor adds, "Mrs. Bethune keeps me busier than all other Daytona citizens combined."

Mr. Gamble laughs. "I can believe that."

While the men join in the laughter, I sip on my tea. The mayor speaks the truth. At my behest, he's served the Negro neighborhoods by improving the sewer system and building a new recreation center. Most recently, he approved a proposal to begin installing streetlights in the colored sections of the city. Mayor Armstrong has done what few Southern mayors have: He's met the basic needs of *all* his citizens, ignored white detractors and segregation laws to work with me, and won the Negro vote in landslides as a result.

"It sounds as though I've got you to thank for raising the city's property values, Mrs. Bethune," Mr. Gamble says, lifting his glass to me.

Our conversation turns to the Lindbergh transatlantic flight and how I believe Amelia Earhart will be next. From the corner of my eye, I see Albert wander outside onto the patio. I suppose he found it awkward to mingle. I pray he doesn't stroll onto the "Whites Only" beach on the edge of the Gamble property. He may be my son, but we are both aware of my limited capacity in this Jim Crow city, even as I'm celebrated at the home of one of the richest men in town.

Mr. Gamble taps on his crystal flute with a silver spoon. Silhouetted against the vivid oranges and reds of the setting sun glowing through the window, he announces, "Thank you for joining me this evening. I decided it would be best for me to give my little speech before dinner because, these days, I never know what shape I'll be in after dinner."

Light laughter fills the room, and as Albert reenters, I see the pride on his face as he watches me at the center of these luminaries' attention.

"As most of you know, I've been coming to Daytona Beach for about seventy years now, and it was twenty years ago when I first met Mrs. Bethune." He glances at me, and I smile. "She was selling pies for her school in front of Henry Flagler's resort, and every time I saw her, we engaged in wonderful conversations. My goodness, I'd never met anyone who could go from talking about God to the Constitution to music in one sentence." Laughter rises once again, and I join in, remembering some of our talks.

"There were times," Mr. Gamble continues, "when I purchased a pie just to chat with her, especially when she talked about her school. She spoke with such passion, and the description of the buildings and the campus was so vivid, I felt like I was right there. Still, I was surprised when she asked me if I would join her school's board.

"I didn't tell her yes or no; first, I wanted to see this marvelous place for myself. So the next day, I hopped into a buggy and made my way over to the school. And do you know what I found?" He pauses. "Nothing! There was nothing there. No buildings, no campus. Just Mrs. Bethune, a few students, and an old shack sitting on Hell's Hole," he says, referring to the garbage dump that I purchased from the city.

There is more laughter as Mr. Gamble turns to me. "Do you remember what you said to me when you stepped out of that building and I confronted you about the school?"

"Of course I do, but you're doing a great job telling the story." I chuckle.

Mr. Gamble continues, "Mrs. Bethune apologized because she

hadn't meant to mislead me. She said when she talked about her school, the vision was so clear in her mind that it *was* real. She asked me if I would help turn her vision of educating underprivileged colored girls into reality. On that very day, I wrote a check and joined the board. We've been educating students at Bethune-Cookman ever since."

Applause breaks out, and he waits for it to die down before speaking again. "I have worked with titans of business all over the world. But our partnership, Mrs. Bethune, is one of my most fulfilling associations. You are a woman of action who has never seen a barrier you cannot overcome. The force of your will has accomplished so much for so many. My goodness, you went from building a school to, just a few years later, opening a hospital right on the same plot of land."

As proud as Mr. Gamble was to join me in erecting Bethune-Cookman, I believe he found greater joy in our opening McLeod Hospital. Owning a hospital had never been my goal. But what else could I do when the only hospital in the city turned away one of my students because she was colored? When I told Mr. Gamble about that incident and that my hospital would also serve as a training ground for the nursing students at Bethune-Cookman, he saw it as an extension of our plan and helped raise the funds.

Mr. Gamble continues, "I've made many decisions in my life, but one of the best was to become a member of your board. Oh"—he pauses as if he has had a sudden thought—"did I tell you that I was the *only* board member at the time I joined?"

The guests erupt in laughter. "But I wouldn't have had it any other way. To everything that you have accomplished at this school, in this city, and in our country. Here's to you, Mrs. Mary McLeod Bethune."

I raise my glass, pretending to adjust my glasses so I can wipe away a tear. Mr. Gamble leans over and asks, "Is there anything you want to add?"

I could provide details on the hundreds of students we educate each year. I could tell everyone how he and Mr. Thomas White purchased one of the best houses in Daytona Beach and gifted it to me. Or I could share that, because of this man's magnanimity, I can provide for my son and grandson in ways my parents would have never dreamed possible when they toiled away on a South Carolina rice plantation.

Instead, I shake my head. "How could I possibly capture my gratitude in words?"

I clink my glass to his and turn to the guests. "To Mr. James Gamble and the twenty-year partnership that changed my life."

CHAPTER 6

ELEANOR

Hyde Park, New York
February 2, 1928

I race toward the front door of Val-Kill Cottage, dodging to avoid Marion's snowball. Nan screeches in delight behind me, as do my two youngest boys. I hear the snowball whiz past me just as I manage to open the heavy wooden door, usher the group inside, and slam the door behind us.

Laughing, we catch our breath in the cottage entryway. Thirteen-year-old Franklin Jr. and eleven-year-old John struggle to get out of their boots and snow clothes—leaving them in a slushy heap—and run into the kitchen to make hot cocoa. Nan and I take off our outerwear until we are in only our sweaters and the wool knickerbocker pants my mother-in-law so loathes.

Nan smiles over at me. "Think Marion is stockpiling snowballs for a later ambush?"

I giggle. "Why else would she still be out there?"

We retreat to the main room, taking over the comfortable brown chintz sofa in front of the fire. I am so grateful for the refuge of Val-Kill Cottage, where I can live informally with Marion and Nan when I'm in Hyde Park at the Roosevelt family estate. No airs and graces required here, as they are in my mother-in-law's main house,

Springwood. No pretense of convention as in larger Hyde Park and New York society, or even the Vanderbilt estate down the road. Only honest conversation, heartfelt laughter, and strategic planning for our many projects.

Did I think these two women would be the catalyst for a changed life when I met them in June of 1922 at the New York Democratic Women's fundraiser? I'd just finished presenting my first speech before a large audience in the Waldorf-Astoria's ballroom. Franklin's political adviser and our close friend, Louis Howe, had prepared me well, and I'd followed his sage advice—"Speak your piece and sit down"—and was astonished to receive a round of enthusiastic applause.

In the midst of that applause, a diminutive, curly-haired brunette approached me with a small bouquet of violets. Nancy Cook was the executive secretary for the Women's Division of the New York Democratic Party, and we both burst into laughter when I thrust an identical bouquet of violets toward her. I suppose it shouldn't have been a surprise. After all, violets are a symbol of friendship for women. But it added to the evening's conviviality.

She pulled on the arm of a taller woman standing nearby and brought her into our conversation. "May I introduce you to my dear friend Miss Marion Dickerman? She spends most of her time teaching young women at the Todhunter School."

With her narrow face and her dark hair severely parted down the center, I expected a dour expression, but instead, Marion beamed at me. For the next half hour and then in our conversations that followed, I didn't have to make painful, empty small talk. I didn't have to pretend at levity to hide my otherwise unacceptable serious nature. Within weeks, as we traversed New York to try to recruit women for the Democratic Party, Nan, Marion, and I formed a circle of our own. They introduced me to a life of purpose I hadn't known existed.

Is it strange that Franklin and my mother-in-law not only accepted but welcomed these non-patrician women into our homes? Were they simply relieved to see me smiling after so many years of intermittent crying jags? Whatever the reason, on one fine summer afternoon a few years ago while we were picnicking with Marion and Nan and the youngest boys down by the Val-Kill brook on the Hyde Park estate, Franklin offered us the acreage for Val-Kill Cottage. Then he enthusiastically planned the cottage, sourced the materials, and oversaw the construction. I've come to see it as his olive branch for Lucy Mercer.

"Hot cocoa coming!" John calls out, stepping into the main room with two mugs. Franklin Junior—whom we call Brud, short for "brother"—follows, precariously balancing three mugs.

"Did you make one for me?" Marion cries out from the entryway.

"Of course!" John calls back, overly proud of his one culinary skill. And I suppose he should be; I only have one as well—scrambling eggs. My boys adore these substitute aunties, and Marion and Nan have stepped into the familial role with gusto.

When the boys get out a deck of cards, I beg off. While the foursome engages in an animated game, I breathe in the peace of our surroundings. The gleam of the copper fire tools. The vast stone fireplace with the large Navajo rug hanging above it, a gift from my Arizonan friend Isabella Greenway. The naval prints and landscape paintings—housewarming presents from Franklin—covering the walls to the left and right of the fireplace. The comfortable Val-Kill Industries furniture, including my own desk in the corner and several lounge chairs scattered around the sofa. The warm pool of light on the rummy players from the rustic chandelier overhead.

This is my first real home after a life spent in the houses of others. There is nowhere in the world I'd rather be. Certainly not at Springwood, certainly not at our New York City town house or at the social events that used to be my mainstay, and not even at our summer home on Campobello Island, where I spent many happy summers with my five children and, occasionally, Franklin.

The bright white snow outside has become violet and pink as the sun begins to set. The dinner hour approaches. "Boys, I hate to be the bearer of bad news—"

Brud interrupts, "No, Mom! Please don't make us go back to Springwood."

"We don't want to dress up for dinner with Granny," John chimes in. "Can't we stay here with you three?"

I am delighted that they'd rather be here, having a simple meal of cheese, bread, and apples before the fire. After enduring so many years of my mother-in-law inserting herself into my parenting and losing my older children to her wiles—spoiling them with gifts of cars and apartments—I feel jubilant that I've forged a steadier relationship with my youngest two. Bit by bit, I've pushed past my own uncertainties to do right by my sons.

I pull them close to me. "Marion and I have Todhunter work to do this evening, but I'll attend family breakfast tomorrow." Kissing them each on the cheek, I gently guide the shuffling twosome toward the door and hand them over to my mother-in-law's driver, who'll deliver them to Springwood for the formal evening meal.

After they're gone, Nan and Marion settle closer to each other in front of the fire and tenderly hold hands. They are in a Boston marriage and have been for some years. Around my family and friends, however, they avoid such demonstrations.

Marion asks, "Will Franklin be at dinner with the boys?"

"No," I answer. "I almost feel badly sending them up to dine with Sara, unshielded by me or Franklin."

"She isn't *all* terrible," Marion remarks. "Remember what a champion she was at that awful club luncheon in the fall? Not only did she suggest inviting Mrs. Bethune, but she railed against those terrible racist women who wouldn't eat with her."

"True enough," I concede.

"Let me guess," Nan ventures. "Franklin is at the local Democratic Party meeting."

I nod. "You know how he likes to rub elbows with his fellow Dutchess County Democrats."

"He does like to stay in the thick of things," Marion observes.

"While never committing to one particular path," I say dryly. My friends have heard about my years as a politician's wife and know I don't welcome a return to that life.

Nan nods in sympathy. "I still think the chances that he'll resume an active political role are slim to none. Walking again is too important to him."

I agree, but I still worry and can't help asking, "Have you heard anything, though?" Nan is at the epicenter of all Democratic Party gossip.

"Only rumors that Governor Smith is destined to be one of the presidential candidates."

This news delights me. Franklin and I admire Smith's championship of the average citizen and his advocacy for women and children. Marion, Nan, and I worked on his reelection campaign in 1924, and I grew to appreciate him on a personal level. Along with my daughter, Anna, and several other young women, we traveled the state raising women's awareness of Smith in a Buick touring car that had a replica teapot on the roof, a not-so-subtle nod to the Republican Party's so-called Teapot Dome Scandal of the Harding administration. It was great fun, even though it led to the defeat of Smith's opponent, my cousin Theodore Roosevelt Jr., and some attendant acrimony among the Roosevelt relatives.

"Well, wouldn't that be grand? That's a campaign I could get behind," I muse. "But nothing about Franklin?"

"No, no rumblings."

I exhale. "That's a relief. I've built such a lovely life here with you and Marion. All that would end if I became a politician's wife."

CHAPTER 7

MARY

Daytona Beach, Florida
May 28, 1928

I love the sheen on my new hazel walking stick. This cane gives me more swank than any of my others. The sun warms my shoulders as I stroll through Daytona's Second Avenue business district. This is one of my favorite diversions, but I don't often have time for it.

Between my work at the college, the National Association of Colored Women's Clubs, the NAACP, and the Urban League, I am most often tethered to my desk—unless I'm on a train or sleeping inside boarding-houses or hotels throughout the country. And given that there's a pres-idential election in November, for which I'll be working hard to get Herbert Hoover into office, this could be my last idle time of 1928.

The rattling engine of a passing car tugs me away from my thoughts, and I turn when I hear a horn honk. "Hey, Mrs. Bethune." A gentleman wearing overalls leans over and waves.

I recognize the man; he's done some construction work at the col-lege, although I can't recall his name. But I return the greeting and then step back from the curb when the car's tires kick up dust as it rolls over the unpaved street. I frown; I need to speak to Mayor Arm-strong. It's time to get *all* the streets throughout the city paved.

When the car is far enough away, I continue my stroll, slowing as

I pass by Hattie's. My chest swells with pride whenever I peek into the windows of this diner. Even though this is Midway, one of the colored sections of the city, every business on Second Avenue was white owned until two years ago.

It started to change when I went before the city council to petition for a business for my son—the Tea Room. The only Negro businesses in town were in the worst sections, and I wanted Albert's Tea Room to be right here on Second Avenue. The city council denied my first request. So I left that meeting and returned every month for five months until they agreed—and we opened the first colored business in Midway.

A year later, when my friend Hattie Johnson told me she had an idea for a diner, I marched right back to the city council. This time, they approved my request within days, and now four applications for colored businesses are before the council. By the time I finish, half of these storefronts will be colored businesses serving colored patrons. As it should be.

Several blocks down, I make a left on Walnut, and at that turn, there is a subtle shift, maybe imperceptible to outsiders, but evident to the city's residents. Now I pass several newly erected storefronts, and there is no rising dust from passing cars as drivers maneuver over paved streets. With each step, I edge closer to the beachside community of Seabreeze, and here, there are fewer faces whose complexions match mine.

I pause in front of the glass door to Miss Esther's Fancy Fashions. I've been a longtime patron of Miss Esther, having met her for the first time more than fifteen years ago. A friend of the Gambles, Miss Esther has become something like my own shopping assistant, making sure my wardrobe is up-to-date.

When I push open the door, the bell above rings, and Miss Esther and her customer turn toward me. "Mrs. Bethune," Miss Esther exclaims. The forty-year-old woman bubbles over with the same energy she had when I met her all those years ago, still as fiery as her red hair, now twisted up into a chignon instead of flowing down her back in a single plait as it once did. "It's so good to see you. Can you give me just a minute?" She eyes her customer, an older woman with skin so pale it's almost translucent.

"Of course." I nod at the other customer, then turn to the rack of dresses along the wall, shaking my head in amazement. Whose idea was it to shorten the hemlines? These new fashions. Almost indecent.

I long for the days when dresses had lots of material that covered the multitude of sins that have expanded my frame since Albert Sr.'s birth. I was much more comfortable when every inch from my neck to my ankles was hidden. But no more, it seems.

"Excuse me."

The Southern drawl makes me tense. But then I remember: I'm home. I face Esther's customer.

She says, "Are you Mary McLeod Bethune?"

"I am."

"I thought that was you," she says, drawing out her words. Her lips, as red as Miss Esther's hair, spread into a smile. "It is very nice to meet you. I'm Mrs. Wallace." She pauses as if I'm supposed to know who she is. Then she keeps on. "My husband is on the city council."

"Oh, yes," I say.

"He's spoken about you over the years and the things you've done for Daytona, particularly your community," she drawls on.

I'm not sure how I'm supposed to respond, so I don't.

She continues, "And my husband and I came to your Sunday community meeting last month to hear Langston Hughes speak."

"Ah yes. Well, I hope you enjoyed Mr. Hughes. He is quite talented."

"He certainly is. I enjoyed Langston's presentation, although it was"—she pauses as if she's searching for the right word, then says—"different."

By "different," I'm sure she means she never expected to be sitting in an auditorium shoulder to shoulder with Negroes. Unlike at other venues, including other colored colleges, I don't allow segregated seating at my school. When I call my gathering a community meeting, I mean that. Everyone from the community is treated the same.

Mrs. Wallace continues, "But in spite of it being different, we did have a good time. We'll be on the lookout for some of your other programs, and perhaps we'll return."

Just as she finishes, Miss Esther joins us and hands a shopping bag to Mrs. Wallace. With a broad smile, Mrs. Wallace says, "Well, it was nice meeting you, Mary."

I flinch, then paste the smile back onto my face and tell Mrs. Wallace, "Mrs. Bethune is fine."

She blinks. "What?" she asks, as if she hasn't understood the English I've just spoken.

"You called me Mary," I say, staring into her shocked blue eyes. "My name is Mrs. Bethune."

Her smile fades and her lips press together, forming a straight line. Without another word to me or Esther, she spins and marches to the exit. The bell above the door jingles as she stomps away.

I watch her for only a moment and then turn back to the dresses on the rack.

"Oh, Mrs. Bethune." Miss Esther giggles so hard, her face turns red. But I don't chuckle with her.

As a child, I heard white children disrespect my parents, calling them Sam and Patsy. My parents never had a single day of honor, were never addressed as Mr. or Mrs. McLeod, and I declared back then that would change with me. Every white person I met would call *me* Miss McLeod. And if I ever got married, then I'd demand they call me by my married name.

"I bet Mrs. Wallace has never had anyone speak to her that way," Miss Esther says.

"I wasn't trying to be rude," I say with a shrug. "She introduced herself as Mrs. Wallace, expecting me to address her properly. Yet she felt it was fine to address Mr. Hughes and me otherwise. She needed to understand that respect goes both ways."

"So true. Well, enough about her." Miss Esther clasps her hands together. "I haven't seen you since the day of the Gamble dinner. How was it?"

"It was wonderful, but, Miss Esther, how did I let you talk me into that gown?"

Her eyes widen. "What are you talking about? You looked lovely."

"Are you kidding? That dress, these hips, and 'lovely' shouldn't be used in the same sentence."

Miss Esther laughs, but I'm only half joking.

"Well, you looked gorgeous, and I'm sure you were the most beautiful woman in the room."

Miss Esther often says that, and as she explained long ago, her words weren't flattery—she meant what she said. "Oh, Mrs. Bethune, your dark skin is perfect for just about any color. You should be a model."

The last part always makes me laugh. No one is searching for a five-foot-nothing thickset Negro model.

"So what brings you into the shop today?" Miss Esther asks. "Another special event, or are you going back to Washington, D.C.? Oh, let me guess! You must be going to a party to celebrate your new business. I read in the paper you're now part owner of Central Life Insurance."

"I am."

"Congratulations!" She shakes her head. "I don't know how you do it, Mrs. Bethune. I spend eight hours here in the shop, and when I get home, I can't get up from my sofa. But you—you're just amazing, acquiring another company."

I don't tell Miss Esther that I'm not amazing at all. This is another situation where I was left without a choice. This time, it was one of my teachers, who complained she couldn't get insurance because of the skin she'd been born with. I had to do something about that.

"Don't shortchange yourself, Miss Esther," I say. "But today I'm not looking for anything formal; I need business attire for the upcoming presidential campaign."

Within minutes, Miss Esther's arms are filled with dresses, and I enter the dressing room to begin the harrowing task of trying on each one.

"Oh, Miss Esther," I say moments later, stepping out to see myself in the mirror. "This is really lovely." The purple crepe and satin dress is dramatic in color and style, particularly with the long scarf hanging over one shoulder. "I love it—except, why is it so short? I can practically see my knees."

She laughs. "You cannot. It's several inches below your knee, and you look so pretty in that purple."

Perhaps the tailor can add a few inches to the hem? For the next forty minutes, I try on dress after dress, skirt after skirt, until Miss Esther wraps up six different outfits for me.

Just as I'm paying, the bell above the door jingles. "Mother Dear, are you ready?" The voice of my seven-year-old grandson is better than hearing my favorite song. Albert Jr. bolts toward me. "Mrs. Davis is outside in the car," he says, referring to one of his two nannies, who do more than help me with Albert; they are also the organizers of my life.

"Okay!"

"She's gonna give us a ride to Miss Hattie's. I hope we can get a table by the window." Even though Albert loves Mrs. Davis' cooking, he's bouncing with excitement at the thought of eating at the restaurant.

"Let me pay for these dresses, and I'll be right there."

"Okay, Mother Dear. Hurry." He dashes out of the store as fast as he came in.

Miss Esther smiles. "I always love it when he calls you Mother Dear."

"Now, Miss Esther, you know every colored grandmother in the South is called that."

"I know." She nods. "But it's so endearing and sweet the way your grandson says it. You must be so proud of him."

"I am," I say. "I'm grateful to be raising him."

She packs up my purchases and hands me the bag. "Thank you, Mrs. Bethune. Thank you for always supporting my business and telling everyone about me. I appreciate you."

As I step back into the sunlight, two young girls passing by call out to me, "Hi, Mrs. Bethune."

"Hello, young ladies." Moving toward the curb, I begin to hum that Louis Armstrong hit "Melancholy Blues," although there is nothing sad about the way Louis blows that horn.

Now it's time to do my absolute favorite thing—spend time with one of my two loves, Albert Jr.

CHAPTER 8

ELEANOR

Hyde Park, New York
May 28, 1928

"Sorry I'm late!" I call into the dining room from the airy entry hall of Springwood.

The sound of silver on china echoes into the vast foyer. I hastily unpin my hat and practically toss it to the waiting maid with an apology as I rush into the dining room. As I expected, Marion, Nan, Franklin, John, Brud, and Sara—in proper evening dresses and suits—have already gathered around the oval table in the ornately carved wood chairs. From their aggrieved expressions, I see my tardiness has already been discussed.

I decide not to allow my mother-in-law's disappointment to ruin the meal for which I raced from New York City, and that includes ignoring her clear disapproval of the plain blue cotton shirtwaist I am still wearing from my workday. It was no mean feat to catch the train to Hyde Park from Governor Smith's campaign headquarters to arrive here anywhere close to dinnertime. Only with the help of my new assistant, Miss Malvina Thompson, did I make it at all.

I was flattered and overjoyed when Governor Smith selected me to be in charge of the women's activities for his presidential campaign. This election will be the first in which women voters will play a significant role in choosing the president. Of course, I didn't realize that my workdays would stretch from eight o'clock in the morning to nearly midnight as I coordinate the women's voting efforts in forty-eight states, interrupted only by the demands of teaching and helping manage Todhunter. Still, I adore being at the center of this historic moment. What a gift I've been given.

I lift my spoon and, as the utensil hovers over my clear consommé, I ask, "So what have I missed?"

Franklin, handsome in his black-and-white evening suit with his hair just beginning to turn silver-gray at the temples, picks up on my light approach and answers, "A very spirited discussion by the boys on their summer plans now that they're home from Groton."

"Let me guess," I say with a grin, thrilled that the boys are home from the boarding school that Franklin and my mother-in-law insisted we ship them to starting at the innocent age of twelve. "It involves a lot of time swimming at the pool at Val-Kill Cottage, followed by sailing at Campobello."

This is the usual summer pattern—and I anticipate that the plan will remain the same this summer, even with the Smith campaign. I hope so, anyway, as our vacation home on the Canada island of Campobello is one of my favorite places on earth. The scent of pine trees mixed with sea air. The sight of lighthouses against the foggy, craggy coast. The sandy inlets and inviting coves. The vermillion sunsets. It's heavenly.

"How did you know?" Brud smiles back with a matching grin. *How attractive and like his father Brud is*, I think. Even the horrible pea-green walls of the dining room cannot cast a pall on his appearance.

Franklin chimes in, "It might not be all fun and games, boys. I have a few projects around the estate for you—"

Sara interrupts her beloved son. "Now, Franklin, the boys deserve their summer holiday. You always had yours. Remember all the summers you spent with me and your father on Campobello?"

This reference to Franklin's long-deceased father is one of Sara's regular tricks to wrangle her son back to her usual position of spoiling the children. My suspicion that it's been effective is confirmed when Franklin replies, "Of course I do, Mama. Boys, we will see what the summer holds."

A flicker of relief passes over the boys' faces as they recognize that their father has retreated from inflicting a list of jobs upon them. But I think some physical work might be good for the boys, might even help address some of the waywardness we've seen in our older boys, twenty-year-old James and seventeen-year-old Elliott, who haven't taken college as seriously as we'd like and have launched into romantic relationships too quickly. I wander into the fray of this conversation, something I would never have done as a younger mother.

"Well, if your father doesn't have anything for you boys to do, I can bring you down to the campaign headquarters and find an outlet for your energy. We always need help stuffing envelopes, don't we, Nan?" I ask with a wink. Nan sometimes works alongside me at Smith's offices, although her responsibilities as the Democratic Party executive secretary extend much further than his campaign alone.

Nan joins in. "Oh, yes—"

"Eleanor! You cannot possibly be serious about bringing your sons down to that awful headquarters in the city heat. It's bad enough that you spend your days and nights there. But think of the boys and the riffraff they'd encounter!" Sara practically screeches out this last point.

"Now, Mrs. Roosevelt," Nan teases Sara in her sweet, singsong tone, "are you calling me riffraff?"

Even Sara smiles at this; no one can resist the kindly, diminutive Nan. Soon the entire table breaks into laughter. This is one of the many reasons I adore Nan and Marion. Their cheery presence serves not only as buffer but as unifier for this disjointed family. Even though my friends aren't part of our social stratum and are tied to the family only through their friendship with me, Sara first tolerated and now welcomes Marion and Nan. She knows I'm happier, and thus the family dynamic is more harmonious, with Marion and Nan present. And my mother-in-law has always enjoyed an audience.

"Ma'am?" A maid appears at Sara's side.

"Yes?" she answers.

"There is a telephone call."

"We are at dinner," Sara replies imperiously without bothering to look at her. Formal meals are sacrosanct for Sara.

"It is Governor Smith, ma'am," the poor girl says, her voice quivering a little. Sara inspires terror in the staff.

Everyone freezes. Sara knows she cannot refuse a call from the governor, but that doesn't mean she has to be happy about it. Governor Smith has called me from time to time at Springwood, but I am surprised he's phoning during the dinner hour—particularly as I saw him earlier today and nothing urgent seemed to be on the agenda.

I push back from the table. "Apologies, I'll just be a minute. Please continue with the meal."

"Oh!" the maid says with a small gasp. "I apologize that I wasn't clear, ma'am. Governor Smith requested to speak to *Mr.* Roosevelt, ma'am. Not you."

I glance at Franklin, then at Nan—both of whom look as perplexed as I feel. Why on earth would Smith be calling Franklin? True, he supports Smith's bid for the presidency, but Franklin has made clear that his paralysis—a word we only use in the company of family— makes substantive campaigning impossible.

Franklin wheels himself away from the table with an apologetic smile to his mother. "Can't say no to a summoning by the governor," he says as he leaves the room.

Nan and I shoot each other a confused glance. I want to ask her if she knows anything, but I hesitate in the presence of Sara. Then I realize my reluctance is silly. My mother-in-law will not allow this strange occurrence to go undiscussed.

"You two are thick as thieves with this Governor Smith. What is this about?" Sara demands, looking at Nan and me.

"I don't know, Mrs. Roosevelt," Nan is quick to answer.

"Neither do I, Mama," I reply honestly.

"I certainly hope that Catholic Smith character isn't trying to rope Franklin into campaigning. Franklin isn't ready—physically, I mean—and he's made that abundantly clear. Perhaps one day, but certainly not yet." While Sara derived a certain amount of joy from Franklin's prior positions, she's fearful of him returning to public service just now.

On this, Sara and I are in rare, perfect agreement—although for somewhat different reasons. I don't want Franklin to return to politics because I don't want to be a politician's wife again.

"I have heard nothing of the sort," Nan assures her.

"That's a relief, dear Nan. Thank you," Sara says, and I try not to let her kindness to Nan irritate me simply because she so rarely shows it to me.

Conversation resumes among the six of us until Franklin wheels himself back into the dining room a few minutes later. "What did Governor Smith want?" I ask in as casual a tone as I can muster.

"Well, he asked me for something. Something a bit surprising," he says, taking a large sip of his wine before continuing. "He's asked me to give the speech nominating him for president at the Democratic National Convention later this summer in Texas."

My heart sinks; I know what this means. "Did you agree?"

"Of course," he answers lightly. "It's only a speech. A bit of fun."

Nan, Sara, and I peek at one another with a knowing look. This is no mere speech. This invitation means he's being courted to run for governor of New York, to replace Smith when he presumably wins the presidency.

CHAPTER 9

MARY

Daytona Beach, Florida
November 6, 1928

The moment Albert Jr. and I step into the Daytona Beach Republican campaign headquarters—a storefront I've rented temporarily—cheers arise.

"Isn't this exciting?" Helen, the campaign manager for this office, rushes to my side. She gestures around the room, which has been transformed from a workplace into a celebratory space. Red, white, and blue balloons hang from the ceiling and complement the Herbert Hoover posters plastered along the wall. Just as many signs feature W. J. Howey, the Republican candidate for governor of Florida. A "Hoover, Howey, and Happiness" banner hangs from the center of the room.

There are about seventy exuberant volunteers milling about, a third of them students from Bethune-Cookman. Even though most of my students are not yet old enough to vote, I've encouraged their involvement in politics in preparation for their twenty-first birthdays. I teach the basics of civics, as well as the history of the Republican Party. The history is easy. Most of my students, like my son, have grandparents who were slaves, so their political sensibilities line up with mine.

I move through the room, shaking hands and thanking everyone for voting. A small group has gathered near the radio, and one of the young ladies says, "Mrs. Bethune, I didn't know how important voting was until you registered my parents."

I nod. "Most people don't know the value of our vote, but the Democrats understand. That's why they work so hard to make sure colored people never vote. So when you're old enough, remember that," I finish, always wanting to teach a lesson.

An older man standing nearby says, "That's exactly what you told me when I registered. I swear, Mrs. Bethune, every Negro in Florida votes because of you."

We all laugh. I know he's kidding, but right now, I feel his words all the way down to my tired bones. Over the last few months, it seems as though I have visited every colored church, business, and community in Florida. As I've done throughout the years, I registered thousands, always with the hope it will benefit the Republicans.

"Hey, everybody!" one of the young men shouts. "They're getting ready to make an announcement."

The reporter's voice crackles through the radio. "There are many important elections across the nation tonight. As we're watching the presidential results, thirty-five states have gubernatorial contests, and we're ready to report on four. The Republican governor of Connecticut, John Trumbull, has been reelected, and the Republicans have won the governor's seat in Delaware."

Polite applause fills the room only because the victory has gone to the Republicans. I'm sure no one here has even heard that man's name before.

"And in the Southern states of Georgia and Florida"—we all inhale at once—"in Georgia, the Democratic incumbent, Governor Hardman, has won reelection, and Florida has a new governor. The Democrat, Doyle E. Carlton, has handily defeated the Republican candidate, W. J. Howey."

A collective moan echoes through the office, although it's more about the Democrats' victory rather than our defeat. I supported

Howey only because of the alternative. But with Howey's embrace of lily-whitism and his desire to bring white voters back to the Republican Party to the detriment of Black voters, I saw little difference between Carlton and Howey.

"Don't worry, Mother Dear," Albert says, interrupting my musings. "Hoover is going to win . . . because of you."

The room cheers; my seven-year-old grandson is a political activist already.

"Ssshhh," the young man closest to the radio calls out. "Another announcement."

I wonder if this will be for president or if another governor will be announced—New York, perhaps. I am very interested in the New York gubernatorial race, especially after meeting Mrs. Roosevelt. Over the last year, she and I have exchanged letters, and we've seen each other in passing on three occasions when we found ourselves in the same city for conferences. She has never spoken of her husband's decision to run for the governor's office. Still, I feel invested in that electoral outcome because of her, even if we don't share the same party affiliation.

I wonder what Mrs. Roosevelt must think about her husband being in the gubernatorial race. Was it as surprising to her as it was to the rest of the country when Mr. Roosevelt stepped in as a candidate for governor once the current governor, Al Smith, decided to run for president? Did she really think her husband would run after his illness? And now, does she relish the idea of becoming First Lady of New York?

The radio interrupts my musings. "I have it on good authority that the winner of the New York gubernatorial race is the Democratic candidate, Franklin Delano Roosevelt!"

Sighs of disappointment rise through the room again. "Not another Democrat," my grandson says.

But I smile. I have become a believer in Mrs. Roosevelt. With her commitment to education, there is so much good she can do in the role of governor's wife.

Then the announcer's voice breaks into the room once again. "And now, in what appears to be a landslide, the Republican Herbert Hoover has defeated the Democratic candidate Governor Al Smith! Herbert Hoover has been elected the thirty-first president of the United States!"

A roar reverberates through the room. There are hugs and back-slaps all around, and everyone rushes to congratulate me.

"You did it, Mrs. Bethune. Congratulations!"

"I hope Herbert Hoover knows how much you helped him."

"One day, Mrs. Bethune, you should run for president! I'd vote for you!"

Laughter takes the place of the cheers with that last statement. I accept the congratulations, but I am not surprised. I knew Hoover would win; the only mystery was how great the victory would be. Al Smith is impressive and has done much for New York as the four-term governor. But his accomplishments couldn't overcome the anti-Catholic sentiment that rages throughout the country. There are too many forces in America that would prevent a Catholic from ever be-coming president.

I take a seat by the door and revel in the sight of the celebration with my grandson at the center. Watching my community makes my heart sing, because I understand nothing will change in this country without the political engagement of Negroes, especially our colored youth.

But I'm a little concerned that the wind is shifting. This was the first election in my lifetime where Negroes were willing to walk away from the Republican Party. It was almost blasphemy, and that's what I told Walter White, the young assistant executive secretary of the NAACP, who first expressed this sentiment to me.

"Mary," Walter had said, "I don't expect anything from the

Democrats—the devil will do what the devil will do—but Negroes must end this chronic Republicanism that is holding us hostage to the promises of Lincoln. Election after election, Republicans give us guarantees to get our vote . . . and they never deliver. I'm considering supporting Smith this time, just so Republicans will see they can't take my vote for granted."

I am not oblivious to the shortcomings of the Republican Party. But I cannot see myself turning on the party of Abraham Lincoln and Frederick Douglass—the party that freed my parents, my grandmother, and my siblings from slavery.

Just then, the front door opens, and my son steps inside. He saunters over and kisses my cheek, and I beam at my only child. "Congratulations, Mother Dear." He glances around the room. "Seems like there're lots of happy people in Daytona Beach tonight, and I'm one of them."

My son's political leanings align with mine. No surprise, given he's heard me speak with passion about the Republican Party his whole life—first as I fought with the suffrage movement and then with the voter registration drives I've held. But I wonder if he's ever had the sort of doubt that Walter has. Is the unrest a generational thing? Does my son have angst about the Republican Party as well?

"I'm going to get Albert home," Albert Sr. says. "Do you want to ride with us, or will someone else bring you?"

Even though few seem like they want to leave the festivities, I'm ready. Within five minutes we are inside Albert's car, and by the time we pick up a little speed, Albert Jr. is asleep in the back seat.

My son and I share a smile as we glance back at him. Albert says, "Thanks for bringing him tonight, Mother Dear. He's always happier when he gets to spend time with you."

There is no judgment in my son's voice, but guilt still tugs at me. Albert Jr. was only six weeks old when I became his guardian. Since that time, my life has been a whirlwind because of my political activism, yes, but primarily because of Bethune-Cookman. Over the years, the school has expanded—the enrollment, the academic program, the faculty—and although I have Mr. Gamble and other benefactors, I do not depend on that alone. Relentless fundraising has kept me on the road.

Albert and I are silent for a few moments, and then I ask, "So how's business?"

Right away, Albert's shoulders hunch and his jaw tightens. "Business is fine, Mother Dear." His tone is sharp.

"I was just asking, Albert. No need for you to get upset."

"I'm not," he says, his eyes straight ahead.

This reaction is always the first indicator that there's something my son is not saying. He heard more in my question than I meant to ask, but his own failure is upsetting him, not my inquiry.

I had great aspirations for Albert's Tea Room after a number of businesses I financed for him collapsed. I hope this business venture will sustain him, although I'm not optimistic. Especially not after the meeting I had with our accountant yesterday.

We stay silent until Albert stops the car at the side of our house. Without looking at me, he lifts his sleeping son. Inside, all Albert says is "Good night, Mother Dear" before he makes his way up the stairs. The steps creak under his weight.

With a sigh, I sink onto the sofa. Less than half an hour ago, I was elated that my presidential candidate had won. Now my heart weighs heavy. My life has many blessings, but my shoulders carry the burden of the responsibility I feel for my family, my school, and this country.

"Lord," I begin a whispered prayer, and I go on to ask that, should anything go wrong in my life, He step in and make the crooked road straight.

CHAPTER 10

ELEANOR

Albany, New York
November 6, 1928

This evening feels unreal. Ticker tape soars through the air as revelers grab handfuls of confetti from the floor and toss them high. Trays of golden liquid circulate through the ballroom, and the crowd is abuzz with excitement fueled by drink, a false levity that always makes me apprehensive, as it conjures memories of my father's binges. A line has formed to congratulate Franklin on his victory in securing the governorship of the state of New York, but my feelings are mixed—Smith lost the presidential election, after all, and I wonder if we would even be on this stage tonight if I wasn't so close to Smith.

What on earth have I done? What if I hadn't been home on that October afternoon only a month ago? Could I have avoided the fate of being a politician's wife once again?

I had just placed the telephone receiver back in its cradle on my study desk in the New York City town house. Franklin and I had finished our daily call, and the exchange had been typical, even banal—mostly about the sorts of exercises his therapist had him doing in the Warm Springs facility in Georgia, a place he established for his recuperation. I felt relief that this day might mercifully pass without change. It was the day the gubernatorial nominations were due, and I'd been hearing rumors that Smith wanted Franklin to run, presumably to take the governor role when Smith himself won the presidency. But nothing had happened, and if Franklin's name wasn't submitted today, then he could not run.

Just then, our housemaid peeked into the study, an apologetic expression on her face. "Sorry for disturbing you, ma'am, but there are two men here to see you."

I had no appointments in my calendar. "Who is it?"

Her voice dropped to a whisper. "The governor and another man."

My stomach flipped, and as I followed the maid to the foyer, I said a silent prayer that there was an emergency with Smith's presidential campaign, something he needed my help with. Anything but what I suspected. As I stepped onto the marble floor of the entry, I saw not only Smith but Mr. John Raskob, chair of the Democratic National Committee.

Bracing myself, I said, "How lovely to see you both. How may I be of service?"

His blue eyes upon me, the dapper, silver-haired Smith turned his bright charm my way. "You've already done so much for my campaign; I hate to ask for one more thing."

"You know you can count on me, Governor," I said, because what else could I say?

The more somber, salt-and-pepper-haired Raskob stepped forward, and it was clear this entire exchange had been carefully orchestrated. "That's a relief to hear, Mrs. Roosevelt, because our request is a large one. We've been thinking"—at this, he glanced over at Smith, who nodded—"that your husband would make a fine governor should our candidate here win the presidential election as we all hope."

I squared my shoulders and said, "What a lovely compliment, gentlemen, and I am certain Franklin will be moved. But I think you know how seriously my husband and his doctors take his recovery from polio. He's actually away at our Georgia home undertaking treatment right now."

This time, Smith took a step closer to me. "We would never want to do anything to interfere with his recuperation, but we have been trying to reach him in Warm Springs all day and he hasn't been available to take any of our calls. We just want to make certain he knows about this offer. If he declines it based on his health, of course we understand."

"Gentlemen, given that I hung up with my husband only minutes before you arrived, I think you can interpret his unavailability to take your calls as the answer to your offer. Surely he knows why you are calling, and in making himself unreachable, he is politely refusing," I said.

"That may well be the case," Raskob blustered, "but we'd feel a whole sight better if we heard it directly from him. We don't want him to miss out on this opportunity through some sort of miscommunication."

Smith fixed his blue eyes on me. "Mrs. Roosevelt, I know if you implore your husband to accept our call, he will. He values your guidance, as do I."

I knew he was manipulating me, but when I stared in the face of this man I hoped would be our next president, a man who had overcome his immigrant Catholic background to mobilize the people of New York these past few years, I felt myself soften. Closing my eyes for a brief moment, I pictured Franklin, trying so hard to walk again for over seven years. Would the governorship put his ability to walk again in jeopardy? But what would waiting and living on the sidelines of life do to his self-image?

I answered Smith, "I have never interfered with Franklin's decision-making. And as you know, his doctors have advised ongoing treatment."

Smith changed his approach. "You misunderstand me, Mrs. Roosevelt. Of course I would never ask you to interfere, particularly when the stakes are so high. But if it's any consolation, we would be in the background helping lighten his load as governor if he proceeded." Unabashed, he continued, "All I ask is that you place a phone call to Mr. Roosevelt."

I felt my eyebrows rise at this rather audacious request, even though I understood the urgency of the timing. "Wouldn't that be tantamount to interfering? After all, by not taking your calls, Franklin has conveyed his decision."

"Mrs. Roosevelt, I'm only asking you to inform your husband or connect us with him. *Not* interfere."

My stomach churned. Should I put Smith on the phone with Franklin and force the issue of a gubernatorial run? I wished I had the time to consult with Marion and Nan. For months, I'd told myself that the reasons Franklin should *not* run for office all stemmed from his best interests, and it had been easy to do, since no one in our circle thought his running was wise or likely.

But was that true? Did I have my own list of reasons for not wanting him to run? I thought of the wonderful freedom I had in my life, and I knew all that privacy and liberty would disappear if Franklin became governor. It had been the same for Uncle Teddy's wife when he became governor and then president—something she'd forewarned me about. But were Aunt Edith's views the right basis upon which to consider Franklin's decision? After all, there might be good that *both* of us could do with Franklin as governor.

Suddenly, I knew what to do.

"All right, Governor. Please hand me the phone."

Thanks to that one decision, we now stand in the town hall in Albany, celebrating Franklin's victory while a consolation gathering happens for Smith's loss down the street.

I hope my new friend Mrs. Bethune is having a more celebratory, less conflicted election day than I am. After all, the candidate she publicly embraced will be the new president of the United States. I hope Herbert Hoover's triumph brings her causes the success they deserve, since for me, this day can only be bittersweet.

As one constituent comes to the front of the line, elated to shake Franklin's hand, another—a well-heeled woman with a triple strand of pearls, a slash of red lipstick, and sharp black birdlike eyes—cuts the queue and makes a beeline toward me. "You must be absolutely delighted with your husband's triumph, Mrs. Roosevelt!" she coos, taking my hand in hers. "I'm Mrs. Broadstreet, and I cannot wait to welcome you and your family to the Executive Mansion. I just know we will be fast friends."

Suddenly, the burly, dark-haired man who'd been assigned as the head of our security—Mr. Earl Miller—rushes to the woman's side, admonishing her for breaking protocol and asking her to leave.

I protest. The woman seems a tad bossy but not a threat, and I suggest as much. To which Mr. Miller replies, "Rules are rules, and protocol is protocol. They're there for your protection, ma'am." And then he promptly escorts her from the hall.

Once he returns, Mr. Miller leans toward me and says, "Ma'am, please know that I will always have eyes on you and will ensure your protection and that of the governor."

On this fraught day, I find his words comforting. "Thank you, Mr. Miller."

"Please call me Earl, ma'am," he says, then recedes into the background again.

Glancing down at my husband—now the governor—I see that behind all of that bullish good cheer, he's exhausted. Although he's seated as he greets his citizens, he spent a goodly portion of the day standing and "walking" on braced legs with my support and the use of a cane. Franklin will not be able to keep up the facade for much longer, but I'll make the excuse of exhaustion when the time comes. He can reveal nary a chink in his armor.

I hear a clinking of crystal, only to see the new lieutenant governor, Herbert Lehman, raising a glass to Franklin. I wonder what the future holds. Regardless, it seems that I must become comfortable with both loss and triumph. With the demise of my marriage came success in my professional endeavors. With the defeat of Smith came the victory of Franklin. With the winning of the governorship comes the loss of my freedom.

CHAPTER 11

MARY

Daytona Beach, Florida
November 16, 1930

I straighten my navy lace dress; then, with my valise in one hand and cane in the other, I enter the train depot. Even though the ride will be long, I don't change my formal garb. My skin is the color of a black sapphire; that is the first thing people notice. But since the next thing they'll examine is my attire, I understand that I must be draped down as if I'm the most important person in the room.

Traveling in the South is one of the greatest reminders of what America thinks of its Negro citizens. Here I am, on my way to a meeting where the president will be in attendance, yet I must enter through the banged-up doors marked "Coloreds Only."

The train's whistle signals its arrival, and soon it chugs to a stop. The stationmaster opens the "Whites Only" door, greeting each of the white passengers. Once all the white travelers have boarded, the stationmaster's smile twists into a scowl as we file past him. But we don't react. His disdainful treatment is what we expect.

Inside the colored car, I can tell this part of the train hasn't seen a broom or a good washing in months, and if my hands were not full, I'd hold my nose to save me from the rank odor that assaults my nostrils.

These are so different from the white cars, which are cleaned in between every route, and certainly not the "separate but equal" anticipated by the court in the more than thirty-year-old *Plessy v. Ferguson* decision.

I find an aisle seat and smile at the young girl sitting by the soot-covered window. She offers a shy smile in return as I slide my bag and my cane along the filthy floor because there are no overhead racks. My legs will be cramped between these wooden benches, and if I have to get up to use the restroom, with my . . . well . . . healthy girth, I won't be able to turn to the right or to the left.

Settling in my seat, I check for the invitation in my handbag again. I make out the gleam of the gold lettering on the heavy ivory stationery—*President Herbert Hoover cordially invites you to attend the White House National Conference on Child Health and Protection.*

As a fifty-five-year-old colored woman from Mayesville, South Carolina, a town so small most couldn't locate it on the map, I never dreamed of an invitation to speak at the White House. But whenever something special like this happens, I think of my grandma Sophie. She wouldn't have been surprised.

My grandmother, who had been kidnapped in Africa and brought to America, believed I had a special destiny before I was born. *It's a special gift coming,* she'd told my parents every day during my mother's pregnancy. Everyone assumed Grandma Sophie was talking about the fact that I was my parents' fifteenth child, the first born free.

But then I came into the world with a veil over my face, the significance of which Mama and Grandma Sophie explained to me when I was five. The veil—the thin piece of skin that kept me safe inside Mama's belly but didn't disappear upon my birth—was a sign that God had a special plan for my life.

Grandma Sophie explained it best: *You may not be much to look at, Mary Jane, but that's not what's important. That veil makes you special. You're beautiful because God made you in His image; you were born with a purpose.*

The train lurches to a start, and the wheels churn slowly. I tried to prepare for the eighteen-hour trip, but no matter how many times I shift, it's impossible to find comfort. The young girl next to me hasn't looked away from the window. Is she trying to see the countryside through the grime? "Is this your first train ride?" I ask.

Her eyes shine with delight. "Yes, ma'am, how can you tell?"

"The way you're peeking out that window." I adjust my glasses. "That's how I was the first time I rode on a train."

"I'm going to New York to see my grandmother," she explains. "If I like it, my mama said I can stay and go to school up there." Her smile fades a little when she adds, "'Cause things are getting hard here at home since the Wall Street crash."

My heart twists at her last words. Lord, will Negro children ever be afforded the privilege of youth? I've spoken to this girl for less than a minute, but I know her story. I'm sure she has no understanding of what she's just spoken, yet she carries the burdens of those words. Just like the adults in her household, she's worried about whether her family will have enough to eat or a place to live next week. She bears the weight of these uncertainties right alongside her school lessons—if she's in school at all. My prayer is that there will be new hope for her in New York.

"Well, I've been to New York a few times. I think you may like it."

"If New York is as nice as this train, then I'll like it a lot."

When she turns back to the window, I shake my head. Her life has given her no expectations. If only her first train trip could have been like mine.

On that day, I was leaving Mayesville for the first time, heading to Scotia Seminary on a scholarship. My hope was to become a missionary in Africa. There, in the land of my grandmother, I would teach the people about God, or so I planned.

The colored townsfolk had banded together to give me everything I needed for my trip: shirtwaists, skirts, aprons, a long dress, and stockings knitted by Miss Pearlene. Even the white man who owned the general store gave me a pair of scruffy brown men's boots that almost fit.

My teacher, Miss Wilson, had arranged not only for my schooling but for my train ticket to North Carolina, too. After dozens of tearful farewells, Miss Wilson handed me an official-looking document.

"Here is your ticket, Mary Jane, to give the conductor. Once you get to North Carolina, someone from the school will meet you at the station."

"Yes, ma'am," I said.

She took my hands. "I'm so proud of you."

I blinked back more tears. There was so much I wanted to say to Miss Wilson about what she'd done for me. She was the first colored person I'd met who didn't work in the fields, or clean or wash for white people. And she was the first colored person I'd ever heard addressed properly. Everybody called her Miss Wilson, even the pastor at the church.

After I waved goodbye again to everyone, I stepped onto the train. The gleam of the wooden floor and the shine of the red seats were a distraction from my sadness. Every surface sparkled, just like in the Big House.

I found an empty window seat, claimed it as my own, and slid my bag onto the overhead rack. When I lowered myself onto the seat, I squealed; the cushion felt like a cloud. The train lurched, and before I knew it, we were moving so fast, it felt like we were about to fly. Homes and farmhouses and fields sped by. It was 1887, I was twelve years old, and anything seemed possible for me.

"Tickets! Tickets!" The conductor's voice returns me to the present. I pull my ticket and Langston Hughes' novel, *Not Without Laughter*, from my bag.

The young girl passes the man her ticket, but before I can do the same, he says, "Auntie, I need your ticket, too."

I stare at the pale-skinned, blue-coated conductor, his face sprinkled with pimples. He can't be a day past twenty. Instead of handing him my ticket, I open Langston's book and commence reading.

My eyes are on the pages, but I feel the conductor standing there and envision his deep frown. A few seconds pass before he continues down the aisle, and I sigh with relief.

Less than five minutes later, the conductor returns. "Auntie, you ready to give me your ticket?"

I do not look up.

"Auntie?" he repeats a little louder, now with a tinge of anger. When I still don't respond, he taps my arm hard. "Auntie, you don't hear me talking to you? What are you, deaf? I need your ticket."

Slowly, I raise my head until my eyes meet his. "Oh," I say, pressing my hand against my pearls, "were you speaking to me?"

The lines etched in his forehead deepen, making plain the young man's confusion. "Yeah. Who else would I be talking to? Do you have a ticket?"

"I do." I nod and smile, even as rage rises inside of me. "I was just a little confused because you called me 'auntie.'"

The man in the seat behind me snickers, and the conductor shifts from one foot to the other. "Yeah, so what's wrong with that?"

"Well . . ." I pause, dragging this out so I'm certain he hears me. "I keep looking at you and searching my memory, yet I cannot figure out which of my sisters' boys you are."

The train fills with laughter, and the conductor's face reddens. He says nothing as he reaches for my ticket. Our gazes lock; we are in a battle. I win when he looks away and down at my ticket.

As he hands me back my receipt, I say to him, "My name is Mrs. Mary McLeod Bethune."

Without a word, he hurries from the car, and the laughter follows him. But I don't crack a smile. There is nothing funny about a white man thinking he can and should address me or any grown Negro woman that way.

I am an educator, and today I taught a lesson. I only hope it was learned.

CHAPTER 12

ELEANOR

Washington, D.C.
November 22, 1930

Franklin and I arrive early for the final evening of the Governors'
Conference so that no one will witness his slow, painful progress toward the state dinner that President Hoover is hosting. Step by painful
step, Franklin advances down what seems an endless carpeted corridor,
swinging his iron-braced legs from his hips as he supports himself on
a cane and my arm. It would be a stretch to call this walking, although
we do. Franklin cannot arrive at the dinner in a wheelchair, as he cannot be perceived as disabled. So walk he must.

"Nearly there," I whisper as beads of sweat break out on his upper lip.

"Thank God," he manages to mutter back through gritted teeth.

We allow ourselves small smiles as we cross the threshold into the
East Room before a single other guest arrives. Tonight, the carefully
orchestrated and mapped-out plan has worked. How my mother-in-
law would love to be here, watching her beloved son amidst the other
governors of our country. Only the strangeness of arriving with two
guests instead of one stopped Franklin from giving in to her pressure
to be included. That and my pointed reference to all that must be done
to ready Springwood for the impending Thanksgiving holidays, for

which all five of our children; Marion and Nan; and my brother Hall, his second wife, and all his children will be present. Given the special maternal role I've played in Hall's life since the untimely death of our parents, I endeavor to create magical holidays for my little brother.

While Franklin rests for a moment on a gilt upholstered bench, I calm my mind by wandering around the largest room in the White House, one in which I spent considerable time while visiting Uncle Teddy, Aunt Edith, and their children while they lived here. Not until both my parents died did I have a significant amount of contact with them, as Uncle Teddy became my guardian.

After my mother passed from diphtheria when I was eight, taking my beloved brother Elliott with her, Hall and I were sent to live with my maternal grandmother, a stern and parsimonious woman, at her brownstone on 37th Street in Manhattan. My father was lost to drink by then and unable to care for us. By the time he passed away, he hadn't been a regular part of the family for well over a year, but still I missed him terribly. His was the only unconditional love I'd ever experienced.

Hall and I were overseen by a governess who loathed me from the start, and the primary relief in my days were the hours spent at the makeshift Roser school, semiprivate tutoring that took place with other girls my age at various homes on Fifth Avenue, and then Allenswood School in England. Loss and loneliness were otherwise my chief companions until I was finally able to loosen the grips that Grandmother Hall kept on me.

Once we could regularly reunite with our father's family, I became swept up in the affection of my dear, ebullient Uncle Teddy, of whom I was the favorite. It was during those weekends and summer holidays at his home in Sagamore Hill that I first came to know him and Aunt Edith, and that relationship deepened during their years in the White House.

I visited during holiday trips home from my English boarding school, my debutante season, my youthful days in society, and even during the early years of my marriage. One of my most romantic moments with Franklin took place in this very room, just weeks before our wedding on March 17, 1905. Franklin and I were guests at Uncle Teddy's second Inaugural Ball. I'd felt positively princess-like stepping out on the dance floor in the East Room in my pale celadon silk ball gown, embroidered in metallic thread in a feathery pattern, with my handsome fiancé at my side.

"You look radiant, Eleanor," Franklin whispered as he wrapped his arm around my tiny corseted waist and led me onto the dance floor for the very first song. He waltzed me expertly around the crowds, in perfect time to Strauss' "Tales from the Vienna Woods," played by William Haley's Orchestra. I felt shivers at his touch and began dreaming about the honeymoon we'd take after our wedding, which would take place on a date chosen because Uncle Teddy wanted to give me away and he would be in New York then, presiding over the St. Patrick's Day Parade.

As Franklin whirled me around the floor, I saw flashes of Uncle Teddy's beaming face and the euphoric grins of cousins and aunts and even my brother Hall. I floated through the evening feeling pretty and adored and hopeful all at once. My skirts swirling, I was at the center of a great historical moment, hand in hand with the love of my life, and I believed the exhilaration was just beginning.

How I miss Uncle Teddy, I think. His energy, his zest for life, his abundant love. Sadly, Uncle Teddy never really got over the death of my cousin Quentin. The jovial, fun-loving Quentin—a close friend of Hall's and a solid fellow despite growing up in the White House—was one of the first fighter pilots in the Great War, and when the Germans discovered they'd shot down a former president's son in a skirmish in which three of their planes took on Quentin, they buried my cousin with military honors and marked his grave in Chamery, France, with a cross. Quentin was Uncle Teddy's favorite, and his death broke the unbreakable Theodore Roosevelt; Uncle Teddy died six months later, a loss that left me bereft—then and now—and one that continues to haunt Hall, who was a fighter pilot who survived.

Finally, Franklin and I hear footsteps outside the entryway, and I push aside my memories and race back to Franklin's side. As I help hoist him upright, I almost falter as he makes his own effort to stand. How much easier this would be if Earl could be on hand to assist, but no other governor is bringing personal security, and Earl's presence would only make Franklin stand out more. Stumbling, I manage to right myself and keep him erect, just in time for Governor Cooper of Ohio and his wife to enter the room.

As we exchange small talk about the history of the East Room and the rumors that Abigail Adams used to hang her laundry to dry here in the winter, the room begins to fill. Politicians and their wives accept glasses of wine that white-gloved waiters pass on silver trays, although of course Franklin and I decline. He needs both his hands to remain stable, and even if I did not have to support him with mine, I would refuse. Having watched my father transform utterly and then die a painful death from his alcohol addiction even after lengthy sanatorium stays, I would never consider imbibing. *How drink ruined him,* I think. It lured him to do things he wouldn't otherwise, like engage in an affair with our household maid.

A gentle bell rings. It's time to line up in the receiving line to greet the president.

We assemble, and then we wait. Franklin leans half his weight on his cane, and I support the other half with the arm I have slipped through his. His legs can't bear a single pound. It is a stance we practiced time and again before he won the governorship. We knew, from that point forward, that we needed to conjure an image of physical health for him. And sometimes it does indeed feel like a magician's trick.

The minutes tick by with molasses slowness. Five minutes, then ten, until twenty-five minutes pass. My arm quivers with the strain of holding Franklin upright, and I can see that his cane is shaking with

his effort to remain "standing." When will President Hoover enter the
room? For a man known for his punctuality, this delay seems out of
character.

Suddenly I realize what's happening. Franklin has just handily won
reelection for another two-year term as governor, and he has emerged
from the campaign as a formidable contender for the Democratic nom-
ination for president when it's time. Hoover is trying to exercise his
power over Franklin in a most devious manner.

An aide in a nondescript suit appears. Bypassing the long line of
governors and their wives, the heavily mustachioed man walks directly over to Franklin and me and asks, "Would you like a chair?"

I want to slap the man for the audacity, even though I know he's
not responsible for this sick gamesmanship. Hoover sent him.

There is nothing more in the world that Franklin would welcome
than a chair. But he cannot show weakness, not in the face of this terrible show of dominance by President Hoover. Somehow managing to
make himself stand even more upright, Franklin answers, "Of course
not. I am perfectly fine to wait all night for President Hoover."

Echoing his words, I emphasize, "We understand that important
national business may delay President Hoover and are prepared to
wait until he finishes."

The aide raises an eyebrow; he recognizes it as the criticism of his
boss that I intend. He then exits the East Room without a second
glance at the long line of waiting governors.

Once we reach the thirty-minute mark, I am in a full-blown rage.
But I can only ignore the pitying looks of nearby governors and their
wives, who can see the sweat dripping down Franklin's face and my
own. What sort of monster does this to a man, political opponent or
not? Hoover *must* know how hard this is for Franklin, even if the full
extent of his paralysis is a secret. Then again, didn't his people start a
rumor that my husband did not have polio but a progressive muscle
disease that would eventually impact his brain and leave him addled?
This is part of Hoover's nasty scheme.

How can Mrs. Bethune admire Hoover, a man who would shame Franklin to gain a momentary advantage? A man who steadfastly denied the terrible financial threat to our country, even on the eve of the stock market crash last year? A man who even now fails to give Americans the support they need to survive, the kind of infrastructure and opportunities that Franklin is working hard to provide for New Yorkers?

I may not have known much about politics and social issues when I married Franklin—after all, on my marriage, I switched from the Republicanism embraced by the Oyster Bay Roosevelts to the progressive Democratic Party of the Hyde Park Roosevelts without really understanding either—but I certainly do now. And I've come to fully embrace this forward-thinking side of the Democratic Party. I believe that it places a higher priority on human values than the Republican Party, which seems to focus on the commercial sector to the exclusion of the citizens' needs. I've always viewed Uncle Teddy as an exception to *that* sort of Republican, and in fact he always hearkened back to the old Republican Party, which did indeed value social reform.

Mrs. Bethune and I have never discussed politics overtly, and I'm certain it won't come up tomorrow during our meeting. The president's decision to give Mrs. Bethune a position on one of his commissions, after the Republicans have repeatedly failed Negroes, speaks well of him. But I feel nothing but anger toward him at the moment.

Until now, I've been less than bullish about Franklin's time as governor and reluctant about the next step—a run for president. Serving as First Lady of New York has required personal sacrifices. While I've been clinging to my pre-governor life by continuing my work at Todhunter and spending time at Val-Kill Cottage with Marion and Nan when I can, I spend much of my time on the train between Albany, New York City, and Hyde Park, and it takes its toll. On my health. On my friendship with Marion and Nan. On my teaching. On my family.

But Hoover's behavior tonight has softened my hesitations and fortified my commitment. A thought occurs to me: If Mrs. Bethune learned of President Hoover's behavior tonight, might it prompt a shift away from him toward some projects with me instead? The sort I thought might happen after that first luncheon meeting? Even if she's a steadfast Republican? Perhaps she might not align with the Democrats, but maybe, just maybe, she might align with me.

CHAPTER 13

MARY

Washington, D.C.
November 23, 1930

The lovely young attendant of the Whitelaw Hotel places the tea tray laden with flowered china on the table in front of the window. She has taken excellent care of me for the last five days. "Thank you, Shirley."

"You're welcome, Mrs. Bethune. I know the *Washington Post* was delivered to you this morning, but I wanted to bring you the *Pittsburgh Courier* also."

"Thank you," I say as she hands me the newspaper.

"There's an article mentioning you on the front page," Shirley gushes. "About how you were at the White House with President Hoover."

"I'll make sure to read it," I say. My friend Robert Vann is the editor of the *Pittsburgh Courier*, the largest Negro newspaper in the country, and he keeps tabs on my travels better than I do.

Shirley shifts from one foot to the other. "Mrs. Bethune, I hope you won't think of this as rude or as an imposition," she begins, the words spilling out of her, "but my mother loves you. She says you're the first colored woman in the White House who wasn't there to work as a maid or a cook, and that you've done more for Negroes in this country than anybody. Every time she sees you in the newspaper or in a magazine, she cuts out your picture! When you're done with the paper, would you mind signing it for her?"

"Of course," I say. "I'll drop it off at the desk for you."

She exhales. "Thank you so much. Is there anything else I can get for you?"

"I'll need a taxicab in a couple of hours, maybe a little before noon."

"I'll make sure a car is waiting," Shirley says before she finally hurries from the room.

Bless her heart. The small luxury of having tea brought to my D.C. hotel room reminds me of my first visit to the District of Columbia sometime around 1913. I had to stay in a tiny space in one of the rooming houses not far from here because Negroes weren't welcome in any of the D.C. hotels.

But Negroes have options now. Ten years ago, the elegant Whitelaw Hotel was planned, designed, and built by Negroes—even the financing came from colored people in this Shaw community.

I'm not as interested in the *Pittsburgh Courier* article as Shirley. The White House conference should have been a tremendous opportunity for me to give voice to the needs of Negro children in America, but it was not. I was hopeful as I looked into the audience of white men—members of President Hoover's cabinet and corporate presidents.

I explained that, from my front-row seat to young Negro life, we were facing a national crisis. I told them that while I was born free, I grew up slave-poor, and that it was unacceptable that I should encounter Negro children throughout this country living in conditions as destitute as the conditions I lived in over fifty years ago.

The men's expressions remained unchanged, even at the end when they gave me polite applause. My words had fallen on ears that would never hear my call to "strengthen Negro America in order to strengthen our entire country." So now I wonder: What is the purpose of this conference—and my presence at it?

I pick up the *Washington Post.* Although the country's largest newspapers rarely acknowledge its darker-skinned citizens, I am a student of the world, and I read far beyond the *Pittsburgh Courier*.

I turn through the pages announcing the Republicans' midterm losses; Hoover's plans to generate jobs; and, of course, the sort of heart-wrenching stories of suffering that are our daily fare. Unemployment has risen to close to ten percent, and it's expected to go even higher. Another bank has declared bankruptcy. And weary men and women stand in long lines in front of shelters and charities that can't keep up with the needs of Americans.

As I always do when I read about the suffering in our nation, I pause to thank God for the blessings I've received and pray this country will soon find a way to rise. When I turn the page, the headline of a small article makes me sit up straight: SOUTHERN WOMEN CONVENE TO STOP LYNCHING. Every colored person knows about the ever-present threat of lynching, but it's hardly addressed in the pages of mainstream newspapers.

Slowly I read:

> *Texas suffragist and civil rights activist Mrs. Jessie Daniel Ames gathered twenty-six prominent women from around the country to discuss the practice of lynching. They shared their concerns about the escalation of lynchings and discussed how they could use their own community standing to end this practice. The statistics are staggering: 4,287 citizens were lynched between 1885 and 1929; and in 1929 alone, there were 21 hangings of Negroes.*

Tears burn my eyes, but it's the final line that strikes me to my core:

> *Mrs. Ames and the other women have declared that every American who is silent about lynching is as culpable as if they participated in the heinous act. Every American who stands by and does nothing must accept a share of the guilt.*

I've never heard such a proclamation. White women saying that silence is equal to the violent act itself? How long have I waited to hear these words? The newspaper slips through my fingers as a memory takes hold, one that I've carried for almost fifty years.

Daddy told me to sit still on the ground, but I was too excited. We were celebrating my seventh birthday, and Daddy and I were at the mule auction. I'd never seen so many people in one place. White people and colored people—mostly men—milled around the field. But it was the mules that I really wanted to see. So while Daddy was a few feet away, talking to Mr. Lewis, his best friend, I snuck toward the barn.

Then I felt a tap on my shoulder. Squeezing my eyes shut tight and praying that Daddy wasn't too mad, I turned around and faced him. His feet were wide apart and his arms were crossed, but he was smiling. Reaching down, he swooped me up and hoisted me onto his shoulders. Now I could see everything!

Green fields spread out before us, and a rickety gray barn was in the middle. A man stood on a wooden step in front of the barn, the way Reverend Bowen did in church on Sundays.

Daddy called up to me, "It's getting ready to start."

A different man walked out of the barn, dragging a reluctant mule, while men started shouting out numbers. There was so much noise, until the man on the step yelled out, "Sold!"

About ten mules later, Daddy lowered me to the ground. "Let's go get a treat." He held my hand as we walked to one side of the field and stopped at one of the tables. "Give me a roasted corn and a cup of lemonade."

My mouth dropped open; I'd never had food away from our cabin.

When we returned to the crowd, Daddy left me alone for a minute to talk to Mr. Lewis again while I enjoyed my treats. Then I heard a loud shout.

"Get that away from me!"

My eyes opened wide when I saw that it was Mr. Lewis yelling. A white man stood in front of him, holding a lit match right in front of his nose.

Daddy began to back away as the white man brought the match closer and closer to Mr. Lewis. But he wasn't too far away when Mr. Lewis smacked the match right out of that man's hand. Everybody screamed. Dozens of white men pounced upon Mr. Lewis. Daddy snatched me up; the corn and lemonade slid from my hands, hitting the grass with a thud.

"Daddy!" I called, wanting him to take me back to get my treats. But he kept running.

All around us, colored men raced one way while white men, angrily shouting, ran in the other direction. Finally, Daddy reached our wagon, tossed me inside, and somehow got Old Bush, our decrepit mule, to move faster than ever over the dirt path.

"Daddy?" I clutched the side of the wagon.

Daddy gave me a sharp look. "Be quiet, Mary Jane," he snapped.

I shrank back into the seat. Once we arrived home, Daddy jumped off, grabbed my hand, and snatched Mama away from the laundry and into the house. My parents stood in the corner of our cabin, Daddy whispering and Mama pressing her hand to her mouth.

Grandma Sophie had been standing next to the wash bin, and she crept over to me. "What's going on, Mary Jane?"

"At the mule auction, Mr. Lewis got into a fight with a white man. But he—"

Grandma Sophie pulled me into the room where we slept and ordered me to shush. From her tone, I knew there was no room for me to say another word unless I wanted to feel a switch on my legs.

Later that night, when my siblings were asleep, I slid off my pallet. My parents and grandma were in the front room, talking in hushed tones. Mama, Daddy, and Grandma Sophie sat around the table, the room aglow from the kerosene lamp.

"We done talked it all out, Patsy. You and Mama need to go to bed. I'll stay up and keep watch," Daddy whispered.

"No," Mama said. "I'm staying with you."

"And I am, too," Grandma Sophie said. "We all need to sit watch. That way, if they come, we'll get everyone out in time."

Everyone out of where?

Mama whispered, "You think they already did it?"

"They got him right away," Daddy muttered, a sob catching in his throat. "Probably had Lewis swinging from a tree within an hour."

I gasped, but no one heard me, because Mama was sobbing.

"I hope that's how it was," Grandma Sophie said. "I hope they killed him right away and it wasn't one of those long, drawn-out lynchings where . . ." My grandmother's words trailed off.

Through her tears, my mother said, "I just hope they didn't burn him. I hope Anna and the boys will have some part of him to bury."

"Lord have mercy," Grandma Sophie said. "Ain't nobody been lynched 'round these parts for about a year now. You sure you didn't say anything to any of those white men, Samuel?"

My daddy shook his head, and when he turned a little, I gasped again. Even in the low glow of the light, I saw something I'd never seen—his eyes glistening with tears. "I didn't say a word, Mama. I ran like a coward. I let them kill my friend."

"What were you supposed to do?" Grandma Sophie snapped. "You have a wife and all these children. You couldn't fight those white men. All you could do was run, or else they'd have killed you, too."

"My God. They would've had Mary Jane swinging from a tree!" Mama cried. "So just stop it. You did what you had to do."

I tiptoed back to my pallet. When I laid my head down, the words I'd heard played over in my mind. Mr. Lewis swinging from a tree. Me swinging from a tree.

I swipe at the tears on my cheek that come with this memory. The next morning I learned that Mr. Lewis had been lynched. The pain of my first lynching has stayed with me since that day. Could twenty-six white women make a difference? Maybe not. But perhaps a governor's wife has some power that can be harnessed toward this cause. I must discuss it with Mrs. Eleanor Roosevelt today.

CHAPTER 14

ELEANOR

Washington, D.C.
November 23, 1930

I stand at the entrance of the Mayflower Hotel, and even though I am
behind the glass doors, I shiver in the frigid autumnal air. Normally,
I would have asked the hotel staff to direct my guest to the restaurant,
but today I withstand the cold because I want to personally greet Mrs.
Bethune.

A young doorman asks if he can help, and I decline, saying, "I'm
waiting for a friend to arrive. She should be here any minute."

Yes, a friend is what Mrs. Bethune feels like to me. Even though we've
only met in person sporadically, our letters over the last three years
have been intimate. We write of our families, our work in women's
organizations, and our hopes for our country—all of a nonpolitical
nature, of course.

Just then, a taxi edges to the curb and one of the older doormen
opens the cab's door. But when Mrs. Bethune steps out, he hesitates. I
do not want her to face anything negative that might spoil our tea, so
I rush over.

"Mrs. Bethune." I greet her with a smile. "How wonderful it is to
see you again."

She smiles back. "And you as well, Mrs. Roosevelt."

I'd almost forgotten the sound of her rich voice, with just the slightest hint of a Southern lilt. I feel dowdy in my simple flowered dress compared to her charcoal-gray belted-waist wool coat with a full round fur collar and a matching dress peeking from underneath.

Earl follows us, as he usually does. His constant presence has taken getting used to, but Earl is pleasant and makes it easy.

"I've arranged for us to have tea in the Palm Court. It is a lovely—"

"Uh, Mrs. Roosevelt."

I face the friendly young doorman from earlier. "Yes?"

His eyes move from mine as he glances at Mrs. Bethune. "Mrs. Roosevelt, may I speak with you privately, please?"

I feel the heat rise to my face. Because of what happened the last time we were together, I have already checked the Jim Crow situation in the capital and was informed that there were no segregation laws in the district.

"Excuse me a moment," I say to Mrs. Bethune. Earl comes closer to me from the shadows of the lobby.

"What on earth is it?" I ask the doorman.

"There are no colored guests allowed in the Palm Court," the doorman says, his face turning beet red.

I feel sick. Segregation may not be the law, but it is in fact the practice. Racism doesn't need laws, I suppose, only people.

"Let me speak to the manager in charge." I square my shoulders, and Earl asks me quietly if he should handle it, but I decline.

I watch the doorman hurry away; then I return to Mrs. Bethune's side. "I am so sorry, Mrs. Bethune. I didn't expect anything like this, not at a hotel such as the Mayflower."

But before she can answer, an austere-looking gentleman hurries to our side. "Mrs. Roosevelt? I understand you asked for a word."

I have a decision to make. Should I have this conversation in front of Mrs. Bethune? Or should I step away so she will not have to hear? As I consider, I think the shame is the hotel's to bear.

"Yes. Well, indeed. As you know, I'm Mrs. Roosevelt, the wife of the governor of New York, Mr. Franklin Delano Roosevelt. And my friend Mrs. Bethune and I are going to have tea in the Palm Court."

For the first time, the manager glances at Mrs. Bethune. Almost imperceptibly, he hesitates, and then he nods. "I'll escort the two of you to the restaurant."

Stares and whispers follow us as we cross the lobby. For a mere moment, I am experiencing the world as Mrs. Bethune does, and I am horrified. How can this be her daily cross to bear?

I elect not to complain when we are seated in the back. Several empty tables surround us, but at least it will afford us privacy to talk.

"Mrs. Bethune—"

Before I can begin my apology, she holds up her hand, stopping me. "Please, Mrs. Roosevelt, say no more. As I mentioned before, there is no need to apologize for others. We have too much to chat about to waste our time on that."

"Mrs. Bethune," I implore her, "if you would like to go somewhere else—"

"This is so lovely, with the palm trees and fountain. It has such a tropical feel; I rather like it. Anyway, I was invited for tea, and I'd like to stay."

She's right; I don't want to waste my all-too-limited time with Mrs. Bethune. There is nothing frivolous about her, which is one of the reasons I admire her and enjoy her company so much. With most others—excepting Marion, Nan, and my family—I'm meant to transform into a cheery, shallow version of myself, to jettison my earnestness and preference for meaty discussions and replace that with a light gentility that is more socially acceptable.

As the waiter delivers an elaborate tea service—brought to our table before we even placed an order, either as an olive branch or a way of hurrying us along from the manager—we settle into easy conversation about our children.

"So how are you adjusting to life in Albany?" Her dark brown eyes are soft and empathetic.

Something about Mrs. Bethune's question and expression moves me. Everyone else assumes that I should be delighted to be the governor's wife and that living and serving in the state capital should thrill me. I realize that she understands. She and I both wear many, many hats in our professional and private lives, and somehow she understands that becoming the governor's wife might make that difficult.

"I am thrilled for Franklin. And of course I am happy to do whatever I can for the people of New York." This is the beginning and the end of what I usually say. But the truth is brimming just beneath the surface, eager to be let out, and the lies are sticking in my throat.

"But?" She supplies the logical next word for me.

"But I've never loved all the smiling and hand-shaking and small talk and hosting teas and dinners. I like to *get meaningful things done*, and that isn't considered the purview of the governor's wife," I admit. "For example, midway through the last dinner we had for the state's mayors at the Executive Mansion, I got so frustrated with the inane chatter over college sports that I slid out of the room to do some work right after the main course. And no one noticed, a fact that became clear the next day when I ran into one of our dinner guests and he mentioned how much he enjoyed our conversation over dessert! Meanwhile, the work I'm permitted to do—socializing, mostly—is a strange mix of exhaustingly busy and very dull."

"So I am guessing the Governors' Conference was more of the same?" Mrs. Bethune asks.

"You guess right," I say, and then shift focus. I'm not going to tell her about the president's dirty trick. As tempting as that might be, it now feels beneath me. "And what about you? How is the work on the Commission on Child Welfare proceeding? Are you pleased that President Hoover appointed you?"

Mrs. Bethune stirs honey into her tea and then sits back before answering. "'Pleased' is a strong word, Mrs. Roosevelt, and it suggests a certain contentment. While I am 'pleased' to have a seat at the table, I don't have any real power. That was plain enough at the conference.

So I am not content. President Hoover indicated I'd be given a role imbued with authority that I do not have."

"I'm sorry to hear that. You are capable of more," I say, angry but not surprised. No president has given any colored person any sort of authority.

She sighs and sips her tea, finally adding, "We *both* are capable of more, and yet here we sit. Me diminished by President Hoover, and you diminished by the rigid expectations for politicians' wives. Part of the struggle to make change is the struggle to get the right change-makers in place."

How astute, I think. Before I can comment, she continues. "Mrs. Roosevelt, we know we're not going to change the minds of men and the country at tea. But there is one specific issue that I want to talk to you about."

"Please, Mrs. Bethune." I lean forward.

"A civil rights activist, a woman by the name of Mrs. Jessie Daniel Ames, convened a group of like-minded white women from all over the country."

"Oh?" I ask politely. I see that Mrs. Bethune came to this meeting with an agenda of her own. *How alike we are in that regard.*

"Mrs. Ames brought the women together to help persuade Southern men to end lynching."

Lynching? I take a deep breath. We are embarking on a most distressing topic, a subject that's assiduously avoided in polite company. I feel like I'm about to plunge into a murky, deep lake, uncertain whether I'll find my way back to the bright surface.

"That meeting ended with a report," Mrs. Bethune continues. "The number of lynchings happening across our country is astronomically high, and they happen not only in the former slave states but in the North as well, including your own fair state. This is contrary to what most people think, of course."

Why have I never heard about this? And what is being done about it in New York? I'm not much of a First Lady of New York if I don't know what's happening to our citizens.

"Now, you won't read about many of these atrocities in the mainstream newspapers or in the formal reports that Governor Roosevelt receives." She pauses for a bite of ginger cake. "But over four thousand people have been lynched in this country, and while many believe the problem is vanishing, it is not. Dozens of Negroes were lynched in the last year alone."

I gasp. "No!"

At this outburst, Earl steps forward, but I wave him away.

Mrs. Bethune's gaze does not waver, and neither does the conviction in her voice. "Yes, Mrs. Roosevelt, I am sorry to say. And there's more. For the first time, a critical sentiment was set forth—one I've long believed to be true but have never been able to articulate."

"What is that, Mrs. Bethune?" I know I must hear what she has to say, yet part of me dreads her next statement.

"Mrs. Jessie Daniel Ames and the women she convened concluded that one of the reasons these numbers are so high is the silence around the lynchings. No one takes a stand against them for fear of retribution, and no one speaks about them afterward, either to the authorities or the newspapers, out of that same fear. It's a stance you can understand when it comes to colored people in those communities, as the threat of revenge is real. But people who are in a position to stop it or punish those involved—white people—aren't doing anything either. Her report asserts that silence on the issue of lynching is tantamount to guilt."

I consider her words. I have never perceived silence around violence or racist actions to be the same as the acts themselves. But why shouldn't it be? Silence suggests agreement, and anyone who knows about these terrible acts—including me—*should* take a stand against them. Mrs. Bethune has offered me an entirely different lens through which I should be examining the racism in our country.

Unconsciously, I reach for her hand and give it a small squeeze. "I don't want to remain silent, but I don't know where to begin."

It feels strange to admit this ignorance. After years of congratulating myself for advocating for the common man and woman, I am starting fresh here. It dawns on me that today's discussion will not involve a pitch for the Democratic Party or even a shared project.

Mrs. Bethune squeezes my hand back, then glances down to where my long, spindly, pale white fingers are intertwined with her strong, dark ones. I'd reached out to grasp her hand without thinking, inadvertently breaking one of the unspoken rules governing race relations—white and black people must never, ever touch.

When we look up at each other, she says, "You have already begun."

CHAPTER 15

MARY

Washington, D.C.
November 25, 1930

I latch the final strap on my luggage so the Whitelaw bellman can carry it down to the cab. The inhospitable greeting at the Mayflower and the somber teatime discussion notwithstanding, I enjoyed my afternoon with the First Lady of New York. It's funny to think of the earnest, warmhearted, surprisingly frumpy Mrs. Roosevelt as the wife of a governor and niece of a president. She seems too sincere, too wishful of doing good, to be part of the political machine.

Could I ever see myself working with her? Despite the gulf in our origins, we have so many commonalities: a belief that the youth are our future, the desire to elevate women, a drive for service, and a dedication to education. But she is a Democrat, if nothing like the Southern Democrats, who have tried to terrorize me more than once, the last time being just nine years ago.

On that terrible day, Mr. Robinson, Bethune-Cookman's groundskeeper, rushed into my office. "I apologize for barging in, Mrs. Bethune, but I just got this note from my cousin Melvin."

He handed me the paper: KKK march 8:00 at Bethune.

There had been rumors for weeks, but I didn't believe the Klan would come back. Two years earlier, after I'd registered so many colored voters that we outnumbered new white voters in the city, the Klan marched across my campus. But it had neither scared nor stopped me. Why did they think another march would intimidate me now?

"Melvin says there's talk of burning down buildings. But we're not gonna let that happen." He shook his head. "Melvin's already gathering men, and we're gonna put the word out. Let the Klan know they can march, but they better not try to burn. We'll be ready."

Mr. Robinson didn't have to explain what "ready" meant. Melvin and his friends were already gathering and counting their weapons. "Thank you," I said, although those words seemed inadequate.

"Of course, Mrs. Bethune, don't you worry." With a single nod, he left my office.

Mr. Robinson had his plan, and now I had to put together mine. The three hundred girls and twenty-five teachers on campus were my priority. As long as they were safe, I didn't care about the property. Anything that Satan tore down, God would restore.

The last class of the day was letting out, so it only took ten minutes to gather the teachers inside the conference room. After I shared the plan and calmed everyone's nerves, I returned to my office and watched the mantelpiece clock tick the minutes away. I bowed my head; my plans were in place. Now it was in God's hands. When I told the teachers what I was going to do that night, I didn't expect any would join me. This was my school, my burden, my battle.

Wrapping myself in my overcoat, I stepped into the hallway—and stopped. Ten teachers were lined up against the wall, many with their heads lowered as if in prayer, including Mrs. Powell, the first teacher I'd hired, almost seventeen years before.

Mrs. Powell stepped toward me. "The girls are in the dormitory," she said with a tremble in her voice. "They're under guard with the other teachers, and that building is secured with a few men. The other buildings"—she inhaled, then continued—"are totally cleared."

"Thank you. But like I told you all this afternoon, I'm not asking any of you to stand with me. You are all free—"

Before I could finish, every one of those teachers shook their heads. "We are with you, Mrs. Bethune," Mrs. Powell said. "We've been sitting down for too long. It's time to stand up to these bigots."

I reached for Mrs. Powell's hand, then nodded my appreciation to the others. The teachers filed out behind me as I walked to the center of the campus, glancing at my home at the edge of the grounds. I was so grateful that my son and grandson were out of town.

As we stood together, I could see the horrific sight approaching. Even though the grounds were dark and empty, the night sky glowed from the flickering flames of the Klan's torches. Then voices from the dormitory next to White Hall floated into the air: "Be not dismayed whate'er betide, God will take care of you . . ."

Behind me, the teachers joined in on the song. "Beneath His wings of love abide . . ."

The white-hooded, white-robed Klansmen rounded the corner, marching in formation. The first five Klansmen didn't carry torches. Instead, they held a huge white sign with bold black letters: **WHITE SUPREMACY.**

As they marched toward me, I lifted my chin, squared my shoulders, and joined the others: "God will take care of you, through every day, o'er all the way . . ."

The ominous parade of white moved closer; I felt the heat from their torches. I hoped the teachers guarding the girls kept them from the windows. No child should ever witness this.

They marched past, five at a time. I ceased counting at sixty-five, as I could not see an end to the procession. Each Klansman stared at me with glaring eyes through slitted hoods. And I met every gaze, raising my head higher, singing louder: "God will take care of you!" Our voices echoed through the night air.

Then those Klansmen, well, they just marched right off my property. Without a word, without any violence, they left the campus and all of us untouched.

My sigh brings me back to the present. Those same Klansmen and their brethren still march, still burn crosses, and still perpetrate violent injustice. Every one of those men was a Democrat. So, can I work with Mrs. Roosevelt, knowing that her husband works side by side with some people who abhor me? She is different, this I know. But will I be able to keep her politics distinct from her person?

This is a question I'll continue to ask, and I will continue to pray.

CHAPTER 16

ELEANOR

Albany, New York
February 12, 1932

"How do you think we'd fare in Pennsylvania?" Franklin sits behind his desk in the Executive Mansion, glasses perched on the tip of his nose, with a sheaf of papers before him. The subject is whether he will or won't run for president.

"It might be one of the trickier states to win over," Louis Howe replies, staring out of his gaunt face with those piercing eyes of his.

Louis is a former reporter and has been with Franklin since his first political run in the New York State Senate over twenty years ago. In my earlier years I was leery of the older, plain-talking, assertive Louis, but he's been a dear friend and a sage adviser for Franklin, tempering any impetuousness over the years with his steady guidance. More than anything, though, I'll never forget how he stepped in when Franklin developed polio.

We were at Campobello when Franklin complained of fatigue and an odd sensation in his legs. Walking out of the ocean onto the beach, he nearly fell. Louis helped him back to the house and stayed at his side as his condition deteriorated throughout the day and I fetched the doctor. He held my hand at Franklin's bedside when the terrible diagnosis was delivered.

In the bleak months that followed—when I didn't know if Franklin would *ever* get out of that bed—Louis became a member of our household. He carried Franklin throughout the house, read aloud to him from the newspapers for hours, even tended to his bedpan. He undertook all the little jobs and roles Franklin usually tackled with the children and in the house. Like the best sports coaches, he managed to lift Franklin's spirits and push him to work his legs. While Franklin dedicated himself to recovery, Louis spoke for him—keeping his face and voice out in the world, keeping alive Franklin's prospects.

"*If* you decide to proceed," I say, reminding both men that no decision has been made yet.

"If I decide to proceed," Franklin echoes absently, something else clearly on his mind, while Louis rolls his eyes. He understands me, even if he doesn't always agree with me.

The presidential campaign of 1932. This topic crowds out all others, whether it is gubernatorial work, heated debate about the economy, or crises with our children who refuse to settle on traditional paths—most recently, the marital troubles that Anna's having with her husband, Curtis. This back-and-forth about Franklin's chances in each state has been droning on for hours, and so I return to grading my students' papers.

Louis coughs, a deep, racking sound. Asthmatic and sickly since childhood, Louis periodically has these bouts, which he assures us are nothing. He becomes furious when we fuss over them, so Franklin and I steel ourselves for them to pass.

"We do have something else we could consider," Louis says after the coughing subsides. "Something different than a state-by-state analysis and approach."

"What's that? I feel like we've reviewed every demographic and toyed with every strategy," Franklin answers.

"The colored vote."

I sit up straight and begin listening more closely. Obviously, I'm thinking of Mrs. Bethune, with whom I have stayed in close touch since our tea at the Mayflower.

"You've got to be joking, Louis. The colored vote has always gone to the Republican candidate. No one can break that bond with Lincoln," Franklin says, referring to the historical alliance between the colored voters and the Republicans.

I've turned this thought over in my mind as I've considered how I might partner with Mrs. Bethune. What if she saw how much more the Democratic Party could do for her and her people?

"There might be a new opportunity," Louis says with his singular brand of authority. "I met with Guffey yesterday."

I recognize Mr. Guffey's name. Joseph Guffey is a businessman from Pennsylvania who's been instrumental in the rise of the Democratic Party in his state.

"And?" Franklin asks, unimpressed.

"And he had a most intriguing proposal. It relates to Mr. Robert Vann. He's a colored attorney in Pittsburgh who also served as assistant city solicitor, and, most importantly, he founded and runs the *Pittsburgh Courier.*"

"I know the *Pittsburgh Courier,*" Franklin interjects.

"I should hope so. It's one of the largest and most popular colored newspapers, and—"

For all the trust he places in Louis, Franklin does not like his scolding, know-it-all tone. I'm better able to ignore it because I see the almost fatherly concern underneath it.

"So what's this proposal about Vann?"

"Well, it seems as though Mr. Vann has grown disillusioned with the Republican Party, in part because of the false promises of securing federal positions for colored folks. But he's intrigued by the policies of the Democratic Party and your track record as governor in particular."

"What does Vann suggest?" Franklin asks Louis.

"He is willing to give his public support to the Democratic Party generally and to you specifically as president. This would include the backing of the *Pittsburgh Courier*."

"In exchange for what?" Franklin asks.

I used to believe that people should adopt political views for purely ideological reasons. But I've come to realize I was naive. This tit for tat is a typical, if unpleasant, part of the process.

"In exchange for including colored units in the United States military and a federal position of some power for him," Louis answers.

I understand why Mr. Vann would seek this goal. The worldwide economic depression has hit the colored community particularly hard. Opening up employment opportunities for Negroes in the military would not only provide much-needed jobs but would also buoy arguments that they should be given all the privileges of full citizenship.

"What do you think, Eleanor?" Franklin looks at me. No matter the failure in our relationship as man and wife, nothing has weakened our political partnership and his trust in most of my opinions.

I pause, wanting to gather my thoughts. "I think Mr. Vann's ask is not only reasonable but something we *should* do. We would do so much more for the colored community than the Republicans. Far beyond merely including them in the military. Think of how the welfare and job training programs you've instituted in New York might help the colored population." My voice grows increasingly loud and animated at the thought.

"That's an excellent point, Eleanor," Franklin says.

Louis agrees with a hearty nod, adding with a wink, "We will make a politician of you yet, Eleanor." He loves to tease me.

I ignore his jab and press my point. "But I don't think we need Mr. Vann."

"No?" Franklin's eyebrows rise in surprise.

"No," I answer firmly. "What if I could get the most powerful colored person in the country to join our campaign? A person who's a symbol and an inspiration to many, and one of the best-known, most trusted colored people in the nation."

"I'd say that's a hell of an idea, Eleanor. And I'd also say, why didn't you raise it earlier?" Louis asks, looking impressed, shocked, and upset all at once. I feel as though I've won an enormous victory.

"Timing is everything, Louis," I say with a smile. "Didn't you teach me that?"

He snorts with laughter. Louis is rarely happy and nearly never satisfied. "Touché," he says, puffing up. He's as proud as if I was his child.

"Who do you have in mind?" Franklin asks, his voice calmer than Louis', although his expression is no less surprised.

"I'm thinking of my friend Mrs. Mary McLeod Bethune."

CHAPTER 17

MARY

New York, New York
March 10, 1932

This is no Mayflower Hotel. The moment I step into the restaurant, I am greeted like an old friend. "Mrs. Bethune, how lovely to see you," Roberto Marino, the proprietor of the restaurant, welcomes me in a singsong voice, spreading his arms wide. "Welcome back to Marino's."

With its red-checked tablecloths and family pictures on the walls, Marino's is every bit as cozy as when Roberto's father arrived in America from Sicily thirty years ago. It's one of the only white-owned restaurants in East Harlem that welcomes me.

Spotting Mrs. Roosevelt against the bright red wall, I smile. I've begun to think of Mrs. Roosevelt as my friend. From the moment I discussed lynching with her in our last meeting, all she has wanted to do is help. In the letters we've exchanged since, her offers to learn and assist have only grown. This has not been my experience with other white people, not even Mr. Gamble and Mr. White, who limit their contributions to the struggle to writing checks.

When Mrs. Roosevelt sees me, her smile is as wide as Roberto's. "Mrs. Bethune, it's so good to see you again. It's been too long."

Earl, her security guard, stands several feet behind Mrs. Roosevelt and nods at me in greeting. Is he here because she's the governor's wife or because she's in Harlem? Either way, I'm not offended.

Roberto takes my fur-trimmed wrap as I slide into my chair. "I hope this restaurant is fine with you."

"Oh, yes," she says, looking around, "it's charming."

"It's not only charming, but the food is marvelous," I say. "Whether you have the pork chops or their famous meatballs, we will have a fantastic meal."

"Fantastic meals are something I always look forward to."

"Me too, Mrs. Roosevelt. I think you can tell by looking at me that few fantastic meals have passed me by." I laugh, but Mrs. Roosevelt does not. Instead her eyes twinkle and her lips quiver as if she's trying to hold her composure. But she loses the battle, giggles, and, finally, releases a high-pitched laugh that makes other patrons turn toward us. I laugh even louder.

"Oh, Mrs. Bethune," she finally says as she covers her mouth, still fighting to stifle her laughter. "You look absolutely beautiful." Her tone is sincere.

"Thank you, but we both know I could stand to lose a little weight—a pound or twenty." I sigh. "But what I always tell my doctor is that good food is my weakness. It started when I was a child."

Mrs. Roosevelt tilts her head with curiosity. From what I already know about her, she's too polite to ask how the poor child of former slaves had access to good food.

I explain, "Food has always been a way for Negroes to hold on to a bit of dignity in the most undignified circumstances. That's a lesson I learned from my mother and grandmother. They poured their love into the food they prepared, and I'm telling you, Mrs. Roosevelt, you haven't tasted anything until you've had some pickled pigs' feet, hog maws, and smothered oxtails." When Mrs. Roosevelt's lips twist in horror, I laugh again.

Mrs. Roosevelt swallows before she stutters, "I . . . can't say . . . I've ever heard . . . of those dishes."

"I'm sure. Most of the food I grew up loving, my mother and grand-mother learned to prepare from scraps they were given on the planta-tion. After the owner took the best part of the cow, he left the slaves with the tongue or the tail. With the pig, we were given the feet, the stomach, and the intestines."

"Oh," Mrs. Roosevelt gasps. "That sounds horrible."

I think for a moment of those meals I've come to love. "Maybe that's how it was intended, but that was the first lesson in what colored folks call 'making a way out of no way.' Those parts of the pig are some of the tastiest food you'll ever have. But not now. Today, we'll feast on Marino's specialties."

"Well, I'm glad we were able to find a place more welcoming than last time," she says.

I nod, pleased that Mrs. Roosevelt doesn't try to apologize again for something she didn't do. "Moving through this country, I've learned the racial challenges stretch far beyond the South. Segrega-tion is as much a fact in the North."

"You've taught me that," she says.

A waiter takes our drink orders, and I explain there is no menu. Marino's simply makes fresh dishes daily and serves them.

Once we are alone, Mrs. Roosevelt says, "So, Mrs. Bethune, given what you've told me about your mother and grandmother, I assume you're a good cook."

Now I rattle the walls with laughter. "Absolutely not. I don't cook at all."

"I would've thought . . ." She trails off.

"No. Once I went away to school, I determined to focus on all things academic. What about you? Do you enjoy cooking?"

Eleanor laughs as deeply as I just did. "Unless you count the scram-bled eggs I serve on Sunday evening for supper, no. But I'm embar-rassed to admit I don't cook for a very different reason—there was always the assumption I'd have a cook, so I wouldn't need to learn."

The conversation shifts again, toward the work in which we've each been engaged. Our exchange continues to be smooth, easy, as if we're decades-long friends. A rogue thought enters my mind, one I've never considered about a white person.

Since I decided as a child how I wanted white people to address me, I've never given a white person permission to call me anything except for Mrs. Bethune. With this lovely woman before me now, however, I feel differently. There are moments when I hardly notice the difference in our skin tones. So this kind of formality—"Mrs. Bethune" and "Mrs. Roosevelt"—when we've laughed about everything from our favorite foods to my weight feels too formal.

When there is a pause in our conversation, I say, "I really enjoy you, Mrs. Roosevelt, and consider you a friend."

Her smile is wide when she says, "I feel the same way."

"Well, I've been thinking. Given the candor of our conversations, the formal use of our names seems too rigid among friends. Perhaps it's time to address each other by Eleanor and Mary?"

She clasps her hands together. "Oh, Mrs. Bethune—I mean, Mary." We share a laugh again. "I'd be honored."

"Well then, 'Eleanor' and 'Mary' it is."

We clink our glasses and laugh again. Then Eleanor says, "I'm so glad you took this detour north from Washington before going home to Florida."

"Any excuse to come to the city. Who doesn't love New York?"

"As the governor's wife, I'm glad to hear that." The waiter serves our meal, and once he steps away, Eleanor leans toward me. Her eyes twinkle a little more brightly as she says, "Especially since there is something particular I wanted to speak with you about today. When we last met, I'd planned to discuss ways in which we might work together."

I nod. "I've considered the same thing. Maybe an education project? Focusing on young women, perhaps?"

She beams. "Yes, a project focused on education might be just the ticket someday. But in the meantime"—she pauses for a second—"there's something else I'm excited to share with you."

I fold my hands, curious about what she might propose.

Eleanor says, "For a long time now, I've wondered about the Republican Party and whether they're meeting their responsibilities to the colored people of this country. It's certainly no longer the party Abraham Lincoln represented, and that's why I've never been able to understand why the Democratic Party hasn't tried to appeal to colored voters. We have so much to offer."

My smile begins to fade. Does she really not know that while some Republicans may ignore us, many of the men and women in her party go far beyond that and hold appalling views of Negroes?

She plows ahead, unaware of my diminishing enthusiasm. "My husband shares my concerns about the colored population, and as the governor of New York, he has made inroads into helping Negroes during these hard economic times. If he runs for president, he's already laid out a national plan following along the same lines."

Her words tumble out so fast that I wonder if she's registering my reaction at all. I press back in my chair.

"His plan will uplift everyone," she continues. "He won't be like those politicians in the past who say what Negroes want to hear and then, once elected, renege on those promises. My husband will give his word and stand by his commitments."

She pauses only to catch her breath. "That's why, when he and I discussed the colored vote, I told him that, if he wants to win this election and help everyone in this country, there was only one person he should speak to—Mary McLeod Bethune!" Her smile is so wide, I can see every large tooth. "I told him *you*—the most esteemed and persuasive colored leader—are the one he needs to speak to. Then, once you understand what the Democrats can do for our colored population, you'll want to join our campaign."

Eleanor sits back and smiles as if she's just given the speech of her life. Her gaze is on me, but she doesn't really see me. She is in the thrall of her own idea, so she misses the fact that my arms are folded, my smile has faded, and I'm silent.

I am shocked when she continues, "Now, at your convenience, of course, Mary"—she smiles at the use of my name—"we'll begin by setting up a meeting for you to meet my husband and his staff. I already told them they must do whatever you say and give you whatever you ask for."

When Eleanor quiets, I nod slowly, but my expression and stance do not waver. Comprehension finally flickers across her face, and her bright eyes dim, and deep lines surface on her forehead.

"Is something wrong?" she asks.

I am still reeling and unsure where to begin. "You're asking me to consider campaigning for a Democratic candidate?"

"Yes," she answers, although now her voice falters.

I cannot believe the timing of this moment. Eleanor and I have just declared ourselves friends, close enough for me to ask her to call me Mary. Yet, after this little speech, I wonder if she has *ever* seen me.

Pushing my half-eaten plate aside, I lean forward. I want to be close enough so that *Mrs. Roosevelt* will not only hear but fully understand how much—and why—she has offended me.

CHAPTER 18

ELEANOR

New York, New York
March 10, 1932

I am reeling.

"I apologize, Mary. I have offended you; I can see that," I plead, my voice cracking and becoming unpleasantly high.

"I *am* a little miffed"—she pauses and then says my name, as if she's forcing herself to—"Eleanor. Maybe more than a little."

"I hope you know that I would never intentionally do anything to harm our friendship. That is important to me above all else," I squeak.

"I do know that you are invested in our friendship," she says, yet her words sound cautious.

"I am," I reiterate, then ask, "Can you accept my apology? Obviously, I've made a terrible blunder." I still don't know the nature of my misstep, but it seems best to move ahead rather than step backward.

"I'd like to do that, but first we need to discuss it." Mary's tone remains even and firm.

A waiter approaches at this inopportune moment, and I wave him away. But Mary stops me and instead instructs him to refill our drinks.

"There is no way to move forward until we look back—not only to the beginnings of our own relationship but to the history behind all these tricky politics," she says once the man has departed. "The request you just made on behalf of Governor Roosevelt feels like a wall that we've got to scale. Either we can climb it together or, I'm sorry to say, that wall will remain between us—becoming a barricade to friendship."

"Anything, Mary," I say, using her name with trepidation, wondering if she even wants me to call her that now.

"Eleanor, do you have any sense of why I'm upset?"

She's asked the very question I'm most mortified to attempt to answer. But I must offer *some* explanation, so I say, "I overstepped my bounds and asked too much of you."

"No," she says with a shake of her head. "In my world, a friend can ask anything of another friend. Whether or not the friend can grant the request is another matter entirely, but there would never be anger for asking. I am not upset with you for making your appeal."

"Then I'm embarrassed to admit that I don't know what I've done wrong."

"Eleanor," she says, and I realize she will not say anything more until I meet her eyes. When I look up, she continues, "What upsets me is the presumptuousness with which you ask for my support. Do you realize this is the first time we've ever talked about anything political?"

It's true. I don't recall an exchange about our distinct political parties; I deliberately skirt the topic to focus on our common ground rather than our differences.

She continues, "Except for the fact that I'm Republican, we've never discussed my personal political sensibilities. Certain terrible racial issues and struggles women face, yes, but politics, no. So, without speaking to me, you assumed several things. First, you assumed what *I* feel about the Republican and Democratic Parties. For all you know, I could be satisfied with our progress under Republicans."

"You're right," I reply, my voice heavy with apology and regret. "I just assumed you would be as frustrated with the Republicans as I am."

"Yes. It was then you made a second assumption. You took for granted that, simply because you asked me to do something, I would necessarily agree and follow your command."

I gasp. My hand flies to my mouth. *Did* I approach our conversation with that level of audacity?

Mary continues, "You gave no thought to my individual will or the thousands of colored folks to whom I am beholden. So let me make this clear: I believe in the policies of the Republican Party, even if some have fallen short."

When I met with Mary today, I actually assumed she'd accept, but why? Thinking back on my offer to Franklin and Louis to reach out to her, I felt confident that I could deliver her, and the colored vote along with her.

Before I can offer another apology, she says, "But there is a final assumption that you made, and it's one that Negroes often face. It's one that wounds us perhaps more than any other. White folks—even well-meaning ones—routinely presume they know what's best for us. And it pains me to say it, Eleanor, but that's exactly what happened here."

"I am horrified," I say, not even trying to regulate my wavering voice or to hold back my tears. I look anywhere and everywhere but at her. I am afraid to meet her gaze, scared what I might learn about myself in it. "I know an apology can never suffice," I manage to say, staring at the red-checkered tablecloth.

Finally, I force myself to look at her straight on. I see a terrible mix of disappointment and resignation and weariness—with a hint of compassion. It is to that compassion that I say a silent prayer for forgiveness. Not only for my presumptuousness but for my ignorance.

She sighs a heavy, deep breath. Only then does she speak. "Well, you might be in for a hard conversation here—and it might pain you to hear about some of my experiences with Southern Democrats and the Klan—but let us see if we can scale this wall together."

CHAPTER 19

MARY

Washington, D.C.
September 29, 1932

When I step into Gray's Café, I'm a little surprised. This upscale, Negro-owned restaurant, just steps away from the Lincoln Theatre, is one of my favorite spots on U Street, even if I have often had to wait for one of the gold-and-black-clothed tables. But today, the eatery is only half-full, even though it's the lunch hour.

I sigh. It's a sign of the times. The economic downturn has come to Black Broadway and even one of its upmarket businesses. I spot my friend Mary Church Terrell sitting in the center of the room and I make my way to her. Mary, the founder of the largest colored women's club, the National Association of Colored Women's Clubs, has been a friend since I was in my twenties and the president of the Florida chapter of NACW.

We greet each other with a hug, after which the waitress is quick to take our orders. Gray's Café is known for its down-home Southern cuisine, and I already know what I want: the creamed chicken over biscuits. Mary orders the chicken and dumplings. And of course we both have an order of their specialty, Southern spoon bread.

We chat for a few minutes as the waitress returns with tea. Mary catches me up on what's happening with the women's club and I tell her why I'm in Washington—another fundraiser for Bethune-Cookman.

When our food is served, we bow our heads to bless our plates, and then Mary exclaims, "Let me tell you how tickled I was to see your name in Ida Tarbell's newspaper article as one of the 'Fifty Most Distinguished Women of Our Day.' Congratulations."

"Thank you, but I'm sure that honor isn't why you invited me to lunch."

"Always so forthright, Mary." She laughs, but then the corners of her lips curve downward. She glances over her shoulders to see if anyone is listening, but the tables closest to us are empty. So she says, "I'm worried about Hoover's chances of winning reelection."

I nod, putting down my teacup. "I haven't been able to rally the voters this time. How can I get people to care about Hoover when half of all Negroes can't feed their families and are on the cusp of being evicted from their homes?"

"Times are terribly hard, but people have to understand," Mary pleads, "the stock market crash was not Hoover's fault."

"That's not the way the voters see it." I shake my head. "You've seen the newspaper headlines—'In Hoover We Trusted and Now We Are Busted.'"

Mary groans. "When will the people realize the president is not God?"

"People know he's not responsible for the Depression. But Americans expect him to get us out of it, and that's not happening," I say.

"Well, we'll just have to put together a strategy to change people's minds. Like we did with Hoover's last election."

I shake my head. "Hoover himself hasn't made this easy. Besides the economy, he made an enemy of colored folks when he nominated John Parker to the Supreme Court. Can you imagine if the Senate had confirmed someone to the Supreme Court who called Negro participation in politics evil?"

She waves her hand. "There have been worse on the court before, and I'm convinced Hoover didn't know about Parker's racist comments. My goodness, this is America. It's hard to keep track of all the horrible things white people say. But it'll be far worse for Negroes with a Democrat in the White House."

Mary's words remind me of what Eleanor said during our last meeting. The memory makes me want to share that conversation, but I hesitate. Although I remain miffed, I still consider Eleanor a friend, and I am reluctant to betray her confidences.

But my hesitation lasts only a moment. Mary has always been more than a friend; she's been an adviser. Even though I feel somewhat uncomfortable because Eleanor and I have made peace, what we discussed is relevant to this conversation.

I put down my fork and say, "The Roosevelts believe that a Democrat in the White House *will* be very good for Negroes. Their campaign is aggressively courting the colored vote."

"I know." She leans forward as if she's about to share a secret. "Have you heard about Robert Vann and how he's working with them now?" She shakes her head as if the thought of the editor of the *Pittsburgh Courier* crossing to the other side disgusts her. "He's even going around saying that it's time for Negroes to turn around that picture of Lincoln to face the wall! Can you believe that?"

I look Mary straight in her eyes. "The Roosevelts are working with Robert—and they tried to work with me."

Mary recoils. "What?"

"Eleanor Roosevelt asked me to join their campaign." I reference the conversation and the now-active presidential campaign; Governor Roosevelt was nominated at the Democratic National Convention this summer. "Saying she asked me to join is too generous. Mrs. Roosevelt came to me and *assumed* I would join their campaign just because she asked."

Her eyes are wide. "I didn't even realize you knew Eleanor Roosevelt."

I can't tell if Mary is appalled or impressed. "I met her through her mother-in-law a few years back. We've stayed in touch, and during our last meeting in New York, she made her assumptions."

Mary leans forward, her eyes and mouth wide with astonishment. "No!"

I nod. "She had an entire plan without soliciting my input; I was just expected to follow."

"Oh." Mary nods as if she knows what I'm talking about. "I've been in more of those situations than I care to remember."

"I have as well, but this was unexpected. Mrs. Roosevelt is a friend and a good person. She's shown a genuine interest in the plight of our people." Mary's eyebrows rise, but she stays quiet, so I continue, "I doubt she realized how presumptuous she sounded, how presumptuous it was for her to assume she knew what was best for colored people all over the world."

"Ah yes, the white woman who's going to save the Negro race."

"Or the white man."

"Indeed," Mary agrees. "So in all of your conversations, this was the first time you've run into this sort of exchange with Mrs. Roosevelt?"

"Yes. Circumstances forced us to talk a bit about race when she invited me to tea at the Mayflower." I take a sip of tea and glance at Mary over the rim of the cup, knowing she will be tickled.

"The Mayflower?" Her eyes are wide at the thought of me at the famous hotel. "And you went?"

"Of course. I was invited, wasn't I?" I say with a shrug.

Mary's laughter relieves the tension. "That's why I love you, Mary. So what did you tell her? I'm hoping you won't join her and that you'll still support President Hoover."

"Of course I'm with Hoover." My response comes quickly. "I will continue to support the president."

"Good," Mary says with a curt nod. "And I hope you corrected her 'presumption.' We don't need white people to save us; we just need white people to be fair and enact laws that guarantee equality."

"It's as simple as that, isn't it?" I say.

"It should be, but I'm beginning to believe it's impossible for many white people to see us as equal, no matter our achievements." Then she gives me a pointed stare. "Even if they say we're friends."

Her words make me flinch, even as I nod along. Although I criticized Eleanor just minutes before, this idea about her doesn't ring true. Or maybe it does—does she see me as her equal?

"I hope Mrs. Roosevelt understands that she can stand beside you, but there is no need for her to walk in front of you," Mary adds. "And if Mrs. Roosevelt ever gets confused again, tell her to read Miss Tarbell's article. A distinguished woman is never a follower—she is always a leader—and you, Mary, are a distinguished woman. You and Mrs. Roosevelt must lead together, or not at all."

CHAPTER 20

ELEANOR

Sioux City, Iowa
September 29, 1932

"What do you think of this, Eleanor?" Franklin asks, his voice raised
to compete with the roar of the train over the tracks.

He sits in his wheelchair behind a portable desk in our private Pull-
man train car. We are on the return leg of his multistate whistle-stop
tour of America, a trip that Louis didn't want Franklin to take. He
thought it might be too taxing, but Franklin was right to insist. By
touring through cities in a convertible car and giving speeches on
podiums and on the balcony on the back of this train, he's eviscerated
claims by the Republicans that he shouldn't be president because he's
a cripple. He presents as very vivid and very able, and just last night,
Louis admitted he'd been wrong to naysay the tour. It isn't often that
our adviser confesses to a mistake.

I don't answer Franklin at first, as I'm immersed in a letter I'm
writing to Mary. In fact, I'm agonizing over the very first line; should
I even call her Mary? Since our last meeting, I've been particularly
cautious with my language and topics when corresponding with her.
How desperately I wish I could undo that encounter, I think. Even though
we patched things up, I fear it'll take some time before we return to
our original level of comfort with each other.

"Eleanor?" he asks again over the rhythmic sound of the train. When I look up, Franklin launches into a campaign speech railing against Hoover's failings. After I give my opinions on his speech—sharing my admiration for the phrase "new deal"—we each return to our work, Franklin to his speech and me to my letter. Until a knock sounds on the train compartment door, anyway.

"Come in," Franklin calls out.

An aide sticks his head into the small space. "We arrive in Sioux City in thirty minutes, sir."

I rise and grab Franklin's leg braces. Together we strap them on so that he can pretend to walk before the supporters waiting for him at the station. The presidential candidate the crowds will see in thirty minutes' time is not the same wheelchair-bound man sitting before me now.

"This trip has shown me that the American people," he says as I secure the final buckle, "are strong. They have the tenacity to create a powerful new nation and overcome this terrible financial crisis, if only we support them."

I look into his blue eyes, glimpsing the young man with whom I fell in love. I remember well that serendipitous day when I ran into him on the train to my grandmother's summer house along the Hudson River, near a town called Tivoli. I recognized the pleasant Hyde Park Roosevelt distant cousin I used to see at holiday parties at the homes of my Oyster Bay Roosevelt relatives. We greeted each other and then launched into an easy conversation about literature and other summertime pleasures. By the time he asked me to follow him to another train compartment to visit with his mother, I felt a subtle shift in the trajectory of my life.

But then Franklin blinks. That trustworthy young man is long gone. He disappeared for good when he betrayed me with Lucy Mercer. But Franklin's political and social ideals have remained. In that, I have some solace. In fact, if he and I weren't in such perfect accord about the American people—and if I didn't believe that he was the best person to lead them at this precarious juncture—I would not be on this train today.

I only wish that the role I was destined to play wasn't that of the supportive spouse and that I didn't have to sacrifice my own wishes. Marion and Nan cannot understand my inner conflict. Their lifestyle does not pull them away from their professional passions, doesn't require personal sacrifices. No one else quite comprehends my situation.

Wait, I think, *what about Mary?* Although our upbringing is very different, we do share the same passion for the welfare of the people and yet feel the pull of other responsibilities. Could I ever consider discussing my feelings about Franklin's presidency with her?

No. How could I express reservations about Franklin's victory after I tried to bring her on board with his campaign? The only other person who comes to mind is my new friend, the reporter Lorena Hickok. The witty, energetic, stout journalist has been assigned to follow us on the campaign trail. Of course, she's the very last sort of person to whom I should confide. But still, I take such pleasure in our effortless exchanges.

The train comes to a sudden stop. I brace Franklin's wheelchair and help hoist him up from it. I bear his weight until he gets his balance and then assist him from our compartment into the train corridor.

"Ready?" I ask him.

"Ready," he says with a curt nod, and we exit our car only to run into Steve Woodburn. The gray-templed, narrow-faced former journalist has recently joined the campaign. Somehow he got the reporters covering the campaign to agree to photograph Franklin only standing behind a podium—thereby masking his crutches and braces—or in his convertible. Never in his wheelchair; never with evidence of his braces; and never, ever in the process of "walking." This is an enormous coup, and I think Franklin will always feel beholden to Mr. Woodburn.

"Apologies, Mr. and Mrs. Roosevelt. I just wanted to let you know we are all set for a question and answer session with the press after the speech—with all conditions confirmed," Mr. Woodburn says, subtly referring to the limitations on photographs.

"Excellent," Franklin says, gifting him one of his widest smiles.

Another face peers in the open train car door, the smiling face of the dark-haired, apple-cheeked Lorena Hickock. "Any chance of a quick statement from Mrs. Roosevelt before she and the governor appear before the Iowan people?"

Hick, as she likes to be called, initially didn't want to take the Associated Press "puff" assignment of covering me during the presidential campaign; in fact, she lobbied to cover Franklin instead. It isn't that she doesn't like me; we met several years ago when she was reporting on Al Smith's campaign, and we got on well. Still, when she resurfaced on the election trail, we had our initial meeting in an empty restaurant train car, and I served her tea from a silver tea service. Apparently, this gesture was unusual for politicians' wives, who would never serve tea themselves, especially not to a reporter. At this, Hick decided to accept the assignment. Since then, she's come to impress me with her political savvy, tenacity, and droll banter. We've spent long hours of train travel laughing together.

"Now, Hick." Mr. Woodburn turns toward her with a wide smile and a teasing tone. This is a much more charming Steve Woodburn than I've ever been privy to, managing the press for Franklin. "You know better than to ask right before the Roosevelts go onstage."

Hick returns the engaging grin. "Now, Steve, what better time than right before they go onstage?"

As he shakes his head no, she gives me a wink, and then the strains of Franklin's campaign song, "Happy Days Are Here Again," grow louder. The crowd applauds and cheers as the first stanza of the Jack Yellen tune begins to play: "Happy days are here again . . . The clouds above are clear again . . ." The tune is catchy, and that's what Franklin wants—to have the citizens singing his song as they cast their vote. And believing that he can deliver those "happy days."

We step into the final car with the balcony positioned off the back. There, Franklin will make his speech to the Sioux City crowd while I stand at his side. With each step toward the balcony, I think how—no matter my misgivings—Franklin does want to make life better for all Americans. But then I think about Mary and her son and her son's son, and I wonder. When Franklin says he wants to make life better for every man, woman, and child, does he really mean *every*?

CHAPTER 21

MARY

Daytona Beach, Florida
March 4, 1933

I switch off the radio, deciding I don't want to hear the swearing in of the thirty-second president of the United States after all. I still can't believe a Democrat will be in the White House again. It is some consolation that Franklin Delano Roosevelt is no Woodrow Wilson—thank the Lord—and I will know the First Lady of the United States.

The day after the election, I sent Eleanor a congratulatory letter, and she responded with only a brief note. What this stretch has been like for her, I cannot imagine, and I'm sure I'll hear more from her once she's settled.

But I wonder what will happen with our friendship, particularly since, while I didn't campaign against Roosevelt directly, I took as many swipes as I could against his vice presidential candidate, John Nance Garner, the Stetson-wearing Texas lawyer turned congressman who supported poll taxes. The campaign against him was easy; I just told colored voters that one-half of the Roosevelt ticket didn't believe in the Negroes' right to vote. But that had not been enough.

Standing in front of my office window, I look out onto the campus quadrangle. The sun beams down on the few eager students sitting on benches with textbooks, committed to their studies, even on the weekend. And then I take in the sight of the black rosebushes. In a few weeks, those roses will bloom, just in time for graduation.

I've started calling my students Black Roses and giving each a fully bloomed rose at graduation. This is my gift, a reminder to each that they are equal in beauty and stature to every other rose, no matter the color. I expect my students to thrive alongside every rose in the world.

I move back to my desk, past the wall decorated with my certificates and diplomas, including the three that are closest to my heart: my degrees from Scotia Seminary and Moody Bible Institute, and my honorary certificate of membership into Delta Sigma Theta Sorority, Inc. I am not a proud woman, but I do take a certain satisfaction in these accomplishments. I believe my grandma Sophie would be pleased with all I've achieved.

Interesting that I think of my grandmother, as thoughts of her come to me when she's sending a message. What is she telling me today? That I should turn my eyes from the government and focus on what I've already been given to lead—namely, Bethune-Cookman College? Maybe the landslide defeat of President Hoover is what I needed so I can nurture more Black Roses.

Yes, Hoover's loss can become my school's gain. The notion heartens me until I hear, "Mother Dear! Mother Dear!"

I jump up when I hear my grandson's cries. Albert Jr. barrels into my office, almost knocking me over as he wraps his arms around my waist. He's trembling, so I squeeze him tighter. "Albert, what's wrong, baby?"

After a moment he settles down. I lift his chin and study the unshed tears glistening in his eyes. "Tell me what's going on," I say as I lead him to the sofa.

He scoots even closer, then folds his hands in his lap, finally allowing his tears to come. "They called us niggers."

I feel as though I've been stabbed, but my voice is shockingly calm when I ask, "Who called you that?"

"The men at the beach," he says.

I squint, confused. The beach is almost two miles away. "You went to the beach? How did you get there?"

"I was playing with Carl; he came over to see Freddie," he says, and then adds, "Then Freddie came out of the dormitory."

Ah, I think as the scene becomes clear. Carl, Albert's best friend, came to the campus to see his brother Freddie, a student enrolled here. Freddie must have taken them to the beach.

"We just wanted to get in the water for a little while. I promise, Mother Dear. We weren't going to do anything bad."

"Of course not," I say, taking his hands into mine. "It's a beautiful day outside; it makes sense you'd want to go to the beach."

He nods, but his shoulders slump, and my heart dips to my feet as I reach for the right words. "Albert, tell me exactly what happened."

He takes a deep breath as if he's inhaling courage. "We weren't going to stay long. Freddie said we'd just run in the water and get our feet wet."

Freddie, along with other students, had been turned away from the "Whites Only" beach more times than I wanted to count. But Freddie seemed as determined to get into that water as the white people were determined to keep him out. Did he think today would be different as he escorted two twelve-year-old colored boys to the beach?

"But before we could even get on the sand, these two white men came running to us like they were gonna beat us up. One of them was yelling, saying we couldn't get into the water 'cause niggers weren't allowed. I asked him why and his face got real red and he told me to shut up and go 'cause they didn't want niggers dirtying up their ocean."

Raising colored boys in this country is not for the weak. I've tried to protect Albert from those who hate him only because of the color of his skin. But there is no defense for this day—when Albert came face-to-face with the ugly side of America.

"Mother Dear?" he says softly. Although his tears have dried, he's still shaken.

"Yes, baby?"

"Do white people think colored people are dirty?"

Now I'm the one fighting back tears. I roll my shoulders back and lift my head high. It's my duty to give him the truth so he'll stand tall in the face of the lies he'll be told about his race. "Albert, you are neither that name those men called you nor are you dirty. But let me tell you who you are. You come from a long line of royalty. Royal blood flows through your veins."

At first, Albert just stares. Then he says, "Royalty, like kings and queens?"

"Exactly like kings and queens. This comes from my grandmother herself, who is your great-great-grandmother."

"She was a queen?" Albert asks.

"Grandma Sophie was a princess," I say. "She would have been a queen had she not been stolen from Africa and forced to come to this country, where she was made to work in the rice fields."

"Oh," he says, like he has some understanding. "Was she a slave?"

I wish I could tell my grandson that, no, my grandmother was not a slave. That none of the Africans who were stolen from their homeland were slaves; they were teachers and doctors and lawyers and scientists. But he needs the truth. "She was a slave when she came to this country. But she never forgot who she was raised to be. Your great-great-grandmother, the princess, was a stately woman who was well-spoken, disciplined, diligent, and strong. Even though she was taken away from her home in shackles, she always remembered the days when she wore ivory around her neck, gold on her wrists, and fancy embroidered gowns. She remembered that she was a princess and *not* a slave."

"I wish I had met her," he says, his eyes wide.

"And you should know that your great-grandmother and great-grandfather were special people, too. Neither your great-grandfather Sam nor your great-grandmother Patsy could read, yet they bought five acres of land when most white people couldn't, and they built the house on that land where I grew up. And your great-grandfather Sam made all of our furniture."

"Wow! I want to learn how to make furniture." For the first time since he entered my office, my grandson smiles.

"One day maybe you will. But in the meantime, I was thinking that after this long talk, we could do something special this afternoon. Do you know what I'm thinking?"

"No, ma'am."

"It has something to do with Second Avenue."

"Oh," Albert shouts, filling my office with joy. "Are we going to Miss Hattie's?"

"I think we both deserve a big piece of banana cream pie. What do you think?"

"Yes, we do! Can Carl go with us?" He dashes to the door before I can even answer. But then he suddenly runs back and pulls me into a hug. "Thank you, Mother Dear."

I exhale when I am alone, not having realized I've been holding my breath. No wonder Grandma Sophie came to me today. I needed her for Albert, and I need her as my rage rises. I want to cry or scream, but I won't. Victory comes in never allowing the hateful words that are spoken to draw out those emotions in me.

It is insane that two white men—who probably have no more than a grade school education—think they can tell my grandson, a young boy who has played with the Rockefeller children and traveled with me throughout this country, that he's not worthy of sharing God's creation. Do they believe that God gave the ocean to white people only?

The thought of that makes me angrier, but I cannot allow my rage to rule me. Instead, I must focus on a solution. I will find a way to end this practice. My grandson, my students, and every colored person in Daytona will be allowed to go to the beach somehow. That is my vow.

CHAPTER 22

ELEANOR

Washington, D.C.
March 4, 1933

Franklin's hand rests on his family Bible as he listens to the oath recited by Chief Justice Charles Evan Hughes. That seventeenth-century Dutch Bible is the oldest ever used for an inauguration and the only non-English one. I only hope that Franklin's presidency will contain other unconventionalities, including the nature of my First Lady role.

I see that his hand on the Bible begins to quiver, as does the hand clutching his cane. Although we have our eldest son, James, at his side in the event Franklin falters, I wish the chief justice would hurry. A hundred and fifty thousand people's eyes are upon us, and we've worked too hard to project an image of strength to have it ruined on his Inauguration Day.

Finally, the chief justice ends, and Franklin begins, "I do solemnly swear that I will faithfully execute the Office of President of the United States . . ."

The sunlight was plentiful earlier in the day, during the brief service performed at St. John's Episcopal Church and the painfully long and awkward car ride to the Capitol with the Hoovers. But now, as Franklin finishes his oath and walks to the podium on James' arm, the sun hides behind the increasing clouds. A shiver passes through me, and I try to shake off the mounting chill as the Marine Band sounds out the first chords of "Hail to the Chief."

The crowd grows quiet as he takes the podium. Franklin's speech will be broadcast on the radio, and if the estimates are correct, tens of millions of citizens are listening. American citizens who need hope and guidance now more than ever. Although the country has endured financial despair for some time, this very morning, the situation turned dire. The Federal Reserve Bank of New York suffered a $36 million loss, and banks in dozens of states shuttered. The New York Stock Exchange and the Chicago Board of Trade made the unprecedented decision to close. All seems in a desperate flux, and much hinges on Franklin.

I stare out at the throngs impatiently waiting for Franklin to throw them a lifeline. I muster a smile for our children and their families, who are assembled around us: our eldest, Anna, with her husband and two small children; James and his wife; Elliott and his new bride; my two youngest boys, Brud and John, both here from school for the ceremony; and close friends like Marion and Nan.

No one looks prouder at this moment than my mother-in-law. I wonder whether Sara will decide to move into the White House with us. Fortunately, she loathed Albany. Our time together was dramatically reduced, and our relationship improved—as did my relationship with my children without my mother-in-law's interference.

Finally, Franklin greets the crowd and then speaks aloud the phrases over which he labored: "So, first of all, let me assert my firm belief that the only thing we have to fear is fear itself . . ."

I heard these words over and over as I listened to Franklin practice. But now it feels as if they've been spoken for the first time, and I feel like cheering. I can see how fear has had a stranglehold in my own life.

But why must that be the case? Why should I allow fear to diminish me? Franklin is the leader who can guide the American people through this crisis; of that, I've always been certain. It's been *my* role in his presidency about which I've had doubts. But the time for my own hesitations is past.

I think about the advice that Uncle Teddy's widow, Aunt Edith, gave me just a few weeks ago. She pulled me aside during the large family party thrown in honor of Franklin's victory and whispered to me: "One day, you'll be scrutinized and scorned, and the next, you'll be celebrated and lauded. Sometimes by the very same people. You will not be able to control the narrative, but you can act according to your conscience, particularly in your personal life. And at the end of the day, that should be the only measure that matters."

In fact, it should be my refrain. As the First Lady, I will stand by Franklin's side and act as expected. But I will not become like Mrs. Hoover, who told me the thing she'd miss most about the White House would be having her travel arrangements taken care of. I will not, cannot, allow the role's constrictions to limit my professional work. Why can't I continue my efforts for women and children? And why can't I continue with my newspaper and magazine columns, and even my radio appearances and speeches? Simply because no First Lady has ever done so before does not mean it cannot be done. A certain buoyancy infuses me, and I feel lighter than I have in some months.

Could I even tackle equality for our colored citizens? I think about the conversations I've had with Mary. The experience of seeing the world through her eyes, however briefly, has not only lingered but intensified. Together, could we test Franklin's commitment to *every* man, woman, and child? I will have to tread lightly and make no presumptions in our friendship.

I consider my friendships with Marion and Nan. While they'll remain living and working at Val-Kill Cottage and at the Todhunter School, I know I can't teach anymore or work with Val-Kill Industries. I'll have to put in a greater effort to stay in touch with them than I did as First Lady of New York.

But what about Hick? What a twist she has introduced. This morning, she arrived at my suite at the Mayflower for a last interview as just plain Mrs. Roosevelt. But as I poured her tea, she made a disclosure. "I confess that I'm not here as a journalist. I have no plan to conduct a last interview." Her already ruddy cheeks were now bright red.

I've only ever known Hick to be a straight shooter, even about her abusive and poverty-stricken childhood. So deception felt out of character and off-putting.

"What's going on?" I asked warily.

"I'm here to give you a gift and ask you a question—off the record." She stammered a bit, unusual for the self-possessed Hick. "But first, the gift." She handed me a tiny, beautifully wrapped box.

I stared at my brilliant friend and said, "I feel like I should be giving *you* a present. You worked so hard on the campaign—on the train, at Hyde Park, in Albany, and in New York City. And you always gave me the courtesy of reviewing your articles about me in advance."

"Please open it," she said.

After I peeled back the cellophane and the wrapping paper, I realized that the box came from a jewelry store. Inside there was an exquisite sapphire ring resting on velvet.

I gasped. "It's beautiful."

"And now my question," she said, her voice quivering the slightest bit. "Eleanor, I've grown to have feelings for you over the past few months. More than friendship, if you understand what I'm saying."

I nodded. Of course I understood.

"I would never ask this question if I didn't know the nature of your relationship with your husband." Although I've never told her about Franklin's infidelity, we've exchanged several pointed glances that revealed her understanding, and I'm sure she's heard the rumors. She also knows I've changed since the early days of my marriage. I've told her that when I married as a young, besotted bride eager to start a family to create the stability I never had, I simply followed where Franklin led—until a shift happened between us and I began creating a life of my own.

"Is there any chance you could ever have those sorts of feelings for me?"

I have wondered at this very question over the past few months. I know I feel *something* for her—something different than what I once felt for Franklin, and distinct from my emotions for other women friends. But is this the sort of affection that Marion and Nan share? I simply don't know. I've never experienced it before. And even if I did, could I really form a tie to a woman just as I become the First Lady? And with a journalist, of all people?

I reached out to touch her cheek. "Can you give me some time?"

She placed her hand over mine and said, "Of course."

Glancing down at my hand now, I see the simple sapphire band she gave me. My cheeks grow warm as I think of the tender, unexpected moment that passed between us. Time will tell what course our relationship will take.

But regardless of what happens with Hick, I *will* forge a new path. Tonight, after the parade, after the White House tea where we'll toast Franklin and after the fireworks display, I will put on the blue lamé dress that's been staring at me from my closet—taunting me and my tall, gangly body. I can almost hear my mother's insults, but I will wear it to the Washington Auditorium for the inaugural ball with a confidence I might not feel. I will become as fearless as Franklin has encouraged the American people to be.

CHAPTER 23

MARY

Washington, D.C.
May 11, 1933

Around us, the din in the Whitelaw Hotel is low and the mood is somber, the result of the morning's presentations. I was looking forward to attending the Rosenwald Fund's Conference on the Economic Status of the Negro. It was supposed to bring together black laborers with white workers and union leaders to pose fresh ideas for broad employment. At the end of the conference, we were to leave with a plan to put everyone back to work. It was an ambitious goal, and an empty one. The white workers and union leaders didn't show up.

"You can't blame the conference," I say after Eugene Kinckle Jones notes that he's certainly attended more uplifting conferences in his time. Eugene, one of the founders of the Alpha Phi Alpha Fraternity, has been to as many conferences as I have.

"I suppose it wasn't *all* bleak," Eugene says, brushing his handlebar mustache with his finger, something I've noticed that he does when he's deep in thought.

"William DuBois' speech gave me some hope," I agree, thinking about how my friend dominated the stage, undiminished at sixty-five. "Even though the statistics were shocking and the Depression is severe, it was satisfying to learn that, at least in the iron and steel industry, Negro workers are holding their own. I was encouraged to hear that in some plants, Negro and white employment is almost equal."

Walter White says, "That's fine, Mary, but it's such a small part of this country. Did you hear what William said about what's going on in the major cities? Like New York and Philadelphia?"

Of course I heard, but Walter is going to repeat it anyway. "Sixty-four percent of Negroes in Harlem are unemployed. As a colored man, that is a jarring number."

Even though I've known Walter since before he became the head of the NAACP four years ago, it always gives me pause when he says something like this. Because, for all the world, he is like his last name— he is white. Yet this blue-eyed, blond-haired, fair-skinned man identifies as a Negro and is a formidable Negro activist.

"And if William's statistics weren't bad enough," Howard professor and recent Harvard law school graduate Ralph Bunche says, interrupting my musings, "the next speaker warned that colored unemployment could go as high as ninety percent."

We all shake our heads, despondent at that thought.

"Sometimes the truth is hard," I say, unsure what else I can offer. "But the truth helps us decide what we have to do, where we have to start."

"Start?" Eugene says. "Feels like this is more of an ending than a beginning. Today it became clear that there's no plan to save all those people who are living on the streets. It's no longer about economics; it's about survival."

"And where were the white people who were supposed to be at the conference?" Ralph asks.

"I was always skeptical." Walter folds his arms. "Why should they attend? None of them want to stop the practice of firing Negroes to provide employment for white workers."

Eugene jumps in. "Look, it's time for us to bypass the workers, bypass the unions, and go straight to the top. We need to speak to the president."

Ralph says, "I agree. I was surprised no one mentioned President Roosevelt or where Negro workers fit into his plans."

Walter shakes his head and chuckles as he asks, "Do you think Roosevelt is any different from other white employers? Do you think he wants to work with us?"

"He should," Ralph says. "He won more colored votes than any Democratic president in history."

"That's no great feat." Walter waves his hand, swatting away Ralph's words. "Negroes aren't a powerful enough voting bloc, especially since there are all kinds of ways to suppress our votes."

"Still," Ralph says, pushing further, "the colored vote helped him, and he's promised to give back."

Walter chuckles again. "Do you honestly think a man like Roosevelt, a man who fancies himself a son of the South, who chose Garner as his VP, cares a bit about Negroes?"

Ralph isn't finished. "No matter what you say, we need to hold Roosevelt accountable. He must include Negro Americans in this New Deal he keeps talking about."

Walter says, "I don't trust President Roosevelt, but that wouldn't stop me from speaking to him—if he'd listen. We've reached out several times, and do you know the president's response?" The younger men watch Walter, but I already know what he's about to say. If President Roosevelt had responded, Walter would have taken out a full-page ad in the *Pittsburgh Courier.* "No response. This means the president thinks the New Deal is like everything else in America—for whites only."

Ralph's mouth forms an astonished circle. "The president didn't respond to the leader of the NAACP?"

"No!" Walter snaps. "We tried going through his advisers, even speaking to Louis Howe and Steve Woodburn, and that still wasn't enough to get a colored man in front of Roosevelt."

I hate the way Ralph slouches in his seat after Walter snatched away that young man's hope. In truth, Walter's skepticism is warranted. Nothing has come of the president's promises. Even Robert Vann, who was given *some* kind of promise of a federal appointment for his endorsement, continues to live in Pittsburgh.

An unsettled feeling comes over me. Would things be different if I had accepted Eleanor's offer to help with the campaign? Would Walter have already secured a meeting with the president if I'd stumped for Roosevelt? Would I have a seat at the table? Maybe I made a terrible mistake—all for the sake of holding fast to the Republican Party.

"Well," Eugene finally speaks up again, "you may not have been able to get in front of the president, but there may be another way. We may have a conduit right here." Eugene turns to me. "I've heard you have a friendship that could lead us right to the front doors of the White House."

How on earth does Eugene know about my friendship with Eleanor? It's not that I've kept it a secret, but I do keep it private. *To whom has Eugene talked?* Then I remember my conversation with Mary Church Terrell.

Eugene interrupts my musing. "You *are* friends with Mrs. Roosevelt, aren't you?"

I watch all of their eyes widen, and Walter leans forward. *"You're* friends with Eleanor Roosevelt?"

I don't have to answer Walter, because I am bombarded with questions from everyone at the table:

"You know the First Lady?"

"When did you meet her?"

"How long have you been friends?"

But Walter's last question silences everyone. "Can you get us in to see the president?" When I stay silent, Walter snaps, "Do you know the First Lady or not?"

I arch my brows at Walter's tone until he leans back. "This whole conversation started with a rumor Eugene heard," I finally answer.

"You all know that I would neither confirm nor deny any rumor of which I was the subject. That would only feed the gossip, and I'll never be part of that."

I pick up my menu, and after a few more seconds of staring at me, the others do the same. When I'm sure their eyes are on the menu, I exhale. I may have skirted that line of questioning for now, but Walter will be at it again. There is only one person on earth as persistent as me—Walter. At some point, he will ask again, and I will have no choice except to answer.

CHAPTER 24

ELEANOR

Washington, D.C.
May 14, 1933

It became clear that, if I wanted the life I dreamed about on Inauguration Day, I'd have to take a hatchet to a thicket of household management chores. There were no political endeavors for me, just menus and wallpaper choices and furniture arrangement and invitations. I didn't blame the staff; after all, this was the typical purview of the First Lady.

To carve out more time for my own interests, I've come up with a plan. Every morning, I meet with Mrs. Henry Nesbitt, whom I'd known as a baker in Hyde Park and then hired as White House housekeeper. Next up is the White House usher in charge of vetting and attending guests entering the house, and then Mrs. Edith Helm, my social secretary. And finally, I meet with my most important staff member, Miss Malvina Thompson—or Tommy, as she likes to be called—and we tackle the endeavors nearest to my heart. In her inimitable earnestness, she helps as I write newspaper columns, books, radio scripts, and broadcasts that focus on my causes. Tommy handles the scheduling and details of my visits across the country. Interspersed among these tasks, we plan the teas and meals for the many groups that align with my beliefs. We also arrange ways for me to introduce Franklin's New Deal to different constituencies.

Perhaps my most revolutionary act as First Lady is to hold my own press conferences in the Red Room. It was Hick who suggested it.

One evening, as she and I ate supper together several weeks after the inauguration, she asked, "How's it *really* going?"

"I might be drowning in other people's expectations," I answered honestly, peering at her over a table piled high with unpacked boxes.

Shaking her head at me fondly, she said, "You know, I've covered a lot of First Ladies as a journalist, and I've learned there is no rule book for the job. Who says you can't write the rule book for yourself? Why don't you begin by announcing your intentions and your plans directly to the American people?"

"How?" I asked, intrigued by the idea.

"By holding regular press conferences. Oh, and what if you hold them exclusively for women reporters? It would not only keep the larger population abreast of your activities and views, but you could help provide stable employment for female journalists by giving them exclusive stories." She explained that women journalists in Washington, D.C., were in constant danger of losing their jobs, and this would give them an exclusive that would provide job security.

"It's a clever idea, Hick, but would people really be that interested in hearing and seeing *me*?"

"If they witness even a fraction of the brilliance and beauty that I encounter when I'm in your presence, they will be hanging on your every word," Hick said, her voice low.

She reached for my hand, and we scooted closer to each other. We sat that way, our fingers interlaced, for a long moment. Not since Inauguration Day had she asked about my feelings, and our physical interaction had been limited to hand-holding and a few stolen caresses. But every time I thought about her, my cheeks became hot, and every time we were together, I felt closer and closer to her. I never imagined that I would find myself in a Boston marriage, and I still hadn't made up my mind about entering into one. But then, after so many years alone with no thought that I might find affection again, I never dreamed I'd find someone like Hick.

The door shakes with a hard knock. Glancing up from the pile of correspondence I'm sorting with Tommy, I see Mrs. Helm standing in the doorway. It's unusual for the social secretary to visit my private chambers after we've already had our morning meeting. "Yes, Mrs. Helm? Can we help you with something?" I ask.

"Do you have a tea appointment in your calendar for this morning? I don't see anything on the schedule, but the security guards rang to say your guest is here."

Having last served as social secretary to the First Lady under President Wilson, Mrs. Helm holds fast to protocol. I think I have her a little frazzled.

"I do. It is an unofficial visit with a friend, so I didn't think it necessary to run by you."

Her narrow face pinches at my words. "Mrs. Roosevelt, you are the First Lady. Every visit is official and must be placed in your diary."

"Thank you for your guidance, Mrs. Helm. If you could let the guards know that they may show my guest up, I would appreciate it."

She doesn't move, but her mouth opens and closes several times. "There is another issue with your appointment."

"Yes?" I know what she's going to say, but I want to make her speak the objection aloud so she may learn such words will never be uttered again.

"It seems your guest is colored," she says without her usual authoritative tone.

"And?" I ask, standing up from my upholstered chair. Tommy rises as well.

Mrs. Helm freezes for a moment and then, with her typical briskness, says, "And nothing, ma'am. I will advise the security guards to send her up. Will you be meeting here?"

"Yes."

"Then I'll ensure a tea service arrives in a few minutes."

"Excellent. Thank you, Mrs. Helm."

Tommy shoots me a glance but says nothing. Wordlessly, she and I sort through the few remaining letters in the pile, and as Mrs. Helm exits my sitting room, she passes by my arriving guest and half curtsies. I stride toward the door and stretch out my hand in a hearty greeting.

"What a delight to see you!" My pitch is higher than I'd like. Louis has me practicing a lower timbre with an expert, as he believes I can be a tremendous asset to Franklin on the road giving rousing speeches. But anxiety and nerves always cause the timbre to rise, and I'm nervous to see Mary again. My voice betrays me.

"And you as well, Eleanor." She returns the smile and the handshake.

I feel such relief that she is still calling me Eleanor. I was worried that she'd revert to Mrs. Roosevelt.

"It's an honor to have an appointment with the First Lady," she continues, and I cannot tell if she is serious or gently teasing.

That high-pitched laugh of mine escapes, quite against my wishes. "It will never stop sounding strange to be called the First Lady."

Mary smiles. "I can only imagine."

"Especially since a change in title doesn't mean there's a change in person."

Mary gestures around the area I've converted from a bedroom suite into a work space. "What a lovely room—and the view is striking."

Together we wander over to one of the wide windows, which look out onto the South Lawn. "I'm partial to those magnolia trees, which I hear Andrew Jackson planted."

"History literally springs up all around you here," she says.

"What a thoughtful way to put it. Please sit." I gesture to the brown chintz sofa. When we toured the White House some weeks before we moved in, Franklin, the children, and I found the furniture unspeakably uncomfortable, so we moved some of our well-loved pieces here, no matter how unseemly for the space. Mary and I settle onto the comfortable upholstery as a maid arranges the tea service and a tray of some of Mrs. Nesbitt's best doughnuts and cream-filled pastries.

After an awkward silence, I ask, "How are things at Bethune-Cookman?"

"As well as can be expected during these hard financial times. I spend more time fundraising than educating these days," she says, her eyes looking unusually weary. "How about your beloved Todhunter?"

"Sadly, I had to give up my teaching there." I hope I don't sound as despondent as I feel. Relinquishing the role that's given me unadulterated joy—teaching—has been difficult, yet I don't want to sound ungrateful for being in the role of First Lady.

"I imagine you have a full plate—a heaping one, in fact," Mary comments.

"Sometimes I wish it was piled high with Mrs. Nesbitt's delicacies"—I gesture to the tray in front of us—"instead of the thorny problems our country faces. But I am blessed to be in a position to help."

At this, we each reach for a doughnut. "These are scrumptious," Mary says as she bites into a cinnamon one. "You've got yourself a gem in the kitchen."

"I don't know about a gem. She is a gifted baker, but I've been having her try out some of the economical meals I learned about in a domestic science course—the White House needs to set a good example, after all—and they are not exactly Marino's."

"No delectable meatballs?" Mary asks with a half smile.

"Not even close," I answer with a shake of my head. "But tell me, what brings you to Washington, D.C.?"

As soon as I ask the question, I chide myself. Does my query suggest that she has no real reason to be here now that Hoover is out of office and her federal committee positions are gone along with him? I'm trying so hard to be careful that my nerves are getting the better of me.

"The conference organized by the Rosenwald Fund," she says, then describes the disappointing turnout of white businessmen and union representatives and her worries over a place for Negroes in the New Deal.

"We must address this concern about the colored population's access to the New Deal programs." I realize my words sound hollow without a plan. Neither Franklin nor anyone on his staff is going to provide me with the opportunity to do work on projects related to equality, especially since his staff is populated with Southern Democrats who are historically ill-disposed to civil rights or those inclined to protect them—Assistant White House Press Secretary Steve Woodburn being a prime example.

To my surprise, Mary doesn't seem interested in pursuing this discussion and attempts to change the subject to living at the White House. *How should I interpret her reaction?* If I have learned anything from Mary, it's that I should not make any presumptions—about her views on a topic, my knowledge on a subject, or her interest in working with me. If I want to pursue this possibility, I need to speak plainly, inviting her insights.

"I am just beginning to find a way to make the First Lady role my own. While I admire my predecessors who found great joy in entertaining and decorating, that work isn't in my nature, as I think you know. Especially not after I've seen the state of the country. I would like to use whatever power I have to help, particularly women and the colored community. I am not exactly sure how to do that, but I am listening if you have ideas."

Mary's usually strong and confident voice grows quiet. "I didn't come here to ask you for anything, Eleanor, and I hope I didn't give you that impression in my letter. I didn't even want to talk about the conference or politics or issues involving race. I only came to check on my friend and her transition."

I reach over, covering her hand with mine. "I appreciate your kindness, Mary, and I hope my missteps the last time we talked haven't scared you away from having these conversations with me again. But I am offering to help, and I am asking you how best I can do that."

She seems receptive, so I go on. "I feel the timing might be auspicious because Franklin is having such tremendous victories getting his various New Deal programs passed."

In his first two months in office, Franklin has had singular success moving along his agenda. During a special session of Congress, Franklin presented nearly fifteen bills geared toward financial assistance for citizens and bolstering the economy. One by one, these bills are passing into laws.

"I appreciate your offer." She squeezes my hand. "It's heartfelt, and we need the assistance. And I appreciate your approach this time. I think there is much we can accomplish together."

I am honored by her words. Is this the moment I rise up and become a *very* different First Lady? "How shall we begin to ensure that the New Deal is indeed for *everyone*?"

CHAPTER 25

MARY

Washington, D.C.
May 14, 1933

We began with tea, moved on to lunch, and now empty dinner plates sit before us. We canceled our appointments as the day went on, and now fountain pens and stacks of papers are strewn about.

First, we made lists of the pressing needs for Negro Americans and then cross-referenced those with the corresponding New Deal programs. After reviewing our final list, I ask, "Would you like me to summarize?"

Eleanor nods, and I stand to face her.

"There are four primary goals: first, immediate relief for the unemployed and their families; second, job creation specifically apportioned for Negroes."

"Yes," Eleanor says. "These first two goals will be directly funded through the New Deal programs, the list of which I have here."

"The third," I continue, "focuses on anti-lynching—specifically, supporting the bill that is currently being underwritten by the two Democratic senators."

"Costigan and Wagner," she adds.

The thought of having federal legislation to punish this heinous act fills me with hope that I've never felt before. "Do you really think it's possible to get an anti-lynching bill on the president's desk within his first year or two?"

"Perhaps." Her tone does not sound as optimistic as I'd like. "Franklin is sympathetic to issues impacting the colored population, but he can be difficult on how those issues are addressed."

"What do you mean?" I squint in confusion. "He doesn't see the racial issues in this country?"

"Oh, he does. He's just steadfast in his belief that discrimination is not totally a social issue. He thinks with a strong economy, most of the racial issues will go away."

I shake my head. "No matter how many jobs are created, no matter how strong the economy, discrimination will remain, because it's in the fabric of this country; it's systemic. Negroes aren't hired because we're colored; Negroes aren't rented apartments because we're colored. Negroes can't go to certain schools, cannot eat at certain restaurants or stay in certain hotels not because of any economic conditions. I'm not allowed into places where I have more money than the proprietor. Because of the color of my skin, the doors are closed. If Negroes are not specifically included in the New Deal programs, we will be left out."

"If only he'd listen to you," Eleanor laments. "You make it so clear, and you're so persuasive."

"Just let me know if you want me to show up at the door of the Oval Office tomorrow," I offer, only half joking.

Eleanor shakes her head, her eyes sad. "I wish that would work. Even if Franklin were so inclined, the Southern Democrats control much of the power in the party, and they won't get behind him if the New Deal contains explicit provisions about race. I'll do my best to put our objectives before him, but we'll need a broader, more flexible approach, because"—she becomes excited again—"our fourth goal, to get Negroes appointed to key positions in the administration, will change everything. If we can get Negroes into some positions, Franklin will have to listen to those men about the issues facing the Negro community."

"I agree. Having a Negro adviser in each of the New Deal agencies will give my community the voice it needs."

She nods.

It is difficult to believe I'm sitting in the residence of the White House, speaking about putting Negroes in meaningful presidential cabinet positions.

"I feel hopeful, Eleanor. For the first time in a long time." I sink into the sofa, overwhelmed by both work and optimism.

"We've got our four-pronged strategy in place," Eleanor says, sighing, "but we'll have to work on our patience, I suppose. We can't solve the problems of this country all in one day."

"Exactly." I pause, pondering her words. "Let's give ourselves at least forty-eight hours."

We give each other a sidelong glance, and then our giggles fill the room until we are crying tears of laughter. We are like delirious schoolgirls, punchy with exhaustion and giddy with hope.

Wiping away her tears, Eleanor says, "Mary, this has been the best day! When was the last time I sat down and strategized on something important with a friend?"

"I don't remember a time when I've laughed so much while working."

Her smile fades. "The laughter is welcome. There hasn't been a lot of it lately."

"I can imagine. You and the president have gone from the governor's mansion to the White House in four short years. It must be daunting—even when it's exciting."

Her eyes narrow, and a shadow crosses her face. "'Exciting' is not the word I'd use for Franklin and me. Things haven't been as you might expect between spouses for some time."

"Oh," I whisper, reaching for her hand. "I'm here to listen for as much or as little as you want to say. And if you want to be quiet, that's fine, too."

She glances down at our hands, mine on top of hers. When she looks up, a heavy sadness shrouds her eyes. Eleanor is the First Lady of the United States, and yet, despite her background and position in life, she carries such melancholy.

Eleanor blurts out, "Many years ago, Franklin had a long-term affair, and I've never really recovered in some ways. Especially since I was betrayed not only by him but by a friend, a woman I trusted with my personal and professional life." She takes a long breath. "She was my social secretary, Lucy Mercer. And it happened right under my nose."

My friend has no idea how much I understand.

Without waiting for my reaction, she races forward. "The two of them carried on for years before I found out. Franklin's unfaithfulness hurt me deeply, of course, but it was exacerbated by the fact that many in our circle knew. And no one told me. I was the perfect cliché of the wife being the last to know."

"How did you find out?" I whisper.

"He was careless. I discovered letters in his suitcase," Eleanor says, her pain audible. "He vowed to be my husband, and she pretended to be my friend. I've never forgiven him—never forgiven either of them." Suddenly, she shakes her head as if forcing herself from a trance. "Look at me. I'm sure you don't want to hear all of this."

"I want to hear anything my friend wants to tell me."

Her lips curve upward, but the smile doesn't reach her eyes. "I didn't mean to go on."

"You were just confiding in a friend, someone who shares a similar pain." She leans back as if she wants to get a better look at me so she can understand. I explain, "My husband had an affair with a woman I considered a friend, too." Even though I loathe talking about my husband, I force myself to continue, "The only difference between you and me is that you stayed, and I kicked him out that night when I returned home from a trip. I found my son asleep in his bedroom and my husband in our bedroom with one of my best teachers."

"Oh, Mary." Eleanor's eyes well with tears.

"She was one of the first teachers I hired, and we became dear friends," I say. It's been years since I've spoken about this, and now the story tumbles out. "It was a shock, so I understand how you feel. We were each betrayed by two people we trusted the most."

"I can't believe it happened to you, too. How could they have deceived us like that?" she asks.

"Is there any acceptable explanation for being unfaithful? Nothing my husband could have said would reason away his decision or mine. The moment I saw the two of them in *my* bed, there was no turning back. I told him to pack his bags. He did, and I never saw him again. Of course, she never came back to the school."

"It was that simple for you?" Eleanor's shock makes me wonder if she never considered splitting with her husband after her discovery. "Your husband just left and never came back?"

"Never came back, never spoke to him. I've hardly spoken his name since, and he died not too long after."

"I knew you'd been married, but I assumed you were a widow."

"I am, technically. We never divorced, so I became a widow when he died. Few people know the truth. There were a lot of rumors back then, but most decided that when Albertus couldn't find work in Florida, he left. Others thought he had just abandoned my son and me. Whatever people thought, I let them believe. The truth is no one's business but mine—and whomever I care to share it with."

Eleanor studies me. "I admired you before, but knowing what you've been through and how you persisted and prevailed, I have even more respect for you."

"I feel the same about you. Neither of us shows the pain we've been through. We just persevere, even though few know our true story."

Eleanor sighs. "I *wish* fewer knew my story. There were people in my life who supported their relationship. My uncle Teddy's daughter Alice—my own cousin—invited Franklin and Lucy to dinner when I was out of town and provided other opportunities for them to be alone together. Apparently, she used to say that Franklin deserved the fun

Lucy could provide, since I was 'an old fuddy-duddy.' That's actually how she described me." She pauses as if she is still astonished. "I was terribly wounded by that, and it made me question myself."

"How so?"

Sorrow imbues her tone when she says, "I wondered if the affair was my fault."

"No, Eleanor." I reach for her hand. "Your husband committed that sin. It doesn't belong to you."

"I want to believe that, but how did you get through it, Mary?"

Her question makes me thoughtful, because the strength Eleanor sees on the outside hasn't always been inside of me. There were mornings I couldn't drag myself out of the new bed that I'd bought. Times when I had to face people with a smile while tears squeezed from my heart. So, how *did* I get from there to here? "Time, of course," I finally say. "Time is the great healer. Albertus' infidelity happened over twenty years ago, so that helps. But most of all, I think forgiving him helped me the most."

Eleanor's jaw drops as if such a notion is inconceivable. "You forgave him? But you told him to leave."

"Oh, he had to go. But there is a difference between forgiving and forgetting," I say. "There was no way he would ever share my bed again. I'll never forget what I saw with my own eyes. But as far as holding on to the hurt and the anger and even the pain, I forgave him and my friend. Otherwise, the hurt I held would gnaw at me. I gave myself time to be human, I grieved, but every day I released a little bitterness from my heart and forgave him the tiniest bit more. Then, one day, I felt whole again."

"What a powerful lesson, Mary," Eleanor says after a long pause. "One of many today."

I squeeze her hand. "We're learning together, because that's what friends do."

CHAPTER 26

ELEANOR

Washington, D.C.
July 6, 1933

"I'll be perfectly safe driving myself," I insist, looking out the rolled-down window at the low-level Secret Service agent. The poor fellow is attempting an air of authority, but all I can see is his youth. And his nervousness.

"Ma'am, we are required to drive you to all your activities and appointments," he says, unable to mask a slight quivering in his voice.

"Or at the very least accompany you, ma'am," another voice chimes in, sounding as young as the first agent.

"Gentlemen, I assure you I am fully capable of handling myself. I've been making my own travel arrangements since I was a girl of fifteen, and I drove myself around New York City only last week."

I know this is out of the ordinary for the First Lady, but I don't want anyone inside the White House to know my whereabouts today. This is the next step in the plan Mary and I put together almost two months ago.

"Is there a problem?" A deep, familiar voice sounds out from farther away in the garage. "Ma'am, can I assist?"

Darn. It is Earl, who now serves as head of my security detail and who has become a trusted friend. I was honored when he popped into

Val-Kill Cottage and asked if he could follow me to Washington, D.C. Instinctively, I leapt up and embraced him, yelling, "Of course!" Marion and Nan gave each other a disapproving glance; they've always been jealous of my easy friendship with Earl. In truth, they are jealous of anyone with whom I form a friendship outside of our threesome.

I give Earl my winningest smile. "Your fine gents want to accompany me or drive me themselves, but I'd prefer to travel alone today, Earl."

"The boys are just trying to do their job, ma'am. Orders are Secret Service presence around you at all times," he says, giving me *his* winningest smile. "You are too important to risk."

While I appreciate his sentiments—and, of course, I always enjoy his handsome smile—this will not do, especially today but also in the months to come. Soon, at Franklin's request, I will be touring the country as Franklin's eyes and ears in the communities hit hardest by the Depression. This is a role I undertook as First Lady of New York, and Franklin appreciates the insights I bring back to him. I plan on having Hick join me on some of these trips, explaining to Franklin that her long years as a journalist will be helpful in getting us extra newspaper coverage.

Does he suspect that there might be something more between us than friendship or political advantage? I don't know; certainly he's aware of Marion and Nan's relationship and so is familiar with Boston marriages, not that my relationship with Hick has reached anywhere near that level. But he never makes any allusion to that, just as I never speculate over his warm interactions with his secretary Missy LeHand or the other young women in his orbit.

In any case, I can't have the Secret Service ruining my trips by making me appear unapproachable to the citizens I come to meet, and I certainly don't want them spoiling my time with Hick. So I must set the stage for those solo drives *now*.

"I'm grateful for your concern, Earl, but I must maintain my position. I will be going out today for a meeting, and I will do so alone, driving myself."

He sighs in defeat but does not appear surprised. Then, as if he expected this all along, he walks over to a cabinet against the garage wall, pulls out a wrapped present, and hands it to me.

"I sensed this day was coming. I was going to give this to you for your birthday, but I suppose you'll need it before then."

The rectangular box covered in thick silver wrapping paper is far heavier than I'd anticipated. Perplexed, I raise my eyebrow, and he gives me an enigmatic smile in reply.

Peeling off the wrapping paper, I gasp when I see what's inside. "It's a gun!"

"A revolver, to be exact. A .22 Smith and Wesson Outdoorsman." He is beaming, and his already broad chest puffs up.

I hold it in my hands, feeling strangely powerful.

"Here, let me show you how to operate it," he says, placing his hand over mine on the revolver. "This comes with a price. You must promise me that, when you travel anywhere without the Secret Service—even if it's on the sidewalk in front of the White House—you will carry this with you at all times. I selected a model that will fit in your purse."

I look into his dark blue eyes. "I promise."

"Come on," he says, pulling me from the front seat of the car. "Let's get you trained with this gun."

The car roars down the avenues of the capital, the wind feeling wonderfully cool on my face. As I press the gas pedal and the tires squeal, I feel a rush of freedom that I haven't experienced since becoming First Lady.

As I approach U Street, I take the intersection a little too quickly and slide across the front seat as the car navigates the curve, but instead of feeling scared, I feel exhilarated. By the time I pull into a parking spot in front of my destination—an attractive tan brick building emblazoned with the sign "The Whitelaw Hotel"—I'm laughing. A tiny slice of my treasured privacy and independence has returned to me.

"Good afternoon, Mary," I call to my friend as she opens the car door and slides in.

"Good afternoon, Eleanor." Mary studies me and then returns my smile. "You look positively joyful."

"You know, I feel jubilant. The sun is shining, and I am behind the wheel of an automobile with my friend at my side. What isn't to love about this day?" I say, then rev the engine again. "So, are you ready for this meeting?" But then, as I edge away from the curb, I rush to say, "No, first tell me about the two Alberts."

I expect Mary to laugh delightedly, the way she always does when I ask about her son and grandson in that way. But today, she sighs. "Well, Albert Sr. is still trying to find his way. That hasn't changed since we last spoke."

In her voice, I hear exhaustion. She's shared some of her frustration with her son and her efforts to help him become self-sustaining, and I have disclosed my similar concerns about my own children. Elliott, for example, has caused a mountain of worry; after college, he bounced from job to job—advertising, broadcasting, sales—until we indulged his fascination with flying and helped him secure a position at a small airline company in California owned by my friend Isabella Greenway.

"What's going on?" I ask, keeping my eyes on the road but my ears focused on her.

"You know," she continues, "we closed the Tea Room and we're looking for a new venture for him. He's not interested in my insurance company. I guess we'll just see what happens." Then, after a pause, her tone changes, and her eyes become bright. "But now, Albert Jr., he's a joy. It's still a year away, but you know he'll be thirteen, and he's already planning the biggest celebration."

"Thirteen?" I say. "My goodness, time passes. He was only six, I think, when we met."

"Exactly. I wish I could slow down time. In my mind, he's still six months old."

"Mary," I begin, but then pause, considering whether I should ask my next question.

"What is it?" Mary prompts.

"I was just wondering, how did you come to raise Albert Jr.?" But then I quickly add, "Of course, if it's too personal . . ."

"Would you stop it," Mary scolds me, but I hear a bit of teasing in her tone. "We're friends. Nothing is too personal, and I'm actually surprised we haven't talked about this before." She pauses, and the seriousness returns to her voice. "During his first year at Fisk University, Albert told me college was a waste and he was ready to be an entrepreneur. He broke my heart when he dropped out; nothing is more important to me than education, you know that."

"Of course," I say.

"But I wanted to be supportive, so we opened his first business—a sundry shop in Miami. But he was doing more down there than just managing his business. He got involved with a young lady."

"Oh." I nod, the picture forming in my mind.

But when Mary adds "A young *white* lady," I almost stop the car in the middle of the road. Instead, I make a right turn onto 9th Street and park safely to give her my full attention.

She continues. "As you can imagine, a white woman with a colored baby in the Deep South—and Miami, of all places—presents a difficult situation. It wasn't a good thing for her or the baby. But honestly, Eleanor, I wanted to get my son out of Miami, too." She shakes her head. "I had images of white-hooded men waiting for Albert every night when he came home from work or outside the sundry shop. I didn't sleep until I finally convinced Albert and the young lady that the baby would be better off with me. In the end, my son's lady friend decided that it was best for her to stay behind and build her life in Miami."

Mary glances away when she says softly, "I can't say I'm sorry about that."

The joy returns to her voice when she says, "Albert Jr. was a sickly little thing when he arrived, but the doctors at my hospital got him healthy. And now here we are, all these wonderful years later."

"My goodness," I say before I start up the car again. "I had no idea."

"Few people do," she says as I pull out of my parking spot. "Only my close friends know."

Before I proceed down 9th Street, I reach for her hand. "Thank you for sharing that with me. It only makes me admire you more."

"It's nothing special," she says as I maneuver the car through the intersection. "But Albert Jr. is one of the reasons why I fight."

"I'm so proud to fight along with you. And I think this could be our most productive meeting yet. A leap toward getting someone other than Robert Vann a federal appointment," I say.

As Franklin has unfurled his New Deal programs, Mary and I have gotten to work on one of the primary prongs of our plan: securing federal appointments for colored folks. To date, only Robert Vann has succeeded in that lofty goal, with a post as an attorney in the claims department in the Department of Justice. Here we are, several meetings and months later. I've been trying to lay groundwork within the administration by getting to know those at the helm of the different departments to gauge their receptivity to colored appointees. Behind the scenes, Mary and I have conducted meetings—separately up until this point—to assess various candidates. This will be the first meeting that we approach together, another reason for my excitement.

I turn onto Rhode Island Avenue and park in front of the lovely redbrick Phyllis Wheatley YWCA building, elegant with its corbeled brick cornice. As I open the car door, I hesitate. Should I really bring the gun? There can hardly be danger, but I promised Earl. I wait until Mary gets out of the car and then pull it out of the glove box and slide it into my handbag.

When I join Mary on the sidewalk, she looks at me askance. "What do you have in your bag?"

"A gun," I answer sheepishly.

"A gun? I hope you don't think you've got to protect yourself from anyone inside the Phyllis Wheatley YWCA." Her voice is stern.

Oh God, I think, *I have offended her.* "Mary, that might be how it looks, but it has nothing to do with the YWCA. I had to fight to take the car out on my own—without guards—and Earl only relented if I promised to bring a gun when I'm alone. Every single time."

Her voice is softer. "You aren't allowed to go out alone without a gun?"

"No. I have to bring it everywhere if Earl and his men aren't around," I answer. "I'm sorry."

Her expression changes. "I'm the one who's sorry. I made an assumption, and I was completely wrong. Here I am, having lectured you about making assumptions, and I am guilty myself."

I squeeze her arm affectionately. "There's nothing to forgive. What is it you tell me? We are friends, and we are learning together."

Smiling at each other, we walk toward the oldest Y in the capital, founded by a group of colored women and named after the eighteenth-century poet.

As we approach the front door, I straighten my skirt and hat. Today's meeting is with the Commission on Interracial Cooperation. Mary thinks they might be an excellent partner for our project.

We have other meetings planned, and my list of allies grows longer. Could I approach Harry Hopkins to see if he'd place a colored leader in his program? The bright, loyal man did an excellent job for Franklin in New York administering work relief programs, and now he's with the federal Civil Works Administration.

What about Harold Ickes, the secretary of the interior and director of the Public Works Administration? Might he consider giving a federal appointment to a colored man or woman? After all, he supported the recommendation that Hick, Louis, and I made to purchase a tract of West Virginia land so that hundreds of out-of-work miners and their families could establish a farming community. We're calling it Arthurdale.

As I gesture for Mary to enter, I automatically look behind me. Have I been followed by the Secret Service, despite Earl's reassurance? I feel like a clandestine agent instead of the First Lady. *Well*, I tell myself, *at least I'm spying for the right side.*

CHAPTER 27

MARY

Washington, D.C.
August 22, 1933

"Isn't this lovely?" Eleanor says, spreading her arms wide as we walk through the White House Rose Garden. "Sometimes I can't believe I live here."

When I asked Eleanor if we could meet, I had no idea she'd select such stunning surroundings. I inhale the sweet fragrance, and I'm reminded of my trip to Europe. Oh, how I wish I could forget the reason I asked to meet with my friend today. This place is too beautiful for us to have such an ugly discussion.

"Breathtaking," I finally reply. "All that's missing are a few black roses."

Eleanor laughs. "I agree! We need a few black roses out here, and definitely some in the White House."

Even though my mind is focused on the unpleasant discussion before me, I nod. I told her about my students and the black roses some time back. It's soothing that she remembers.

"I would venture to guess that my uncle Teddy's wife, Edith, didn't see too many black roses in her life. She was the one who fashioned the Rose Garden," Eleanor says as we stroll along the stone walkway past flower beds abundant in red, pink, and white blooms. "Through the years it's been updated, of course, and now Franklin and I want to put a more modern stamp on it."

Before I can reply, Tommy strides toward us and whispers something to Eleanor, and then my friend turns to me. "Would you excuse me for a moment? I have to sign an urgent letter."

"Of course." I point to a bench on one side of the garden. "I'll wait for you over there."

I settle down, grateful that a breeze cools me a bit on this hot August morning. After a few moments, I reach into my bag for the *Pittsburgh Courier*.

I begin reviewing the headlines, and my back straightens as I read: PRESIDENT ROOSEVELT CREATES THE OFFICE OF THE SPECIAL ADVISER ON THE ECONOMIC STATUS OF THE NEGROES. My eyes cannot scan this article fast enough. It is so exciting to see the plans that Eleanor and I began just three months ago coming to fruition.

After our meeting last month with the Commission on Interracial Cooperation, Eleanor presented our strategy to the president. She said he listened to our idea about giving federal appointments to Negroes in each of the New Deal agencies. Then she gave him the list of candidates the commission recommended. According to Eleanor, President Roosevelt was receptive to all of it, although he didn't make any promises.

Why didn't Eleanor tell me this was going to be announced today? As I wonder, I read the president's selection to head up the office, and my excitement fades.

I glance up when I hear Eleanor's footsteps. She's smiling, but her smile disappears when she sees my expression. "What's wrong?"

I hand the newspaper to her, and she reads the first line aloud. "Through the secretary of the interior, Harold Ickes, President Roosevelt has created the Office of the Special Adviser on the Economic Status of the Negroes." Grinning, she adds, "This is wonderful, Mary. This is the central office we wanted. Franklin listened to us."

Then she reads the rest of the article as I stand and pace in front of the roses. Finally, Eleanor looks up. "Clark Foreman will be appointed as the special adviser." Her expression has changed from joyful to confused. "But Mr. Foreman, he's . . . he's . . ."

"He's white!" I explode, finishing the sentence for her.

We are both familiar with Clark Foreman, as he works for the Commission on Interracial Cooperation, the organization that gave us the suggested list of names, and his wasn't on it! Yes, Mr. Foreman is a fine advocate for equality, but he is white—the precise opposite of what Eleanor advocated for with the president.

"They chose a white man?" Eleanor sounds as astonished as I feel.

"How could President Roosevelt do this?" I say, feeling like I want to punch the air.

Eleanor shakes her head. "I cannot believe he went forward with this without even doing me the courtesy of informing me. I shouldn't have to find this out in the newspaper." When she glances toward the White House, her face now flushed with anger, I remember that the president could very well be just feet away in the Oval Office. For a moment, I imagine the two of us storming into his office, demanding answers.

I say, "It seems the president is not taking our request seriously. He's not only ignoring us—he's insulting us."

For a moment, she's silent. When she speaks, her voice is calmer, steadier. "Mary, I'm as shocked and disappointed as you are, but I want both of us to consider something. Is it possible that this appointment might make sense?"

I want to grab my friend by her shoulders and shake her. "Make sense? How? The president has established an office for Negro affairs and put an overseer in charge."

Eleanor flinches. "That's a bit harsh. Mr. Foreman has a good reputation with the Commission on Interracial Cooperation. He's quite progressive, from what I understand."

Every inch of me is weary when I plop back onto the bench next to Eleanor. I am overtired from the struggle and my efforts that often leave me like this—frustrated and angry. But the fact that I allowed Eleanor to see me venting shows how much I trust her. I learned long ago, especially as a colored woman, never to show any emotion. Today with Eleanor, I forgot. For the first time, I showed her Mary Jane.

"I may have overstated the situation," I say, "but as you and I have discussed, we don't want white people deciding what's best for Negroes. That's why this appointment doesn't make sense."

Eleanor focuses her blue eyes on me. "I understand why you're frustrated, but please hear me out. I agree this is the wrong way to go about it, but if there is a white man who can make a difference in this position, it is Clark Foreman. I've heard him speak about how profoundly he was changed in college by a lynching he witnessed."

I hold up my hand before she can continue. "I know his story, and I know he's nothing like his slave-owning grandparents. I applaud him and his fight for equality. However, whatever transformation he's been through, nothing can transform his white skin. He can only see the world through white eyes, and for that reason, his appointment is a slap in the face to every Negro."

I expect Eleanor to have a retort, but she's quiet. Eventually, she says, "I understand, but with the way this country is, maybe we do need Mr. Foreman. Maybe the best thing is to have a white man who has more than just white eyes—he has white skin that gives him access to go places where Negroes cannot go and to make inroads Negroes cannot make. Yes, Mary, it is sad, unfair, and unjust. But if it gets us the results we want, does his skin color matter?"

For a second, I wish I hadn't invited Eleanor to speak so freely to me. Because her words sting. Only a white man can accomplish what we're trying to do? Only a white face can move this country forward for Negroes?

When my silence continues, Eleanor says, "Mary? What do you think?"

What I think is that Eleanor's words cut deep—because they are true. In fact, they reflect the strategy I've used my whole life. Years ago, Booker T. Washington advised me of the benefit of white benefactors. He was right. My school would have never moved forward without the endorsement, the financial backing, and the faces of James Gamble, Thomas White, and John D. Rockefeller. In this country, at this time, maybe a white man is needed to bring Negroes into the administration and to ensure that they have a place in the New Deal.

It takes all the energy I have to say, "You're right, even if it's the opposite of what I want, and even if it hurts." What I don't say is *I guess there is a place for a white savior.* I keep that harrowing thought to myself.

We sit quietly, staring out at the garden. Then Eleanor looks at me. "If we had any doubts before, we now know we can speak the truth to each other, even when it's painful." I nod, and she adds, "We will watch and hold Mr. Foreman accountable."

"Well, even though I'm not pleased, there may be another benefit to this appointment. If Mr. Foreman is going to be responsible for getting Negroes appointed to the New Deal agencies, then maybe that will free up our time and we can turn our attention to the third item on our agenda."

"Lynching?" she asks, and when I nod, she says, "I've been trying to find out all I can about the Costigan-Wagner Bill, and—"

I raise my hand before interrupting her. "This is why I wanted to see you today. Have you heard about the recent lynching in Maryland?"

Eleanor stiffens and shakes her head.

I take a deep breath, and with all the beauty surrounding me, I share the ugliness of this country. "His name was George Armwood." Then, giving the young man the respect in death that he never received in life, I correct myself. "Mr. Armwood was twenty-two years old, a quiet, uncomplaining young man, according to those who knew him. He was accused of assaulting and raping a seventy-one-year-old white woman."

The pictures I've seen play through my mind like a film reel, and I have to press through my disgust and dismay. "Without any evidence or any sort of due process, Mr. Armwood was dragged to a field right across from his mother's house. And do you know what happened?" I don't pause for Eleanor to respond. "His mother watched her child being stabbed and beaten."

Eleanor presses her hand against her chest as if she's trying to hold back her emotions. I keep on. "That should have been enough for the mob, but it wasn't. Even after he was arrested, they wanted his blood. And so, as always, the mob became Mr. Armwood's judge and jury."

Eleanor shakes her head, and I haven't even begun the horrific story.

"Mr. Armwood was dragged for miles before they decided it was time to torture him." I shake my head and take a breath, because this particular lynching is almost too much to bear. "I hope Mr. Armwood was already dead by the time they hung him from that tree. Because even that wasn't enough."

"What do you mean? They beat him, they hung him, they killed him," Eleanor cries. "What more can there be?"

"They burned him." Even though her eyes become glassy and she looks like she might be ill, I proceed. "And then they celebrated, dancing around his body before they cut him down and distributed pieces of that rope as keepsakes. Because no good lynching can end without souvenirs."

"How—" She pauses, swallows, continues. "How can people be so evil?"

"I don't know." I feel my shoulders slump. I slide a clipping from one of the colored newspapers across the bench. "This is a photograph of Mr. Armwood."

When Eleanor glances down, she whimpers. I told her this was a picture of George Armwood, but it is not. This isn't a picture of a man; this is the picture of the charred remains of someone who was treated as if he wasn't human.

As I slide another clipping to her, I add, "As disgusting as that one is, I find this one worse."

Eleanor braces herself but then she frowns as she takes in the image of rows and rows of white men dressed in their Sunday best, looking up at the scorched body swinging from a tree's limb. "I don't understand," she whispers.

"The lynching of Mr. Armwood was advertised in the newspapers as a social event that shouldn't be missed. Thousands showed up."

Eleanor's hand shakes as she touches one of the pictures. "When I said I wanted to fight against lynching with you, I thought I understood this wickedness. But I didn't; I thought lynchings were just hangings, which, of course, are horrible enough." Tears stream down her cheeks as she looks up at me. "But this—I'm sorry, I didn't know—"

I shake my head. "How would you know if you were never exposed?"

She sighs. "Mary, I know we didn't make it our first priority, but we must focus on this now. We have to get that anti-lynching bill passed."

This is why I wanted to speak to Eleanor today. "It won't be easy, thanks to the Southern Democrats."

"I know, but if we can get Franklin behind this bill, he can get both parties to support it. Imagine, he'd be the first president to sign an anti-lynching bill into law"—she pauses, her expression filling with contempt—"ending this savagery."

I'm grateful for her determination and faith. "That will be a giant step forward," I say, feeling a fresh spark in this fight.

"If it's all right with you, Mary, I'd like to keep these." She lifts the newspaper clippings, stares at both photographs, and shakes her head. "These are images Franklin must see, and once he does, he's *got* to understand the importance of eradicating this horrible practice."

Eleanor's words give me hope, and for the first time since we entered the Rose Garden, I smile.

CHAPTER 28

ELEANOR

Washington, D.C.
August 23, 1933

I dress with more care than usual, selecting a sweater set and skirt in colors I know Franklin prefers. Rather than quickly rolling my hair into a simple chignon and surrounding it with a hairnet to keep it in place, I make a more complicated style, without the hairnet that Franklin so dislikes. Hick dislikes it, too, and Hick's opinion matters more and more to me.

Just yesterday, she stopped by my sitting room in the late afternoon before a dinner with Franklin, Louis, his wife, and several other couples who are formidable Democratic Party donors. "What will you wear tonight?" she asked after I told her about my evening plans.

Her question surprised me, particularly since Hick's predilection for baggy, masculine clothes means she is no dandy herself. "What's wrong with this?" I exclaimed, glancing down at the full-skirted floral dress in muted shades of brown I'd been wearing all day.

She laughed. "One of the things I love about you is your obliviousness to some of the unimportant minutiae most women are obsessed with—like clothes. Even still, you *could* get gussied up sometimes. What about wearing one of those solid-hued silk dresses that hugs your figure a little more?"

Love? Did she say "love"? The word thrilled and scared me. I was temporarily speechless. We whispered words of affection to each other in the dark of the night in the White House guest bedroom or in hotel rooms when we traveled together, but those always came on the heels of physical affection. And neither one of us had ever said the word "love" about our feelings for the other before.

Hick didn't seem to notice my reaction. "And that love is one of the reasons that I cannot be a journalist covering the White House any longer."

I stammered. "W-what do you mean?"

"Eleanor." She folded her fingers around mine. "I've told you how I feel before, even if I haven't specifically mentioned 'love' until today. And I know you aren't ready for that sort of commitment in our relationship, which is fine. But I cannot sit idly by, pretending to cover you and your husband's presidential term for the AP with anything close to objectivity. I've got to go."

A desperate pang took hold of me, and I blurted out, "But I don't want you to go." I knew I was being selfish, because I had Hick to myself whenever convenient—nearly every day I inhabited the White House—without making any sort of promises to her. "What if there was a job for you with Harry, assessing the New Deal programs?"

Her eyes lit up at the idea of working for Harry Hopkins, the chief administrator for three huge New Deal departments, but she didn't smile. "It's not just about the job, Eleanor. It's too hard being here with you and not knowing where I stand."

I touched her soft cheek with my free hand and said, "What if I told you that you belong here with me, at my side?" And I kissed her.

The memory of that kiss makes me flush. I didn't sleep well last night, and I'm still not sure what to call our relationship, but it's so pleasant to have someone in my corner who's just mine.

In the morning, as I step out of my bedroom to walk through the many corridors to the South Portico, I feel strange. It's as if I've gotten gussied up for another date with my estranged husband rather than for what it really is: a business meeting masquerading as breakfast.

Although Franklin and I don't often have breakfast together—in fact, he almost always has a breakfast tray served to him in his bedroom—I know his schedule and patterns well. On this particular morning, I learned from Mrs. Nesbitt that he'll be up and at the informal breakfast table on the cool South Portico instead of taking breakfast in his bedroom, due to an early meeting. I arrive at the table before he wheels in, bracing myself with a cup of the dark, bitter coffee he likes, an unusual blend made from ground green coffee beans. I thank my lucky stars that my mother-in-law is in Campobello instead of breakfasting with her beloved son, as she likes to do whenever possible. Her presence could easily make my strategy go awry.

Franklin's eyebrows rise in undisguised surprise to see me, but he doesn't say anything other than "Good morning."

We chat pleasantly about the day's schedule and less pleasantly about the state of Anna's divorce as plates of his favorite corned beef hash with poached eggs arrive on the arm of a maid. I usually stick to tea and toast in the mornings, but I take a bite of the dish and shudder. The eggs are barely cooked and the corned beef hash is somehow hard. Franklin continues on as if the meal is delicious. He's used to it.

Mrs. Nesbitt may have sanitized the White House kitchens and modernized the equipment, but with the exception of dessert, she hasn't elevated the food, even after I supplied her with shelves of recipe books. I see why guests grumble over official meals and cartoonists have taken to lambasting our offerings. But I will not make a fuss. Countless Americans are struggling to feed their families. The White House fare should be simple and nutritious, not lavish and fussy, and I try to serve what the average citizen can afford.

"What about you, Eleanor?" Franklin asks. "What does your schedule hold today? Hosting one of your famously well-attended teas?"

I see that he has been paying attention. My teas, which usually have a theme and host a couple of hundred people and, in one instance,

nearly two thousand, are my way of highlighting issues and connect-
ing numerous like-minded people at once, primarily women.

Smiling, I say, "Yes, although we'll be serving cool lemonade and
iced tea, since the day promises to be sweltering."

"Sounds wise."

"I do have one unusual item on my agenda today to discuss with
you."

"Ah? And what's that?" he asks, his attention more on the eggs
than on me.

I sip his bitter coffee, trying not to wince. "Well, if something
rather catastrophic hadn't happened recently, I might be here today to
discuss your creation of the Office of the Special Adviser on the Economic Status of the Negroes." I cross my arms as I speak.

He removes his glasses, places them on the table, and grins. "I
thought you'd be pleased with that."

"So pleased that it would override the courtesy of keeping me informed about a decision in which I am very invested? So pleased that
it's fine I found out in the newspaper like everyone else?"

Placing his glasses back on—his subtle way of distancing himself
from me—he says, "I thought you'd be happy that the needs of the
Negro are being addressed."

"I don't like finding out through the headlines. Not to mention I
was very clear about the importance of placing a colored person in that
role. I gave you a long list of candidates."

"Ickes told me Foreman was the man for the job, and his is the
recommendation I have to follow. Maybe I should have discussed it
with you first, but I thought you might find it a welcome surprise." He
looks—and sounds—like a disappointed child. This is my signal to
abandon this part of the conversation.

"In any event, that's not the most pressing agenda item."

"What, then?" His petulant tone remains, and I wonder if I've erred
by leading with my disappointment over the special adviser announcement. *How we continually add salt to each other's wounds.*

"I want to talk about George Armwood."

"Not this," he says, wheeling back from the edge of the dining table.

"Yes, this," I say, my voice firm.

"It's not that I don't feel terrible about what happened to George Armwood. This business of lynching is abominable. But it's a veritable quagmire for me; you know that better than anyone." He lowers his glasses to stare at me, knowing that I'm vulnerable to his naked gaze. When I don't agree with him, he continues, "If I back the anti-lynching bill, I can kiss the rest of the New Deal goodbye. I'll give up the ability to help millions of desperate Americans with my legislation, rather than a few persecuted Negroes."

"'A few persecuted Negroes'?" I squeal. "Do you know that ninety people are lynched each year? How can you call the horrific murder of ninety human beings the loss of a few Negroes?"

I notice a figure silhouetted in the screen door to the South Portico. As the person presses his face closer to the screen, I realize it's Earl. He's always looking out for me, whether I realize it or not.

"Eleanor," Franklin says in a tone so unerringly calm I want to scream, "how can I walk away from lifting up millions of citizens from starvation and poverty and homelessness and joblessness with the New Deal—to save ninety people a year?"

This sounds like one of the arguments he makes to the parade of Northern politicians who pass his office day after day. But I am not one of his supplicants, and I am determined to wield the limited power I've been given as the First Lady in the way in which my Aunt Edith urged—in accordance with my own sense of justice. Political expediency cannot rule the day. My conversation with Mary about this most recent, terrible lynching in Maryland has my compass pointing in a very specific direction, and I cannot allow the horror of lynching to go unaddressed.

Bracing myself, I recite some of the horrifying description Mary shared with me, details Franklin is unlikely to hear from anyone else. Franklin looks sick and pale. He pushes away his plate, with the remains of the eggs and hash still piled high. I have his full attention.

I then slide the images of George Armwood's body and the smiling mob across the table. "How can you stay silent about lynching now? It's more than a gruesome murder. It is a wielding of power. And if the president of the United States doesn't condemn it, then it could continue in perpetuity."

"I will do something about it, Eleanor," he says in a near-whisper.

I watch as he lifts the newspaper photographs up and examines them one by one.

"Good. Because otherwise, *this* could be the legacy you leave this country."

CHAPTER 29

MARY

New York, New York
December 16, 1933

The moment I step into the reception area of the NAACP office, I am swarmed by nearly a dozen young men and women, all calling out for "Mrs. Bethune." Although I smile as they gather around me, Walter frowns. "Let's give Mrs. Bethune some space. She's here for a meeting, but perhaps she'll say a few words on her departure."

The smartly dressed women in day dresses with waists cinched by belts and the men in dark suits return to their seats behind the rows and rows of desks to toil away at the business of seeking justice in America. In the five years since Walter White has been the executive secretary, this staff has made headway. Whether it's successfully blocking Supreme Court justice appointments or advocating for the nine young men in Alabama who were falsely accused of raping two white women, the NAACP is a force.

As Walter leads me to his office, I scold him, "You needn't have been so harsh with those young folks."

He chuckles. "If I let one person ask a question, I have to let a dozen. And we'd never have our meeting." He gestures for me to take a seat in front of his desk. "I guess that's the plight of the most famous Negro in the country." He laughs, but I give him a smirk. He says, "I'm just glad our schedules aligned. I wasn't sure I'd be back from Maryland before you left New York."

"You were there for the George Armwood case?" When he nods, I add, "Please tell me you didn't infiltrate any meetings." From the time Walter started as an NAACP investigator sixteen years ago, he's been involved in dangerous undercover work, gathering information from sources such as the Ku Klux Klan while posing as a white man.

"No, not this time," he says, giving me that reassuring smile.

"Thank goodness. You've put your life on the line too many times, and tension must be higher than ever in Maryland."

"When you're a colored man in America, your life is always on the line." He shrugs. Despite the shade of his skin and the bright blue of his eyes, he's never wavered in his Negro identity. "But there's no need to worry. You know only colored folks recognize colored folks. White people see only my white skin. That defines me."

"As my dark skin defines me," I respond.

"Exactly," he says. "And because of that definition, we've both been underestimated. So don't worry about me."

"Walter, after what almost happened to you, you can never tell me not to worry," I say, knowing his memory lands exactly where mine does.

In 1919, when Walter was a new investigator, he posed as a white journalist and traveled to Arkansas right after the Elaine Massacre. It took only days for him to cozy up to the white supremacists, and he collected a mountain of information to pass on to the authorities— including the names of the murderers. But Walter's cover was blown, and he escaped in the darkness of night with the help of a trio of colored pastors. They rushed him to a train before the mob found him and "made sure he never passed for white again."

"One close call in more than one hundred investigations. I'll take those odds, and I'd say my work has been a success."

"Certainly the NAACP is better for all you've done."

"Getting better is always the goal. Now, if you can answer a question for me?"

"Of course. I figured there was a reason you invited me here."

"Initially, I simply wanted to take you to lunch, but then this morning I saw this." He holds up a copy of the *Pittsburgh Courier*, and I read the headline: MRS. MARY MCLEOD BETHUNE PRAISES PRESIDENT ROOSEVELT.

"Ah," I say, sitting back in my chair. I knew this headline would be shocking, since my devout loyalty to the Republican Party is well-known. When Robert Vann's newspaper reached out to me for comment, I praised President Roosevelt because he has done something that neither President Coolidge nor President Hoover dared. After Eleanor shared the clippings about George Armwood, the president made a bold move, giving a public radio statement to millions of Americans decrying lynching as a "vile" and "murderous" practice that must end. President Roosevelt's action deserved my praise.

Since I've been working with Eleanor, I've reconsidered my politics. The more we collaborate, the more I realize I'm not loyal to a party— only to my people. Whichever party and president has policies to help Negroes, that's the president I will support.

I say to Walter, "Have you read the article?"

"I have, and I was surprised. And I'm not the only one. I've had about six or seven calls just this morning. You and I have always been frank with each other, correct?"

I nod. "Absolutely. I wouldn't want it any other way."

"Then I have to ask"—his tone turns stern—"what were you thinking? Why would you go on the record commending the president when he's done nothing worthy of Mary McLeod Bethune's praise?"

"I disagree, Walter; he made a public statement to America about lynching." I sit up straight, prepared to defend my words. "No other American leader has ever done that."

"He said a few negative words about lynching, and now, with your public support, President Roosevelt will probably think he's done enough. But his watered-down statement will not suffice. Stopping lynching is why we're here. And lynching, for me . . ." His voice lowers and drops off, and I know his mind has drifted to the time when he was thirteen years old and a violent mob attacked Negroes in the streets of Atlanta. He was caught up in the crowds that day and witnessed men being beaten and hung from lampposts. It was only because white men saw him as a white boy that he escaped.

"Mary," he continues, returning to our conversation, "we cannot give an inch. Lynching won't stop with words. I'll give Roosevelt credit when the anti-lynching law is passed."

"I agree, but I will not ignore progress, and that's what I commended."

"Progress? This is not progress! This is not action. Did you know Roosevelt still won't meet with us, even though we call and send letters regularly? His excuse? He's too busy with the New Deal to focus on social issues, and so colored men continue to be murdered in the streets."

"I understand your skepticism, but I've learned the best way to move forward is to encourage Roosevelt for what he has done, not condemn him for what he hasn't. And look at the action he *has* taken," I keep on. "He's created an environment in the New Deal that's encouraging *colored* appointments in the federal government—Robert Vann, of course, but more recently Eugene Kinckle Jones was assigned to the Commerce Department; Robert Weaver will work directly for Clark Foreman; and that Harvard lawyer, Bill Hastie, will serve as legal investigator for the Department of the Interior. And that's just the beginning of the federal appointments."

"Having appointees is good, but don't you think they should be functional?" His question is rhetorical, because he doesn't pause. "Some of the men you've mentioned are frustrated. They do nothing all day but sit in those buildings, sometimes at desks in hallways, without being given any assignments!" Walter shakes his head like it's all impossible. "So forgive me if I don't share your high praise for the president. And this"—he picks up the newspaper, then tosses it aside—"won't help as we try to push Roosevelt to action, especially about lynching."

I let his words settle in the air before I say, "I've heard about the struggles of the men who've been appointed, but, Walter, having the men in those federal positions *is* progress. Just like the president's words are progress." When Walter rolls his eyes to the heavens, I chuckle, then, in all seriousness, add, "There's something you should know. The president didn't do all of this on his own. The First Lady pressured him to make those statements about lynching and to get more federal appointments for us."

Walter frowns. "So the two of you are friends?" he asks, and I remember him asking that question seven months ago.

"We are," I say, and then explain all that Eleanor and I have done over the past months. I've shared our friendship and partnership with very few, but today, I finally add Walter to that number.

"You're really working with Eleanor Roosevelt?" He sounds skeptical and incredulous.

"Yes, and she's an active ally. She wants this anti-lynching legislation passed as much as we do, and the president's statement proves her commitment. He would have never spoken up that way, so publicly, so strongly, without the First Lady pushing him to do so."

"It's hard for me to imagine that she would care anything about this, especially with her privileged background."

My eyes narrow. "Don't be so limited in your thinking, my friend. People don't have to be poor to care about the poor; people don't have to be lynched to care about lynching."

"Really, Mary?" he says at my preposterous statement.

"I think I've made my point."

"Well, clearly, I understand that," he says, his tone as sharp as mine now. But then he softens. "Even assuming that everything you're saying about Mrs. Roosevelt is true, how do we know her husband will listen to her—beyond that little speech?"

After a pause, I say, "Maybe she should talk to you about this herself."

His eyebrows rise. "I doubt the president will let me anywhere near the White House, even if I have an invitation from the First Lady." He releases a rueful laugh.

"I don't believe I said anything about the president or the White House. Why would you need to meet with Mrs. Roosevelt there when you can meet with her here? Right in the offices where the fight against lynching began." Tapping my finger on his desk, I say, "Maybe *this* office is the road to the White House and will lead us all to the end that we so desperately want."

CHAPTER 30

ELEANOR

New York, New York
January 8, 1934

"Are you sure about this, Eleanor?" Mary asks as I slow the Cadillac and pull into a parking spot on Fifth Avenue.

It appears that my fearless friend is worried. Even though she's the one who instigated the meeting today.

"Of course I am. I can't allow Franklin's opinions to be mine." I am still trying to squelch my fury. Why does Franklin's resistance to doing the right thing enrage me more in this context than any other? Is it because lynching is so clearly evil? Or is it because I'm used to operating as his external conscience and he usually listens? Hick thinks it's because I derive so much of my self-worth from doing good—a vestige of my mother's saying that "you're plain, so you must be good"—and Franklin is stymieing that effort. "Anyway, Hick says this is a sound next step, and I trust her opinion."

"Remind me who Hick is again?" Mary asks. "You've mentioned her before."

I can't meet Mary's eyes without worrying I'll reveal the truth—that Hick is closer to me than anyone in my life. That she is my secret love.

"She's a dear friend who was a journalist and is well versed in political machinations. You might know her better as Lorena Hickock."

"Ah yes," Mary exclaims. "She's practically famous. You said she 'was' a journalist—has she left the field?"

I can sense my cheeks redden. I feel guilty about Hick's career change. "She's taking a break for a bit."

"That's a loss. I'll miss her articles until she returns," Mary says, and my stomach knots, thinking of what our relationship costs Hick.

When I don't trust myself to speak, Mary returns to our original conversation. "In any event, your husband *has* done something by mentioning lynching more than once in two public speeches. I was pleased when he echoed his original words in the State of the Union address. No other president has gone that far," she offers, trying to soften my rage. "That's something."

I nod begrudgingly. "He did, and I appreciate your public support of those statements, Mary, especially since I know how much criticism you've received. But Franklin's words are empty without action."

I've never spoken about Franklin with anyone as honestly as I do with Mary. Mary gives me a half nod. She knows I'm right, but she doesn't want me to alienate Franklin. We need him.

I reach across the car and squeeze her hand. "It'll be all right. What Franklin doesn't know at this precise moment won't hurt him," I say with a conspiratorial grin. "And by the time he learns about it, the deed will be done."

She winks and says, "I'm a good one for a secret. I haven't told anyone about your gun, have I?"

Her words make me smile even wider. With Mary, I feel like a girl again, full of vim and vigor, ready to do what's right and necessary— even if I've got to do it on the sly. Having an accomplice emboldens me.

By the time we step out of the car, the presence of the Secret Service vehicle parked behind us hardly matters anymore. When I first spotted them following me from our East 65th Street town house to pick up

Mary at the Hotel Olga, I was annoyed. I wanted to do this on my own. But I realize now that was selfish; it's their job to protect me. And I bet the fact that I am sitting in the front seat of a car in New York with a colored woman has them on high alert, even though it shouldn't.

Mary and I walk the half block from the parking spot to a lovely brownstone at the corner of Fifth Avenue and 14th Street. Passersby stare at us, and I wonder if it's because the sight of a colored and a white woman walking and talking companionably down a city street is such a rarity or because they recognize one of us.

Suddenly, I have the answer to my question when a young man shouts out, "Hey, Mrs. Bethune."

She gives him a smile and a nod without breaking stride. I am so tickled. Because as Franklin's wife, I may be famous, but Mary is more—she's a celebrity.

As we approach 69 Fifth Avenue, a white man gives us a little wave from the entryway. Could he be reacting to the sight of a white and a colored woman together? I look back toward the Secret Service agents, suddenly relieved they're here. The stranger draws closer, but oddly, Mary doesn't appear alarmed. In fact, she steps toward the man.

"Mrs. Roosevelt, I'd like you to meet Mr. Walter White."

This man is Walter White? This pale, blue-eyed, Irish-looking man with blond hair and spectacles? How could this be the formidable Negro activist? I'm fairly certain my mouth is agape.

Instead of ignoring my reaction, Mary addresses it. "Mrs. Roosevelt, Mr. White often uses his apparent whiteness to pass in dangerous situations, like when he's conducting investigations of lynchings. It's quite the secret weapon."

I try to mask my astonishment better, then stretch out my hand. "It is a pleasure to meet you, Mr. White."

As he shakes my hand, he says, "I assure you that the pleasure is all mine, Mrs. Roosevelt. Any friend of Mrs. Bethune's is a friend of the NAACP. She was one of our first members, and there's hardly a more important advocate for Negroes anywhere. But to combine that with an introduction to the First Lady, well, that is a rare and fine honor indeed. Won't you both come in?"

As we step into the NAACP reception area, the staff crane their necks as we pass. Once we settle in two chairs across from Mr. White's desk, he takes the lead. "Mrs. Bethune tells me you are interested in becoming more involved in the fight against lynching."

"Indeed," I say with a brisk nod of my head.

"And you are familiar with the status of our legislative efforts?" I can hear his skepticism. Am I just another white woman, he can't help thinking, who knows nothing about the Negro struggle but who wants to be perceived as sympathetic to the cause?

"I believe so," I say, hoping I haven't missed out on a recent development. "I've kept up-to-date on the status of Senators Costigan and Wagner's anti-lynching bill."

"Good. Then you know that it should allow for federal prosecution of those involved in lynch mobs, even law enforcement officials. As you may know, local sheriffs or mayors often fuel the fires of a lynching— so it's hard to get prosecution of lynching on a local or state level."

I shudder. "Yes, my understanding is that the senators may propose their bill later this year."

"That's right. It will be the first time since the Dyer Bill in 1922 that we've had a chance at an anti-lynching law."

"Hard to believe it's been that long."

He nods. "But of course it will take much more than simply proposing the bill for it to become a law. What happened with the Dyer Bill is a case in point. The House of Representatives passed it, but the Senate filibustered it."

Since we both know I don't need a primer on how a bill becomes a law, Mr. White's statement can be read only one way—a subtle reference to the work Franklin and I can do behind the scenes and in public to lobby for the bill. We both know that, even if the bill garners strong support, it may not get to the floor for a vote without Franklin's endorsement.

"I cannot promise to deliver the president's personal commitment to the bill," I say, meeting his blue eyes directly. "Only my own."

Mr. White looks shocked. "Mrs. Roosevelt, I would never dare ask for such a thing. It is enough that you are here today, talking about these issues with me and expressing your solidarity."

"She *is* with us, I can attest to that," Mary says.

"I am. But please understand that my support will not be in name only. Not just words—but actions, too. And as part of those actions, I'd like to invite you as the representative of the NAACP to a meeting with me at the White House."

"The White House?" he asks, practically slack-jawed. He's been working for nearly a year to get anyone in the Roosevelt administration to even answer a letter, and now he has an invitation to the White House from the First Lady? Sometimes I do see the appeal of power.

"The White House."

"I—I'd be honored."

"Wonderful. I need to be educated on the struggle and on what I can do. But in the meantime I want to make plain publicly where my allegiances lie: I want to join the NAACP."

"You what?" Mr. White blurts out. I know how unusual this is. For a First Lady to take any sort of controversial stance, let alone one regarding race, is unheard of. But I don't want to be like any other First Lady.

CHAPTER 31

MARY

Washington, D.C.
April 28, 1934

It's been no easy matter to engage President Roosevelt on the issue of lynchings. Eleanor has been urging a meeting with Walter White, and the president has been resistant. But that is of no matter. My people have been waiting for decades to redress this wrong. We must all be patient—and strategic.

"Mary!" a voice calls out from across the Whitelaw Hotel restaurant, taking me away from my musings.

Three young men, all decked out in dark three-piece suits, walk toward me. I greet Robert Vann and tease Eugene Kinckle Jones about that mustache of his, but it is the third gentleman, a fresh-faced young man, who has my attention. Although his name was on the list that we drew up for federal appointment consideration, this is my first time meeting the recent Harvard doctoral program graduate Robert Weaver, who is also known as a great debater.

He reaches to shake my hand and introduce himself. "It is an honor to meet you, Mrs. Bethune."

I nod. "I've been looking forward to meeting the young man who put the 'Negro' into the Office of the Economic Status of Negroes."

The three laugh, but I don't join in. I mean what I said, even though

Eleanor was right in her assessment of Mr. Foreman. He has done a good job, first by hiring Robert Weaver to work with him and then by getting Negroes federal appointments.

After the men order drinks and study their menus, Robert Vann looks up at me. "So, you called us here to draft a thank-you letter to President Roosevelt," he says, crossing his arms. "Of course, we want to talk you out of that, since Roosevelt hasn't done a damn thing."

"I'll excuse your language," I say.

He holds up his hands. "I apologize. It's just that I'm amazed you want to do this."

"That's surprising coming from the newspaper editor who reached out to me for that exact statement about the president four months ago."

"My reporters, not me."

Of course, I know that. "And you were one of the first Negroes appointed to the Roosevelt administration," I add.

He shakes his head. "Mary, my appointment, like all the others, is in name only. Forget about an office; they didn't even have a desk for me when I arrived. To this day, none of the white secretaries will work with me. And how am I supposed to be the special adviser to the attorney general when Cummings will not even put me on his schedule for a meeting? So tell me how my appointment or any of the others have made a difference." Robert shrugs. "I'm thinking about going back to my law practice."

"And give all of this up?" I ask, trying to kid him just a little.

Robert slaps his hands on his thighs. "Give up what? Have you not heard anything I've said?"

"Of course I have. But even with all of that, you're still there. You still have a seat at the table, Robert. Change won't happen unless you're sitting there and not in Pittsburgh."

"In theory, I agree with you," Eugene pipes in. "But are we really at the table if they won't sit down with us? My experience is not much different than Robert's." Eugene describes his spacious office but lack of responsibilities. "I feel like my hire was just a way for them to send out a new press release and say, 'Look, we have another Negro in the Roosevelt administration.'"

I knew that Robert Vann and Eugene would be difficult about the letter, which is why I invited Robert Weaver. Turning to him, I ask, "What about you, young man? Are you being pushed to the side, too?"

Robert Weaver shifts in his seat. "Uh, no, ma'am. I haven't been there as long as Mr. Vann and Mr. Jones, but my experience has been a tad different. In fact, it's been mostly positive. Mr. Foreman and I work well together, and I just compiled a memorandum for him outlining all the New Deal agencies, showing their strengths as well as the inequities for Negroes."

"And it was well received?"

"Yes, ma'am. And not only that, but Mr. Foreman has terminated contracts with any companies where racism has been proven. I understand what's been going on with my brethren here, but it's different with Mr. Foreman. I've seen and experienced progress."

Robert Vann and Eugene exchange a long glance. Directing my words to them, I say, "You two are justifiably frustrated, but I think my proposal will help with that."

"Even with everything we just told you, you still think a letter to Roosevelt is a good idea?" Robert Vann is mystified.

"Yes, and here's why. While I want all the Negro appointees to have significant roles and responsibilities, our number one issue is getting that lynching bill through. If we play offense and thank Roosevelt for the progress to date and express enthusiasm about his future decisions—rather than complain about what he *hasn't* done—we will get the most positive response from him. For your federal appointments *and* the anti-lynching bill."

Eugene and Robert Weaver slowly nod, but Robert Vann remains immobile. His reaction doesn't stop me, and I pull a notepad and pen from my purse.

Robert Vann says, "So you're going to do this no matter what?"

His words surprise me, because he's known me long enough. "Yes, Robert, I didn't ask you here today for your *consent*, but I had hoped for your participation. I'd like to see your name on this letter, but"—I shrug—"you're free to abstain. Others will sign."

He sits in silent contemplation for a minute, glances at the other two men, and then says with a sigh, "Well, we'll need more than four names on this letter to make an impact. And we'll need to do more than just mail it to the White House."

"Okay," I say, "what are your thoughts?"

"If you want this letter to move Roosevelt, it needs to be public. So . . . what would you think about publishing it in the newspaper?"

My friend is right. What good would this letter do if it was to just sit on the president's desk? "That's an excellent idea."

"Then it's settled," he says. "I won't sign it, but I'll arrange for it to be published in the *Courier* once it's written and you've procured signatures."

"Well, gentlemen, let's get started," I say, picking up my pen.

Robert Vann holds up his hand. "Just one caveat, Mary."

"Of course." I give him a smile, because he's come a long way from where this conversation began.

"The language in this letter cannot go too far. Not only because Roosevelt hasn't earned it but also because you haven't fully embraced the Democratic Party. I don't think you've turned around that picture of Lincoln yet." He grins, and the men erupt in laughter.

"You raise a good point. We'll thread the needle so people know that, while we are encouraged by the fact that a president has finally spoken out against lynching, we haven't become Democrats yet."

"Excuse me, Mrs. Bethune." Glancing up, I smile at one of the hotel's front desk attendants. "There's a call for you."

"Thank you, my dear. Who is it?"

"I don't know, ma'am. It's a woman with a high-pitched voice who said it was important."

"Excuse me," I say to the men, and all three stand up as I push back my chair. "Keep sharing your ideas on the letter." When I hand Robert Vann the pen, he smirks, and then I follow the attendant to a desk near the reception area. *Why is Eleanor calling?* She knows about this meeting and wouldn't interrupt unless it's important.

Picking up the receiver, I say, "This is Mrs. Bethune."

"Mary, my apologies for the interruption."

"I always welcome a call from you, my friend."

"I wanted to catch you before you finalized your declaration. While you know I'm thrilled with this idea, I want to make sure the language in the letter isn't *too* exuberant."

Her words are so close to Robert Vann's. "Why?"

"Well, Franklin will not commit to meeting with Walter, no matter how many times I ask or reasons I offer. He has no intention of doing anything about lynching beyond what he's already said."

"Oh." My shoulders slump. The meeting with Walter is as important as the letter. This is a two-pronged approach. Eleanor and I have decided that the letter will *pull* the president closer to where we need him to be and a meeting with the head of the NAACP will be the final *push* that is needed.

Giving up on this meeting is not an option, and a thought comes to mind. "I have an idea. Are you willing to engage in a touch of subterfuge to get Walter before your husband?"

"Yes," she says, no hesitation at all. "What are you thinking?"

"Now, before you say yes, think. And if you're not able to do it, I'll understand and we'll come up with something else. I don't want to compromise your morals; I know how important honesty is to you."

"Please, Mary. Would you just tell me? I mean, a *little* flexibility in my values is a small sacrifice to stop this reprehensible practice."

"All right." I take a deep breath. "Your husband won't commit to an appointment, but that's not the only way for him to meet with Walter. What if the president simply finds himself in a meeting with Walter at the White House by happenstance?"

Eleanor is quiet, and I'm afraid I've overstepped our boundaries. But then I hear a laugh. "Why, Mary, what a splendid idea. And I know just the way to make it happen."

CHAPTER 32

ELEANOR

Washington, D.C.
May 7, 1934

"Would you like another cup of tea?" my mother-in-law asks. Watching Sara Delano Roosevelt fill Mr. White's Lenox blue-and-white china cup, I am sure this is the first time that a family member of the president has served a Negro.

We have had forty minutes of small talk while we wait for Franklin to return from his excursion on the Potomac River. Not that we've discussed this tardiness, of course. As far as formal invitations are concerned, my mother-in-law and I simply asked Walter White to the White House in his capacity as leader of the NAACP to discuss issues of race facing our nation.

Mr. White understands—without my having to explain it to him—the subtle deceit in making this meeting happen. The fact that his visit happens to coincide with Franklin's return from a sailing jaunt that will put the two gentlemen in direct contact, well, we can't help that, can we?

Although I forewarned my mother-in-law about Mr. White's fairness, it didn't prepare her for the pale fellow who entered the lovely six-pillared South Portico, where we were sitting. While she handled the introductions with her usual aplomb, I notice that she keeps stealing glances at him.

Sara has been a staunch ally on the issue of lynching, and in situations such as this, I can almost forgive her past manipulations. My husband has sidestepped every attempt I've made to bring him and Mr. White together, and I was distraught until Sara approached me with an offer of help and Mary made this excellent suggestion.

Our conversation trails off when we hear voices outside the door. As one, we smooth our attire and place our teacups in their saucers. Yet when a guard opens the door and Franklin wheels himself in, nothing could have readied us for his expression.

Fury. A cold, controlled fury simmers beneath the forced smile on his lips. It's a terrifying expression that I've had turned on me only once or twice. Either he knows this is Walter White and he's irate that we've bamboozled him, or he's seething because we've allowed someone other than family and close advisers to see him in his wheelchair. Either way, has our scheme been a terrible mistake?

We all rise, but I'm the first to speak. "Franklin, I would like to introduce you to Mr. Walter White, who serves as the director of the National Association for the Advancement of Colored People. Mama"—I gesture to Franklin's mother—"and I have been having a most illuminating conversation with Mr. White. Would you care to join us?"

I can see that he's formulating one of his famous excuses. But before a single word can escape from his lips, his mother says, "Oh, do join us, dear. It would be most pleasing to your old mother."

Oh my, I think, *Sara has trotted out her secret weapon. Guilt.* I almost laugh, as this powerful ammunition is usually only used against me. But I am tickled to see it in play, as I know it will force his hand.

"Of course, Mama," he says, and wheels himself to the table.

Having brought him to the battlefield, she withdraws and pours him a cup of tea. This is my signal to begin my opening, which I practiced with Hick until I got it just right.

"Franklin, we began discussing the thousands of letters I've been receiving from hard-hit colored families, describing their experiences with homelessness, joblessness, and racial hostilities. Mr. White has some excellent suggestions on steps I might take for these poor folks." We decided we should lead with issues other than lynching.

A look of relief flashes over Franklin's face. I can almost hear him think, *Perhaps this is the extent of it. Perhaps this isn't the diatribe about the anti-lynching bill I expected.* He turns to Mr. White and says, "The First Lady and I have been discussing the plight of those poor folks for some time, and while I know she's involved Mr. Hopkins, who runs the Federal Emergency Relief Administration, your advice is most welcome."

So far, so good. Gazing out at the South Lawn, lovely on this warm spring day, Sara and I stay quiet as their conversation continues, speaking again only when it begins to die down. It is then that I leap into the breach. "Franklin, as you may be aware, Mr. White is also working hard on behalf of the anti-lynching bill that's being floated in Congress. He's made believers out of your mother and me, and we'd like to give you the opportunity to hear his perspective."

Franklin is silent, but I know that, inwardly, he's groaning. With his mother present, though, he won't lash out or be rude. "I do believe I am familiar with Mr. White's views on the anti-lynching bill. He's sent them in letter format to the Oval Office often enough, and though I wasn't present, I do believe he espoused them at the Capitol, which was reported in the newspapers."

"It's one thing to read the arguments in favor of the anti-lynching bill and quite another to hear them. Mr. White feels deeply the violence that's been done to his people. As should we," my mother-in-law announces in her most imperious tone.

If I had made this statement, it would have been ignored or marginalized. After all, I have been in hot water at the White House since it became known that I joined the NAACP; Steve Woodburn had what I can only describe as a temper tantrum when he found out.

Franklin knows when he's defeated. "Go ahead, then, Mr. White," he says with a sigh.

Mr. White stands and addresses Franklin. "Mr. President, our nation's understanding of lynching—what it is, where it happens, how frequently it occurs, and why—is false. Lynching isn't a historic event that occurred rarely in the South when a colored man was accused of attacking a white woman. Lynching is a brutal murder undertaken by and in front of a mob, and it happens with surprising frequency in both the South *and* the North—to the tune of five thousand in the past fifty years alone, which translates to ninety lynchings a year, or an average of one every four days." Mr. White pauses for a breath, and Franklin takes the opportunity to interject.

"Contrary to popular opinion, I am familiar with the numbers on lynching." Franklin's tone is growing angrier.

"Of course, sir, but we are talking about the majority of the American people here. And what those citizens don't understand is that state and local governments rarely stop a lynching once it's in progress.

"We need federal authorities to prevent this miscarriage of justice. But they can't, because there is no federal law that assigns the government the authority to stop the mobs of vigilantes who are acting as judge and jury. They are murdering American citizens without recourse. The only word for this is 'anarchy.'"

Franklin is quiet as Mr. White pauses. I see that the well-phrased, calm, persuasive argument has resonated with my husband. Perhaps Mr. White has raised points about lynching that Franklin's never heard before, forcing him to see lynching not only as an abomination but as a symptom of a government in disrepair. Or perhaps Franklin has never really listened closely to the NAACP's arguments until now.

Suddenly Franklin's expression changes from open and considerate to stormy, even enraged. I can guess what's occurred. Instead of allowing himself to really hear the truth about this terrible practice, he's thinking about what sacrifices he'll have to make if he supports the anti-lynching bill.

Mr. White has launched back into his argument, and from his heightened tone, I am guessing it's reaching its crescendo. "So I hope that I have made a clear case in support of the Costigan-Wagner Bill. A bill that will unfortunately fail without your backing.

"It's fairly simple, President Roosevelt—either the federal laws are strong enough to pursue those who lynch, or they aren't. We cannot allow these hideous murders to happen and then go unpunished."

Mr. White remains standing, facing Franklin, even though his speech has concluded. Franklin holds his gaze. And then, without shifting his eyes, he says, "Someone has been priming you, Mr. White. Someone has provided you with all my anticipated responses and the best replies you might offer, so that you can include them in your pre-sentation. And I think I know who that someone is." He turns and stares at me.

The entire room has gone quiet.

"Was it my wife?" he asks.

I open my mouth, about to take full credit—and full blame—when my mother-in-law stands up and says, "It was me, Franklin. I am the one who called this meeting, and I am the one who invited Mr. White here in an effort to convince you to put an end to this evil practice."

I have never cared for her more.

But who is this man I married? The young fellow I encountered on the train, full of enthusiasm to fight for what's right, would have been horrified by the realities of lynching. Where has his integrity gone? Did it go by the wayside when polio struck and he had to claw his way back to some semblance of walking? Or was it squeezed out of him one handshake at a time as he built up enough support to become president of the United States?

Franklin's eyes widen and the anger fades from his face. He swivels back to Mr. White. "You see, Mr. White, no matter what anyone has told you, I am sympathetic to your cause and your bill. I wish I could publicly declare my support. But you are a smart man, and I think you know what would happen. The Southern Democrats would abandon me, and I would lose all their votes for the New Deal legislation I'm rolling out. Every bill I ask Congress to pass would be blocked, and that would be disastrous—perhaps even fatal—to the millions of people who need the federal government's help. I wish I could help the ninety people who fall victim to the horrors of lynching every year, but I can't risk the future of millions. There will have to be another way to stop lynching besides this blasted Costigan-Wagner Bill, because I will not be supporting it."

CHAPTER 33

ELEANOR

New York, New York
February 23, 1935

"Are you sure this is the right address? This doesn't look like an art gallery."

Earl peers over the passenger seat and replies with a rascal's smile. "Now, I may lead you astray from time to time, but have I ever been guilty of delivering you to the wrong destination, ma'am?"

"No," I concede, thinking of all the times he's shepherded me to events and rallies and meetings all around the country in all kinds of weather using all sorts of transportation, from cars to trains to planes and—in one strange instance—a horse and buggy.

"This is indeed the Arthur U. Newton Gallery, an address that I personally triple-checked. Because the art exhibit had to be relocated at the last minute to this gallery—due to the death threats—I inspected the premises earlier today to ensure we could protect you here."

"Thank you for going above and beyond, Earl."

"Ma'am, there is no such thing as above and beyond when it comes to you."

He leaps out of the car to open my door, and I enter the frigid, velvety blue night. As I step up to the landing of the elegant six-story building, I hear footsteps behind me. On edge from my conversation with Walter White, who detailed the threats of violence the NAACP received for organizing the show, I pivot, only to see Earl.

"What are you doing?" I ask, astonished—and admittedly a bit relieved—to see him. Earl never accompanies me to my appointments. He only lurks in the shadows.

"I'll be at your side every step of the way tonight," he says.

"That really isn't necessary, Earl. I'm sure you can manage my safety from the periphery."

"I am acting on the order of President Roosevelt, ma'am."

Earl's insistence on a procession of vehicles now makes sense. Franklin and I had an enormous battle over my desire to come to this exhibit; he railed at the "unnecessary risks" of attendance, given the threats sent to the NAACP and the protests staged outside the prestigious Jacques Seligmann gallery, where the anti-lynching exhibit had originally been scheduled. Only after heated exchanges and two more lynchings of young men, Jerome Wilson and Claude Neal, did he finally relent.

Arm in arm, Earl and I step into the foyer of the gallery, where we are greeted by marble floors, creamy walls, and the hint of brass, gilt, and wooden frames peeking out from adjoining rooms. And Mary and Mr. White, of course.

"Mrs. Roosevelt, it is such an honor to host you at *An Art Commentary on Lynching*," Mr. White says.

I reach out my hand to shake Mr. White's hand and then Mary's. In my peripheral vision, I see both white and colored guests at the gallery gawk at this gesture.

After I introduce Earl, I say, "I would not have missed this exhibit for the world. You certainly took Franklin at his word when he suggested that we find another way to stop lynching."

The sadness and anger I felt on that day nine months ago when my husband declared he would not support the anti-lynching bill is still with me. I haven't given up, but Mary and I have decided to focus more widely—and look for innovative ways to raise awareness, like Mr. White's exhibit.

"We cried enough tears, didn't we?" Mary says. "But now we move forward, and this ingenious idea of Walter's will raise national awareness about lynching in all sorts of communities."

Turning to Mr. White, I say, "Well, I am proud to be here tonight to support your brainchild."

"I can't tell you how much your words move me, Mrs. Roosevelt. Please call me Walter, if you are comfortable with that. Shall we enter the first gallery room?"

Guests mill about, studying the pieces of art. Mary nods hello to two young colored women in professional attire who call out "Mrs. Bethune" in greeting, and several people stare at me as I pass. As we walk toward a specific painting, Mary says, "Walter, you have to be pleased with the many white and colored folks in the crowd. How far your message will spread."

Walter's smile is wide and his blue eyes twinkle, but it doesn't last. His expression quickly turns somber. I understand. He needs to maintain a grave countenance, given the theme of the exhibit. "I *am* pleased. I hope this will bring lynching into the mainstream news and not only the colored papers. My greatest desire is that people will be moved to act against lynching." He lowers his voice and adds, "Let us allow the images of renowned artists like Isamu Noguchi, Thomas Hart Benton, and José Clemente Orozco to speak to us rather than words."

A black-and-white picture hangs on the wall before us. The smallness of its scale—possibly two feet by one and a half feet—prompts us to lean toward it for a closer look.

Walter then presents a fair-skinned colored man in his thirties to us. "Mrs. Roosevelt. Mrs. Bethune. Will you do me the honor of allowing me to introduce you to Mr. Hale Woodruff? He is the artist of this painting, called *By Parties Unknown*, and he also teaches at Atlanta University, where he's founded an art department."

Dapper in a striped suit, the mustachioed young artist bows toward us. I say, "It is a pleasure, Mr. Woodruff."

"The pl-pleasure is all mine, Mrs. Roosevelt," he replies. I don't imagine he expected to see the First Lady here.

"Nice to meet you, Mr. Woodruff," Mary adds. "I'm a fan of what you're doing at Atlanta University for our young colored boys and girls, giving them opportunities in a field not known for welcoming them."

"Thank you, ma'am. It's an honor to meet *the* Mrs. Bethune."

Niceties aside, Walter launches into his purpose. As always. "Mrs. Roosevelt and Mrs. Bethune, when I invited the artists to participate in this exhibit, I asked each to focus on the brutality of lynching without concern for how violent or disturbing the images might be." Turning to the young man, Walter says, "Mr. Woodruff, would you mind telling us about your picture?"

As Mr. Woodruff takes a big breath, I lean in to examine the black-and-white piece. At first, all I can make out is the image of a somewhat run-down church, complete with stained glass windows. Then I realize there is a body laid out on the church's front steps, a man with his hands bound behind his back and a noose around his neck.

"As you can probably see, my subject is the victim of a lynching. I used black to render the image of a lifeless young Negro who's been cut down from a tree where he was hung and deposited by the mob on the church steps."

"It's very moving," I say, unable to take my eyes off the sad, striking composition.

"Thank you, ma'am," he says. "That was my intention."

"Do you mind if I ask about the title, *By Parties Unknown*? Why did you choose that?"

Mary, Walter, and Mr. Woodruff give each other a curious look. Did I say something wrong? I'm not an art aficionado, but I would have guessed that a query about the title was acceptable.

"The phrase 'By Parties Unknown' is often used in sheriff or governmental reports or in the press as a way to evade naming the lynchers, even if their identity is well-known," he says almost apologetically.

I see why they exchanged glances. The phrase is familiar to those in the colored community because lynching and the efforts by lynchers to avoid punishment, often aided by local law enforcement, are common. How little I know.

"Why is the poor man on the church steps?" Mary asks. "I don't think I've ever heard of such a thing."

"I hoped to highlight the hypocrisy of the lynchers and the mob— that dichotomy between their actions and the beliefs they profess to hold," Mr. Woodruff says.

"How powerful," I say. "We tell people that all the time, but it's quite a different experience to *see* it. It allows you to feel the terror and inhumanity of lynching in a visceral way." Earl makes a small noise, and I realize this exhibit is affecting him as well.

Walter practically jumps up and down with excitement. "Mrs. Roosevelt, that is it exactly—the entire purpose of this exhibit. To have viewers experience what it's like to be a colored person in the South and ask how we can consider ourselves a civilized country if torture and murder routinely happen without regard or punishment."

We move through the pictures in the gallery. Mr. Woodruff gets pulled away at one point, and it is just us four as we stand before the final image. It appears to be a charcoal sketch of a white crowd standing before a farmhouse, all wearing the sorts of hats and bonnets that might be worn by farm folk, as an older woman holds a young girl on her shoulders. The mood is merry and therefore incongruous in the context of this exhibit.

"You look a little confused, Mrs. Roosevelt?" Walter asks.

"Well, for the life of me, I cannot image what this scene has to do with the anti-lynching theme."

"This sketch is by the *New Yorker* magazine illustrator Reginald Marsh," Walter says as Mary leans close to see the caption at the bottom of the drawing.

"This is her first lynching," she reads to us.

Suddenly the entire picture changes. No longer is this a jolly farm crowd gathered together to watch something out of sight in the sketch, such as an auction or a traveling performer. Instead, this group turns into an ugly mob, witnessing a man being lynched for entertainment. They are so evil, they deem a lynching pleasant enough to bring a child.

I reach for Mary's hand, clasping it as I stare at this horrible sight, this induction of a young child into ritualized, accepted racial bloodshed. "This may well be the most disturbing piece in the entire exhibit."

As Mary murmurs her agreement, Walter probes further. "Why is that, Mrs. Roosevelt?" His tone does not bear any surprise, and I'm guessing my reaction is the whole point.

"Because it evokes a terrible truth that Mary revealed to me not long ago. Inaction in the face of racism is acquiescence to it."

CHAPTER 34

ELEANOR

Washington, D.C.
June 14, 1935

Did I hear someone shout my name? The sound startles me. Decorum rules the day at the White House.

But then I hear it again. I have just walked Mary to her cab after we finished up a meeting about the speech I'll be giving on her behalf at the upcoming NAACP annual conference. I glance behind me, but there's no one at the base of the stairs.

Turning toward my sitting room, I collide with a looming Steve Woodburn, the only person who'd dare take such liberties.

"Mr. Woodburn, you startled me." I dislike having any contact with this man. The more time I spend with him, the more I see his Southern Democrat roots. I suppose this shouldn't surprise me, as I've heard rumors that his ancestors served in senior Confederate positions.

I often wonder if Steve would be as ensconced in his position—and have Franklin's ear—if Louis were well. In the past year, my husband's longtime adviser, who holds the position of secretary to the president and resides in the Lincoln bedroom in the White House so Franklin has constant, immediate access to him, has struggled with breathing difficulties. When Louis isn't himself or is at the hospital, Steve seems to always step into the fray.

"Mrs. Roosevelt, a word," he instructs rather than asks.

Part of me wants to excoriate him for his presumptuousness, but since I'm the one always advocating for less formality in the White House, I hold my tongue. "Yes, Mr. Woodburn?"

"I didn't make a huge fuss when you joined the NAACP, never mind how it impacted the Democratic base when the news was leaked. I kept my mouth shut when you attended that ridiculous art exhibit about lynching, no matter how awfully it played out in the press and how much work I had to do on damage control. But now your man Walter White has gone too far in the constant communications he sends directly to the president, including inappropriate reports and images, despite the fact that the president has made clear he has no intention in getting involved with that anti-lynching bill. You really must do something about your people and their overreaching requests," he barks at me.

Oh, how I wish Earl was waiting in the shadows, as he often seems to be. Not because I cannot manage Steve, but because I would love to see Steve's face as Earl managed him.

"*I* must do something about Mr. White? *My* people have gone too far? Mr. Woodburn, you make a terrible assumption in your demands."

"And what is that, Mrs. Roosevelt?" He says my name with a sneer.

"That Mr. White is mine to command." I pivot away from the man, toward my sitting room. I wisely step away before I regret my words. I need to speak to Louis about this behavior. *He* is in charge of Franklin's staff.

When I slam the door behind me, Tommy jumps up from her desk and cries out, "Jeepers!" and then, seeing my face, says, "Apologies, ma'am."

"I'm the one that's sorry, Tommy," I apologize for startling her, "but that Steve Woodburn gets under my skin like no one else. He practically accosted me in the hallway."

Hesitating, she hands me a single-page memorandum, saying, "Then I am extra sorry to have to deliver this missive from said Steve Woodburn."

Skimming over the document, I can't believe what I see. "Well, doesn't this just beat all. How dare he? The audacity."

"I know," Tommy says. "The gall."

I read aloud, "'Walter White's letters to the president are insulting. . . . He is to be considered one of the worst troublemakers. . . . He must stop his barrage of letters and telegrams and requests immediately. . . . His requests are wholly inappropriate.'"

I ask the rhetorical question. "Who does Steve Woodburn think he is?"

"I cannot imagine, ma'am."

Memorandum in hand, I march to the Oval Office, barge past the guards, and stride inside.

As usual, Franklin sits behind his handsome desk, constructed with Michigan maple veneer by the Robert W. Irwin Company for former president Hoover. He's using his wheelchair instead of the designated desk chair, a sure sign that he's not expecting guests. A plethora of objects clutters the surface—practical items like letter openers and pens compete with comical objects like figures of donkeys and elephants—and I often wonder how he can work amidst the jumble.

"Do you know what Steve Woodburn did today?" I have to keep myself from shrieking.

Franklin lowers his glasses. "Not specifically, but he seems to ruffle feathers on a regular basis."

I lay the memorandum in front of Franklin. "Ah, I see," he says.

"What do you see, Franklin?"

"I see you're upset that Steve has asked you to rein in your Mr. White."

Franklin's words make me incensed. "You are no better than Mr. Woodburn—calling Walter 'my' Mr. White and speaking as though he is mine to control. That's beyond insulting, Franklin. To him and to me and to the work we are trying to accomplish."

"I apologize, Eleanor. You might have a point there. But while Steve's approach may be all wrong—and I will speak to him about it—his point is not unfounded. Mr. White has made a nuisance of himself with his persistence, and by associating yourself with him so plainly, you are opening yourself up to criticism that might undermine your projects. Just yesterday, I overheard one senator speculate to another that you are so amenable to the colored folks that you must have Negro blood. I think that's the sort of thing Steve is worried about."

My God, what a thing for someone to say and my husband to repeat. And then to suggest that I should disassociate myself from Walter because others find his work uncomfortable. Where is the Franklin I once knew and loved?

"I'd be proud to have Negro blood, and I suppose that if I did, and if my relatives and people were regularly tortured, murdered, and mutilated, I might make a nuisance of myself, too." I stare him down. "I'll make sure to tell Walter that I'd do exactly as he's doing if I was colored. In fact, I'll mention it to him at the NAACP National Conference."

"I don't think it's a good idea for you to attend that." Now I understand. Steve has already discussed the conference with Franklin, on top of everything else he raised in his letter and in the hallway.

"Mary is winning the Spingarn Medal, and I've promised to give a speech on her behalf. I've already written it, in fact, and plans have been made."

The Spingarn Medal, the highest honor granted by the NAACP, is awarded to a colored person who's made outstanding contributions to the community, and Mary will be only the second woman to receive it. I was touched when she asked if I'd give the keynote address.

"I'm going to ask you to skip that event, Eleanor." Franklin says it pleasantly, but I can tell from the intensity in his eyes that he's very serious. He rarely makes edicts about my activities, always professing to others that he "cannot do anything about" me.

"Are you serious?" I am incredulous at this overt effort to control me.

"Very."

"I can't believe it. I thought we had an understanding." I refer obliquely to the agreement we reached after his affair: that I would stay with him if I were free to live my own life. And that included pursuing my own projects and holding my own opinions.

"Eleanor, we are so close to enacting the Social Security Act. I can't risk you irritating one of the Southern Democrats." His expression turns pleading. "Just think of the millions we can help with that bill."

Even though I know this is a manipulation on both Franklin's and Steve's parts, I understand what he is saying. Could I hurt these New Deal endeavors, in which I believe as well? Have I become too tainted, too controversial? Am I too hemmed in by Franklin's agenda to do the work Mary and I have started? Have his lighthearted protests that he "cannot do anything about" me been empty words, as he has no intention of letting me pursue the policies to which he pays lip service? Does he use my work and words as a way of appeasing Negroes and women, when he has no intention of alienating his Southern supporters? My mind is spinning. How far can I go in defying the president of the United States, even if he is my husband?

I feel sick at the thought of disappointing Mary and Walter. Not to mention the colored citizens of our country. Will I really leave behind my hard-won boldness to fight for equality—which includes standing at the dais at the NAACP conference to honor my friend—because Franklin has asked me to?

My cheeks grow warm as an idea forms in my mind. Perhaps I will do as Franklin requests, but not because he asked it. I will do it because I might just be able to turn this setback into an opportunity to get *Mary* a seat at the federal New Deal table.

CHAPTER 35

MARY

Washington, D.C.
September 24, 1935

As I step out of the train from Florida into Union Station in Washington, D.C., the irony of my situation makes me laugh. After having spent nearly an entire day and night in a hot, squalid colored train car, I'm on my way to accept a federal position, an appointment made by the president.

Union Station is buzzing with the chatter of arriving and departing passengers. Typically, I take my time as I pass through this terminal—its architecture is a balm that calms me after the hardship of traveling as a colored woman. But today, I do not slow down, for I cannot be late.

Eleanor managed to make the impossible happen. While we were focused on getting colored men into federal positions, she secured this federal role for me, behind the scenes, anyway. It was an idea that came to Eleanor when she was unable to attend the NAACP convention. She sent the influential Miss Josephine Roche in her stead. Eleanor knew that as the assistant secretary of the treasury and cochair of the National Youth Administration's executive committee, Miss Roche would be an important ally. Sure enough, after hearing my speech, Miss Roche returned to the White House with a glowing review. And when

Eleanor suggested that I be considered for a position with the NYA, Miss Roche agreed and recommended me to the chair of the Executive Committee.

How excited I was to receive the call. The National Youth Administration is forming an advisory council, and as one of the members, I'll have input into federal programs that specifically focus on colored youth. I'll be part of a team that ensures New Deal monies are being directed into Negro communities, and today is our first meeting.

As I step out of Union Station, the sun is blinding. Is this a sign of the bright future that lies ahead as I return to federal work?

Squinting, I move to the roped-off colored section for taxis, but the line is long. I glance at my wristwatch and begin to feel anxious. There are plenty of taxicabs for white passengers, but only a few for us colored travelers.

By the time I arrive at the federal building on Constitution Avenue, I am fifteen minutes late. *Not the impression I wanted to make on my first day.* I locate the conference room and push the door open. A sea of white male faces look up from around the table, deep frowns on their faces. I can almost hear their thoughts: *What are you doing here? You don't belong.*

I stand at the door, the heat rising beneath my skin. *Yes, I belong here,* I want to shout. *Yes, my skin is one hundred shades darker than yours, and still, I belong in this conference room as much as you do.*

Pressing my lips together, I push my anger into my fingers and grip the handle of my valise tighter.

"Excuse me," the gentleman at the head of the table says, but he does not stand. "I think you're in the wrong place."

My chin juts forward, and I glare at each of the dozen men peering at me. "My name is Mrs. Mary McLeod Bethune," I say, my voice resounding through the room. "I. Belong. Here."

They exchange glances, but no one speaks in reply. This angers me more. "I was invited," I say, my words clipped, "by Mr. Aubrey Williams." Then, with my cane, I stomp across the room, moving to the one empty seat at the table.

"Mrs. Bethune," the man at the head of the table says, "I'm afraid you *are* in the wrong room. Mr. Williams' meeting is in the conference room one floor below."

I blink in confusion.

He continues, "The room you're looking for is 232. This is 332."

Once again, my skin warms, but now from embarrassment. "Excuse me for interrupting," I apologize, finally turning around.

It feels as though it takes me thirty minutes to leave the room, and when I finally step into the hallway, I lean against the closed door. I was ready to put every single one of those men in *their* places. But *I* was the one in the wrong.

Well, I think as I push myself off the wall, *lesson learned, and when I return to Florida, I'll have a new lesson to teach Albert.* Not every "no" is a rejection, and not every "no" spoken by a white man is uttered through the lips of a bigot.

Minutes later, I find the correct conference room, and I cautiously peek inside. The first person I see is a white man sitting at the head of the conference table. But this time, a smile accompanies his glance. He rises from his seat. "Mrs. Bethune," he says, his tone filled with ardor. "I'm Aubrey Williams, the executive director of the NYA, and it is such a pleasure to meet you."

I exhale, and only after we exchange greetings do I notice Miss Roche and my friend Dr. Mordecai Johnson, the first colored president of Howard University. Eleanor mentioned that Mordecai would be an adviser as well.

After the perfunctory welcomes and compliments, we settle at the broad cherrywood conference table. "Mrs. Bethune, I cannot tell you how pleased Miss Roche and I are to have you and Dr. Johnson joining us today. My goal is simple—to make sure that every NYA program works for everyone. No one will be left behind, especially not the colored young people in this country. That's why you and Dr. Johnson are here."

Mordecai and I each express our enthusiasm for the opportunity, and then Mr. Williams continues, "Our plan is to review all of our federal programs with the two of you and have you advise us on how we can use each program to help the Negro youth. But also, my focus extends beyond the federal level; we hope to appoint state directors who will be working on the ground, making sure that each program is implemented and funds are used properly at the local level. We want to make sure we have the right people in these positions, and by 'right people,' we mean we need colored directors, particularly in the South."

Already I like what I'm hearing. "That's certainly one area where we'll be able to help. Recommending the right people," I say, glancing at Mordecai, who nods.

"Your recommendations will be crucial. We have made one state appointment I'm excited about. He's not colored, but this young man is very committed to making sure all Texas youth benefit from this program—Lyndon Baines Johnson. He'll be excellent."

"We'll arrange for Mr. Johnson to meet and speak with both of you," Miss Roche says.

From there, the four of us chat about the ideas Mordecai and I have. I want to work with the poorest and most vulnerable children, particularly in rural areas, while Mordecai talks about increasing federal support for Negro colleges and universities. At the two-hour mark, an aide pops in to alert Mr. Williams of his next meeting.

Mr. Williams clasps his hands together. "What a productive start. Miss Roche and I will make sure you get the schedule for our biannual meetings."

I nod and smile, but I have no intention of meeting with Mr. Williams only on a biannual basis. *Oh, no.* I plan on turning this small seat at the New Deal table into a vast and expansive one.

CHAPTER 36

ELEANOR

Washington, D.C.
September 24, 1935

As I wait for my friend to emerge from her meeting, I feel as youthful and excited as I did during my time at Allenswood School. Each of those days in London brought the delight of learning, the warm support of the headmistress Madame Souvestre, and the company of like-minded fellow students. *Why do I feel like a schoolgirl?* Is it because Mary has, at last, found an official, Roosevelt-sanctioned place in the administration?

Or could it be the lovely stint I just spent at Hyde Park? Lots of meetings for both Franklin and me, but time with friends and family as well. I caught up with Marion and Nan at Val-Kill; it had been months since I'd had more than a stolen hour with them. Our mild-mannered, nineteen-year-old John took the train down from Harvard and we spent a wonderful weekend together. I don't know if the reason I share a closer bond with him and Brud is because they have easier temperaments or because I'm a different person and parent with them than I was with my older ones. Even Sara was more tranquil than usual. And the best news of all—we got a positive update about Louis' condition.

Dark-suited white men begin to trickle out of meeting rooms. I stop pacing and wait for Mary. *What is taking her so long?*

As two of the gentlemen continue past me, I hear one of the men say the word "Bethune" to the other. When the other man mutters something like "above her station" in response, I realize I've got to keep my ear to the ground. The very self-assurance I so admire and which makes Mary powerful and effective can also be perceived as a threat.

Finally, Dr. Johnson, Mr. Williams, Miss Roche, and Mary exit the conference room. Part of me wants to race toward Mary and beg for details, but as far as anyone but Mary is concerned, I'm here for my own meetings. I wait for a break in their conversation and endeavor to catch her eye.

Mr. Williams notices me first. "Why," he exclaims, "is that Mrs. Roosevelt?"

Mary and I give each other a knowing smile as Mr. Williams bounds toward me. The dark-haired administrator has such stern features that I shied away from him upon first introduction, but Hick scolded me. I was judging him unfairly on his appearances, she said. I should know better. She told me about his hardscrabble background as an impoverished, self-educated Southerner and how he'd dedicated himself to the underprivileged, and now my opinion of him soars.

"What a delight running into you, Mr. Williams. And you as well, Mrs. Bethune and Dr. Johnson," I say.

"Why, Mrs. Roosevelt, I didn't expect to see you here," Mary says with the slightest wink.

"The first meeting of the NYA's advisory board just concluded," Miss Roche says with a proud nod in my friend's direction, her upswept graying hair bobbing with the gesture.

I clap, as if surprised. "Well, that's a wondrous coincidence. As I think you know, the work you do is very dear to me."

"Your support means the world to us at the NYA." Mr. Williams beams.

"You are so fortunate to have two brilliant luminaries on your advisory board. You do well to rely upon their expertise," I add, glancing at Mary and Dr. Johnson.

"We are lucky to have them," Mr. Williams says, his voice passionate.

"There will be many more grateful, employed, and well-educated young citizens as a result. Otherwise, we could lose this entire generation of youth," I say, hunting for a way to end the conversation politely and extricate Mary. We've arranged to get together after the meeting, and I have a plan.

Finally, we say our farewells, and Mary and I, followed by Earl, stroll out through an obscure hallway into the bright sun, where our vehicle waits to whisk us away. Sometimes there is magic in being the First Lady.

Mary looks at me quizzically when I gesture at the automobile. "Is that for us?"

"It is," I answer with what I hope is an enigmatic smile.

"Where are we going?"

As we slide into the back seat, Earl stores Mary's valise in the trunk, and I answer, "It's a surprise."

She gives me a glance of astonished delight, and I ask, "How did the meeting go?"

"Lots of aspirational language bandied about, but not a lot of details. As expected," she answers with a sigh. "Even though I think Mr. Williams and Miss Roche very much want to include young Negroes in the NYA."

"But there's room for expansion in the role, I imagine? And room for firm plans, instead of the nebulous sorts of conversations your colleagues are having elsewhere in New Deal agencies?" I'm relieved to be able to talk with our usual frankness instead of the polite stiffness we used in the presence of Mr. Williams, Miss Roche, and Dr. Johnson.

"Yes. But now I'm hoping for your counsel on something specific."

"Whatever you need, I'm here," I say.

"I see enormous possibilities for the NYA. I could give you a litany of all the things that agency is in a position to do, but not much can be accomplished with a council that meets only twice a year. I need to be in D.C. much more frequently."

"I agree," I say. "From the beginning, we talked about this council spot as an entrée to something larger."

"Yes. And I think that if I spoke not only as Mary McLeod Bethune but as the voice of thousands of colored women, that would encourage Mr. Williams to expand my position—and could lead to much more."

I don't understand. "What do you have in mind?"

She explains, "I'm thinking of starting a new women's organization."

My confusion is not lifted. What does the creation of another women's organization have to do with expanding Mary's federal role with the NYA? After a moment, I say, "You're already a leader in countless organizations: the NACW, the NAACP, Delta Sigma Theta, and the YWCA. How would another group help your efforts to secure a bigger New Deal job?"

Mary smiles. "This would be a new organization that brings consolidated Negro power to Washington."

I press my lips together, holding my thoughts inside. Those are two words one never hears spoken together—"Negro" and "power."

She speaks into my silence. "I'm thinking of an organization that is bigger than any of the ones you named. It would unite groups of all sorts, including important non-clubs like the colored sororities and the YWCA. Every organization would maintain their own structure, of course; this would be a separate entity, a kind of umbrella, where we would all come together to discuss and promote shared goals. Imagine bringing that kind of power to Washington."

I'm still confused. It would certainly be a large organization, and definitely unique, but power?

She adds, "It would be the largest organization of Negro women in the country. An organization of women whose voices are currently disparate and unchanneled but would now be unified. And in my federal role, I could be their voice. I would no longer speak as Mary McLeod Bethune, lone colored woman. I would be raising the voices of thousands." She pauses. "Thousands of Negro women who vote."

Suddenly the veil lifts. As the head of this organization, Mary would be connected to thousands and thousands of voters. Every New Deal agency would want her in an expanded role at their table, and even Franklin would want her at his side. I'm stunned by her vision.

"Mary, it's brilliant."

Just then, the car pulls alongside a four-story brick building with a brown-and-white awning emblazoned with the word "Reeves."

"We're here," I announce, and practically leap out of the vehicle.

"What's this?" Mary asks.

"Only the very best bakery and candy store in all of Washington, D.C.," I announce, then add with a smirk, "Although if you tell Mrs. Nesbitt I said that, I'll deny it."

As Mary laughs and the bells on the front door chime, we step into a homey restaurant filled with a cross section of D.C. society. Earl had concerns about securing the safety of a bakery and café that seats one hundred and fifty people at the counter and a slew of tables on the first, second, and third floors, so he and I made a compromise: Mary and I would take over a small private room on the first floor, which Earl and his men could guard effectively. This has the added benefit of shielding Mary from any raised eyebrows over a colored and a white woman dining together.

Earl shepherds us to the reserved space, where we are greeted with an exquisite platter of finger sandwiches and a stacked triple tray of Reeves' most popular sweets. Slices of the bakery's famous strawberry pie, fruit turnovers, cinnamon bow ties, tea cookies, chocolate drops, and iced gingerbread all sit side by side. "Congratulations!" I tell Mary.

"Well, well, isn't this a delectable display. I'm not sure what I've done to deserve all this."

"I think becoming part of the NYA is worthy of celebrating with the capital's finest desserts, don't you?" I say, then add, "Maybe not the fanciest, but certainly the most delicious."

"Of course! But I think *I* should be hosting this celebration. You're the one who made it all happen," she insists.

"Now, Mary," I reply, considering the slices of strawberry pie, *"you* are the one who impressed Miss Roche, not me. I just made sure she was in the right place at the right time. Shall we toast to your new role?"

"I'd like that." Mary glances down at her teacup but then points to the dessert tray. "Should we toast with one of these treats instead? You know that gingerbread is calling to me."

"Sounds perfect," I answer, reaching for a tempting piece of pie. As my dessert plate touches the corner of Mary's bowl of gingerbread, I say, "To the beginning of your work at the NYA."

"To a sweet future!"

CHAPTER 37

MARY

Washington, D.C.
April 3, 1936

I have become a fixture in the capital. A regular in Union Station. A frequent guest in the corridors of federal buildings and even the White House. The only place where I've become a stranger is my home in Daytona Beach. Although my school is being well managed and my grandson has two dedicated caretakers, his father, and the eyes of an entire campus upon him, guilt is a constant companion as I travel by train from Florida to Washington, D.C., over and over again.

To assuage my guilt, I remind myself of the gains we are making. In the six short months since I've been named to the advisory council for the NYA, I've formed the National Council of Negro Women. All the women see the strength in unification and coordination, and we've even secured a Washington, D.C., town house to serve as our head-quarters.

I enter Union Station and approach the long corridor that leads to the special track for the presidential train. In front of me, a colored porter is speaking to two white men in dark suits, both of whom I recognize as members of the NYA. When the porter steps aside for the men to enter the corridor, he faces me.

With a smile, I greet him. "Good morning, young man." I reach inside my pocketbook for my ticket. "I'm Mrs. Mary—"

"This train isn't for you," he interrupts, sounding as if he has no patience. He points to the sign above. "The sign says this is a special entrance," he tells me as if he's not sure I can read. "This is a train for passengers going to see the president."

My voice is filled with disappointment. "Do you not realize that it is possible for a Negro to be on this train? I am one of President Roosevelt's advisers, and I've been invited to meet with him at his home."

The porter's mouth opens as wide as his eyes. I'm not sure what saddens me more—his assumption or his astonishment. This young man has never imagined a colored woman could enter a train car filled with white people, all of us on our way to see the president.

As I move away from the porter and follow the train tracks, I remind myself that his view of what Negroes can and cannot do has been shaped by the limits he's experienced. What he thinks, what he believes, is not his fault.

The moment I step onto the train, Mr. Williams calls out, "Mrs. Bethune!"

Once I set my bag down, I join Mr. Williams, Miss Roche, and the other NYA members around a small table at one end of the car and we discuss the presentations we will be making to the president today. Each of us will speak about our area of focus; my presentation will highlight the desperate need for special funding for colored youth. When we finish our review, we return to our seats.

I have given hundreds of presentations to thousands. Yet the presentation I will make in a few hours is daunting. I will have an audience of one, but he is the president of the United States, and this first meeting has me a bit unsettled.

So while Mr. Williams, Miss Roche, and the others chat, I lean back and close my eyes. I want to go before the president with a calm and grateful heart. And so, I pray.

How grand the Roosevelts' home is, I think as our car slows in front of the three-story house called Springwood. Few of the impressive homes in Daytona can compare to this vast brick estate with its white pillars, green shutters, wide stone entrance, and views over the Hudson River. Given Eleanor and the president's heritage, I would have expected nothing less than this historic stateliness. This place the president depends on to renew his spirit is impressive indeed.

Eleanor greets us at the door, and I am surprised as I step into the airy foyer. With such a formal exterior, I expected the inside to be decorated like the White House. Instead, this house feels like a home. From the warm, rich tones in the walnut doors and staircase to the dozens and dozens of family photos on the walls and atop every surface to the upholstered chintz chairs and settees scattered around every room, it all feels lived-in and inviting.

Eleanor welcomes Mr. Williams first, then me. "Mrs. Bethune," she says with a smile.

Following Eleanor's lead, we wind through a warren of hallways to the president's study. While the room isn't small, it feels cozy with its abundance of comfortable sitting areas. Bookcases line one wall, each shelf stuffed with leather-bound books, and more family photographs are displayed around the room.

Six pale green damask chairs have been arranged in a semicircle in front of the wide mahogany desk where the president sits. He's dressed in a cardigan, although he still wears a starched white shirt and a tie. But his appearance and expression are so casual, I'm put at ease.

"I'm going to step away," Eleanor says to everyone before Mr. Williams introduces each of us to the president.

When he gets to me, the president bestows a smile so warm, it feels like an embrace. "Ah, Mrs. Bethune." He nods in greeting. "I've heard so much about you from my wife that I feel I know you already."

At his remark, the others in the room study me, surprised. "It is an honor to meet you, Mr. President."

We settle into the chairs, and Mr. Williams begins, "Thank you for seeing us, Mr. President. I'd like to go over the agenda." Once he's finished, he passes the meeting to Miss Roche, who delivers the first report. I have chosen to go last, believing the final voice in any presentation is the one that lingers in the minds of the attendees.

As I listen to each of the speakers, I shift in my seat. Not impatiently but anxiously. I am eager for the president to hear the needs of my people. I am here for hundreds of thousands of faces I've never seen, voices of men and women I've never heard. Yet I know them, and what happens in this room will impact their lives.

"And now, Mr. President, it is Mrs. Mary McLeod Bethune's turn to present her *report*," Mr. Williams says, his emphasis a reminder that he wants me to just state the facts on the status of Negroes under the NYA and not go off script, which I tend to do.

I move to the edge of my seat. Although I am used to standing when presenting, everyone has remained seated, a polite nod to the president.

"Mr. President, as you know, my focus with the NYA has been ensuring that Negro youth are included in this federal program. I've concentrated on two distinct groups. First, children under the age of ten, particularly those who live in rural communities. And second, because I am the president of a college, I'm focused on preparing young people to attend higher institutions of learning. So my report will cover these two groups." I begin by sharing statistics: the number of Negro children living in poverty; the number of Negro children who never attend school; and then, at the other extreme, the number of Negro youth who enter college but are unable to complete their education because of lack of financial resources.

But as I continue, my report sounds like the others, and I realize I'm talking about numbers and not people. Pushing my papers aside,

I look the president in the eye. "President Roosevelt, as I was walking through Union Station today, I could see the impact your New Deal programs are having on the recovery. After two years, people are returning to work and traveling again. For many, happy days are here again, or at least they can see happier days on the horizon. However, Mr. President, there is a group that has been completely left behind. For them, there is no hope for happier days . . . and that's Negro youth."

I point to the papers I've laid on his desk. "I've given you statistics, but these girls and boys shouldn't be reduced to numbers. The statistics don't begin to describe their plight. Let's start with the youngest of these.

"There are colored children in this country who live in conditions no different than how I grew up—in dirt-floor sharecropper cabins with no electricity, no running water, and, what's most important, no access to a better life. This is 1935, President Roosevelt. No one, no matter the color of their skin, should live this way.

"And then there are the Negro children who live in conditions that are slightly better, and their parents have hope for their future. These families struggle and sacrifice to secure that rare opportunity to send their children to college. That, of course, is the key to opening the door to the American dream.

"But that key is broken, and that door is locked for Negro youth. Even for those few who obtain college degrees, they are still defined by the color of their skin. Often when those college graduates actually find a job, it's either not befitting of their education or short-lived because, months later, they are fired to make room for a new white hire.

"Whether a child is faced with living with no indoor plumbing or a young person is living with the challenges of discrimination and racism after college, both are unacceptable in a country that's called the *United* States. Both are unacceptable for a country that promises the American Dream."

The room is silent—rapt, I'd say—as I continue, "The New Deal is leaving these citizens behind, and America is losing as well. Our country can only be great when we recognize the potential of greatness in every child in this country." I then tell the president, "I do not believe in presenting problems without providing solutions. Mr. President, I hope you'll consider the following: in order to reach these forgotten citizens, Negroes must take the lead. I understand that every effort has been made to include Negroes as advisers in the New Deal agencies, but in order to address the problems I've presented, in order for real change to happen, Negroes have to be more than advisers. Negroes must lead some of the New Deal programs."

When the president takes a deep breath, I inhale as well, wondering if I've gone too far. Well, it's too late now, so I take the bet and double down. "When you ran for president, you said you were going to be the president for every American—and beginning today, you can be that president. The one who keeps his word. The one who changes lives for the good. The one who delivers for my people." I tap my finger on his desk with each word that I speak. "Negroes love this country, and you, Mr. President, can be the one to show Negroes that America loves us back."

No one speaks when I finish. I ask myself, *Did I just lecture the president? Did I just tap on his desk like a teacher making a point of emphasis? Oh Lord.*

"President Roosevelt, I apologize. I got carried away by the—" I blurt out.

The president holds up his hand to stop me, but he has to blink a couple of times before he speaks. "Mrs. Bethune, please don't apologize. I thank you for your words, and you're right. We must provide as much aid as we can to our Negro youth, especially those living in dire conditions." He pauses and covers my hand with his. His blue eyes glisten. "I promise you, I will do whatever I can to help your people."

CHAPTER 38

ELEANOR

Hyde Park, New York
April 3, 1936

"Are you ready to leave, Mrs. Bethune?" Mr. Williams asks. The meeting came to an end a few minutes ago and now the presidential train will return everyone to the capital.

"I'm staying here," Mary responds.

"You are?" Mr. Williams appears confused.

"Mrs. Roosevelt has invited me to stay the night," she answers, not meeting his shocked gaze or those of her fellow board members. We all know how unusual this is, to invite a colored person to stay at the president's home. But we will not engage with this reaction. *Onward.*

"Indeed." I leap into the awkwardness. "The president's mother has created stunning gardens with rosebushes that bloom later in the spring, and we promised to walk the grounds with Mrs. Bethune. It would be too late for her to return to the capital after that."

As if on cue, my mother-in-law steps into the room. "Ah, I was wondering when you all would finish. Lovely to see you again, Mrs. Bethune."

Mary gives my mother-in-law one of her rare, beautiful, wide grins. "And you as well, Mrs. Roosevelt."

As the two women launch into an animated conversation about the gardens, I watch Mr. Williams. He's frozen, and I can almost hear him wonder how Mary knows the Roosevelt family so well. I can see that things might get a bit awkward, so I begin to usher the others to the front door. "Well, we don't want to keep the special train waiting, do we?"

Two hours later, after we've explored every inch of the exquisite gardens, my mother-in-law retires to her room for a rest before supper. I am finally free to bring Mary to Val-Kill Cottage.

As we drive the short distance, I point out the charming cottage where Earl stays when we are in Hyde Park, and as we approach Val-Kill Cottage, I say, "Of course, I don't think either Franklin or Sara ever anticipated that Val-Kill would become my true home. I think they thought I'd use it as an occasional getaway from the main house with my friends who live there year-round."

Mary laughs. "Seems like you'd need more than an occasional getaway with a mother-in-law like the president's mother."

We are still laughing when I push open the front door to my picturesque stone cottage, fragrant with the scent of the blooming trees and bushes. Marion and Nan await us just inside the door, dressed in skirts and sweaters, a bit more formal than their usual, unconventional habit of wearing pants at home. "Mrs. Bethune," Nan calls out, "we are so happy to meet you!"

As Mary shakes Nan's hand, Marion waits impatiently for her turn. "Eleanor talks about you incessantly; we've almost begun to feel jealous!"

I wince. I'm sure she and Nan *have* become jealous of Mary, as I mention her often and fondly. Since Franklin became president, I've seen less and less of Marion and Nan. Although I still care for them, of course, my workload is overwhelming. But they aren't happy about it and, in response, seem to have become more demanding of me.

They ask to attend White House events and stay overnight; they appeal for New York theater tickets; they call Tommy and request she put speaking engagements for their various organizations on my schedule; they seek personal letters for family members and friends and Todhunter students and parents; they beg me to give personal tours of the White House to various school and educational groups, as well as political friends. We've had several intense spats about the demands, as they sometimes put me in a conflicted position and require I bend the rules. But that hasn't stopped them asking.

When I feel as though Marion and Nan are taking advantage, I remind myself that they provided me with their friendship and an entrée to a new life at a time when I desperately needed it. I replay those happy days and evenings at the cottage when we joyfully set about our tasks and enjoyed simple meals before the fire. I recall the picnics they've hosted on the property for our guests. Lately, however, those reminders and memories haven't repaired the rift between us, and civility in the presence of others is the best we can manage.

Fortunately, Mary doesn't sense the undercurrent, and she laughs at this overly exuberant greeting. To soften the latent tension, I say, "Ladies, let's not overwhelm poor Mrs. Bethune. She's had a long day already. She may need to take this welcome sitting down."

I lead the ladies from the foyer into the comfortable parlor, which has a soft dusty-rose sofa and several matching upholstered chairs—all made at Val-Kill Industries, of course—arranged around the stone hearth. Although the early evening still bears the warmth of the afternoon, the fire is lit and inviting. We settle into our chairs, a cup of tea and a cookie in each of our hands.

Easy conversation ensues. Marion and Mary connect on schools for girls, and Mary and Nan forge an immediate bond over political matters. As I sit back quietly, a rare contentment passes through me, and I feel like our little group has been waiting for Mary to be complete.

At first, I dismiss the knocking I hear. For a fleeting second, I imagine it might be Hick. *How lovely it would be to introduce Mary to her.*

I quickly dismiss the idea. Not only is Hick in the Midwest for work, but Marion and Nan have never gotten along with her. Each is too covetous of my time to enjoy the other.

Nan jumps up, but I wave her off. "You three keep chatting. I'll get it."

I'm surprised to see one of Franklin's assistants at the door. "Mrs. Roosevelt, ma'am, the president is wondering if he might have a word."

"Did he say what it's in reference to?" I gesture back into the parlor. "I am entertaining, as you see, and I wouldn't want to break away unless it was urgent."

"President Roosevelt did not specify, but I would imagine it is a matter of some importance," the assistant says.

Taking leave of my friends—and explaining that Mary will accompany Marion and Nan to Springwood for dinner, where I'll meet them—I ride back to the main house with the assistant. I find Franklin in his study, as always, and I don't bother to hide my irritation when I step into the room. "Whatever is so critical that it couldn't wait for dinner, Franklin? I just introduced Mary to Marion and Nan."

"No doubt they'll get on like a house on fire and won't even notice your absence," he says, swatting away my complaint like a fly, and then adds, "I wanted to see you before dinner because we need to talk outside the presence of Mrs. Bethune."

I lower myself into one of the chairs in front of his desk. "I'm listening," I say, curious and somewhat concerned.

"Mrs. Bethune made a most impressive and persuasive speech during the NYA meeting."

"She is an excellent speaker," I say warily.

"Toward the end of the presentation, she talked about the impact the NYA has made—and *could* make—in the lives of colored youth. She explained that, in order to ensure that Negroes are being properly served, we need to have colored people more actively involved in running the programs." He pauses, and I hold my breath. This notion is one of the central tenets of our plan, but I didn't anticipate that Mary would raise it so plainly and so early. The opportunity must have been perfect.

"Her argument in favor of colored folks helping manage New Deal plans got me thinking. What if we created a division within the NYA that specifically addressed the needs of our Negro citizens? A department unto itself?"

Is Franklin suggesting what I think he is? If so, he's exceeding our highest hopes. With great care, I say slowly, "I think that's a fine idea, Franklin."

He nods, then continues. "What if that office was run by a colored person?"

My heart is pounding so hard that I'm certain he can hear it. If Franklin moves forward with this idea, it would place a colored person in a very senior role in federal government. In an overabundance of caution, I nod and say, "That makes perfect sense."

"I am pleased to hear that, Eleanor," he says, and his tone is ebullient. We find ourselves at odds frequently enough that I'm sure he is both relieved and tickled to present this decision to me. "And I think you'll be very happy with who I have in mind."

"Who is that?" I ask, not daring to hope.

"I'd like to appoint Mrs. Bethune to the role."

CHAPTER 39

MARY

Hyde Park, New York
April 3, 1936

I fasten the top button of my nightgown, then, with my book in my lap, I settle into the overstuffed brown chenille chair and sigh. I could sit here for hours, and maybe I will. Turning over the book, I study the cover of *The Ways of White Folks*. Langston sent this book to me a while ago, and it has finally risen to the top of my reading list.

Just as I open to the first short story, there is a knock on my door and Eleanor peeks inside. "Is everything to your liking?" she asks as she steps into the bedroom, dressed in her nightclothes as well.

"How can it not be?" I open my arms as if I'm presenting the lovely surroundings to her. The walnut-framed bed is the centerpiece of the room, covered in a crisp white linen sheet and a gold-and-coffee-colored bedspread that matches the brown settee at the foot of the bed. "This chair is so comfortable, I just might sleep in it."

She laughs. "I promise the bed is better yet." Eleanor sits on the edge of the bed facing me and tilts her head to peek at my book. "What are you reading now, Mary?"

"*The Ways of White Folks*." I hold it up and then hand it to her.

Eleanor turns the book over and studies the back cover. "Ah, Langston," she says as if she knows him, although they've never met.

She only knows Langston through the stories I've shared with her, but she always reacts as if she loves him as much as I do. "I didn't know he had a new book."

"I'm ashamed to say it's not new. It's just new to me. I haven't had a chance to read it, but this chair presented the perfect place to curl up and begin."

"Short stories," Eleanor says. "I'll have to buy a copy. I've enjoyed all of his poetry."

"Once we finish, we'll have to talk about this one, too."

"I'm intrigued by the title. I'll look forward to that," Eleanor says, then her tone changes. The lightheartedness is gone when she says, "But there's something I want to discuss with you now." She stands, hands me the book, and begins to pace.

"Okay. This sounds important." I lay the book aside and fold my hands in my lap. I knew there was something on my friend's mind. Throughout dinner, Eleanor kept glancing across the table, and whenever our eyes connected, she looked away. The same thing happened as we traveled back to the cottage tonight, but I didn't question her since Nan and Marion were with us.

At the time, I thought Eleanor was just making sure I felt comfortable here in Hyde Park. She didn't have to worry about that, though. I've been heady since I arrived. I pinched myself more than a few times tonight as I sat at the vast walnut dining table in an ornately carved high-back chair before floral-patterned plates that Mrs. Sara Roosevelt informed me came from her childhood days in China. As we chatted through dinner, it was hard for me to believe that I, Mary Jane McLeod Bethune, was actually having dinner at the private home of the president.

But now, as I watch Eleanor pacing across the wooden floorboards, I ask, "What's going on with you?"

She turns to face me, and her smile is bright. "Oh, Mary. I've been holding something in, but if I don't say something I'm going to burst."

"What is it?"

She sits across from me once again. "First, you must promise not to repeat what I say."

"All right."

"I mean it. You can't say anything to anyone before the appointed time."

"I said all right," I repeat. "Just tell me."

"Well. You made quite an impression on Franklin today."

I press my hand against my chest. "Did he say something?" Through dinner, I kept checking for signs that the president wished I'd left with the other NYA folks. But he was gracious and kind and engaging.

The news erupts from Eleanor. "Franklin wants to create a division within the NYA specifically for Negroes, and he wants that office to be managed by a colored person."

"Oh my goodness," I say. "I mentioned something akin to that to him, but I wasn't even sure he heard me. This is fantastic news."

"No, Mary, you haven't even heard the best part." She pauses. "He wants you! He wants you to be the director of that office."

I stare at Eleanor, my mouth agape. Surely I have not heard her correctly.

"Mary, did you hear what I said?"

Still I cannot speak. Eleanor leans back and laughs. "Oh, Mary, you should see your face."

I am shocked and honored. Afraid and determined. Most of all, I'm hopeful and grateful.

"Mary." Eleanor leans forward and takes my hands so that I must look at her. "You wanted to change this country and you're doing it. There is so much you'll be able to do for colored youth, the people you care most about." She squeezes my hand before she stands. "This calls for a celebration."

When Eleanor steps from the bedroom, I do not follow her. I just bow my head and say, "Thank you, Lord."

Minutes later, Eleanor sits across from me in another chair, each of us balancing bowls of gingerbread and vanilla ice cream on our knees. "What a celebration." The aroma of my favorite dessert has brought me around from the daze that overtook me with her news.

"Indeed." Eleanor takes a bite of her gingerbread.

"Thank you for this," I say.

"Of course. I couldn't let you come to my home and not serve your favorite dessert."

"I'm not just talking about this," I say, holding up the bowl, "but all of this, Eleanor. For inviting me here, for this time, for sharing your home with me."

"I am so happy to have you here. This is where I'm at my best, and it was hard to imagine you never visiting me here. Val-Kill is a special place."

"Well, it will always be special to me because this is where I heard the best news." I shake my head, still astonished.

"Isn't it exciting?"

"I'm not sure I'm at the excitement level yet. I have to get past this first stage of shock."

"When Franklin told me, I was as stunned as you are. But now, all I can think about is how much good you're going to do." She clasps her hands together. "Just promise me that when he finally delivers the news, you will act sufficiently surprised."

"Oh, I will. And I promise you, I won't be acting."

She laughs. "I cannot wait for you to tell the two Alberts. They'll be so proud."

"Who knows? They've both had to grow up with me being in so many roles. I think they might be more impressed with this gingerbread." I pick up the bowl again and savor another spoonful. "I can hear them now. I'll tell them about my appointment and they'll say, 'Oh, Mother Dear, this is the best dessert I've ever tasted.'"

Eleanor chuckles and tilts her head. "'Mother Dear'? Is that what they call you?"

I nod.

"I don't think I've ever heard a more lovely term of endearment."

"Oh, I'm not the only Mother Dear. In the South, among colored folks, there are plenty of us. It's a common name for grandmothers, the matriarchs of the family. My son used to call me 'Mother,' but when Albert Jr. came along it became 'Mother Dear.'"

"You love being a grandmother, don't you?"

I nod. "I think it's one of the most important roles God has given to me."

Eleanor exhales a small sigh. "I wish I had the opportunity to spend as much time with my grandchildren as you do with Albert. Your bond with him was evident when he visited the White House with you last year."

"What a day that was!" Mary exclaims. "I loved watching him march down those historic hallways with Anna's boy and girl. And it seemed to me you had a close tie with your grandson and granddaughter. Curtis and Anna adore you."

"Well, I am closer to my daughter's children than my other grandchildren, certainly—they've lived in the White House, after all—but I'm not as close as I'd like. And now they live in Seattle." She smiles, even though sadness shrouds her eyes. But then she blinks that sorrow away. "Well, one day, I'd like you to bring Albert Jr. to Val-Kill. It would be a joy to have him here."

"Oh, he would love it here, but who wouldn't?" I pause. "It seems that your friends Nan and Marion thrive here, too."

She nods.

"So," I begin, needing to satisfy the curiosity that began building this afternoon. It peaked when we entered the cottage after dinner and

Nan and Marion excused themselves to the same bedroom. "I enjoyed speaking with them earlier."

"I'm so pleased. They're wonderful women, even if things have been tense between us."

"Really? I didn't sense anything."

"We don't see each other that much now that I'm in the White House, which they're not happy about, and . . ." She hesitates, then blurts out, "They're always asking me for something."

I freeze for a moment. What is she trying to tell me? "I do the same thing," I say, then ask what I must. "Does that make things tense between us?"

Eleanor shakes her head. "Oh, no! It's completely different. You're fighting for other people, and Marion and Nan are looking for Broadway theater tickets or a private tour of the capital for their families. Not always, but sometimes."

I release a breath of air. "Well, I'm sure if you speak to Marion and Nan, you'll be able to resolve your differences. The two of them— well, they seem rather tight," I say, awkwardly moving forward with curiosity.

Eleanor gives a small laugh. "Are you trying to ask me something, Mary?"

I shrug before I smile. "You know me well."

"I do, but this wasn't your most artful moment. Yes, Nan and Marion are very close. They're in . . . in . . . a relationship. A Boston marriage."

"Oh my," I say, unable to hide my surprise. "I've heard of that, of course. But I can't say I've ever known anyone in such a relationship."

Eleanor glances away, and when she turns back, the smile has faded. Softly, she says, "That may not be true, Mary."

I frown, confused. "What do you mean?"

Eleanor averts her eyes for so long that I ask, "Eleanor, what's going on?"

She faces me, squaring her shoulders as she does when she's standing at a podium summoning her courage. "You know me, and I am in a sort of Boston marriage." Her voice quivers as she speaks.

I try to control my reaction, but my eyes widen in astonishment. In this moment, I have such love for my friend. She seems so vulnerable, and I know she's never had anyone offer her unconditional support. Well, with a disclosure of this magnitude, I'm going to make sure she feels that from me. "Eleanor," I whisper so that she'll face me. "Does this person treat you with the respect and love you deserve?"

"Yes, Hick certainly does." Eleanor's cheeks turn crimson at the mention of Hick.

Ah. The gifted reporter she often mentions. The dots are suddenly connected.

"It feels so strange to be speaking about it out loud," Eleanor says. "I've never told anyone, even though I'm sure some have surmised."

"I'm guessing Franklin doesn't know?"

"I've certainly never told him, and he would never ask. In truth, unless he needs something work-related or we are gathering as a family, he tends to ignore me. And anyway, he has many women who fuss over him the way he likes—and I try not to think about the nature of those relationships."

I'm taken aback at her words—"many women who fuss over him"—but I stay focused on Eleanor. "Well, I'm honored you told me." Reaching for her hand, I say, "Eleanor, we are all entitled to live our lives with love. And if Hick gives you that, I am happy, because you deserve that and so much more."

Eleanor nods, but she doesn't speak. She doesn't have to; I see the gratitude shining in her eyes.

CHAPTER 40

MARY

Washington, D.C.
August 7, 1936

When I hear the rise of baritone and tenor voices from the landing outside the front door, I take a quick glance around at the gleaming wood floors, the polished furniture, the bright brass chandelier, and the marble fireplace. All is in order.

"Welcome!" I say, flinging the front door open.

"Mary!" Eugene Kinckle Jones greets me first, and I notice that he's trimmed down his mustache a bit. Then, one by one, I receive the smiling men with handshakes, pecks on my cheek, and readied compliments. "This town house is beautiful, Mary."

Over the past few months, I purchased this Victorian town house in Northwest Washington for the National Council of Negro Women and turned it into the showcase the organization deserves.

"How did you get this done so quickly?" Robert Weaver asks. "When I last saw you here in Washington, there wasn't even a National Council of Negro Women, let alone a headquarters. Not to mention a directorship in the NYA!"

Eugene pipes in, "Come on, Robert. I can't believe you're asking that question. This," he says, then gestures toward me with relish, "is Mrs. Mary McLeod Bethune, the most powerful Negro in America."

The gentlemen murmur their agreement, and I give Eugene, the only one in the room besides me who's already lived to see fifty years of age, a wink. "Indeed."

Then, to the others, I say, "Gentlemen, it's time to get to the purpose of our meeting. Care to follow me into the conference room?"

The levity ceases and the atmosphere shifts as the men follow me to the adjacent room and take seats around the table.

I stand at the head, but before I can speak, I'm surprised when Bill Hastie, who's recently been appointed as the president's race relations adviser, raises his hand. The young man, a Phi Beta Kappa graduate of Amherst College, is so quiet, at times I have to strain to hear him.

"Mrs. Bethune?" he says softly.

"'Mrs. Bethune'?" I repeat, and tilt my head.

"Mary," he corrects himself.

Every man here is my brother in the struggle; a couple have been alongside me for decades. Behind closed doors, there is no need for formalities.

Bill continues, "Before we begin, we'd be remiss if we didn't officially congratulate you on your appointment by President Roosevelt as director of the NYA's newly formed Division of Negro Affairs."

He begins to clap, and the others stand in an ovation. I appreciate this moment, because after I got the call, I went straight to work, setting up my office, hiring personnel, meeting the heads of the state and federal agencies. I've taken no time to appreciate that I am a close adviser to President Roosevelt.

"Thank you so much for your recognition," I say as the men settle again into their seats, "but this evening isn't about me. I asked you all here, gentlemen, because for the first time since Reconstruction, Negroes have an opportunity to have a real voice in our government's policy. Each one of us is in the position to have the president's ear, and there is power in that." I pause, seeing the glances between Eugene and Robert, then continue, "But our power will be even greater if we band together. Can you imagine working in unison? What if we not only kept one another apprised of what was happening in our divisions but we spoke as one body and advocated with one voice? If we did that, we would be the most powerful group of Negroes ever in government."

Eugene reacts first. "Mary, you know I am happy to see you in your position. But as far as calling us powerful or believing we'll have any kind of impact"—he shakes his head—"that's not happening."

"I agree." Robert Weaver steps in. "Even though things are better for me than most, just about every other Negro with a federal appointment complains about the lack of responsibilities."

As others nod, I say, "Maybe it's because I'm the oldest in the room or because my origins were lower than most of yours, but I see the progress, even if the changes aren't as fast as you'd like. And with this collective that I'm suggesting, we will be able to push for even more progress."

This time, Robert exchanges a glance with Bill, and I understand. The youngest two in the group do not have the patience that I've had to learn. Robert speaks up again. "Any concern you're just a pawn of the president?"

Even though I could, I choose not to take his words as an insult, because I know that was not his intent. In the two years that Robert has been in his position, he's not seen the progress he expected. And now this young man is almost as jaded as the others. It saddens me.

"How would the president be using me?"

"Of course, you are incredibly qualified," he hastens to correct himself. "But aren't you concerned that your appointment is like those of most of the others—fodder for a newspaper story about Negro hires? And then Roosevelt will use that story to get more Negro votes in the next election."

As murmurs of agreement fill the room, Robert continues: "Not to mention, I can't see Roosevelt focusing on any of our issues with all that's going on in Europe with Hitler and Mussolini."

There are more whispers of consensus before I say, "Robert, I wonder if you know how much I have been able to accomplish through the NYA in the three short months that I've been there. Do you realize I've doubled the funding? Do you know I've hired colored directors to run our state and local programs? Are you aware that I've arranged for educational stipends for twenty-six thousand colored children from grades one through twelve? I've ensured that Negro youths will get Civilian Conservation Corps jobs, and I've orchestrated fifty thousand dollars in grant money for colored graduate students. Did you know I am the financial manager?" I pause, noticing how every eyebrow in the room rises when I mention that role. It's a big deal to hold the purse strings. "And I'm just getting started. My goal is to have more than three hundred thousand young colored people back to work within the next year. That's what I'm doing with my division, but together we can move the needle under Roosevelt."

I hear murmurs of astonishment. Glances are exchanged, but otherwise no words are spoken.

"I have one last question for you, Robert," I say. "What's wrong with helping President Roosevelt in his campaign as long as that's the gateway for us to achieve our goals?"

As Robert lets out a low whistle, Eugene sits back in his chair and stretches his long legs in front of him. "So, Mary, are you saying you're willing to support the president—a *Democrat*—for reelection?"

"Yes." I raise my head higher, realizing the statement I'm about to make will change the way Negroes vote in America, maybe even for decades to come. "For the first time in my life, I will support the Democratic nominee for president, and here's why. New Deal funds and resources are being distributed to Negroes, and with all of us in place for his second term, we will push President Roosevelt further. It will benefit us all for Roosevelt to win again." The men shift in their seats, clearly astounded. "Don't be surprised. This is a transactional relationship; we need the New Deal and this president needs us. He gives us what we want, and we'll give him what he needs. I plan on getting as many Negroes as I can to switch their party affiliation from Republican to Democrat."

This time, there are no frowns and even a couple of smiles. I'm sure the news that a fierce Republican like me is finally turning Abraham Lincoln's picture to the wall is shocking, regardless of my relationship with the Roosevelts. But my conversion may be more welcome than I imagined.

I say, "We're in the room, gentlemen, and we have the president's ear. I have access that no Negro has ever had before. Let's use this access and the power of our vote."

I see a few more smiles. "We have three months before the election, and so I propose that we meet on Friday nights. We can gather here to keep one another informed of developments, to make suggestions on how to move forward, and to handle any issues that may come up. I promise you, gentlemen, that planning and working cooperatively will be for the betterment of all Negroes in the country."

Robert slowly nods and finally calls out, "Hear, hear!" I breathe a sigh of relief when the rest echo him, some more enthusiastically than others.

"It seems as if the Black Cabinet rises again," one of the men says, referring to the group of colored men who were appointed to federal positions by President *Theodore* Roosevelt. The group was quickly dismantled when Woodrow Wilson was elected. But while several of the men laugh, the younger gentlemen do not.

With Bill nodding along, Robert says, "I hope you're kidding, because I find the name *Black* Cabinet offensive." The older men sit back, surprised. Robert explains, "I'd prefer either the Negro Cabinet or something that actually describes us, like Afro-American. I am certainly not Black."

Eugene shakes his head. "I cannot believe you're concerned with something like that when you've been called worse."

"It doesn't matter what any of us have been called in the past," Robert snaps. "This is about determining how people will address us in the future."

The men go back and forth, but I'm certainly not going to allow this group to break apart before it even forms. I jump in. "Our name needs to be different from the first Black Cabinet; everyone needs to understand that we are a new force, and I've given this some thought." When all of their eyes have settled on me, I say, "Let's call ourselves the Federal Council of Negro Affairs."

CHAPTER 41

ELEANOR

Washington, D.C.
August 11, 1936

I lift the knocker on the town house on beautiful, brownstone-lined Vermont Avenue, admiring the tidy postage-stamp front lawn as well as the intricate white trim around the front door and wide bay windows. A diminutive colored girl answers, wearing a fashionable sweater and skirt, and I don't know if she's staff or family. Uncertain how to address her, I transform into the fumbling girl of my youth—or the tongue-tied woman I was when Mary and I first met. After an endless second, I regain my composure and say, "I am here to see Mrs. Bethune. I believe she is expecting me."

"But—but—you're the First Lady," she stammers.

"I am indeed. Although that even surprises me sometimes," I say to put her at ease.

The girl smiles. "Please come in, Mrs. Roosevelt. I'm Dovey Johnson. I work with Mrs. Bethune here and at the NYA. I'll get her for you."

As I follow her, I hear Earl's footsteps behind me. He insisted on accompanying me here this evening, something he doesn't always do—since he gave me my gun, anyway. I wonder if it's because I am meeting with my colored friend. Lately, I have received several hateful anonymous letters calling me horrible names and threatening me with violence for my involvement with the colored community. The usual vile commentaries on my unattractive clothes or my bucktoothed profile they were not, and Franklin ordered an investigation and heightened security. Still, since he receives similar mail, he agreed that we shouldn't allow it to stop our work, so he only mandated more precautions.

"Do you mind waiting outside, Earl?" I ask him. "Mrs. Bethune and I have private matters to discuss."

His posture stiffens. "Only if you allow me to wait on the stoop directly in front of the house and allow the other men to stand guard out back and in front."

"That's fine," I agree, and I squeeze his hand in thanks.

Dovey leads me into a small, tastefully decorated parlor with creamy walls, a few comfortable chairs, chandeliers, and a piano. I stand near an open window, hoping for a breeze on this stultifying night, but it's less than a minute before Mary enters, dressed as usual in elegant attire.

"Welcome, Eleanor. I'm so happy to have you here, but I must say, when I got your note, I was surprised. I thought you'd left for Hyde Park."

"Well, that was the plan. But then . . . then . . ." My voice chokes.

"But something happened?" Mary prompts when I drift into my thoughts.

"Louis took a turn for the worst," I say, trying to hold back a sob. "He's been ill for some time; you know that. Since I've known him, he's had breathing problems. But we truly thought that if he rested more and didn't attend so many meetings with and for Franklin, he'd recover. But I just left his hospital room at Walter Reed General Hospital, and he doesn't look good. It doesn't seem as though he has long."

Tears stream down my face, and Mary hands me a linen handkerchief. "You have yourself a good cry. You haven't had many people to rely on, so to lose one—even if this is a temporary downturn and not a permanent loss—is terribly hard."

As I dab my eyes, I say, "That's it exactly, Mary. Louis has been there every step of the way, during the early political days, Franklin's affair, his contracting polio, and this most recent political rise. Most importantly, he's usually been able to help guide Franklin to make solid, moral decisions."

"Do you worry that Steve Woodburn will fill the void Louis would leave behind? That Steve will have your husband's ear?" Mary asks. I've mentioned this to Mary only once, but I shouldn't be astonished that she filed it away.

"I do," I admit.

"Let's not fret just yet. Let's say a prayer for Louis' recovery and focus on what we can control," she says, and suddenly I do feel a bit better. "Stay for dinner. I had my cook make her famous fried chicken."

Having had nothing but cold sandwiches and bruised fruit at the hospital, I relish the thought of a warm, hearty meal. Especially since I'd otherwise be facing Mrs. Nesbitt's cooking—or, worse, her leftovers.

As we discuss the loveliness of the new town house, we move to the inviting little table near the open bay window, just big enough for us to eat at. On top of the perfectly pressed linen tablecloth are delicate porcelain plates and gleaming silver. "Mary, you didn't have to go to all the trouble! I only let you know a couple of hours ago that I'd be stopping by."

"You hush. It isn't every day that I get to host a First Lady at the National Council for Negro Women headquarters—or at my home, for that matter," she says, pouring each of us a tall glass of lemonade from a crystal pitcher.

As Dovey serves dinner, we glance out the window and talk about the latest drama with my children, who seem to swap spouses as easily as I change dresses. "I'm curious," I say, breaking a momentary silence, "how did the meeting go last week with the other colored federal appointees?"

We chat about Mary's success forming her "Federal Council," and then she adds, "I'm looking forward to keeping a president in office who actually abides by his promises."

As I cut into a large piece of chicken, I say, "Please don't hesitate to tell me if Franklin asks too much of you, Mary. I know how much travel you'll do campaigning for my husband. Franklin demands a lot of himself and all those around him. It's taken me years to learn how to set boundaries, and I don't want you to make the same mistakes."

"Eleanor, I would think you'd know by now that I know how to set limits," she mock-scolds.

"I do know that. But lately I've been thinking about his campaign. Without Louis to prod him along, Franklin is rather relaxed about this election. True enough, the Republican candidate, Landon, is lackluster, but I've been contemplating organizing a women's division for the campaign, as well as an outreach effort for the Negro vote. If you are to be deployed on both the NYA and the campaign over the next few months, I want it to be thoughtful and I want promises to be made. You are too valuable for your time to be wasted without meaningful strategy behind it."

"That's an excellent plan," Mary concurs as I bite into the chicken.

"This is the most delicious piece of chicken I've ever tasted, Mary," I exclaim. "How on earth did you get it so crispy and moist all at once?"

"Now, Eleanor, you know better than to ask me how a dish is cooked! I can ask my cook if you like."

I laugh. "I don't know why I asked! And anyway, even if your cook was willing to share, it's not like it would change anything with Mrs. Nesbitt. She simply won't take a hint when it comes to her ghastly repertoire of dishes. For the past three months, Franklin has been asking for chicken à la king, and she hasn't put it on the menu once."

We are laughing when I notice a small group of people have gathered on the sidewalk outside the bay window. *Why are they talking instead of waving or smiling, the sort of reaction I usually get?* I feel panicky.

Suddenly I see Earl and another guard step closer to the group forming near the town house. I realize they are all white, and their faces appear increasingly agitated. We hear Earl raise his voice. I now understand that these people are enraged at the sight of a colored and a white woman eating together.

Mary is the first to speak. "It seems as though we've drawn some attention."

"It does." I will my voice to stay low and calm.

I realize I have a choice. I can let fear and hatemongers and evil words stop me and the good I can do in this world as First Lady. Or I can trust in the safety precautions Earl provides and I can proceed—in this moment and beyond.

I turn to Mary and say, "I am going to have Earl summon the other members of my security detail to dismiss these people. But I'd like to take advantage of this situation to normalize interracial dining. Assuming you are willing?"

A small half smile appears on Mary's face. "You have my attention."

I smile back. "After Earl mobilizes his men, I'm going to call in my journalist friends, the women who have sole access to cover my First Lady press meetings. I am going to have them photograph us happily sharing our meal. It could be the first step toward turning the breaking of bread between colored and white folks into a perfectly ordinary, acceptable event."

CHAPTER 42

MARY

Daytona Beach, Florida
November 5, 1936

I step over the threshold of my house, thinking that if I could hug my home, I would. Since the campaign season began for President Roosevelt's reelection, I haven't been home for more than two consecutive days. When the president won less than forty-eight hours ago, I'm not sure if I was more excited for his victory or the chance to hop on the first train heading south.

"Welcome home," Mrs. Brown says, coming from the kitchen to greet me. "Albert will be so glad to see you. He tried his best to stay home from school today."

I laugh. "I'm sure. But he'll be here in a little while."

She nods. "I'll take your bag upstairs." She pauses as she lifts my valise. "I sure wanted to make all of your favorites for dinner. Are you certain you want to go out?"

"You know if it were up to me, I'd be sitting right there," I say, pointing to my dining room table. "But I promised Albert he could have anything he wanted, and he said he wanted to have dinner with me and his father at Hattie's, so . . ." I shrug.

Mrs. Brown laughs. "He just loves her pies. Well, I'll have a big breakfast waiting for you in the morning."

I spend long, languorous moments strolling through the living room, glancing at the latest edition of *Life* magazine, then moving into the dining room and smiling at my reflection in the sparkling glass of the hutch. Finally, I enter the kitchen, which is Mrs. Brown's domain. Even though I rarely come in here, I am proud of this space just the same, especially my stove with the built-in slow cooker.

Settling in the living room, I make a mental note of all I have to do while I'm home. Most pressing are my staff meetings at the college. Over the last few years, with the death of Mr. Gamble and the Depression, it's been challenging to meet the college's operating expenses, but I know, with God, I will find a way.

Then my latest project for the city needs attention. It's been three years since Albert Jr. was chased off the beach, but since that time, I've identified two and a half miles of beachfront property, the investors are on board, and all that's left is to select the architects and planners so the Bethune Beach project can move forward.

The front door opens, then shuts with a slam, and my fifteen-year-old grandson barrels in. "Mother Dear! I'm so happy to see you," he says, wrapping his arms around me.

"I bet you I'm happier than you are." I squeeze him back. It isn't lost on me that my grandson is now part of the very demographic for which I'm working so hard in my position with the NYA. But while Albert is chronologically a member, he is not financially. My work and my prayer are to give others the kinds of opportunities I've been able to give him.

"Dad said for us to meet him at Miss Hattie's. I can't wait." He pulls me toward the door.

"Okay. Let me get my pocketbook."

As I grab my bag, Albert hands me my cane. "Don't forget this. I want everyone to know that Mother Dear is back!"

Hattie's is less than a mile away. A stroll to her restaurant is a special joy on afternoons like this, when the temperature is at least twenty degrees higher than what I left behind in Washington, D.C. But only a few minutes into our traipse, I find myself struggling to breathe. It's only because he hasn't stopped chatting that Albert doesn't notice. By the time we reach Hattie's, I'm perspiring and exhausted.

When Albert Sr. hugs me in greeting, he steps back and stares. "Are you all right?"

"I am," I say, although I sit down quickly. "I just haven't had a walk like that in a while."

I manage to deflect my son's attention by focusing on Albert Jr., and the three of us spend our time laughing at my grandson's stories about school and his football team. My son is in a buoyant mood. Bethune Funeral Home, which has only been open for a few months, is prospering. He's finally found his place as an entrepreneur.

The biggest blessing is that our talk never turns to politics. Albert has been dismayed with my new alliance with the Democratic Party. On my last trip home, we had quite a disagreement, although the conversation was mostly one-sided. Albert was apoplectic: "How can you switch to the Democratic Party when they have a history of senators who've served as the grand dragons of the KKK? I'm just glad my grandparents aren't alive to see your betrayal."

His words would have hurt if I didn't know much better. My parents and grandmother would be proud of my work. And one day, my son will be, too.

Our dinner is interrupted more than a few times as neighbors stop by. I chat with everyone until I feel like I'm losing my voice and I'm ready to go home. Outside, I'm grateful that Albert drove so we won't have to walk. When my son drops us off at home, I send my grandson to his room to do his homework and I rest on the sofa, wondering why I'm so winded when I only walked from the car to the front door. Must be the schedule I've been keeping.

I lean back, but before I can collar a nod, Mrs. Brown comes into the living room. "Mrs. Bethune, you have a long-distance call from Washington."

Retreating to my office, I pick up the telephone's receiver. "Hello?"

"Mary!" a deep male voice with a hint of Southern twang calls out.

"This is Mrs. Bethune," I say, frowning. "To whom am I speaking?"

"This is Steve Woodburn." His press secretary's tone is filled with arrogance, suggesting that I should know who he is from his voice.

Why on earth is he calling me?

This is not a man I want to speak to. Louis Howe died last spring, leaving a grieving president and First Lady. Since that time, Steve Woodburn has been wreaking havoc. Even when Eleanor and I were trying to help the president's campaign and suggested dispatching several Federal Council members to give speeches, Woodburn stopped that. "The campaign doesn't have the money for that kind of undertaking," he lied. Eleanor had to find separate funding for our travels.

"Mary, I need to—" Woodburn starts.

I interrupt him. "Excuse me, Mr. Woodburn. But have we ever been formally introduced?"

"Uh, no, I don't think so, but—"

I interrupt him again. "Therefore, I would prefer to be called"—I pause—"Dr. Bethune." My tone is firm.

"Doctor?" He chuckles. "Well, in the South, we aren't that formal—Mary."

I inhale, recognizing his words for the slight they're meant to be. I swallow the words I really want to say, then I give him a proper response. "Mr. Woodburn, if we knew each other better, it *might* be proper for you to call me Mary and me to call you Steve. But until then, this call is not appropriate." Without another word, I end the telephone call, rise from my desk, and return to my sofa.

I'm just about to get comfortable when the telephone rings again. I wait and begin counting in my head. Before I get to thirty, Mrs. Brown comes into the living room.

"You have another call from Washington, D.C."

Rise above, I say to myself as I return to my office. "Good evening," I say, as if I don't know who's on the other end.

"Uh . . . Dr. Bethune," Woodburn says, not apologizing, although he seems to have learned the lesson. "If you have a moment, there are a few things of an urgent nature." And then, because I'm sure he doesn't want to risk my hanging up again, he rushes to add, "It's about your upcoming Negro conference."

As intended, now he has my attention. "What do you need to discuss with such urgency about my National Conference on the Problems of the Negro and Negro Youth?"

"There are two things associated with your conference that will have to be changed. First, I don't know if you're aware, but I've been counseling the First Lady so that she appears more positive in the press." I have to hold back a snort of laughter. Eleanor would never allow herself to be "counseled" by Steve Woodburn. "And one of the things we must do is limit her appearances to only those that will enhance and improve her image."

Even though I understand the terrible insult in his words, again I bite back what I really want to say. "That is wonderful, Mr. Woodburn. Thank you for letting me know, and I'll make sure the press gets plenty of photos of Mrs. Roosevelt as she's giving the keynote address at my conference."

"Uh, Mary . . . I mean, Dr. Bethune. You don't understand. I've determined your conference is not the best use of the First Lady's time. She is the First Lady of the United States, after all."

I half expect him to finish the sentence with another insult, like *and therefore she cannot be at your little Negro conference.* "This is interesting, Mr. Woodburn. When Mrs. Roosevelt and I discussed her attendance, the First Lady of the United States thought it was a wonderful use of her time," I say, no longer having the patience for this insulting waste of *my* time. "I'll speak to the First Lady, and someone will get back to you."

"There's really no need for you to speak to her," he rushes to say. "I can handle everything from this end."

Ah, just as I thought. Eleanor has no idea of this call.

"There is no need for you to handle anything that is my business,

Mr. Woodburn. I'll speak to Mrs. Roosevelt for clarification, because your statements contradict her earlier representations. But I thank you for your call." I slam the receiver onto the cradle.

Squeezing my fists, I feel the fury rise within me. And this is only a tiny fraction of Woodburn's insidiousness. Eleanor and I will have to be better prepared. Tonight, however, I do have some solace. I picture Mr. Woodburn still staring at the receiver in his hand, listening to the static of our disconnected telephone call.

CHAPTER 43

ELEANOR

Washington, D.C.
January 3, 1937

I've been waiting for this day since Mary called me from Florida in November. I wanted to storm down the White House hallways to Steve Woodburn's office immediately and admonish him for his disrespectful behavior. But then Mary and I discussed it. Serpent-tongue that Steve is, he'd twist my words, and somehow I'd end up in an acrimonious conversation with Franklin. Instead, we chose a different tact: defiance.

I hear the murmurs of the fully packed auditorium from the hallway. Today we'll be presenting the real-life problems faced by the colored population and will then be offering solutions. Would all these people have attended if rumors hadn't circulated that I might make an appearance?

I do my best to ignore Earl and the phalanx of Secret Service trailing in my wake and stride over to Mary's side.

"Are you ready?" I ask.

She nods, a conspiratorial grin taking over her face. "I am indeed. Thank you for appearing today."

"There's no reason to thank me. We are in this struggle together."

We mount the stage together, but as planned, I center myself directly under the huge banner declaring this to be the "National Conference on the Problems of the Negro and Negro Youth." Mary approaches the podium first; expertly greets the crowd; and then, before she introduces me, turns to me with a wide, satisfied smile. How we've both grown in the ten years of our friendship. I wish Marion and Nan could have grown along with me similarly. The dynamic between us has grown so fraught that I've moved my belongings into Val-Kill's defunct furniture woodshed and transformed it into my solo refuge. One of our last pleasant evenings was during Mary's visit. I suppose she buffered the tensions simmering beneath the surface.

Mary's low, rich voice commands the room. "It is my distinct honor to introduce to you today an esteemed guest who needs no introduction. She is an educator, a writer, a public speaker, an unparalleled champion for equality, and my dear friend—please join me in welcoming Mrs. Eleanor Roosevelt, the First Lady of the United States!"

Painting on my public smile, I approach the podium. The closer I get, the more intense the clapping becomes, until I'm facing a standing ovation. As I reach Mary's side, she gestures for me to take her place, but before she leaves, I whisper, "Can you stay for a moment?"

She looks perplexed. This is not part of our carefully orchestrated plan.

"Thank you all for this warmest of welcomes. The honor to speak to you today is all mine. But I want to thank Mrs. Bethune for the biggest honor of all—being introduced today by another First Lady. The First Lady of the Struggle!" I announce as loud as my usually weak voice can muster and gesture to Mary, who looks astonished but quickly recovers. Another burst of applause erupts.

When the clapping dies down, I begin the keynote that Steve Woodburn so desperately wanted me to cancel. As I speak, I study the white and colored faces of the audience. Most of them seem attentive, although I can see that not everyone is inspired by my message of equality. "We must take whatever steps are necessary—through the New Deal or our own private funding—to make sure that

Negro youths receive equal educational and employment opportunities."

There is astonishment on the faces of some of the white men. A few
sets of eyebrows are raised in shock at the President's wife addressing
such charged issues. One man walks out, and I can almost hear the
detractors' thoughts: *Why is she saying such things in public? Doesn't
she know this is being broadcast on the radio across the country? Doesn't she
realize that the press is in the room and whatever she says will be aired in
newspapers throughout the United States? Surely this isn't what the president would want.*

I reach the crest of my speech. Quite unconsciously, I glance back
at Mary, who gives me a small, close-lipped smile. This almost
imperceptible encouragement bolsters my moral fortitude in a way
that nothing else can. I adjust the white cuff of my navy dress
with a white-gloved hand and then tilt the small brim of my dark blue
hat.

"We must begin by working together and supporting one another,
no matter our color, religion, or background. This country rises or
falls on the strength of all its citizens. Thank you," I conclude.

With all eyes on me, I stride over to Mary.

Mary—I owe this all to her, I think. Her guidance, her trust, the
honesty of our conversations, her willingness to accept me into her
fold and believe that I can help.

"Are you ready?" I whisper to her as I get close.

"Of course. The question is—are you?" she whispers back.

"It's something we've done many times," I say with a bullishness I
don't exactly feel.

"But never in front of a thousand eyes," she points out quietly. "And
reported to who knows how many on the radio and in every newspaper
tomorrow."

"As we planned," I remind her.

We nod at each other, and then our gloved hands meet and clasp,
one white and one colored underneath the white cotton exteriors. The

clapping slows, and the audience's roar begins to hush—until I can hear a few people gasp. Then, still holding hands, we smile into the audience, and the applause resumes and gets louder until it's a cacophony of sound.

Mary and I have publicly broken the hard-and-fast rule that whites and Negroes should never, ever touch. Perhaps this reaction signals that Mary and I are changing hearts one controversial handshake at a time. Will it even move Steve Woodburn when his precious newspapers print stories about my appearance here, the conference he practically forbade me from attending?

Half an hour later, we send Americans—and Steve Woodburn along with them—another message. At exactly noon, my car rolls to a stop in front of 1427 F Street, where Mary waits for me outside the front door. "Be cautious, ma'am, and know that I'll be right outside," Earl says, always my stalwart protector.

Together, Mary and I enter Old Ebbitt Grill. This restaurant is a capital mainstay, even though it moved from right around the corner from the White House several years ago. A tall, thin man with a full, dark mustache rushes toward us as we enter, one of the managers I know well enough.

"Mrs. Roosevelt," he gushes. "We are so glad to have you." He pauses, his eyes darting from me to Mary and then back and forth a few times before settling on me.

"I think my secretary requested a table for two in the front when she made the reservation." Tommy laughed when I gave her my instructions. She is an ardent supporter of the approach Mary and I are taking.

"Yes, yes, but, uh, Mrs. Roosevelt . . ." he says, his voice trailing off.

"Yes? I'm sure you won't have any problem accommodating me and my dear friend, Mrs. Mary McLeod Bethune." I gesture to Mary.

But the manager's eyes stay on me. He's obviously weighing his options. Is he prepared to throw the First Lady out of his restaurant?

What would that do to business? What would happen when the president found out?

Sighing with resignation, he says, "Very well."

The manager leads us to a table toward the front but behind a large fern. I point to another table in the middle of the restaurant's large front window. "I think I'd prefer this one."

His shoulders droop as he seats us at this table and delivers our menus.

Mary and I stifle our smiles.

"I almost feel sorry for him," Mary says.

I wave my hand. "Don't. Segregation needs to be seen for what it is—absurd and damaging." I glance down at my wristwatch. "We have about ten minutes before my photographer friends arrive. I've asked that they take pictures of us not only chatting but eating as well. I want everyone to see us as two friends enjoying our time together." I pause. "Just like at your home, people may start protesting when they pass and see us, but Earl will have it firmly in hand. And I've already instructed him to arrange for you to be driven back directly if that happens."

"I'm not worried," Mary says calmly. "Everything has been going according to plan. Except for that 'First Lady of the Struggle' announcement."

Oh no, I think. I've acted presumptuously again. But then I study her face, and I see a twinkle in her eye.

"I was flabbergasted when you uttered that title. It's one I pray I'll live up to."

"You live it—every single day of your life, Mary. You're an inspiration and *the* leader in this fight, and I want everyone to understand the role you play."

Mary nods, but then the twinkle in her eyes fades. "What's wrong?" I ask.

Instead of answering directly, she says, "Did you know that I wanted to be a missionary when I was growing up?"

I'm surprised by the quick change of subject. "No. I didn't know."

"Because of my grandmother," Mary says, which isn't exactly an explanation for this topic shift. "She was born in Africa, and though she was kidnapped from her country, she never lost her love for her native land. And she passed that love on to me. Then, when I began to learn about God, all I wanted to do was go back to Africa so I could bring the message of the gospel to my people."

"That's amazing. Why didn't you?"

"I spent two years at Moody Bible Institute right after college, the only Negro in the school. All the other students were given missionary assignments, mostly in Africa. But I, the only one in the school who wore the features and bled the blood of Africa, couldn't be a missionary on that continent because my skin wasn't white. I was told there was no place for Negro missionaries in Africa."

"Oh, Mary." I sit up straight. "That's more than horrible—that's ridiculous."

"Yes," she agrees, then says, "but I was able to take the desire I had to become a missionary and turn my heart to the children in this country. What I've come to understand today is that I'm still a missionary, and I'm doing that work with you. With big speeches and actions as well as little gestures like handshakes, and now this." Mary points to the table between us. "We're missionaries in our own land, normalizing the integration of the races."

What an epiphany, I think.

"Yes," I say, enthusiastically, "we're normalizing equality."

We squeeze each other's hands across the table, and right then, a flash from outside makes us blink.

CHAPTER 44

MARY

Washington, D.C.
January 14, 1937

"Mrs. Bethune! What a delightful surprise!" a regal-sounding woman calls to me from the shadowy hallway in the first family's private quarters. Of course, I recognize the voice.

"How lovely to see you, Mrs. Roosevelt," I say.

As Mrs. Sara Delano Roosevelt approaches, I take in her silvery coiffed hair, which matches her pearly-gray fur-trimmed sweater. She offers me a fuchsia-lipsticked smile. "What brings you here?" she asks, and then answers her own question. "Visiting with my daughter-in-law?"

I nod. "Yes, we just spent a lovely afternoon together. And I'm glad to see you, because I want to thank you again for being kind enough to attend my fundraiser for Bethune-Cookman in October."

"It's a pleasure to support your school, and I want to thank you, too, for all the work you did on Franklin's campaign." Then, with excitement, she adds, "You know, Franklin is down the hall in his study. I'm *certain* he'd like to thank you as well." She pivots and marches off in the opposite direction. "Follow me!"

I wish the door to Eleanor's sitting room would suddenly open and she'd step out and intervene. When that miracle doesn't happen, I call after Mrs. Roosevelt. "Oh, no, please! I don't want to disturb President Roosevelt. I'm sure he has so much to do with all that's going on in the world."

"Nonsense," she says without turning around. "You'll only be a few minutes, and I insist."

When she doesn't hear my footsteps falling in line with hers, she finally glances back. "Mrs. Bethune?"

Suddenly, my dark green cape frock that was meant to keep me warm in these January temperatures has me sweating. After my conference, about two weeks ago now, I compiled a bold document—the Blue Book is what I called it—that contained a recommended plan for change, with specific prescriptions to address problems facing Negroes.

Just days ago, I circulated three thousand copies to attendees and government officials. In the copy I hand-delivered to the president, I included a personal note: Mr. President, if you want Negroes' continued support in the voting booth and otherwise, you need to respond to the attached report.

Now I have to figure out what I'm going to say. Should I open with an apology for my audacious, even presumptuous note? Of one thing I am certain: I will not apologize for the Blue Book itself.

Mrs. Roosevelt and I step into the president's personal sitting room, where he's ensconced behind a wide mahogany desk in what looks like a chair but I know to be his wheelchair.

"Mama, to what do I owe the pleasure?" he says with warmth, even though his eyes look red and tired.

"Franklin, dear, look who I found wandering the hallways!" She presents me as if I'm a gift she's discovered under the Christmas tree.

Removing his pince-nez from his nose, he says, "Well, how lovely to see you, Mrs. Bethune. I know I've told you before, but I think it bears repeating how indebted we are to you for your campaign work."

"It was an honor, President Roosevelt."

"I certainly hope you can make it to the inauguration and some of the festivities my wife has planned." He pauses. "And by the way, I was just talking about you, Mrs. Bethune. Isn't that right, Steve?"

"That's right, sir."

Both Mrs. Roosevelt and I jump at the voice that sounds out behind us. Steve Woodburn is sitting in an upholstered chair on the far side of the room.

"Oh, Steve, you scared the daylights out of me. You shouldn't be lurking about in the corners of rooms. It's unseemly," Mrs. Roosevelt admonishes him in a tone that lets me know her feelings toward this man are the same as mine.

"I apologize, Mrs. Roosevelt." He glances at me with undisguised dislike. "*Dr.* Bethune," he says by way of greeting, with a strange emphasis on the "Dr.," as if the title is unimaginable.

President Roosevelt continues, "I just told Steve that I had quite the tome delivered to my office two days ago." His gaze and his grin are steady.

"You don't say, sir," I answer, giving myself time to determine what I'll say next.

"Yes. And though I've been busy with the inauguration, I have had the occasion to flip through your impressive Blue Book. It's a most thorough description of the plight of the Negro population, with quite a few practical solutions."

What a relief. "I'm pleased you think so, Mr. President."

"I do." His tone and his expression are earnest. "I'd like to set up an appointment with you to discuss it. Steve?"

"Yes, sir."

"Let's see if we can find a time on the calendar for me to talk over this Blue Book with Mrs. Bethune," the president instructs, at which Mr. Woodburn nods. "Then perhaps we could craft a public statement about it."

"Yes, sir."

"I'll leave you two to discuss it," President Roosevelt says, then turns to his mother. "Mama, a word about the inauguration."

With a grimace meant to look like a smile, Mr. Woodburn gestures for me to proceed before him out of the room into the reception area.

Away from the president's line of sight, Mr. Woodburn no longer hides his feelings. Leaning toward me until he's unpleasantly close, he says, "I would never defy a direct order of President Roosevelt, *Dr.* Bethune, but the president's calendar is booked for the foreseeable future. Therefore, it will not be possible to schedule a meeting between you and the president of the United States to discuss your little Blue Book."

The heat of anger rises inside me. Does he really believe I can be bullied? "Maybe we need to go back in there and have you explain that to the president."

"We can do that," he says. "And the result will be the same. The president will tell us to work it out. Then we'll leave, and"—he shrugs—"I'll tell you the same thing. You will not get a meeting about the Blue Book with President Roosevelt. Not on my watch."

It takes every bit of restraint to keep my cane beside me and not do with it what I think Mr. Woodburn deserves. Instead, I say, "We'll see about that, Mr. Woodburn." Then I turn my back to him, grateful that my parents raised me to know when to walk away.

CHAPTER 45

ELEANOR

Washington, D.C.
January 20, 1937

I stare out my bedroom window in my White House personal quarters
as one of the maids helps zip me into the blue velvet dress. As I adjust
the matching velvet wrap around my shoulders, the rain pours veritable sheets of water, and I pray the weather does not forebode this
next presidential term. Worldwide economic crises, American racial
unrest, and the rise of fascism across Europe have overwhelmed
Franklin's first term, and I hope that this next four years sees an im-
provement across all fronts.

When there is a knock on my bedroom door, I know who it is. After
asking my maid to leave, I say, "Come in."

"The dress suits you perfectly." Hick is wearing a dressier skirt suit
than usual. She runs her finger along the velvet sleeve of the Arnold
Constable dress she convinced me to wear.

"I have you to thank for that." I know if I meet her intense gaze, I
will only disappoint her, because I can't match her emotion. Although
I once believed that I loved Hick as she loves me, in time I came to
realize that my feelings are more akin to friendship. This truth I had
to share with her as the election approached. I wanted her to be free
to make her own plans for the future, regardless of the election outcome;

I couldn't allow her to forsake her journalistic career any longer for my own selfish need for her company. A decision was made, and she will remain my friend but no longer my lover—and she will return to reporting. But not just yet.

"You always try to hide in your clothes instead of letting everyone see your slender, unique beauty," she insists.

"You are the only one who sees me that way." I finally look up into her face.

"Everyone else is blind, then." Her eyes linger on mine.

"I only wish I could have given you more of myself. You deserve that, Hick, and I apologize."

"Never apologize. It's been a privilege to be close with you."

"Privilege? That's awfully formal and awfully final," I say, attempting lightness. "Even though we cannot be more, I thought we were still good friends."

"We are," she answers warily. "But I may need some time and a little distance."

The skies relent as we travel from the White House to St. John's Episcopal Church in the convertible Franklin has come to know and love. He beams at the citizens lined up along the car route, even turning to me with a wide grin from time to time.

After the service, we return to the Capitol for the ceremony itself. Once again, we've recruited our son James to help maintain Franklin's facade of walking. When we park in front of a side entrance to the building, James races to help his father from the vehicle and then up to the dais.

As our children and their spouses and, of course, my mother-in-law pour out of the automobiles that followed Franklin's convertible, I join them. We chat about the fortunate break in the weather as we take our places on the stage, flanking Franklin. I stand closer to him than anyone besides James, and we quietly greet our guests, important governmental leaders and family members alike. Unlike at Franklin's past inaugurations, Marion and Nan are not here; the break between us means that they're no longer included in the inner circle. But it heartens me to see that Hick's smile beams out from the group, as does that of Earl, who feels almost like family.

I am pleased to see several colored folks among our personal guests, including Franklin's Harvard classmate the esteemed educator G. David Houston. At my prompting, Mr. Houston was appointed to the inauguration committee. He arranged not only for colored press to cover the inauguration but also for a colored soldier who holds the Congressional Medal of Honor to serve in the Honor Guard. It gives me hope to see their faces in the crowd.

The only incongruous face—the only one I fervently wish was not on the stage with us—is Steve Woodburn. He hasn't said a word about my stunt with the conference and lunch. Nor have I said anything to him about the stunt he pulled with Mary and Franklin's schedule. I turn away from him, not wanting the sight of him to ruin this otherwise glorious day.

I stare at the thousands who've come out to celebrate this momentous occasion. Franklin won the election by a mile, and we are indebted to each and every voter, but—if we are being honest—especially the colored votes, under Mary's guidance. It is then that I notice a woman who looks remarkably like Mary approach the white usher overseeing the reserved section nearest the presidential stand.

He examines her ticket for an unconscionably long time and then points her toward a section in the back. *This simply will not stand.* Who knows if this swearing-in ceremony would even be taking place without her? How dare she be denied her place because of unbridled prejudice?

Turning to Franklin and James, I ask, "Do you think I have fifteen minutes before the ceremony begins?"

Franklin's eyes widen in astonishment. I alone know every facet of his inaugural speech and can prompt him if necessary. "Must you?" he replies, more a command than a query.

"Mary has been denied her seat in the reserved section."

"Ah," he says with instant comprehension. "I could ask you to put aside that worry right now, but I know better. You won't let your friend down."

"I'll be back in two shakes of a lamb's tail."

Scooting out behind the low row of stands behind the podium, I catch many glances from our guests, looking on in disbelief as the First Lady leaves the stage just as her husband is about to be sworn in. I take the staircase to the left, close to where I last saw Mary, going as fast as I dare in my heels. Stepping into the cold air, I see my breath cloud, making visible the light drizzle that has started again.

Winding my way through the surprised throngs and the many puddles, I finally reach the seating area where Mary tried to gain access. I study the crowds, but I don't see her anywhere. I approach the guard who rejected her and ask, "Where is the woman you just refused entry?"

His mouth drops open in shock at the sight of me.

"Do I need to speak louder?" I raise my voice. "Where is the woman you just refused entry? Where did you send her?"

"You are M-Mrs.—" he stammers, then stops.

"I know I am Mrs. Roosevelt. Do you realize that the woman you turned away is my personal friend, has a senior position with the president, and is here at my invitation?" I seethe as the man practically crumples in front of me.

"I apologize, Mrs. Roosevelt—"

I interrupt him; apologizing to me isn't enough. He needs to come face-to-face with the person he's insulted. My words morph into a demand. "You will help me find her and give her the best seat in this entire section, even if that means moving other guests."

"Of course, m-ma'am. I am so sorry that I refused your friend."

I draw close to his face, so near that I can see the stubbly spot missed by his razor. "You should be sorry that you denied entry to a ticketed guest on the basis of her race—regardless of whether she is *my* friend or not."

The man quivers, and I am certain it isn't from the chill in the air. "Yes, ma'am."

"Come on," I say. Together we set out to comb the thousands of guests to locate Mary. Just then, I see a familiar silhouette leading not with a cane but an umbrella.

"Is that you, Mrs. Bethune?" I call out.

She chuckles and then shakes her head in astonishment. "It is indeed, but what on earth are you doing among the masses on Inauguration Day?"

Forcing my anger at this injustice aside to laugh, I say, "Why, making certain my dear friend has a good seat for the swearing-in, of course."

CHAPTER 46

MARY

Washington, D.C.
January 17, 1938

Eleanor meets me at the cab when I arrive at the White House, as always. Swinging my cane, I say, "I'm glad you were able to carve away time to see me."

"Me?" she shrieks. "You're the one whose calendar is full, chockablock with all the important work that I brag about the First Lady of the Struggle doing."

When Eleanor declared that I was the First Lady of the Struggle, those very words appeared in the press the next day. Since then, it is how I'm often introduced.

As we enter the White House, we laugh about how—even though I already had an overflowing workload fighting daily for Negroes at the NYA, the NCNW, and Bethune-Cookman College—I now write a regular column for the *Pittsburgh Courier* called From Day to Day. Eleanor's own daily column My Day served as inspiration.

Inside, we settle down to tea, curling into that brown chintz sofa. I say, "So, here we are again with another cup of tea." We glance down at our cups and then burst into laughter.

"I know," Eleanor says. "But what else are we to drink or do, especially in this weather?"

I study the porcelain cup. "You know, I've never had one, but I hear Bloody Marys may just be our cup of tea."

I'm not sure if it's the play on my name, the thought of the two of us indulging, or the absurdity of it all that sends us into another fit of laughter.

It takes minutes for us to gather ourselves, and I suspect Eleanor needed these moments of levity as much as I did. Finally, we check in, and Eleanor tells me how her son James is serving as Franklin's secretary; her daughter, Anna, is out west, running a newspaper with her second husband; and her third-oldest, Elliott, is working in Texas, happy with his second wife and children. Even the younger ones, Brud and John, are adults now. I share how Albert Sr. has finally found his way running Bethune Funeral Home, while Albert Jr. will be graduating from Bethune-Cookman High School next year and then going on to Morehouse College.

"And how's everything going with the beach?" Eleanor asks, another chuckle sneaking out. The notion of buying a beach to address that bout with racism has always tickled and impressed her.

"We're moving forward, albeit slowly. But it doesn't matter if it takes me a decade or three. That Bethune Beach resort will be built."

"I'm so happy to hear that, Mary. You will let me know if there is anything I can do."

"Of course," I say. Then I add, "So, has there been any more news about Amelia Earhart?"

Eleanor's shoulders slump. "No, and it's just so sad. After all that she accomplished, especially as a woman. And all that was still in front of her."

I nod my agreement. Over the last six months, Eleanor and I have discussed the disappearance of Miss Earhart, a dear friend of Eleanor's whose plane vanished on what was supposed to be the first circumnavigational flight flown by a woman. After her plane was lost near her destination in the Pacific Ocean, President Roosevelt authorized an intense two-week search, but to no avail. Neither Miss Earhart nor her navigator has been found.

"I am still hopeful, although . . ."

Eleanor doesn't have to finish her sentence. I know there is little hope, and I pat her hand just as there's a knock on the door. Tommy sticks her head in. "It's almost time," she says.

"Has an hour gone by that quickly?" Eleanor sets her cup aside, stands, and summons a smile. "I hope you are ready for a long night, Mary."

"Your Gridiron Widows parties are legendary. I'm looking forward to this evening."

"I can't believe I never invited you before," she says. "I guess I thought you'd be bored among wives of government officials. Before we go downstairs, there is one thing I must share with you."

She wrings her hands, and I frown. "What is it?"

"I hope you won't be uncomfortable as the only Negro in the room." Her face is full of apology.

Her concern is surprising, and I say, "After all these years, you should know that I find myself in white-only spaces most of the time. Why would this be any different?"

"I know." She sighs. "But I always think back to the day we met."

"I never think about that day, Eleanor," I say, shaking my head, "because focusing on one incident of racism, especially one that happened a decade ago, isn't a luxury I can afford. I'm faced with too many incidents every day to pay particular attention to any one occurrence. Since I'm not thinking about it, you needn't either. And besides, you can't protect me from racism."

"I would if I could."

"I appreciate that." I stand and take a step toward her. "But let me introduce you to Mrs. Mary McLeod Bethune, a woman who needs no protection—in fact, there are a few who just might need a little protection from me. Ask the Klan."

She smiles ruefully. "If only you could travel this country to stare down every racist."

"Wouldn't that be something?"

"Well, tonight we won't have to deal with any of that. After the usual socializing, we'll spend the rest of the evening entertaining one another with skits and poking fun at all things Washington, D.C."

I clap, delighted at the idea of the women dressing up as stuffy old men. "Please tell me someone will be mocking Steve Woodburn."

"You will have to wait and see." Her eyes twinkle. "But I think the funniest skit may be the one where I play the role of the newest Supreme Court justice."

"Oh, that is funny. Can you imagine? A female Supreme Court justice? I cannot wait to see that."

As we enter the East Room, I take in the massive space and all its splendid glory. The chandelier in the center sparkles, illuminating the hundreds of women in the room with a bronze glow. The chatter is easy and the laughter is light, but there is one thing that stands out: there are dozens of Negro men and women dressed in traditional wait-staff garb, serving the guests.

Eleanor's words come back to me: *I hope you won't be uncomfortable as the only Negro in the room.* She didn't count the staff because she doesn't see them. *How horrified she'd be if she realized this.*

Women rush to greet the First Lady. Eleanor is careful to make sure her steps match mine; she's so protective of me. Certainly, when she introduces me, she always denotes me by calling me her "dear friend." I bear the First Lady's stamp of approval.

After drinks, we move into the State Dining Room, another elegant space, where small, white-clothed round tables with seating cards have been arranged. We maneuver through the room and find our seats at a table in front of the makeshift stage. According to the cards, Eleanor has arranged it so that my seat is next to hers.

As I move to sit, though, the stout, plainly dressed dark-haired woman already seated on the other side of Eleanor stands up. The way she and Eleanor greet each other with a lingering hug, I know who she is.

They are holding hands when Eleanor turns to me. "How delighted I am to introduce two of my dearest friends. Mary, I would like you to meet Lorena Hickok."

"Miss Hickok needs no introduction. It's an honor to meet one of the most respected reporters in the country."

"And you as well, Mrs. Bethune. Thank you for the compliment, but it's been some years since I was a reporter—although I'll be returning to some of my old beats soon."

"Well, that's wonderful news. The world needs your discerning journalistic pen these days, especially with the European developments."

As we settle with the others, one of the waitstaff, a young woman, steps up to our table with a teapot. As she moves around filling each cup, the conversations continue and no one gives her a single glance. The young woman's focus remains on her task; she doesn't make eye contact with anyone.

When she moves to me, I say "Thank you" as she fills my cup.

My words surprise her, making her pause, and when she glances at me, I see the recognition in her eyes and her smile. Still, she doesn't speak. She nods, but before she can move on to Eleanor, I touch her arm.

"What's your name, young lady?"

The question makes Eleanor turn from Hick to face me, but I stay focused on this girl, who's no more than twenty years old. She deserves to be seen and acknowledged.

My question, however, seems to have upset her. She stands stiff and straight, her eyes darting from one corner of the room to the other, as if she's afraid.

Then I realize—she's been told not to interact with the guests. She's been trained to be as small as possible. I extend my hand to her. "I'm Mary McLeod Bethune. It's nice to meet you."

She studies my hand for a moment, shakes it, and then turns quickly, her attention now on Eleanor's cup. But before she can pour the tea, Eleanor mutters, "I . . . I want to know your name, too."

Again the young woman stiffens. I touch her arm, this time to reassure her. "This is Mrs. Eleanor Roosevelt. You'll be fine."

"My . . . my name is . . . Mary."

"That's my name," I add, although she already knows.

Nodding, she then whispers, "My mama is from South Carolina, and she told me that I'm named after you."

She scurries off before Eleanor or I can say anything, and for a moment, we stare at each other.

"That's amazing." Eleanor appears stunned.

"It's an honor," I say, although I don't mention how many times I've been blessed to hear those words from young ladies who tell me they're named after me because their parents wanted them to grow up and change the world.

But I also know Eleanor's amazement isn't only with the young Mary. I watch as Eleanor glances around the room, her eyes open to the fact that I am *not* the only Negro in the room. She *sees* the many other Negroes moving about. When she faces me, her expression is filled with sorrow, and her apology is in her eyes. I pat her hand to reassure her. No words need to be spoken. The lesson has been learned.

We turn our attention back to the other ladies, and a few minutes later, Eleanor excuses herself from the table. I notice how Hick's eyes follow Eleanor for a few seconds. When Hick turns back to me, I ask how she got started in journalism, and she tells me she sold stories to the local newspaper for seven dollars, which delights me, and we chat until Eleanor rejoins us. The three of us talk until the overhead lights dim and only a single spotlight on the stage remains. I've been so engrossed with Hick and Eleanor, I didn't notice that women were donning costumes and taking places onstage.

The first skit focuses on a nameless senator rushing to leave his office to catch a train, but every time he gets to the door, the telephone rings. The skit that follows contains a humorous take on Mr. Woodburn and his overbearing personality that makes me laugh out loud.

By the time the third and the fourth skit come onstage, there are merry tears in the eyes of every woman.

Then it is time for the final skit. How Eleanor slipped away from the table, I will never know. The stage fills with women with signs around their necks, representing eight of the current Supreme Court justices. The justices bemoan having a new justice on the court, especially a woman, because they're "always late." Then Eleanor sweeps into the room.

They greet her in unison—"Hello, Justice Roosevelt"—and add a collective moan.

The women in the audience laugh as Eleanor greets all the justices and announces, "Before we review any cases, Mr. Chief Justice, I think there is something we must do first." She reaches into her bag and then piles balls and balls of yarn onto the table.

Laughter fills the room once again as the chief justice asks, "What are you doing?"

"Have you seen these robes? They are boring, and I"—Eleanor pulls out her knitting needles—"am going to liven our costumes up." The roar of the audience makes it hard for Eleanor to continue. "Or maybe I should do a different color," Eleanor finally says as she retrieves a ball of golden yellow yarn. "This would be perfect for spring."

The audience howls now, and even though I laugh, I sit back and fold my arms. *Why not?* The world Eleanor and I are trying to create is vast and wide and equal. What have I dreamed that I haven't been able to accomplish? Why couldn't there be a female justice on the Supreme Court? Maybe even a Negro? Yes, I can see a Negro female on the Supreme Court. Knitting needles and all.

CHAPTER 47

ELEANOR

Birmingham, Alabama
November 20, 1938

Hurry, hurry, I think as my driver proceeds down the winding, bumpy Alabama back roads that lead from the housing project I toured this morning to Municipal Auditorium, where the Southern Conference for Human Welfare is about to begin day two. Usually the poor colored population is allotted the worst housing, but I'd heard glowing reports about this option and wanted to see it for myself. The buildings were indeed newly constructed and freshly painted with pleasant if small yards, and the interiors were well planned and shone with the owners' pride. I could see the corners that had been cut in the construction, but I do understand that compromise is needed in these financially challenging times.

When the driver peels onto the road leading to the auditorium, it's already one o'clock, the time designated for the first speech to begin. And I don't want to be late.

It seems that the conference is causing a stir in Birmingham. On the first day, the local rules about segregation were disregarded and audience members sat willy-nilly, white and colored folks intermixed. But Mary heard rumors that Birmingham's public safety commissioner, Bull Connor, was furious and would be forcing the segregation rules upon the conference attendees today. We hatched a plan to address it, but I hope it doesn't come to that. Still, I peek inside my purse to make sure I've got my equipment.

With Earl's guidance, I hustle in through a side entrance. This conference is meant to promote the New Deal policies supporting Negroes, a more regional version of the big January conferences that Mary has hosted. It is one of the first large interracial meetings of its kind in the South, and perhaps two thousand people are reportedly going to attend. Among them will be Supreme Court justice Hugo Black, Alabama governor Bibb Graves, NYA head Aubrey Williams, business and community leaders, and sharecroppers—over two hundred Negroes among the attendees—and I am proud I'll be in their ranks, alongside Mary.

When I enter the back of the dimly lit auditorium, the program has already begun. *Dang it.* Mary told me she'd reserve seats for us in the front row so we can easily mount the stage for our turns speaking. More than a few police officers line the walls. I spot Mary and the empty seat next to her.

"Sorry I'm late," I whisper. "The tour of the housing project ran long."

"You are here now; that's all that matters."

We'll have time to catch up back at my hotel suite, where I've been assured Mary can stay—secretly, of course. The governor wraps up a moving speech about the needs of his colored constituents and how much the New Deal programs—both federal and state—have helped the people of Alabama. The audience applauds politely as the next speaker, Supreme Court justice Hugo Black, rises from his seat.

It is then that I feel a tap on my shoulder. Turning, I see the beet-red face of a young local police officer. "You are breaking the law, ma'am."

"Excuse me, son?"

"I'm not your son, and you are breaking the law. I am going to have to ask you to move to the white section or place you under arrest."

Suddenly, Earl appears at the policeman's side. "Back away from her. Do you realize this is the First Lady of the United States? How dare you speak to her that way."

"Even the First Lady has to abide by the law." I realize that this police officer knows exactly who I am. "And Birmingham's laws include a segregation statute. Mrs. Roosevelt cannot sit in the colored section. She must move to the whites-only section." He points across the aisle.

This police officer is attempting to get the First Lady of the United States to abide by Jim Crow laws, a legislative system I have spoken against. I glance over at Mary. Her expression is inscrutable, except for a subtle nod to me—the signal to proceed with our plan.

Just as Justice Black begins his speech, another officer appears on the scene. This one's uniform bears more insignia than the first policeman's.

"Ma'am," he says with a deep Southern drawl, "my name is Bull Connor, and I am the former police commissioner of Birmingham, now serving as the city's public safety commissioner."

"Nice to meet you, Mr. Connor." Unfortunately, my high pitch belies my nerves; it cracks on the word "nice." Earl draws close to my chair. Justice Black's voice soars through the room, but almost all eyes are on me, and no one is listening to a word he's saying.

"I am going to have to ask you again to move to the white side of the auditorium, Mrs. Roosevelt." His voice is authoritative and pretends at respect for me, but I hear the latent sneer in his tone. "We follow the law in this state, and our law calls for segregation of the races. You are a white woman sitting in the Negro section, and you must move to the racially appropriate area."

"Mr. Connor, I am here at the invitation of my dear friend Mrs. Bethune"—I gesture to Mary—"and I have every intention of sitting next to her for the duration of this conference."

Earl crosses his arms and stares at Mr. Connor while another one of my security detail joins him. "Then, Mrs. Roosevelt, since you've

told an officer of the law that you plan on breaking it, I am afraid I'll
have to detain you for the duration of this conference. And then we can
let our local courts adjudicate this case and see if it merits further
punishment."

With those words, the face of Steve Woodburn passes through my
mind, and once again I consider what Franklin's reaction will be. This
is not Washington, D.C. Here, racism is legislated, and I cannot imagine how being arrested and turning this into a spectacle will help my
husband's presidency.

Do I have the moxie to go through with the plan? It's risky, but I
can't simply abide by these racist laws without some form of protest.
No matter how it affects Franklin.

Nodding at Earl to let him know I'm fine, I stand up. A smug smile
spreads across Mr. Connor's repugnant face. He thinks he's won. But
instead of walking across the aisle to the open seat to which he points,
I pick up my chair.

I set the chair off to the side while I reach into my purse for the ruler
I brought along. With great care, I measure the distance between the
white side and the colored side of the auditorium seating, then mark the
exact center with the pencil I also brought. I place the chair on that
spot—the precise middle of the aisle. Neither on the colored side nor on
the white. I have neither bowed down to segregation nor done anything
to break their Jim Crow laws. Mr. Connor is in a box.

Not a single eye is on poor Justice Black. As I settle into my chair,
utterly ignoring Mr. Connor and his policemen until they finally depart, I think how appropriate my speech for today is. I'll call out the
recent, horrific Nazi-sanctioned racial violence during Kristallnacht
and hold all American citizens to the highest standards in human
rights. After all, isn't every citizen of the world entitled to the same
freedoms and treatment? Just as the eyes of this conference are fixed
on me today to assess how I reacted to racism, the eyes of the world
are watching us. And we must ensure that justice prevails.

CHAPTER 48

MARY

Washington, D.C.
April 9, 1939

I step up onto the stage and pause to take in the Mall, and the sight helps ease the residual smarting from the last time I stood on a stage before thousands, at the Alabama conference. Tens of thousands of people, colored and white, men and women, stand shoulder to shoulder, dressed in their Easter Sunday best, chatting easily and waiting patiently for the legendary contralto Marian Anderson. The throngs stretch from Lincoln's feet at his memorial all the way back to the Washington Monument. How I wish I was sharing this with Eleanor; it is because of her that we are here today.

My seat is in the front row on the stage. There are two hundred of us up here, all public figures who've provided financial support for this event, including folks like New York senator Robert Wagner, who greets me as he passes. As I settle down, I think of how this all began with a request I made back on a frigid January day.

I'd invited Eleanor to the town house to catch up. But as we sat in front of the fire in the parlor, I told her that, once again, I needed her help. She braced herself, and I remembered when she had told me about Nan and Marion and how their requests never stopped. Those two couldn't have been the only ones—how many times a day did people make requests of the First Lady?

Even with those thoughts, I pressed forward. This request wasn't for me. "Howard University wants to host Marian Anderson for a benefit concert, and the Daughters of the American Revolution refuse to rent Constitution Hall to them."

"Why?" Eleanor frowned. "With the tickets sold, they will certainly be able to afford that venue."

"It has nothing to do with finances. This is all about her race."

I could almost hear her thoughts. *Not again.* But then her wariness turned to eagerness.

"I can help. I have an honorary membership in the DAR. Surely we'll be able to fix this."

Eleanor and I dove into the effort, amassing supporters to put pressure on the DAR—Walter White and the NAACP, NCNW, and dozens of other organizations, church leaders, and activists. We formed the Marian Anderson Citizens Committee and created petitions, arranged protests, and kept the story in the press. All of that was designed to shame the DAR into changing their position.

They did not. Not even when Eleanor orchestrated Marian Anderson's performance to take place during the king and queen of England's upcoming historic visit to America—the first time reigning British monarchs have *ever* traveled to America. Not even when thousands of women quit the DAR and the newspapers turned against the organization. The DAR remained steadfast in their denial.

So Eleanor had an idea, and that idea turned into a plan culminating in today. The only thing that makes me angry about today, though, is that Eleanor had to stay away. But she made the right decision; her safety has to be the priority, and I know she didn't want to serve as a distraction.

Secretary of the Interior Harold Ickes and Miss Anderson finally appear from behind the columns and stand side by side in the middle of the colonnade, and riotous applause explodes through the air. My eyes fix on Miss Anderson. With her ankle-length mink coat and finger wave hairstyle, Miss Anderson looks elegant, almost aristocratic. The statue of Lincoln looms large behind them, and I imagine the emancipator's approval.

At the bottom of the steps, Miss Anderson stops, and Secretary Ickes continues toward the bank of microphones. The crowd becomes silent. "Distinguished guests. In this great auditorium under the sky, all of us are free," Secretary Ickes proclaims.

Again the applause is resounding. When the audience quiets, he speaks about how God makes no distinction between race, creed, or color, and I almost can't believe his words. Having Miss Anderson perform for an integrated audience on the steps of the Lincoln Memorial is a grand victory, but to have a senior Roosevelt administration official make such a bold public statement in favor of equality is monumental. There is a shift happening in America. No matter the resistance in places like Alabama.

Secretary Ickes concludes this fine speech by saying, "Please join me in welcoming a genius in her field, Miss Marian Anderson. Genius, like justice, is blind. Genius draws no color lines."

Once more, the air erupts with applause. Does everyone here recognize this moment for the transcendent experience it is about to be?

CHAPTER 49

ELEANOR

Washington, D.C.
April 9, 1939

"Ma'am," Earl whispers in my ear as thunderous applause breaks out across the crowds in front of the Lincoln Memorial. His voice is uncharacteristically firm. "You really need to stay farther back, behind the curtains, so no one on the Mall can see you."

I know Earl is right, as he is about most things. When he and I discussed my desire to be here today, he cautioned against it. Although I trust Earl with my life—literally and figuratively—and we've grown so close he even shares his personal problems with me, in this instance I had to insist on coming.

No one knows I'm here except Earl; I didn't even tell Mary I'd be here. I do not want to give the protestors spewing vitriol about me any more fodder. All eyes should be exclusively upon Miss Anderson. Earl has different reasons for keeping me backstage: He's worried about the anonymous death threats that poor Tommy had to open up in the mail. Both he and Franklin begged me not to come, but nothing could keep me away.

Everyone on my staff has gotten used to letters—and newspaper articles and cartoons of me, for that matter—blasting my looks or admonishing me to stay at home instead of making appearances out in the world. But these recent hateful missives are a horse of a different color, what with their violent details and, in one case, a gruesome illustration.

The applause crests on the heels of Secretary Ickes' moving speech, and I'm desperate for a peek at Miss Anderson before she approaches the microphone. Craning my neck, I get a glimpse of her elegant profile as her pianist begins the introduction. I keep my eyes fixed on her until I hear the first sweet notes from Miss Anderson. Her confident, rich contralto fills the air, and I allow the music to sweep over me: "My country 'tis of thee, sweet land of liberty, of thee I sing . . ."

How wise to start the concert with this patriotic song, revealing her own citizenship, her patriotism, and her rights in this country. I open my eyes and notice that Miss Anderson has hers closed. I suppose there is no need for her to see the people; all she needs to do is feel the music.

When she finishes, her eyes open and she holds up her hand in appreciation of the applause, then transitions into her next song. This is an Italian aria, and it flows beautifully into her third song, "Ave Maria." The crowd settles into the sacredness, and the clapping before intermission is almost reverent.

As Miss Anderson leaves the stage, a deep sense of peace descends upon me. It was never a foregone conclusion, but all the strife and consternation over the issue of the DAR and Constitution Hall and Miss Anderson and the hate mail and the haggling with Franklin have been worth it.

After Mary's and my initial efforts failed, I labored over two pieces of writing. First, I drafted a letter of resignation to the Daughters of the American Revolution for their refusal to allow Miss Anderson to perform, calling their decision unenlightened. Then I wrote a My Day column about the decision. Without describing my exact quandary— unnecessary, as it had been extensively reported on in the paper—I posed the question of whether one should stay with an organization that acts against one's beliefs, fight from within, or resign because one does not want to suggest approval of their actions.

When I completed the writings, I marched to the Oval Office and past the guards outside the closed doors, who barely batted an eye at my unscheduled visit. They've grown used to this peculiar First Lady, so different from the usual presidential wife. Knocking on the door and then pushing it open, I knew I'd see Secretary of the Interior Ickes sitting in front of Franklin's desk. That part had been planned.

"Good morning, gentlemen," I said, and Franklin and Harold broke into laughter.

Franklin said, "We had a bet on when you'd arrive."

I laughed along with them. "Have I really become that predictable?"

"In matters of race, yes. But you needn't come armed for battle this time around."

"I don't?" I asked, sitting down beside Harold in a chair across from Franklin.

"Oh, no, we fully expected to have a discussion with you about Miss Anderson today. After all, things are coming to a head," Franklin said.

"While it's not my place to speak for the president," Harold said, motioning toward my husband, "I, for one, have been horrified by the intractability of the Daughters of the American Revolution, and I understand you feel similarly."

"I do. It's on par with being ordered by the Birmingham police to sit in a separate section of an auditorium."

Franklin raised an eyebrow. He didn't love my aisle-sitting tactic, but he agreed that the police request had been immoral, if not illegal. "Knowing you—and Mrs. Bethune, for that matter—I am guessing you have a plan. We are listening."

"Before you consider the request, I recommend that you read the letter I'll be sending to the DAR today and the My Day column I'll be publishing tomorrow." I handed the papers first to Franklin, indicating he should pass them to Harold when he finished.

"The reaction will be electric—both positive and negative," Franklin said as Harold reviewed the pages.

"I know, and I know it'll cause a ruffle with your Southern supporters and constituents. But it is what my conscience demands."

As I awaited Franklin's verdict, I thought, *How I miss Louis.* He would have stood silently to the side, his presence serving as quiet encouragement for me and moral prompting for Franklin.

Franklin bestowed on me a wide grin, and I felt unexpected relief. "I would expect nothing less." From his positive reaction, I guessed that Steve's efforts to sway Franklin toward the viewpoint of the DAR had failed—an unusual development. Perhaps the broad-based support of Miss Anderson in the white newspapers had something to do with that. Franklin had little to lose by backing her.

Harold chimed in, "These are powerful and necessary, I think."

"But this isn't the entirety of the plan, is it?" Franklin sounded almost amused, and I could only attribute it to the fact that this situation was so egregious.

"No." This was one of my most ambitious requests to date, and I'd gone directly to the two people who could make it happen: the president and the secretary of the interior, who has control over federal land. "What would you think about hosting Miss Anderson for a public event at the Lincoln Memorial on Easter Sunday? Instead of performing for four thousand people in Constitution Hall, she'd be singing for tens of thousands at the memorial and millions on National Broadcast Radio."

Miss Anderson returns to the stage, belting out a beautiful spiritual song I don't know: "Get on board, little children . . . get on board." She quickly moves on to another. "Though the storms keep raging in my life . . . and sometimes it's hard to tell night from day . . ." A familiar song follows—"Nobody knows the trouble I've seen . . . nobody knows my sorrow . . ."—and one of the guests onstage moves, affording me a view of the back of Mary's head. I see she's dabbing her eyes with a handkerchief.

It takes everything I have not to rush to her side. I long to comfort her if her tears are sad. But even if they're joyful, I want to understand in what manner these songs move her.

I wonder if Franklin is listening from Warm Springs or if he's already begun his train journey back to Washington. He and I plan on attending tomorrow's Easter Egg Roll at the White House. Perhaps he cares less about the concert and music itself and more about the advantage he garnered when the newspaper coverage turned against the Daughters of the American Revolution. Would Franklin be moved by Miss Anderson's performance? I glance up at Earl, and I see unshed tears glimmering in the corners of his eyes.

I refuse to think any negative thoughts on this peaceful day. Miss Anderson started this historic concert with a proclamation of her love for her country and ended with what could be the anthem for the Negroes in this country. She connected two Americas. Might this moment last?

CHAPTER 50

MARY

Daytona Beach, Florida
February 18, 1940

I hold my breath as the presidential train pulls into the Daytona station. The Bethune-Cookman College band is behind me, the mayor is on my left, and my son and grandson are on my right. The arrival of the First Lady in Daytona is a first, and even though I orchestrated this visit for the benefit of my college, I want the entire region to celebrate.

If I'd had my way, there would have been thousands of people here to greet Eleanor. But it has been quite a feat to get her to the city, even for the thirty-fifth anniversary of Bethune-Cookman.

For six months, I've been trying to arrange this, but between her schedule and pushback from the White House, I felt as if Eleanor had serious reservations about attending. Still I pushed, changing dates on my calendar, rearranging the times—everything to accommodate Eleanor. A twinge of guilt passes through me. Through the years, I have asked Eleanor for a lot, but this time, I pressed beyond the limits.

As Eleanor's train slows, I signal the student musicians. They lift their instruments, and once the train comes to a stop, they begin. The door to Eleanor's car opens, and my friend steps out into the simple open-air station. The sound of the rousing horns playing—"Happy Days Are Here Again"—greets her.

I am elated at the sight of my friend, and we walk toward each other. But as she draws close, I frown. Puffy circles darken her eyes, and her energy, the stuff that is of legend, seems to be drained. She arrives in Florida bedraggled.

It must be all that she's had to deal with in Washington. The White House must be a flurry with the war developments, namely Germany and Russia's plans to invade Finland, Norway, and Denmark. But none of these are new developments, and once again, guilt courses through me.

"Mrs. Bethune," she says, and reaches for me.

"It's so good to have you here, Mrs. Roosevelt," I say, nodding at Earl and her other security guards.

We shake hands for the cameras. Then I turn. "I'd like you to meet my son, Albert Bethune Sr., and of course you know Albert Bethune Jr."

When she faces the loves of my life, the grin that I am used to returns. "What a delight to finally meet you, Mr. Bethune." She shakes my son's hand and then she greets Albert Jr., whom she's met before on a few occasions. I introduce her to Mayor Armstrong, who bestows her with the key to the city. Journalists snap pictures and call out questions, but Eleanor doesn't answer any, citing our tight schedule. The band plays again as Eleanor, my son, my grandson, and I get into the car. We have a driver who will take us straight to the campus.

Once we're inside, I say, "It's good to see you, my friend."

"I'm glad to be here. But, Mary, I didn't expect so many people at the train station. Certainly not the press."

I hear a tinge of annoyance, but I wave it away. "I know you wanted to keep this low-key, but you're the First Lady and I wanted you to know that Daytona appreciates your visit. As do I." I press my hand against hers before I pass her the agenda.

Glancing down, she asks, "The school speech is first? How big will the crowd be?"

It's the same resistance I began to hear in her tone when we got into the planning of this thirty-fifth anniversary celebration. Although I understand she may be tired or have reservations about a big speech, I need my friend here. My school still finds itself in dire straits. With the threat of war on top of the Depression, our sources of financial support have all but disappeared. This commemoration with Eleanor is our last, best hope to raise funds.

"The crowd won't be too big," I say. "Is the timing still all right?"

"Yes, I just thought I'd have the chance to freshen up and have a bite to eat first," she says with an exhausted sigh.

Maybe that is what I'm feeling from Eleanor—her fatigue.

"Just because you don't see a stop at my house on the agenda doesn't mean we aren't headed there. I have a bedroom cleared for your use and fresh fried chicken on the table. I know it's not yet noon, but it's your—"

"Favorite," she finishes my sentence, and I see her genuine smile. "Thank you, my friend." She sits back and studies me. "You look lovely, Mary."

My navy day dress with its white lace collar is one of my simplest daytime outfits. Today I wear no fur, no cape, no overlay, but I guess compared to Eleanor, in her plain white blouse and black skirt, I look glamorous.

She says, "Sometimes I feel like I could use a little help with my clothing."

"Oh, no, you're fine." When she looks at me from the corner of her eye, I laugh. "You're the First Lady. You're supposed to be a bit more . . . reserved."

"Reserved? Is that what this"—she motions to her limp blouse—"is called?"

I try to hold back my laughter, but I fail in that effort, and Eleanor laughs with me. "Well, we can always stop by Miss Esther's. She's not too far from my home."

"And miss out on that fried chicken just to get a new dress?" She waves her hand. "We're going to your house for that food."

When we laugh again, I see my son exchange a curious glance with my grandson. Albert Jr. leans over and whispers to his dad, "They're always like this." That makes me laugh even more. Our chatter and laughter continue until we arrive at my home. Eleanor has about a half hour of downtime, and then we're on the move. First the speech and radio address, then a tour of our campus with a meeting with staff and students.

All goes well until we reach a planned gap in the schedule. I'm sure Eleanor assumes that tea will be served during this time, but I'm serving up something much more important.

I lead Eleanor into our college library, another building funded by the late Mr. Gamble. "It's lovely, Mary," she says as I take her through the stacks.

Clearly, she thinks this is just another tour, until we reach the open area toward the back. The study space is brimming with smiling, excited children between the ages of six and ten, all lined up and dressed in the best clothes they have.

Eleanor faces me, confused, but before I can explain, the children break into "Lift Every Voice and Sing." When they finish, Eleanor claps. "Thank you. That song is more beautiful each time I hear it."

The girls curtsy, the boys bow, and then they disband. As she watches them, Eleanor whispers, "I don't understand. I thought all of your students were college aged."

We watch the children form a single line in the back, near tables that are manned by older men and women. "I wanted you to see the role Bethune-Cookman plays not only in the lives of its college students but in the broader Daytona Negro community."

I gesture to the student at the front of the line. The little boy is barefoot, even though the outside temperature is a relatively chilly fifty degrees. His pants are high above his ankles and his button-down shirt is frayed at the collar and cuffs—but this was the best he had.

Eleanor and I watch as he extends a bucket to a gray-haired man, who fills it with fruit, bread, and a generous serving of ham; it's enough food for about two or three meals. Then the gentleman pours him a glass of milk and directs him to the next table.

Eleanor and I watch while the boy moves to the table, where books are piled high. He chats with the woman behind the table, then she hands him a book. She gestures to another area, where the boy settles on the floor, his glass of milk in one hand, his bucket in the other, and his book tucked under his arm.

"Mary?"

That is all Eleanor has to say, and I understand her question. "Every weekend, Bethune-Cookman opens its doors to the community and we provide food and programming for children who need it most. We give them a couple of meals, and once all the children have been served"—I point to where a group of the boys and girls are now sitting—"some of our college students will read with them and work with them on arithmetic, and then we send them home with the food and a book on loan."

"This is amazing."

"For some of these poor youngsters, this is the most food and the only instruction they'll receive all week. And we do the same for their parents on the other side of the campus."

"My God," Eleanor exclaims. "This is a miniature NYA."

"Indeed. This is what I've tried to bring to the federal level, although we've been doing this here for thirty-five years. You see, Eleanor, if Bethune-Cookman fails, then we fail far more than our enrolled students. We let down the entire colored population of Daytona." I'm sure the worry I've been feeling over the last few years is evident on my face. "This is why I was so insistent on you being here. Your visit will help us raise much-needed funds."

She shakes her head. "All these years, and I didn't know how much you did here."

"This is why I asked you to come, even knowing how busy you are. My school, and all that we do, is in financial danger, and I have to do whatever I can to save it." Turning toward the children, I add, "And them."

Eleanor sighs, a heavy sound. "Mary, I hoped I would not have to do this. But we need to talk."

CHAPTER 51

ELEANOR

Daytona Beach, Florida
February 18, 1940

I didn't want to tell Mary about Steve's offensive behavior. How could I? She's poured so much of herself into my visit and made it the centerpiece of her special celebration. Even Tommy—who never complains—commented on how many communications she had with Mary over the details of my visit. How could I spoil the big thirty-fifth anniversary celebration?

"Could we stop by your home?" I ask. The sort of conversation we need to have shouldn't take place in a public space.

"I think some quiet time to talk would be perfect."

I try to keep the conversation light as we stroll across what Mary describes as the quadrangle, then pass several redbrick buildings as we walk toward her pretty, white two-story house, with its deep porch that I imagine provides a cool respite on hot Florida days. It is nearly dusk when we enter, and she hurries off to the kitchen to have her housekeeper fix us some tea. A formal dinner is planned, but it's been several hours since lunch, and I'm happy for the warm tea and pie. We do love our desserts, and this sweet potato pie is outstanding.

"What's on your mind?" she asks as soon as we are alone. "Between the dark circles under your eyes and your weariness, I figured something's wrong."

"You know me well, Mary. I didn't want to sully this occasion with any sort of unpleasantness, but when you made clear the economic stakes at play at Bethune-Cookman, well, I realized that I need to."

Mary sits up a little taller. "All right."

"Steve Woodburn stopped me in a White House hallway late one night—not too long ago—when no one was around, which I am sure was his intention. He ordered me 'absolutely not to visit that colored school that Mary is associated with.' That last bit is a direct quote, which you probably guessed because he called you Mary instead of Dr. Bethune, or even Mrs. Bethune, and he would not name your college."

Mary sucks in her breath. "Who does he think he is, telling the First Lady what she can and cannot do? Did you tell President Roosevelt?"

"I did, the next morning. But Franklin said I must have misunderstood. When I pushed—even suggesting that such impudence warrants termination—Franklin said Steve is too important to his public perception and relationship with the press to fire. He reminded me that Steve's long-standing agreement with the press is why no newspaper or magazine will publish a picture of Franklin in his wheelchair or with visible leg braces."

"The president won't protect you because Steve's too valuable to him."

"Something like that. But that isn't all, Mary. Steve claimed that he got a call from certain senior Democrats in Florida warning that I should not visit Daytona or there would be 'unfortunate' repercussions."

Mary's brow furrows. "Did they say what they would be?"

"Initially, Steve mentioned that Florida might do whatever it can to stand in the way of white voters supporting Franklin in the next election. I told him that's a risk I'm willing to take and turned away."

"What did he do then?" Mary's voice is grave.

"He called my name, and when I refused to turn around, he said that my visit here would present other problems for Bethune-Cookman College, financial ones. I asked him what he meant. With the most sinister smile on his face, he said that a visit to Bethune-Cookman by the First Lady signals a tie between the Roosevelts and the school—and that since Bethune-Cookman applied for federal money through the New Deal, it would present a conflict of interest, rendering the college's request for money null and void."

Mary freezes. "Is that when you called me with all sorts of excuses for not coming?"

"Yes."

"And I begged you to come."

"Yes."

"Why didn't you tell me? Eleanor, I thought we agreed to talk through things." Mary sounds mad.

She's right. I should have told her. She should be angry.

"I wish I had," I say, then try to explain—not excuse. "First of all, I thought it might be an empty threat, but most of all, I wanted to protect you. I—I thought if I kept Steve's warning to myself and I made sure my visit was not a big deal in the press, then we could still have your event without much in the way of risk."

"You hoped these people of Steve Woodburn's wouldn't get wind of your Daytona trip and put my federal money in jeopardy?" Mary asks, and when I nod, she says, "And then I barreled through and disregarded your request. More than that, I invited the press to the train station."

"Yes," I say, trying to stay matter-of-fact. She's angry enough at herself, but she shouldn't be. I'm the one who made the mistake. "I am terribly sorry, Mary. I didn't realize how desperate Bethune-Cookman's financial situation is. I should have told you about the threats. I made a presumption about what is best for you and your school and didn't even give you enough information to make a decision of your own."

"You thought you were doing what was good for me," she says, offering me an out.

"It's inexcusable. Didn't you teach me I should never make such presumptions?"

She nods, a little sadly. "Still, Eleanor, I understand your intentions." Her tone then becomes businesslike. "Now, it's quite possible that Steve Woodburn invented this supposed call from Florida Democrats to scare you away from Bethune-Cookman. You know how he feels about our friendship. There are many schools with some sort of tie to you and your husband that applied for federal funding through the New Deal, which does make his claim somewhat suspicious."

"But it's also possible that it's true, and I'm sorry I came. Not that it's much consolation."

"I accept your apology for the presumption, but otherwise, Eleanor, this is not your fault. What have I told you about apologizing for others' sins? This belongs to Steve, and, truth be told, I am not afraid of him. I always find a way, and I will with the school funding—which I would have told you had you asked," she mock-scolds, and then she smiles. "Eleanor, you are here at Bethune-Cookman. The community knows. We have planned a glorious celebration, and I think we should participate in it, even if Woodburn's Florida cronies catch wind of it. Assuming they even exist. God will provide if the government won't."

"Are you sure?" I ask.

Mary sounds so confident, but I am worried.

"No, but I *am* sure that we deserve to do tonight the one thing we promised each other we'd do the first day we met."

I rack my brain for details about that awkward first luncheon at our New York City town house. I can conjure up the clothes we wore, the unpleasant faces of the other, racist guests—even the soup that was served.

Mary chuckles. "When you mentioned it that day, I couldn't believe it. The fact that you made the suggestion revealed your innocence about segregation. How much you've learned since then!"

"For the life of me, I can't remember. Are you going to let me in on the secret?" I tease.

"You wanted us to see the singer Roland Hayes together."

I slap my leg as the exact exchange comes flooding back to me. "That's right! Oh, I was so naive to think we'd be able to sit together and watch him in the same venue." I smile. "But what does Roland Hayes have to do with tonight?"

Mary beams. "I've arranged for Mr. Hayes to perform a concert in honor of you and Bethune-Cookman's thirty-fifth anniversary. I'm hoping we might attend it together, as we planned all those years ago."

CHAPTER 52

MARY

Baltimore, Maryland
May 28, 1940

It occurs to me that I have become a different sort of victim of racism. Not the overt sort of casualty, as with a lynching. Nor the lesser sort of injury, as is often seen in the economic and social oppression in the colored community. No, I have been made ill by the constant, heavy toll on my body of fighting for equality against the thick, reinforced wall of prejudice. It's a beating I've taken every day of my sixty-five years through the words and actions of others.

I'm not sure what caused my eventual break. It could have been the strain as I worked to save my college. Or maybe it was the worry over Steve Woodburn's threat. Even though we did not see the negative ramifications Woodburn warned about, the weight of that distress could have compounded the damage that the struggle had already taken on my body.

"Are you comfortable, Mother Dear?" my son asks as he fluffs the pillow behind me in my hospital bed.

For the past two months, I've been at Johns Hopkins Hospital. I needed a crucial sinus surgery after having a life-threatening bronchitis and sinus infection. However, my weight threatened my ability to survive such a procedure, so I've been locked away in this room, where the doctors have been monitoring my diet.

"Very comfortable," I tell Albert.

"No pain?"

"None, and, Albert, can you stop hovering, please? It was just a minor operation."

"Mother Dear, you'd be the first to tell your students that 'minor operation' is an oxymoron."

"My time is almost up here, son. One more week, so you needn't worry anymore. What time does your train back to Daytona leave?"

Albert's grin is so bright, I have to fight to keep my smile at bay. "Are you trying to get rid of me?"

"You've been gone too long. That funeral home isn't going to run itself."

He chuckles, and I'm filled with such gratitude. For the last three and a half years, we've been able to speak without arguments about his business because he's doing so well.

"You can go. The surgery is over and I'm fine." I make a big display of huffing, but the truth is, I'm grateful my son took the time to be with me.

"Just make sure you eat your dinner," he says, pushing the bed tray closer to me, then hugs me before he kisses me goodbye.

When I'm alone, I look at my dinner—a plate covered with a teaspoon of mashed potatoes, six green beans, and a boiled chicken thigh with skin so wrinkled, that chicken had to have been more sickly than me. This diet has nearly killed me faster than any bronchitis attack ever could.

Pushing the food tray to the side, I snuggle back into the pillows. *What a time to be hospitalized.* The world was already falling apart before my illness, and the disintegration has accelerated. War rages in Europe, and as America positions itself for possible intervention, Congress has approved increased military spending. This means even more New Deal programming will be cut.

And what that will mean for the country's most vulnerable citizens scares me. My programs are being trimmed down to nothingness. Until these last few days, I've been too ill to gather the key Federal Council members together, but today that begins anew. I am strong enough to set this crooked road straight.

Just when I have that thought, there is a knock on my door, and I call out, "Come in."

Robert Weaver peeks inside. "You awake, Mary?"

"I am," I say, forcing my voice to sound strong. "And I'm delighted you could make it."

"I'm happy you're well enough to have me. And I hope it's okay that I brought another friend."

I tilt my head in surprise when Bill Hastie steps in behind him. "It's good to see you looking so well, Mary," Bill says, his voice as soft as usual. He hands me a bouquet of tulips and magnolias.

"How lovely," I say as I inhale the flowers' fragrance. "Would you mind putting them on the table?"

He has to rearrange the vases already there to find room for his bunch. "My bouquet seems downright paltry next to these. Did your son give you all of these flowers?"

I point to the enormous array of yellow blooms in the center. "Albert gave me those. The others came from the White House gardens."

Bill exchanges a glance with Robert, but I just motion to the chairs opposite my hospital bed. "Please have a seat."

When they do, Robert speaks first. "So, you've had quite a stay."

"Would have been better at a resort." I shift in the bed. "I cannot wait to go home. I'm being released Sunday."

"Well," Robert starts, "sometimes these kinds of setbacks are blessings. An opportunity to get the rest you need."

"I'm getting rest, but there's still work to be done. That's why I asked you to come visit with me. I feel like we have to fortify the Federal Council in light of all the budgetary cuts coming. We have to unite to protect the agencies we represent."

The men glance at each other again. I wait for one of them to say something, but when they don't, I continue, "I'm hoping to enlist your help by having the two of you arrange a Federal Council meeting for this upcoming Monday at the NCNW town house. Now, I've started an agenda and—"

When the men once again look at each other, I can no longer ignore it. "I feel like you two are having a conversation and I'm not included. What's going on?"

Robert finally stammers, "Well, Mary . . . about those meetings— I'm afraid we won't be able to get everyone together that way again."

"Why not?" I snap, although my frustration isn't meant for Robert. It's because he's spoken aloud what I've feared—without my leadership, the Council has already crumbled.

"The group has all but disbanded, Mary," Bill says. I lean forward to hear him better. "And it started long before you were hospitalized. Haven't you noticed?"

"What do you mean?" I say, although of course I noticed enthusiasm had waned not long after the president's reelection. At each meeting there were fewer attendees, until one Friday night, I sat in my parlor alone.

"Well," Bill answers, "most of the men broke off into smaller groups, focusing on their own interests."

I shake my head hard. "This isn't the time for selfish interests. We must be aligned or we will lose all we've gained."

"But are our interests the same, Mary?" Robert asks. "No one questions your commitment and desire to see the New Deal policies work for Negroes. The question is, does the president share that commitment?"

Bill continues, "The president promised so much, Mary—everything from securing voting rights to jobs to better housing and education for Negroes. But what has he delivered? Yes, federal appointments have been made. But just how many times do we have to recap this story? We had no power before, and now, with the war looming, half of us have been reassigned to positions with even less authority." I cross my arms, but that doesn't faze Bill. "That's why there's no motivation among the Federal Council to keep meeting. It feels like a waste of time. We're waiting for empty promises to be fulfilled."

"But the president *has* done many things. Yes, I've been disappointed with the lack of authority you've been given, but look at some of the things that have been implemented. Like Public Law 18."

Both men nod when I mention the law President Roosevelt signed last year mandating that the Army Air Corps train Negroes, with a special focus on colored colleges.

"That alone should keep us encouraged," I continue. "Think about how big that is. Negroes will be able to have military careers and then advance beyond working in the kitchen or other menial positions."

I wait for them to respond, but it seems not even something as impactful as that public law impresses them. "Listen, young men, real change takes time." *How many times have I said those words to a young Negro man or woman?*

"While the public law is good, Mary, we need much more than that, and we've given President Roosevelt more than enough time," Bill says, unwavering. "But like the presidents before him, Roosevelt makes promises to get our votes, and then . . . nothing."

"So, what is your solution?" I ask. "To walk away? That doesn't make sense when I have a relationship with the president and First Lady . . ."

Bill holds up his hands. "I don't mean any disrespect, Mary, but part of the problem *is* your relationship with the Roosevelts." The quietness of his voice does not soften his words.

"It's because of Mrs. Roosevelt that we're in the position we're in today," I snap.

"I would agree with you there," Bill says. "Your friendship with Mrs. Roosevelt has hindered the Council rather than helped it."

I breathe deeply, feeling as if my sinuses and my lungs are closing. "How—how has my friendship with the First Lady hindered us?" I demand to know.

Bill leans forward. "After all the work we did for Roosevelt, after all the votes we gave him, when nothing changed, when we were given no more responsibility, when he didn't address voting rights or jobs or better housing, you didn't push him."

I am aghast. "Push the president? How was I supposed to do that?"

He shrugs and sits back. "You stood in front of us at that Council meeting professing to be our voice and our advocate because you had access to the Roosevelts. But not enough has come of that, and many believe that's because you're not only too soft but you've even pandered to the Roosevelts."

I gasp. "Who thinks this?"

Bill holds up his hands. "I'm not going to name any names, because that's not what's important."

I turn my stare on Robert. It is surprising that Bill has been the one doing the talking, while Robert, usually the most outspoken, has stayed quiet. Is that because he disagrees with his friend?

I ask him, "How do you feel about this?"

"Well, I did think we'd be further along because of your relationship with the Roosevelts."

Is that all he has to say? All I want to do is jump out of this bed and shake these men. How can they be so blind? We may not have made the huge strides that they'd hoped for, but steady progress is being made nonetheless. Young people across the country have positions in libraries and public offices. Colored folks in rural areas are working on farms and in construction. Colored girls have jobs cooking and sewing and as nurses. This is more than has ever been achieved.

And I *have* pushed the president. I think about that meeting in Hyde Park. I think about the Blue Book. I have pushed the president and his wife to the edge. Nothing more would be accomplished if I stormed into the White House demanding action. My God, I would be escorted out, never to be invited back.

Taking a deep breath, I steady my voice. "There is no need for us to debate this point any further. What can I do to bring us together and move us forward? Because we need the collective power we bring to the table now more than ever."

Bill shrugs. "What can any of us do? Even if you agreed to be more aggressive with the Roosevelts, we don't have anything to bargain with. The president has already served his two terms, so we can't negotiate with our votes." This young man is wrong about so much—including the assumption that the president isn't running again. Through Eleanor, I know that President Roosevelt is considering an unprecedented third term *because* he wants to make his social programs and policies part of the fabric of this country.

I can't disclose that, though, so I say, "Well, I'm not ready to give up. Even with the little time we have left, we can unite and together push the president. But it makes no sense to do nothing."

The room is church-quiet until Robert finally says, "You know what? Everyone on the Council loves you, Mary. You've been a beacon of light in this struggle, showing us what's possible. So we'll make some telephone calls and let you know what we can do." He glances at Bill, and together they nod.

I thank them for this, and then they kiss me farewell. Once I'm alone, I consider our conversation. No matter what they say, I am not done. Contrary to their claims of softness, there is more I can accomplish with President Roosevelt, especially if he chooses to run again. He will need the Negro vote if he wants a third term. That alone gives me, and every Negro in this country, a power we've never had before.

CHAPTER 53

ELEANOR

Washington, D.C.
June 2, 1940

Just as Mary and I enter the Oval Office, Franklin's guard ushers out two military men in full regalia. In the past few weeks, Germany has invaded Scandinavia; Belgium has surrendered to the Germans; and much of France has fallen, although the French and British troops stranded at Dunkirk were evacuated. Against this backdrop, orchestrating this meeting between Mary and Franklin has been especially hard-won.

"It's wonderful to see you looking as chipper as ever, Mrs. Bethune," Franklin says brightly as Mary and I settle into the chairs opposite his imposing Oval Office desk.

"Yes, we were quite worried about you," I add, acting as if I'm seeing her for the first time upon her return—although we all know that's not true.

"Thank you both. It's wonderful to be back to my old self. Nothing a little rest couldn't cure, especially with all those White House flowers at my bedside."

"It was my pleasure to send a little cheer," I say, and it's true. Joy flitted through me every time a White House gardener showed me a bouquet destined for Mary.

"Anything to help you return to your health. We've needed you here in Washington." Franklin widens his smile just the tiniest amount. It's the grin he brandishes when he really wants something. "I understand you have some items for discussion?"

"I do indeed, sir," Mary answers, her tone pleasant.

"That's grand." He pauses, his eyes becoming a little dimmer as he turns down the charm and raises his political intensity and wariness. It's a shift I've witnessed many times.

I know what's coming. Mary and I spent over two hours at the Council town house last evening, poring over military data, NAACP reports, and *Pittsburgh Courier* articles as we finalized the strategy for this meeting. Her letters to me during her convalescence politely and precisely described how Franklin's failure to deliver on his promises had led to the breakdown of Mary's Federal Council. She persuaded me that something had to be done.

Mary's posture and expression are as determined as ever. She's a formidable negotiator, even for Franklin, who's taken down the most skilled orators. But I wonder if Mary is up to the task, health-wise. She returned to D.C. from her long stint at Johns Hopkins Hospital only yesterday morning, far sooner than I thought possible, and she does seem a little faded and tired, although she waves away my inquiries.

She sips on her glass of water and then clears her throat before speaking. "Mr. President, as you know from my letter, there is significant unrest in my community regarding the commitments we believed we had in place after our last national NYA conference, when you met with me, Dr. Mordecai Johnson, and three other delegates. For example, you supported calls for progress in education, voting rights, jobs, and better housing through the New Deal plans, as well as more Negroes in federal positions—all of which was laid out in the Blue Book. And yet hardly any of those commitments have been met. Even many of those Negroes who managed to land administration positions have been reassigned to defense division positions, usually with lower rank and authority." Her voice is firm and clear. How much stronger she sounds than so many of the male cabinet heads and military leaders I've heard within these walls.

Franklin lowers his spectacles and stares at Mary, the dark circles under his eyes now more apparent. "I am certain you understand that another world war is nipping at our heels. The federal government's attention and resources have been justifiably diverted from the New Deal to the military. As have my attention and resources."

"That is precisely why I am here, Mr. President. I realize the federal government's plate is full, so I'm here to offer you a solution to the problem at hand," she says with a rueful chuckle. "My proposal would help appease the colored factions that are rightly disgruntled and would also aid you in remaining as the country's leader to help safely guide the United States through this dangerous time. If you should even want that, of course, sir."

How nimbly Mary is dancing around the elephant in the room. Speculation and scuttlebutt are running rampant as to whether Franklin will break tradition and announce running for a third term. From our private discussions, I know he believes—and I agree—that we need strong, consistent leadership at this critical juncture.

"What is your proposal?" he asks. "Assuming, for argument's sake only, that I should consider a third term."

"Given the worldwide crises we are facing, this country will need the support and contributions of *all* of its citizens, and Negroes want to help—we want the right to fight." As Mary pauses, I think about our conversations on this topic. The right to fight fascism abroad and racism within the military ranks is important to the colored community. The more colored soldiers are able to achieve in the military, the stronger their arguments for full equality. How can the rights afforded to most Americans be denied those who've fought valiantly for America's freedom, after all?

Mary continues. "But you know what's going on in this country, Mr. President. Negroes rush to enroll and are met with rejection and barriers, then relegated to the most subservient roles if they make their way through. Inclusion can only strengthen the military. Ongoing racism and segregation in the military—combined with exclusion of Negroes from the active defense of our country—weaken the country at a time when we need to show strength."

She scoots to the edge of her seat, and Franklin watches her intently. "I have several suggestions. If immediate action could be made to include the colored population in pilot training and in combat training, Negroes will no longer be assigned only to the lowest of positions. Instead of consigning the few Negroes admitted to segregated labor battalions, we could include those men in integrated combat units. And I'd like to see some colored officers, and improved barracks, of course." With a nod, Mary finishes, "With those things, I believe Negroes would walk to the polls happy."

We both know how critical this next element of the conversation is. I hold my breath as she says it. "And we would overwhelmingly endorse you as the president, if you should choose to serve a third term."

Franklin stares at Mary with those piercing blue eyes of his. What are we to make of this expression? This unusual silence?

With great care, Franklin finally answers, "Mrs. Bethune, I hope you know how much I respect you and the work you do."

"I thank you for those kind words, sir," Mary says with an appreciative nod, but I can see she is bracing herself. This sounds like the beginnings of a rejection.

"And I appreciate the sentiment behind your proposal. You'd like to further the cause of your people while furthering the cause of our nation."

"That's it exactly, Mr. President."

"If I understand you correctly, if I was to help facilitate these measures for Negroes in the military, then you might see fit to publicly support my presidency. If I should choose to pursue a third term, that is?"

"Mr. President, you know that I'll campaign for you regardless, but in terms of rallying my people, I could be a lot more persuasive if you met the commitments that have already been made." Mary's confidence nearly takes my breath away. Very few people hold firm to their audacious asks in the face of a presidential Socratic inquiry.

Franklin actually laughs. "Well, Mrs. Bethune, you make it hard to say no, do you know that?" From the furrow of his brow, I see that he's assessing her request. "Now, I would have to run everything by General Watson, of course, but I might be able to get you some of this. Certainly we should be able to create a couple of schools for colored pilots and combat training. We should be able to have more colored army units—perhaps some antiaircraft battalions, field artillery regiments, and other types. Also, we may be able to consider applications for the officers' corps from colored reservationists. And I don't see why we wouldn't be able to increase the number of enlisted Negroes."

I am shocked. Never in my wildest imaginings did I think that Franklin would acquiesce to so many of Mary's demands. *Mary must be overjoyed.* When I look at her to gauge her reaction, however, I see no evidence of jubilance.

"What about integration of the combat units?" she asks, holding fast to the ultimate prize. Although Mary and I discussed this request, I assumed she'd included it as a negotiating tactic. She had to understand that this leap was too far and wide for Franklin—even if he wasn't going to seek reelection and didn't have to worry about the Southern Democrats.

"Mrs. Bethune, the federal government doesn't have a policy of segregation."

"Of course not, but we both know that while we may not have a policy, we certainly have a practice of segregation in the military. And if the president was to change this practice, then integration would become policy. Even by executive order."

"Mrs. Bethune," he says, "I would not want to jeopardize the significant advancements we might make here today by insisting on a goal that is not attainable at this time."

No, enough with political expedience. It is time to do what's right. And while the war is a horror looming before us, should we not utilize one of its few gifts—the expansive powers given to Franklin in wartime—to make the moral choice? I am about to stand up and make the case when Mary speaks.

"While it breaks my heart that you are not embracing integration at this juncture, I think that I can give my people some peace with the pledges you've made today. I will await formal word from General Watson, but, Mr. President, I am pleased to say that we have come to an agreement," Mary says.

She rises up and reaches across Franklin's desk. While I know Franklin and Mary have had physical contact before in Hyde Park, I'm not sure they've ever had this kind of handshake. One that symbolizes that an actual agreement has been made.

Franklin hesitates before lifting his right hand. After so many years worrying about war and despairing about the limited inroads we've made in equality, hope returns to me as I watch their hands clasp in unity.

CHAPTER 54

MARY

Washington, D.C.
October 9, 1940

The Federal Council had a few good months of unity when my negotiations with the president back in June bore fruit. General Watson confirmed the agreement I reached with the president, and for that glorious stretch, we banded together again.

But then the reports arrived. Colored volunteers were still being turned away at military recruiting stations; the few who were accepted were assigned to performing mess hall duties, shining shoes, or cleaning latrines—or, if they were lucky, they became cooks. The living situations had not improved either. The barracks remained segregated and the conditions for Negroes were still deplorable.

Was President Roosevelt just appeasing me? That's what the Federal Council believes, and week by week, the Council has splintered under the weight of Roosevelt's inaction.

"Mrs. Bethune." I hear Dovey say my name, and it takes me out of my dark thoughts. "Should I send out invitations for Friday's Federal Council meeting?"

How uncanny is her timing? I think. I've just been musing on this.

When I don't answer, she continues, "I know no one has attended for the last few weeks, but if you don't mind my saying, I think we should still send the invitations. You haven't disbanded, and the invitations let them know your expectations."

My smile returns at this excellent suggestion. "You are a wise woman, Dovey Johnson."

"I'll take care of it," she says with a smile and then scurries to her office, right across from mine.

What a gift that young woman has been for me with my work with the government and here at NCNW. She's smart, well organized, and doesn't mind telling me what she thinks. I bless the day I met her grandmother at a political gathering in Charlotte a decade ago.

I return to the piles of paper on my desk. First on my list are thank-yous to those who have contributed to my college, Eleanor and the president among them. Financially, we're still not where we need to be, but with Eleanor's assistance and connections, we are, if not thriving, surviving.

Before I finish the first letter, Dovey returns to my office. "Mr. White is on the line. He says it's urgent."

"All right." I cross the hallway to her office and press the receiver to my ear. "Hello, Walter."

"The president's office has issued a press release about Negroes in the military," he says without greeting.

"Finally." Eleanor and I have been so frustrated with the delay. Making a statement about our agreement is as important as the agreement itself. Now that the announcement has been made, maybe the Federal Council will work together again. "Does it confirm the terms the president and General Watson agreed to with me?"

"It's bad, Mary. Much worse than we could have ever imagined."

Slowly sitting down, I ask, "Did they back away from their promises of pilot and combat training programs?"

"No, they're giving us that."

"What about the promise of more Negroes in elevated military positions?"

"No, they seem to be fine with that, too."

"Then what, Walter?" I ask, not hiding my frustration. "This news isn't bad, and in fact sounds good."

I hear the rustling of paper before Walter says, "Let me summarize the press release for you. It seems that Mr. Woodburn—"

As soon as Walter mentions his name, I groan. Of course Woodburn would have the final say on what would be released to the public.

Walter continues, "Mr. Woodburn announced there would indeed be a War Department policy on Negroes in the military. Very generally, he mentioned that colored men would be permitted to enlist and fight, and there would be a chance for qualified candidates to advance."

I hold my breath. What Walter has told me so far is good news, but I brace myself for the damage Woodburn has undoubtedly done.

"Woodburn closes the statement with this: 'The War Department will maintain its long-term policy of not intermingling white and colored military men in the same unit.'"

"What?" I ask, working hard not to scream the word.

"Can you believe it?" Through the telephone, I feel Walter's wrath.

"But"—I lower my voice—"what is he talking about? The military has *never* had a *policy* of segregation. Perhaps a practice, but it wasn't their publicly stated policy. This makes segregation in the military sound like it's government sanctioned."

"Exactly. It makes it sound like President Roosevelt is taking segregation from standard custom to almost damn near the law."

I shake my head. "This is not President Roosevelt. Steve Woodburn did this," I say through clenched teeth. "He's hated everything we've tried to accomplish, he's hated the access we've had to the president, and this is his way of putting us in our place."

"I agree," Walter exclaims. "Woodburn saw an opportunity to make segregation in the military formal, without legislation. And he took it."

I am seething, but my focus has to be on moving forward, fixing this, finding a solution. "There has to be a way to pull these words back."

"The president needs to do something, Mary. Because if the statement stands, Steve Woodburn will have single-handedly set back Negroes and our fight for equality by decades."

CHAPTER 55

ELEANOR

Washington, D.C.
October 28, 1940

I've lost count of how many phone calls and letters Mary and I have exchanged about Steve Woodburn's destructive public misstatement. My frustration with his manipulative words—paired with my inability to force a public retraction—has been an undercurrent of this reelection campaign. Today in particular, watching Steve as he whispers in Franklin's ear or guides him through the crowd at this Madison Square Garden rally makes me ill, and I swear I see Earl's lip curl at the sight of Steve. How could Franklin have failed to address Steve's lies to the press, no matter my pleading? Is he so concerned about winning in these final days of the campaign that he's forgotten how to do the right thing? Does he ever think about what this is doing to Mary? *Oh, how I miss Louis.*

Standing at Franklin's side in the wings, I watch as a crowd of twenty thousand from all five of Manhattan's boroughs crowds into Madison Square Garden. Hand-lettered posters mixed in with official campaign boards displaying Franklin's portrait are held aloft. With a phalanx of extra security blocking him from public view, Franklin stands up from his wheelchair. He leans on me more than usual, much more than he did back when he first ran for president. I know how tired he is—all the chatting, hand-shaking, and public speaking. Even I am fatigued, and I am not under the constant pressure to force my unwilling body to walk. Then, as if he is the one escorting me, we walk together out onto the stage toward the podium. The applause grows louder and more animated the closer he gets. Amidst the cacophony, I can even hear individual chants for me. The intensity of the attention is dizzying.

I stay at his side as introductory speeches are offered by the head of the Democratic National Committee and New York governor Lehman. Once these men take their seats behind the podium and Franklin is steady at the microphone, I settle into my designated chair. The cheering finally dies down as Franklin begins.

With a powerful voice, he opens: "Nothing is more important than the pursuit of peace for our country!" He knows this is what the people want to hear.

Franklin then launches into the importance of military preparation—even if we are attempting peace—and how ready our army and navy truly are. Explaining why Republican comments to the contrary must be disregarded, he describes how such statements are misinformation bandied about for cynical election campaigns, and how those same Republicans described the American military as overprepared during federal budget talks mere months earlier. He concludes with a rousing call to end fearmongering and to pray for peace—even as we keep preparing for every eventuality.

Negroes in the crowd are nodding along, and I think how much stronger our country would be if they were permitted to train and fight alongside their fellow white citizens. How can we call people citizens and not allow them the right to fight? How can we position ourselves time and again for the colored vote but not offer them the chance to do what every other voting man of a particular age in our country can do—protect our land? These are the sorts of questions Mary is fending off daily from her fractured Federal Council.

Balloons sail through the air, and the band plays a joyous tune as

Franklin concludes. I walk to his side and wave at the sea of people. "Are you ready?" I whisper, at which he nods.

I slip my arm through his, and we make our way offstage behind a line of security guards both protecting him and masking his walking from the crowds. It's a maneuver we've practiced hundreds if not thousands of times by this point. I still get nervous, though, bracing for that catastrophic fall. All it takes is one tumble.

Backstage, we greet the senior members of the Democratic National Committee, donors, and New York politicians. I say a brief hello to Marion and Nan, who've taken the train from Hyde Park for this momentous campaign event at Sara's invitation, but they are cold to me. Funny how these friends who were instrumental in showing me a fresh way of life for women seem incapable of flexibility. In this way, they are disappointingly like so many others who can see people only through the narrow lens of their own needs. Like Hick, from whom I've also grown apart. I was attracted to her for her strength, but as I got stronger under her tutelage, she seemed to need me more but like me less.

Very quickly, Franklin is ushered to his wheelchair, which resembles a wooden seat, where he receives several more senior folks. My husband appears so jovial and lighthearted, one might almost forget that Italy invaded Greece today; that the British people are suffering through the Blitz as we speak; that the Axis powers of Germany, Italy, and Japan are plotting the downfall of the Allies, and America along with them. Looking at Franklin's wide, easy grin, one might fail to remember that, too soon, our sons could be conscripted onto battlefields.

Suddenly, Steve Woodburn announces, "The president and First Lady will be leaving momentarily so they can return by train to Washington, D.C., this evening. I will remain behind to take a few questions from the press." He nods toward a small group of key reporters from major newspapers who have been granted special access.

Security detail and assistants in tow, Franklin and I make our way by automobile to Penn Station and onto our special train cars. It takes a fair bit of time to get him organized and situated, and when I finally settle on the upholstered bench and tuck my now-wrinkled green silk dress around my legs, the exhaustion hits me immediately. I'm ready to depart and get back to my Washington, D.C., bed, but Steve still hasn't returned by the time Franklin wants to pull out.

"By God, where is Woodburn? I've got meetings in the morning, and I don't want to get back too late," he complains when Steve still doesn't appear fifteen minutes later. "The European developments are coming in fast and furious. Woodburn knows that better than anyone. We will have to leave without him if he doesn't board soon."

"I don't know, Franklin. He's not one for tardiness; something must be holding him back," I answer, half listening as I glance out the window.

A skirmish seems to have broken out near the guarded entrance to the special presidential train. I can only see the backs of two police officers as they attempt to restrain a man trying to push through the security line. More policemen join their fellow officers, and I begin to worry that this might be an angry citizen—or, worse, the rumored agent of the Axis powers who wants to inflict harm upon Franklin.

"Franklin, does this look like something we should be concerned about?"

He wheels himself over to the window. Together we watch as the man lunges at one of the officers, kicking him so hard that the policeman falls to the ground. The officer writhes, and we can see his face clearly through the train car window. The policeman is colored; he must be one of the very few Negroes in the NYPD ranks.

"My God," Franklin says.

"What?" I look away from the poor fallen officer to Franklin. His face is aghast.

While the officers' attention is on their fellow policeman, the perpetrator pushes past them toward the train. And I see why Franklin has reacted—the man is Steve Woodburn.

As Steve races toward the train and sirens sound, I instruct Earl to find out what's going on and to make sure the policeman is all right. Then I return to Franklin. "Enough is enough. Steve Woodburn has done enough damage to our Negro citizens. First and foremost, you must make Steve apologize publicly to the NYPD commissioner for this terrible action and to this policeman specifically. He has physically injured a member of the police force who was just trying to protect us, and that is unacceptable. Steve Woodburn is not above the law. Second, I'm finished with the hemming and hawing on your part and the part of your military leaders. Steve's mischaracterization of the agreement you reached with Mary makes it sound as if the federal government formally approves segregation! You must force him to issue a correction and a public apology."

Franklin's eyes never leave the policeman, who is now being loaded onto a stretcher by medics. "I'll make sure he clarifies his statement and issues an apology in the morning."

"And?" I ask, prompting him for the other piece—the actions he promised.

"And I'll push the generals to incorporate colored soldiers in the army's officer corps and appoint senior colored officers to the War Department, including a brigadier general and an undersecretary of war. I'll make a public statement to that effect."

I nod, but I don't speak. If Franklin thinks I am going to thank him for these actions, he is wrong. This should have been done immediately after Steve issued that spurious statement.

When Franklin looks at me, his eyes are sad and tired. Then, he says the very hardest thing for him to admit. "It seems that Mary has been right all along about Steve. As have you."

CHAPTER 56

MARY

Daytona Beach, Florida
January 20, 1941

The record on my phonograph has just begun playing when my front door opens and Albert steps inside.

> *Southern trees bear a strange fruit*
> *Blood on the leaves . . .*

Our eyes meet as the haunting words reverberate through the room, then he takes a seat across from where I'm sitting on the sofa.

"You have regrets about the election?"

I am shocked those are his first words, without a hello. "Why would you ask me that?"

He shrugs. "I come to visit you, and you don't have the inauguration playing on the radio. Instead, I hear 'Strange Fruit' on the phonograph. What else should I think but that you're having second thoughts about Roosevelt's third term?"

Interesting that he makes a connection between this song about lynching and President Roosevelt. I'm sure my son is thinking about the failure of the anti-lynching bill, which he blames on the president. But I say, "I have no regrets about the election."

"Even after you traveled every road, every byway, in this country, taking the Negro vote away from the party that delivered our freedom to the party that has delivered nothing?" His tone teeters between sadness and anger, but most of all, there is disappointment in his eyes. He seems unable to see my point of view in our political discussions. And yet he's summed up the last few months of my life with great astuteness.

The final months of the campaign were grueling. Not only did I wear myself to the bone with endless speeches in countless Southern counties, but I had to fight to get the splintering Federal Council behind President Roosevelt. It was only after the president corrected Woodburn's pernicious statement and then publicly announced his position on changes he wanted to see in the military that the Council came on board to support Roosevelt's bid for a third term.

Suddenly, Albert begins to slow clap, breaking through my thoughts. "Congratulations on your victory."

I don't respond to my son's sarcasm. Instead, we listen in silence to Billie sing the story. Her voice, filled with gravel and grit, etches the images of the song's words in my mind. I see the strange fruit of the lynched folks about which Billie sings, and tears sting my eyes. The song is slow and poignant, with more words than notes, and my heart constricts with each stanza. When she gets to the last line and sings about the bitter crop, I close my eyes and pray for all the souls who've hung from trees.

Albert's heels click against the wooden floorboards as he crosses the room. By his movements, I know he's at the phonograph turning over the vinyl. When the needle hits the record, Billie sings a new song: "*My man don't love me . . .*"

I open my eyes as Albert loosens his tie, then returns to where he was sitting. "You want some dinner? Mrs. Brown made my favorite." I try to tempt him with the fried chicken, mashed potatoes smothered with butter and gravy, and mustard greens with pork bits that he knows will be served shortly. Most of that dinner, especially the fried chicken, is against my doctor's orders; my weight remains of grave concern as my bronchitis flares again.

He shakes his head. "I'm gonna eat when I get home. Just came by to check on you."

"I'm fine," I insist.

"Between the music and your decision to skip the inauguration, I'm thinking maybe you're not fine."

"Maybe you should stop doing so much thinking and focus on what you know. You know I didn't go because of my doctor's recommendation."

"When have doctors' orders ever stopped you from doing what you want to do?"

Folding my arms, I say, "Sounds like you don't want me to be fine."

I hope he'll carefully choose his words so this conversation will not escalate. "Of course I want you to be fine, Mother Dear, but I'm hoping you'll think about how you helped to elect a white supremacist to the White House and you'll do something about this."

My lips hardly move when I say, "The Roosevelts are not white supremacists!"

Albert gives me a one-shoulder shrug. "You're the one who taught me you're known by the company you keep. And President Roosevelt's company—"

"Did you notice the man you voted for has been a Republican for about two weeks?" I ask, exaggerating only slightly. "Wendell Willkie changed his party affiliation just to run for president. So essentially it was a Democrat running against a Democrat."

He chuckles, although there is no joy in the sound. "Willkie has been fighting against the Klan for years, and what about Roosevelt? He has Southerners in the highest positions in the White House and then stands by while one of his men runs around assaulting Negroes. That colored cop his man attacked in New York was hurt so bad, I heard that even Joe Louis went to see him," my son says, referring to all the newspaper coverage of the heavyweight boxing champion visiting the officer.

I sigh. Albert is right. The president is surrounded by many who obstruct our fight for equality. Some in his inner circle behave as if they don't even want the colored vote, almost as if they'd rather lose without it than win with it.

"Willkie promised that, under his administration, he would fight to end segregation. And what does Roosevelt do about segregation?" Albert stops and waits for me to speak. When I remain silent, he nods. "Exactly. Roosevelt has done nothing, and still, you turned Negroes against Republicans."

My eyes narrow. "I didn't turn Negroes against anything. I turned them toward hope and a future. President Roosevelt developed programs that can greatly benefit us, and that's all I care about, Albert. Using our voices and casting our votes for the party that is going to do the most good . . . or the least harm. We can't afford to be devoted to one party; we must be committed to supporting the best policies for us. And sometimes that may mean supporting the party that will do nothing over the party that will do everything to harm us."

He shakes his head. "That's a hard choice."

I nod and pray that he now understands. Certainly, I've reached thousands of Negroes in the South with those words. After a moment, Albert slaps his hands on his thighs. "Well, I've checked on you, you're good, it's time for me to get home."

"Was it something I said?" I ask, my voice light.

No matter his beliefs, he grins, and it breaks the tension. My son gets his love for our country and politics from me, so I can hardly blame him for his passion. But it's hard to be on opposing sides. Albert believes that I have let him and the party of Lincoln and Frederick Douglass down. But what he has to understand is that, with Roosevelt, we really do have opportunities like never before. And I constantly press for more, deluging Eleanor with letters about getting a Negro judge a federal appointment, giving more federal defense jobs to colored workers, and even asking her to join me at the Delta Sigma Theta Sorority, Inc., national convention in Detroit so that we can rally those women to serve as the country prepares for war. I've pushed for so much that I worry about the pressure my demands put on our friendship.

Albert moves to my side of the table and wraps me in his arms. "Even though you are wrong, I still love you, Mother Dear."

"I love you, too, son." When he walks out the door, I sit for a few moments, the weariness taking hold. This decades-long fight is like a spinning wheel—going round and round, getting nowhere. But it's disingenuous for any of us to say that no progress has been made.

Standing, I move to the phonograph and flip the vinyl back to where I started, and once again, the mournful sounds fill my home. Billie Holiday sings because she never wants us to forget, and I listen for the same reason. White folks want us to move on from all the violence that is perpetrated against us, but how can we, when we're faced with their brutality daily?

Even as I campaigned for President Roosevelt, I met the family of Austin Callaway, a sixteen-year-old who was dragged from a jail in Georgia and murdered by a mob. As Austin's mama sobbed into my bosom, it wasn't lost on me that I was asking her to vote for the man who didn't support punishing the men who killed her son, the man who let the anti-lynching bill die.

That bill is dead, but I am not. As God is my witness, I will continue this fight until an anti-lynching bill is passed through Congress. Whether it happens with President Roosevelt, or the next president, or the next, "Strange Fruit" will play in my home until lynching is no longer in the fabric of America.

CHAPTER 57

ELEANOR

Washington, D.C.
January 20, 1941

How different this formal inaugural occasion is from the carefree assembly at Hyde Park last weekend! Oh, the happiness that coursed through me when Anna and her family arrived from Seattle and stepped into the Big House. The children and their families, Franklin, Sara, and I shared two glorious days, when we walked through the woods, ate entirely too much, and talked until well past midnight. Even a heated discussion between Franklin and me about his choice for a political appointment and the occasional awkward appearance of Marion and Nan at meals didn't affect the merry mood. I was disappointed on Sunday when we had to return to the capital.

The irony is not lost on me. I should be euphoric to be commemorating Franklin's historic victory as a third-term president, but instead I feel torn between happiness for our country and worry over the personal cost to me and Franklin. If I'd stayed closer to Marion and Nan, or even Hick, then I might have shared my inner turmoil with them, but those friendships have long been hobbled. My secret conflict must remain just that. Mary is the only other person I'd consider talking to about it, but how can I burden her with this confession when she's sacrificed so much—even her health—to make this third term happen? And anyway, Franklin's presidency is the best thing for the country.

I try not to think about the weight of this day as we gather on the East Portico of the Capitol Building for the swearing-in ceremony. Instead, I focus on the robin's-egg blue sky and the bright, chunky rays of sun streaming down upon us. Turning my face toward the light, I allow it to warm me on this crisp January day.

As the oath of office finishes, I smile over at my nineteen family members and out at the American people from the dais in front of the Capitol, as if this bright sunny January day brings me nothing but joy. I pointedly arrange my stance so that Earl's profile blocks Steve Woodburn. Unfortunately, Steve has cemented his position with this victory, but today I refuse to consider him.

As James did in the first two inaugurations, he walks Franklin to the podium, where he readies to give his speech. His voice sounds wonderfully strong and reassuring, despite the fact that I can see exhaustion and worry on his face. I hope his speech bolsters the millions of Americans who've spent the past several years battered from within by the Depression and without by threats of fascism.

Subtly, he shifts gears. He draws a parallel between the nation and a human body that needs to be properly "housed and fed and educated"—my suggestion—and I could jump for joy. The mention is brief, and he quickly moves back to our international responsibilities, but Franklin has done as I asked.

Is Mary listening by radio? How unfair that she's too ill to attend. I hope she hears Franklin's words. How hard we've worked these weeks between the election and inauguration to meet some of our goals before the specter of war becomes manifest—in judge appointments, military opportunities, and New Deal postings. But it's not enough; she and I both know that well.

As we move away from the Capitol Plaza ahead of the crowds to the White House to watch the inaugural parade, Anna leans over and whispers to me, "I think it went well, don't you, Mother?"

How lovely my only daughter looks today. I am so touched that she chose a dress, coat, and hat in a shade that the press has dubbed "Eleanor blue." As she gets older, her appreciation for me grows, and our closeness along with it.

"I do, dear," I say. "I am well pleased with the balance of messaging your father managed to pull off."

"It was no mean feat to fit in your aims alongside his," John chimes in behind us, still the eavesdropper at the ripe age of twenty-four. I smile at my handsome youngest. In his career and his beliefs, he is determined to carve out an independent path from that of his father and feels strongly about peace in lieu of war.

John draws closer, and I reach for his hand and Anna's, squeezing tightly as we mount the steps to the replica of Andrew Jackson's Hermitage constructed in front of the White House. There the grinning faces of my other children await us. Anna's husband, James' wife, Elliott and his wife, Brud and his wife, and a gaggle of grandchildren are all arranged on the dais; only James is absent, as he's helping Franklin.

I wonder when war will divide my family. Tears well up at the thought. *No,* I tell myself as I think of all the mothers and sons in the crowd today, *you will not cry.* This nation is in the best hands possible for the crisis ahead, and I must be strong. I paint a smile on my lips and prepare for the parade.

There will be no homemade floats and no spectacle. The news from Europe is too grim for that; in fact, a dreaded meeting between Mussolini and Hitler took place during the inauguration. But our armed forces will be in full regalia, marching down Pennsylvania Avenue.

I hear the clip of military boots proceeding in unison. As the soldiers materialize, a murmur ripples across the replica Hermitage. But I just smile. There, marching before us, is the Virginia colored cavalry regiment. I'm sure Mary will see their presence in the papers and hear about it on the radio. I hope it brings her some satisfaction to see the colored soldiers marching alongside the white ones. Still, watching *all*

316 MARIE BENEDICT AND VICTORIA CHRISTOPHER MURRAY

our boys prepare for war seems a terrible thing to celebrate, even though this brief integration is a victory for which we fought hard.

Our tactics are going to have to change. The New Deal programs will be cut, so we will have to figure out new ways to make progress. But one thing is clear: Mary and I will continue to fight for equality—together. It is a war I'm determined that we will win.

CHAPTER 58

MARY

Washington, D.C.
April 20, 1941

If I had a gavel, I'd shut down all this cross-talking among Federal Council members. "Gentlemen," I call out, glancing around the jam-packed conference room. I feel the judgment in each set of eyes.

"Robert Weaver has asked for the floor, and we must give it to him," I say.

"Thank you, Mary." Robert nods at me. "Because of the coming war, we are being marginalized more than ever. We must find another way to make colored citizens part of the national plans. No one can placate us this time. And a march on Washington, D.C., is the only way the president will understand we mean business," he cries out, as if he's in an auditorium rather than in the conference room in the NCNW town house.

Chatter takes over the room. It's disconcerting that this message is coming from Robert. In the seven years I've known him, the now thirty-four-year-old has always displayed youthful impatience. But because he continually found a way to temper his frustration, he's supported me.

Not anymore, it appears, and although I fiercely disagree, I understand. So much has happened since his early days, when he worked with Clark Foreman and the Office of the Economic Status of Negroes. Since then, Robert has been moved from agency to agency, his responsibilities diminished, and now, like the others, he feels ignored by the administration. So of course he would seek another way. It's not a surprise that, along with these other young men, he has decided that working within the system no longer works. But why must they join A. Philip Randolph and his March on Washington movement?

Mr. Randolph organized this country's first predominately colored labor union. Recently, he's been working with Walter, Robert, and others to move President Roosevelt toward integrating the military and ending racial discrimination in the defense industry. His objectives are no different than mine. But when the president refused to act on integration as Mr. Randolph urged, Mr. Randolph decided a new approach is necessary, one involving a hundred thousand colored people descending on Washington and marching up to the White House doors.

I am not unsympathetic to the Federal Council's anger, but a march will not deliver the results we desire. The president and his men will not see it as the peaceful demonstration that Randolph claims it will be. In fact, I imagine the thousands of Negroes will be up against red-faced policemen slinging batons and leather saps and leaving severely injured and even dead men in their wake.

"Please, gentlemen, your attention!" It is the raising of my voice that finally restores order. "Robert, I agree with many of your points. I just disagree with your strategy."

A few in the room nod in agreement, but most stare me down without a glimpse of a smile.

"You don't seem to have heard a thing I said!" he shouts.

"Robert," I say, careful to keep my tone even and my frustration hidden. "Certainly you don't think there's a correlation between my agreeing and my hearing." A few men snicker, and that lowers the temperature a tad.

"So, if you hear me, what approach would you advocate?" Robert asks, his voice quieter and his tone softer. "I've watched you all these years, Mary, and I've tried it your way. But then Roosevelt allowed Woodburn to make that statement practically establishing segregation in the military—"

I interrupt him, "A statement President Roosevelt retracted because of me."

He nods. "But since that time, Mary, we've only taken baby steps toward our goals, and even then, every step we take is always in danger of being ripped away. We can no longer leave our issues to this intentionally deaf and purposefully blind administration. We must take a step they cannot block out."

A chorus of "Hear, hear!" follows his words.

"There are other ways."

"What other ways?" He feigns wide-eyed innocence. "More pandering? Haven't you done enough of that already? Have the Roosevelts not used you enough?"

Even though this isn't the first time I've heard this, his words sting. While I agree the president moves slowly and always errs on the side of political expediency, the same cannot be said of Eleanor. She has taken every one of our grievances to her husband. She never falters, always supporting me and every man in this room.

"You're supposed to be our leader, Mary, not the cheerleader for the Roosevelts. Without you turning the colored vote to the Democratic Party, that man would have never been reelected for a third time. Hell, he wouldn't have won a second term without us. You did that, Mary." Robert taps his finger against the table, emphasizing each word. "You did that for him, and both you and the president need to remember that. We need you, Mary, to be our leader again. Stop catering to them and start collecting our due."

His words feel like a sharp slap and ring in my ears.

We need you, Mary, to be our leader again. Stop catering to them.

My first instinct is to grab my cane, slam it against the table, and tell Robert and these young upstarts that I have been on the front line

of this struggle since most of them were still waddling around in dia-
pers. But this is business, so I keep my emotions at bay. I meet Robert's
gaze, my eyes blazing with all the anger I feel. "The one thing no one
can ever accuse me of is pandering."

"All I'm saying is that the tactics of the past will not work in the
present. As a third-term president, I'm sure Roosevelt feels invincible.
He's already received our votes, so now Negroes don't matter."

"Why does it always come down to this? Why do I always have to
recite a list of what's been done? Bill," I say, turning to Bill Hastie,
"you have your new appointment in the War Department because the
president was responding to our requests." Then, to all of them, I say,
"The president has appointed the first Negro general, and that's a big
achievement. Everyone in this room has benefited from a gain instituted at the hands of the Roosevelts."

"And that's fine, but, Mary," Robert says, continuing the debate,
"that was the past. We're talking about what needs to be done now.
Look how easily he's gearing this country up to fight fascism when he
has the same issues right here at home. His own colored citizens don't
have the benefits of democracy, yet he's willing to fight for those freedoms across the Atlantic. Should he not have the same concerns for
Negro Americans?" He shakes his head. "Either he takes action or we
march."

More than half of the men in the room cheer. For the first time
since this Federal Council was formed, I feel as if I am the lone voice
of reason. "What do you think will happen if one hundred thousand
Negroes show up in Washington? What do you think Roosevelt will
do? What do you think Congress will do? Who will be on our side
then? And what about Steve Woodburn? You know he'll stir things up
with the press and police."

"None of that frightens me," Robert says. "I'm a colored man in
America, and at any time, I'm very likely to end up on the wrong end
of a white man's bad day. I'd rather go down fighting for my freedoms—
including the right to go into battle for America, even as this country

won't fight for me. I'd rather do that than die a slow death by pandering."

It is time to end this meeting. "We will not be marching."

But Robert stands up, shocking me and staring me down from the other end of the table. "Mary, you're a celebrity out there," he says, pointing over his shoulder. "But in here, you're just one vote. And we say we're marching, and there's nothing you or anyone can do to stop us."

Declarations of "No more," "Exactly," and "Never again" ring out, and I see Walter White, with his arms crossed, standing alone in the corner. He and I have been together in this fight the longest, yet he nods along with the others.

I will not be able to convince them today. I will simply have to find another, compelling way of my own.

CHAPTER 59

ELEANOR

Washington, D.C.
April 22, 1941

I greet my friend on the driveway with an embrace and usher her upstairs to my sitting room as if this was an ordinary visit in ordinary times. Inquiring after the two Alberts as well as her health as we walk, I act as though we're about to sit down for tea and catch up on each other's news. Yet the topics we will cover today won't consist of many personal tidbits.

"Good morning, Miss Thompson," Mary greets Tommy, who's been stationed at my sitting room desk, poring through letters. Tommy stands, and the two women shake hands. They've grown close over the years.

"Jeepers, how many times do I have to ask you to call me Tommy? Everyone else does," Tommy mock-scolds.

"Probably as many times as the First Lady has asked you to call her Eleanor. And you still call her Mrs. Roosevelt," Mary says with a wink, and the two women laugh.

Tommy excuses herself, and a White House maid enters with the tea service I requested and the pastries I know Mary likes. Teacups in hand, we settle onto opposite ends of my deep, cushiony sofa. "I think I know what's brought you here today," I say.

"You mean beyond our usual plans to utterly alter the country through equality for all?" Mary says, and we laugh.

Allowing our laughter to recede, I say, "I'm guessing it's about this March on Washington that Mr. Randolph has planned." The rumors have been percolating for weeks, and I'm alarmed. A large-scale march could erupt in bloodshed.

"Exactly. I wanted you to hear the news from me."

"What news?"

"I am going to have to back the march. There has been a ground-swell of support for it, and people are energized by the thought of this mass nonviolent protest. I will not release any public statements—our enemies would have a field day with that—but I will be bolstering it in practice."

I expected a thorny discussion, but not this. I'm astounded. The press and Democrats will interpret the March as anti-Roosevelt, be-cause it condemns the status quo for Negroes and calls specifically for Franklin to do more. Bolstering it? "Wh-what do you mean?"

"Next week, I'll be announcing that my annual NCNW conference will take place from June 28 to June 30 in Washington, D.C., which will enable attendees to easily attend the march on July 1."

A strange blend of fear, anger, and empathy takes hold of me. Then an almost familiar sense of abandonment crashes over me, and I choke out an accusation of sorts. "So you want to make it easy for thousands of colored women to participate in the march."

"Yes," Mary answers quietly, then stares down at the floor as if the rug's pattern is of utmost interest. "If I do not sanction the march in this way, I fear it will do more harm."

"Funny," I respond, my tone unexpectedly sharp, "I was thinking that supporting the march would do more damage to all our progress than if we stopped it. The only thing such a stance might benefit is maintaining your dominant role with your Federal Council."

Even though I sound angry, I mostly feel hurt. We have worked together for so long—how could Mary take an action that would cast aspersions on my efforts? Does she not have faith that I've done my utmost for the cause of civil rights? I've always thought of Mary as the one person in my life *not* propelled by personal desires and the things I can give her. But it seems as though I haven't done enough, and once more, I am alone.

We sit in silence for an unbearably long and heavy moment. Since some initial missteps, Mary and I have been in sync about our objectives and strategy, and now that we are misaligned, the distance between us feels vast.

"Eleanor, I am sorry," she finally says, her voice heavy with remorse. "I do not want this, and believe me, if I thought that we could slow or halt Randolph's freight train, I would try. In fact, I did try. I offered to pursue the Federal Council's goals behind the scenes in lieu of a march, but they are tired of relying on my connections with you and your husband to make change. In fact, they called it pandering, so Robert and Bill—and even Walter, if you can believe it—rejected my overtures. If I persist in my anti-march stance, then I'll be alienated from the Federal Council forever, and all the private work you and I do will have no support from my community."

Tears of anger and hurt stream down my face. Mary scoots down the sofa to embrace me, but I do not soften. She says, "I apologize. The last thing I wanted was for this news to upset you. I am behind you and the president—not against you—and I know what allies you've been. That's why I wanted to tell you myself, so that you'd understand I'm positioning myself this way only to walk a necessary narrow line, and only temporarily."

I steady myself and try to put myself in her shoes. "Mary, I realize you're in an impossible bind and feel pressure to push for governmental change, but I wonder if supporting the march really is your only option. You know the message it sends. And you can imagine how it makes me feel—" Before I can finish, she interjects.

"I feel terrible."

"I do, too," I say with a sigh, and give myself a minute to think all this through. "I apologize that I took your news so personally. I realize that you and the Federal Council are only fighting for what you are rightly owed. It saddens me that I couldn't make enough of a difference, and I'm upset because I feel like Sisyphus. We keep pushing that boulder up the hill, and time and again, it rolls back on us. The progress we've managed to orchestrate with jobs or education or training or support isn't enough—or there is awful retaliation to it. But I have no right to these tears. Look how much you've suffered and how long you've been in this fight."

"I understand why you feel hurt. Just because you're white doesn't mean you can't get angry or disheartened by racism." She tsks me in a comforting way that's almost maternal. "I just wish it was all different. And I wish I had another choice."

"These tears aren't just about you, Mary. I feel so alone in this White House, just as you must feel sometimes with the Federal Council." Mary nods, and I continue. "The malicious gaze of Steve Woodburn is always upon me, judging me and forcing all eyes on war, war, war. Even the day of the inauguration, the Lend-Lease aid for Britain became the primary focus, and now we are facing Allied defeats in the Middle East, labor strikes across the country delaying defense production, seizure of Axis assets, and constant air raids on Great Britain. And while I do understand we could be fighting for global freedom, I also know that we still need to fight for the rights of our own citizens here at home." I pause for breath, stopping myself before blurting out the possible jeopardy to Mary's precious NYA. It is a bridge that Mary and I will have to cross, but perhaps not today.

Changing tack, I say, "Sometimes I wonder if we are throwing ourselves into this war because it's one way of ceasing this endless Depression."

"Boy, I wish you were the one in the Oval Office," Mary says, chortling to herself as she reaches for a pastry.

I relax. Between the chuckle and the sweet treat, the air has cleared.

I may not like what she's doing with the march, but we can move forward as we always have.

"Louis Howe used to say that, too," I say offhandedly. "He used to say that he'd make me president after Franklin was through with government. I often wonder what would have happened if Louis hadn't died."

"I bet you miss him," Mary says softly.

"I do. Every day."

Thinking of Louis and his faith in me, my resolve returns. I wipe my eyes with the lace handkerchief I keep in my sleeve and say, "Well, that's enough of the self-pity and blubbering and making you feel guilty for something you shouldn't. Never mind my hurt feelings—my biggest fear is that, if the march goes forward, violence will result. I understand the Federal Council believes the march is the only way, but I am wondering what I can do, Mary, to help stop it without tainting you by association. What will it take?"

CHAPTER 60

MARY

Washington, D.C.
June 18, 1941

Pushing aside the curtain from the parlor windows, I peek onto Vermont Avenue as I have every five minutes for the past hour. Are the men en route? It's been over two hours since the White House appointment began. Is that a good sign or a bad one? I am filled with worry over the most important meeting ever to happen between President Roosevelt and Negro leaders.

It took a lot of frank talk and many apologies for the Federal Council members to consider a meeting with the president. But I couldn't serve as go-between as usual. These men, who've been my friends for decades, don't trust me.

After I spoke with Eleanor, she reached out to the men who would make a difference at this meeting: Philip, of course, since the march was his idea; Walter White, because no decision could be made without the head of the NAACP; and Robert Weaver, because the great debater, as I've come to call him, represents all the other men on the Council.

Eleanor told the three that they have her support for ending discrimination in the military and defense industries. Then she invited them to lunch at the White House, where the men presented her with a report on the employment statistics and treatment of Negroes in the military. She promised to take that information straight to the president.

All of that was not enough. Philip, Walter, and Robert told Eleanor a face-to-face meeting would be necessary. And only once the president made certain commitments during that meeting would they consider calling off the march slated for July 1.

Eleanor did everything she could to make it happen. That meeting was scheduled for this morning, and I can hardly wait to see what happened.

Stepping away from the window, I sit on the sofa. Over my shoulder, I hear the whispers from the conference room where some of the men from the Council have been waiting.

"Calm down, Mary Jane," I murmur, and send up a prayer for the Lord's best.

I jump up when I hear the knock. When I swing open the door, Walter walks in first, leading the delegation of three. Each passes by me silently, moving straight through the parlor to the conference room. I search their faces for a sign, but I can read nothing. Once we are all assembled around the table, I am the first to ask, "How did it go?" My heart is racing.

Finally, Philip relieves us from this misery. "Well, the meeting wasn't just with the president. He was surrounded by military men and war advisers, flanked on all sides."

Philip continues, "But from the moment we walked into the Oval Office, Walter, Robert, and I felt like the president was really listening, even though some of his military men were resistant to just about everything we were saying. I think these last weeks of gossip about the march primed the president. He wants to stop it, so he was finally ready to listen and talk today."

"Even still," Walter picks up, "we took nothing for granted. We presented our information and made our case as if these were new ideas, as if we hadn't been asking the president for the same thing for months."

"So after a two-hour meeting—" Walter stands up and announces, "President Roosevelt has agreed to issue an executive order bringing an end to any discrimination that exists in the military." The three men break into the widest smiles.

I grip the edge of the table as the room reverberates with cheers. *The Holy Grail,* I think. Right now, this federal order will be limited to the military, but it is an astonishing precedent for any institution. "So it's done?" I ask, doing my best to keep my breathing even.

Since everyone in the room is standing except for me, Walter reaches for my hand and pulls me up. "Once the president agreed to it, he left us alone with his military advisers to draft an order. We went back and forth, but we agreed upon language banning discrimination in the armed forces and in defense jobs. It will be memorialized by a government lawyer tomorrow and circulated for all of us to review. Then, if we're comfortable, we'll cancel the march."

One of the men calls out, "What about desegregation?"

Walter holds up his hands. "I think we'll get everything but that specific integration language," he admits.

"This is a big first step," Philip reminds them. "What President Roosevelt is doing is unprecedented. When he signs this executive order, it will move the needle. Colored men will be treated equally in the military. The military will provide good jobs so that Negroes will be able to build secure futures in the armed forces. No president has ever taken these steps for us."

My heart swells at his encouraging words.

Then one of the younger members of the Council says, "Mary, it's a good thing I brought that champagne."

As the men shake hands and slap backs, Walter sidles up to me. "I know you don't drink, but can you make an exception today?"

I tilt my head. "Why? We've had victories before."

He nods. "Yes, but this was almost too easy, Mary. The president was ready to do this only because of you and Eleanor. You two made history today. This executive order would not have happened without the two of you. A nation thanks you, and all of us in this room owe you an apology."

I press my hand against my chest. I hope from this point forward these men will see that a seat at the table, even if it's in the back, is better than no seat, no table, no invitation at all.

When the men bring out the champagne and glasses, I tap Walter's arm. "You're right, this is big. Maybe I'll have two sips."

He grins. "Just have one. Save the second sip for when this deal is completely done."

CHAPTER 61

ELEANOR

Campobello Island, Canada
June 25, 1941

I feel lighter than I have for a long time. I've left behind the oppressive humidity of Washington and cast off the heavy weight of the impending war, if only for a few days. Soon after I set out for the holiday home that once brought Franklin and me joy, Germany invaded Russia. This was a move that surprised Russia but wasn't entirely unexpected by the Allies, though it did put American planning in some disarray. Franklin wasn't joining us anyway and we were already en route, so we continued to Campobello Island.

"Mrs. Roosevelt, it's even lovelier than you described," Mr. Lash calls over to me. He is overseeing the unloading of our trunks and baggage from the ferry.

This young man, a former Communist and now an organizer of the Student Leadership Institute, impressed me when we met two years ago. After working with him and his organization, I decided to let him use the Campobello house for a monthlong summer camp for his students. Franklin believes that Mr. Lash is another stray—one of my ragtag rescue projects he likes to tease me about—and, glancing over at the earnest fellow, I chuckle, thinking Franklin might be right. Although my track record is not always successful. Look where my efforts got me with Marion and Nan, although they rescued me in some ways. Or even my poor brother Hall, whose alcoholic ways have landed him in a small cabin on the Hyde Park property since he lost his engineering job and his family cut him off. How I hope this "rescue project" turns out differently.

"It is, Mr. Lash, isn't it?" I answer. Staring out at the vast expanse of navy blue ocean juxtaposed with the dark emerald of the evergreen trees covering the island, I think about the summers we spent here when the children were small. We'd sail together along the Maine coast, returning to the lovely red-shingled house that my mother-in-law gifted to us as a belated wedding present in 1908. Although Sara hasn't yet arrived for the season, our home is next door to her cottage, the same one where Franklin spent his childhood summers. This rock-ringed, evergreen-laden island in the Bay of Fundy across from Maine is indescribably beautiful. I've always lamented the fact that our regular Campobello jaunts as a family dried up when Franklin's illness made it nearly impossible for him to visit. The terrain is simply too hard for him to navigate.

With the bags crammed into the waiting automobile, Mr. Lash, Tommy, Earl, and I squeeze into the back of the already crowded car. As we drive to the house, I congratulate myself on not leaving its seasonal opening to an assistant. That was my initial plan, but when it became clearer that the March on Washington was not going to happen, I leapt at the opportunity to accompany Mr. Lash. With war on the way, who knows when the chance could come again?

As we pass the large hotels established here in the late 1800s to serve the wealthy families from Boston, Philadelphia, Montreal, and New York desperate to escape the sweltering heat, I'm grateful that Franklin's parents adored Campobello Island enough to build their own compound. With its saltwater coves, vast forests, beaches of gravel and sand, high cliffs, and breathtaking array of wildlife, it is truly a place like no other.

Our longtime seasonal housekeeper awaits us, although, to my surprise, she's not lingering at the front door. She strides directly toward me. "Mrs. Roosevelt," she says, handing me an envelope, "this telegraph came for you more than two hours ago. It is marked urgent."

My stomach clenches, and I tear open the envelope. Thankfully, the telegram isn't bad news from Franklin or the White House staff or the children. To my surprise, it is from Mr. Randolph and Mary. They are quite concerned. The draft of the executive order has been languishing on Franklin's desk for weeks and his office is ignoring their repeated efforts to contact him. What happens if the date for the march arrives without him signing it? Or if the terms of the executive order are so whittled down by the military men that it is stripped of all power?

How could Franklin let it come to this? Even though I try my darnedest not to be irritated, I am livid that I have to deal with this from afar, particularly since we have no electricity in the house and no telephone.

"I'll be back shortly," I call out to Tommy and Mr. Lash, waving off the efforts of the security detail to accompany me. I need the walk to clear my thoughts and defuse my fury.

I march the half mile to the home of Mrs. Mitchell, the island's lone telegrapher, who also happens to have one of the only telephones. My anger fades by the time I arrive, replaced by determination. Mrs. Mitchell greets me with no more than raised eyebrows, in typically stoic Canadian fashion. She follows my instruction to telegraph Franklin and then set up a call with him. Knowing from experience that this might take some time, I wait on the front stoop of her small cottage and allow the refreshing breeze to dry the perspiration on my forehead.

Fifteen minutes, then thirty, pass before Mrs. Mitchell finally fetches me. "How's the old stomping ground looking?" Franklin asks, all jocularity, as if he doesn't suspect the reason for my call. This is the man who's able to detach himself from any emotionality when it suits him.

I play along. "The island is in fine form, and the house along with it. The hydrangeas are in full bloom, in fact."

"Lovely, just lovely. I long for that Canadian cool right about now."

"I bet. Why didn't you tell me about the invasion?" I say. There is only so long I can tolerate this small talk.

"It only happened yesterday, and you've been traveling. It's not as if it's easy to reach you in transit or on Campobello."

"Fair enough," I say. "Will the invasion be good or bad for us?"

"Probably good—divide and conquer and all that. I won't be making a statement about it just yet, although we're making plans to provide aid to Russia."

The German invasion of Russia does not seem to be weighing too heavily on him, either, so I will give him no slack. On to the real purpose of my call.

"Franklin, is it true that the draft executive order—the one related to Mr. Randolph and the march—is sitting on your desk? That all the terms have been reached and the lawyer's given it his blessing, but you still haven't signed it?"

The line is silent for so long that I wonder if I've lost the connection. Just as I'm about to call for Mrs. Mitchell, he says, "Yes, that's true."

"What is the reason for the delay? We are days away from the march. Mary and I have worked tirelessly to get it to this point. All it takes to forestall the protest is the signing of this order. Mr. Randolph even walked away from the demand to desegregate the military, so I cannot see what your objection might be. Even your military leaders are willing to agree." I pause for emphasis, then say, "Even Steve."

Franklin exhales with a deep, weary sound. For a moment, the immense weight he bears is visible to me, and I feel pity for my husband as he shoulders the rights of his citizens and quite possibly the future peace of our world. But this is the job, one he sought out for a third term.

"I know, Eleanor. It's just that it's an unprecedented step, and that alone gives me pause."

"It's an overdue step, as well as an unprecedented one," I say firmly.

"It should not give you pause that you are finally correcting the wrongs of your predecessors."

"All right, Eleanor, I hear you." He doesn't mask his irritation at my little diatribe. "Would you like me to read it to you before I sign it?"

"Yes, I would like that very much."

He clears his throat and, sounding very presidential, says, "Executive Order 8802. This order calls upon employers and labor unions alike to provide for the full and equitable participation of all workers in defense industries, without discrimination because of race, creed, color, or national origin." He continues on, detailing the creation of the Fair Employment Practices Committee, which will monitor compliance with the order and investigate complaints.

"It sounds perfect, Franklin." I want no more hemming and hawing over vagaries in language or the groundbreaking nature of this order. This moment must be seized. "Do you have your pen handy?"

"I do."

"No time like the present. I'd like nothing more than to hear the scratching of its tip on that paper," I say, and to his credit, he laughs.

A moment of silence passes, and then he announces, "The deed is done."

A rush of euphoria courses through me, banishing the sense of hopelessness that has been plaguing me of late. Franklin and I say our farewells and I begin the half-mile walk back to the house. I wish Mary was with me to celebrate. An idea occurs to me, and I race back to Mrs. Mitchell's house. Climbing the stoop once more, I call to her through the screen door.

"Can you send another telegram for me, Mrs. Mitchell? To a Mrs. Mary McLeod Bethune."

CHAPTER 62

ELEANOR

Washington, D.C.
December 8, 1941

Although Franklin may have his little superstitions—avoiding the number thirteen, for example—I've always believed myself impervious to such irrationalities. But it's frequently said that bad things happen in threes, and I am now inclined to believe in that particular superstition.

The first sad event was not entirely unexpected. After a summer at Campobello where she increasingly retired to her sitting room, my eighty-six-year-old mother-in-law returned to Hyde Park in September and immediately took to her bed with a disconcerting, mysterious illness. At my urging, Franklin raced by train to her side on September 6 in time to say farewell. At the moment of her death, the biggest tree on the Hyde Park estate—an enormous, ancient oak—crashed to the ground. No gale wind, no crack of lightning, and no raging storm caused it; the sky was a cloudless, azure blue and the sun shone brightly. Could this be the final, otherworldly last word uttered by strong-willed Sara? Her grandchildren certainly thought it possible, and it became a topic of much discussion at her funeral as we celebrated the formidable woman she'd been.

The second thing should have been anticipated, but I'd been denying it for years. My brother Hall passed away from cirrhosis of the liver. He'd been in the grip of alcohol for decades. Twice divorced with five children, he'd somehow managed to build a successful career as an electrical engineer, until the drink overtook him. For the past few years, he lived in a small house on the Hyde Park estate where we could keep an eye on him, but even still, he downed at least a quart of gin a day. Perhaps, like my father, he was too sensitive for this world. I felt like I lost a son rather than a brother.

Should I have expected that third bad thing after Hall's death? Certainly all Americans were consumed by anxiety; we hoped we could avoid another war, but we seemed to be in an inevitable march toward it. As assistant director for volunteer coordination in the Office of Civilian Defense—the first First Lady to ever have a role at a government agency—coordinating citizen-led protection of our country, I experienced this worry up close. Even so, when I heard the news about the bombing of Pearl Harbor, I was stunned and shaken to my core.

Over two thousand Americans were killed in the surprise Japanese attack, primarily military personnel but civilians as well. Nineteen ships were damaged or destroyed. I felt sick with fear over the fate of the American citizens—for what they'd already endured and the horrors to come.

But I cannot show that terror now as I stand by Franklin's side before an anxious Congress in the Capitol Building. I try to summon the calm demeanor I feigned last night during my previously scheduled regular radio address, when I expressed my faith in the American people and urged my listeners to rise above our collective fear.

Franklin gives me that imperceptible nod that signals his readiness to walk down the aisle. Squeezing his arm for luck, I leave him to James' care. I stand at the back of the chamber, watching my husband walk as best he can on the arm of our eldest, in his Marine captain uniform. Then I join former First Lady Mrs. Edith Wilson in the gallery to watch this historic moment.

Partisanship is forgotten, and thunderous applause greets Franklin as he approaches the Speaker's rostrum. He shakes the hands of the vice president and the Speaker of the House. I know the exact words he's about to say; I practiced them with him throughout the night. But hearing them said aloud before Congress and the biggest radio audience in history will be entirely different; I know this. It will make war real.

Franklin stares out at a sea of politicians, calm and authoritative, putting to good use that disconnected quality he can trot out at will. By contrast, my hands are sweaty, gripping the wooden arms of my chair in the gallery, but it isn't because I doubt his leadership. No, Franklin was born for this moment. It's simply that I know the world will change from this time forward.

I try not to think about Brud at sea on a destroyer; my children who live on the coast of the Pacific Ocean, so close to the Japanese; and Elliott about to take to the air. Mary stepped in this morning to lead the National Assembly of Women's Clubs, and I force myself *not* to consider her grandson, who is of age to serve and now can, thanks to our work with Executive Order 8802. Instead, I listen to Franklin say the words I know will reverberate throughout time: "Yesterday, December 7, 1941—a date which will live in infamy . . ."

CHAPTER 63

ELEANOR

Washington, D.C.
August 16, 1942

Someone is knocking. But this darkness has taken a deep, paralyzing hold on me. This isn't the first time that storm clouds—my Griselda moods, I call them—have taken over. They were frequent and black during the terrible days after I discovered Franklin's betrayal. But this is certainly the worst in recent memory.

I know I have no right to surrender to this bleakness. Our soldiers are fighting against the evils of Nazi Germany, Italy, and Japan. They face the horrors of war—death, violence, and fear—and my boys are among them. The final moments with James before he left to train with the Marine Raiders, a commando force, and then Elliott as he departed for the Army Air Corps replay over and over in my mind. Yet I can't seem to answer the calls to leave my bedroom. Even Hick— with whom I've had limited contact for months now—stopped outside my door to check on me. But no amount of begging or scolding on anyone's part has prompted me to move.

What happened to the vitality and fight I felt in the days leading up to and after Pearl Harbor? In September, I threw myself into the relentless work of the Office of Civil Defense, headed up by former New York City mayor Fiorello La Guardia. I traveled the country and spoke about what we must do to protect ourselves on the home front, preparing the people for things like air raids. I felt purposeful and productive. What I had not anticipated was the public backlash to an official appointment for the First Lady, and to spare the agency more criticism, I resigned in February.

After I stepped away, I realized that enterprise had been staving off despondency over the reality of the war. This was compounded by the shock of Franklin's Executive Order 9066, which authorized the immediate evacuation to inland relocation centers of anyone deemed a threat on the West Coast, especially the Japanese.

How could Franklin do this? He didn't even have the decency to tell me about it himself. Tommy was the one who had to inform me. He knew how much time I spent with our Japanese citizens in the fall of 1941 and right after Pearl Harbor. When I raised the blatantly racist order with Franklin, he refused to discuss it with me, forcing me to go underground with my complaints about the violation of basic rights and my efforts to help those unjustly affected by the paranoia about "fifth columnists" that is sweeping our nation.

But even my distress over Executive Order 9066 didn't prompt my plunge into despair right away. I was still producing My Day columns and giving my radio speeches. I was also helping find safe passage and homes for refugees and hosting European royal families, dignitaries, and military leaders—while always continuing to work on civil rights. No, the savagery with which all my efforts were received by many of our citizens and the press—and even Franklin's advisers and some friends—was the final straw that drove me to retreat into my bedroom. I have begun to feel as though I'm damned if I act according to my beliefs and damned if I don't.

The knocking continues. At first, I hear it only faintly and muffled, as if echoing down a long hallway. Bit by bit, it grows louder and louder, until I feel as though Tommy is pounding directly upon my forehead.

"Mrs. Roosevelt, are you in there? Are you quite all right?" She sounds desperate.

Only then do I reply, "Yes, Tommy?"

"Mrs. Bethune is here to see you," Tommy says through the door.

Mary? Do we have an appointment? When I last saw Tommy in my sitting room the day before yesterday, I asked her to clear my schedule for the foreseeable future. Loyal secretary that she is, she did exactly that, although I am sure she alerted my family.

"Shall I tell her to wait in the sitting room while you ready yourself?" she asks. I think about the assumption in Tommy's question—that I'm in any frame of mind to throw off these bedclothes and change out of the nightgown I've been wearing for two days.

"She can come in," I call out from my bed.

"In your bedroom? Now?" Tommy asks.

"Yes. If she wants to see me, this is where it will have to be," I answer resolutely.

Heeled footsteps clap outside my door. In a minute or two, my bedroom door opens with a creak, and in steps Mary, elegantly attired in a cool blue silk dress, with her silver-handled cane entering first. Pausing only for the briefest of seconds at the sight of me—hair disheveled, in my bed, and dressed only in a sleeveless white nightgown—she greets me as if this situation is perfectly ordinary. "Why, hello, Eleanor. It's a delight to see you, as always."

"You as well, Mary." It's a strangely formal exchange, given the circumstances.

Mary pulls my desk chair over to my bedside. She studies my face and the state of my hair. "My goodness, Eleanor, are you all right? The war affects each of us differently, and you know you can always speak frankly to me."

I glimpse such tenderness and concern in her warm brown eyes that it brings tears to my own eyes. When was the last time someone was actually worried about me? Not as the wife of the president, not as the liaison to a federal agency, not as the deliverer of speeches and articles, not as mother or grandmother, not as the person who can dole out important favors. Only as Eleanor.

Mary squeezes my hand. "Don't feel as though you have to answer me. I can see plain as day that a melancholy has taken hold of you. I am here to offer whatever support you need. Even if that means simply sitting quietly." She allows the room to settle into silence.

Melancholy. That's it exactly, I think. A deep melancholy at the state of the world and the futility of my efforts. No one else has ever identified it so precisely.

"How do you know what to call this?" After all, I haven't seen Mary for a few months, due to her illness and the constant travel we've both undertaken. We exchange regular letters, but our periodic congenial meetings of old have no place in this new world.

"I've experienced it enough times myself to recognize it," Mary answers.

"You?" I blurt out. "I've never seen you without a spring in your step and the energy to wage any battle you need to fight."

"I could say the same about you, Eleanor," she says, "until today. But that doesn't mean absorbing others' troubles and fighting for them doesn't take a toll. Especially when we're faced with such strident and merciless detractors in response." I know she's referring to all the hateful press about me—and her.

"You've had days like this?"

"Weeks, sometimes. And then I play Billie Holiday's 'Strange Fruit' over and over on the phonograph and surrender to the melancholy. But then something will happen, and I'll pick myself up again and get back into the struggle."

"What brings you low?" I ask.

"Disagreements with my son. Something that happens more and more these days, with our political differences—and my disapproval of some of his decisions. Recently we've been arguing because he's been canoodling with a woman in a house close to Bethune-Cookman's campus."

I nod. "I've probably had similar arguments with Anna over her divorce—and Elliott and James over theirs. I don't think Franklin and I have been good role models in the marital department."

"Through no fault of your own," Mary interjects, patting my hand. "Is that what's got you down now? Problems with your children?"

"Nothing so selfless. If I was to put a finger on it, I'd say it's all the negative press. That and exhaustion." I shake my head. "How indulgent this sounds in the face of what our boys are facing at war and what you face every day."

"The melancholy doesn't care if you're colored or white, at war here or abroad. It takes hold when *it* feels like it, not when we believe it's justified."

How sage, I think. Her insights move me, and for the first time in a long time, I don't feel so alone.

We smile at each other until the door shudders with a hard knock. Mary pushes herself to standing and says, "Let me deal with that."

From the voices in the hall, I can tell Tommy stands outside. China clinks on silver, and Mary carries in a tea tray with samples of our favorite treats from Mrs. Nesbitt's kitchen.

We don't talk as Mary pours us each a cupful of milky, sugary tea and serves herself a piece of gingerbread and me a slice of the angel food cake I adore. "A bolstering tea and a sweet treat are sometimes the first steps toward leaving my bed. Perhaps they'll be yours."

I do feel a bit better than I have for the past two days. Is it the visit or the tea and dessert? Perhaps it's the honest acknowledgment of my state. And the fact that Mary understands.

"I'm sorry to drag you all the way to the White House on this hot day for a meeting I don't even remember we scheduled. Or why," I say with an apologetic shake of my head.

Mary continues sipping her tea. "Oh, we didn't have an appointment."

"We didn't?"

"No. Miss Thompson called me at the town house and begged me to come over. She thought I might be able to help."

I sit back on my pillows. *How these two women have surprised me.* "Well, you have. As has she."

Mary simply nods and reaches for one of the cookies. "I'm glad."

We lapse into another comfortable silence. Suddenly a notion comes to me, the first such idea I've had over the past two days. "I should be working instead of languishing in this bed."

"Let's not even think about such things right now," she says in a soothing voice.

"You, of all people, are telling me to sit tight and not get back to work? The same woman who was dictating letters and making phone calls from her hospital bed a couple of months ago?"

She laughs. "You've got me there. Although that is not a course I'd recommend to anyone in need of rest and recuperation. I just felt that, if I stepped away from all my projects, they'd fall into further disarray than they already were."

"What makes you think this is any different? How will anything get done if we take our eyes off the goal? Has anyone else been able to make as many strides as we have in the realm of race relations?"

"No," she admits.

"Well then, do you mind helping me out of this bed? We've got work to do."

CHAPTER 64

MARY

Washington, D.C.
September 26, 1942

I pace in front of the taxicab door on the north side of the White House. Never have I come here in this manner. Someone has always been expecting me.

Time is a commodity that I value, so I only made this trip after great consideration. I hope Eleanor will understand that this was my only option. Although we've corresponded by regular letters and phone calls as usual since I helped coax her out of melancholy, this past week, that changed. I left three messages with Tommy, who politely gave me excuses for why Eleanor couldn't speak to me. Tommy's declaration that I couldn't see Eleanor until tomorrow prompted me to just hop in a cab and head to the White House anyway. This matter is too urgent for delay.

For a moment, I stop pacing. Even though it's only noon, I am weary. Sleep has evaded me for the last few weeks. And then yesterday, after the visit from the FBI, I couldn't rest all night.

"Mary." Eleanor is rushing toward me. She seems hurried but still pulls me into her arms. "I didn't expect to see you today."

"I know," I say. "And I'm terribly sorry to barge in like this."

"I have no doubt that, if you made this trip, it is something I must hear."

When she turns to lead me to her quarters, I almost have to trot to keep up as we stride through the corridors. Even though Eleanor is usually fast on her feet, I've never seen her move this quickly. By the time we are in her sitting room, I am almost gasping for air. I'm surprised Eleanor doesn't notice, but I can see that she's distracted as she speaks to Tommy softly, giving her instructions before we are left alone.

Finally, Eleanor sits beside me. "I'm so sorry to keep you waiting outside," she says. "There is so much going on right now, but I do like to greet you myself."

"I promise not to take up too much of your time. It's just that—"

Before I finish, there is a knock on the door, and Tommy peeks in. "I'm so sorry to disturb you, Mrs. Roosevelt, but the president said he cannot wait for that letter to Mrs. Churchill. It must go out within the next hour."

She nods to Tommy, who steps outside. Eleanor then turns to me. "Mary, I very much want to hear your news, but I'm afraid I have a crucial matter to tend to right now."

I stand to face Eleanor and tell myself to breathe slowly. "Eleanor—"

Before I can say more, she holds up her hands to stop me. "Please, Mary." Her tone is sharp. "Whatever news you have will have to wait. I'm sure anything happening with the Federal Council or the NYA will hold until tomorrow."

She turns away, but I stand strong. "What I have to talk to you about won't take too long, and it cannot wait. And I would appreciate you not pushing me aside as if I don't matter at all."

She whips around to face me. "How can you say such a thing to me?" she asks. "You certainly do matter; you know that. But right now, I'm asking for twenty-four hours, because we are at war and I have other urgent business—I cannot always only tend to your issues."

"My issues?" My head rears back. "I never knew that equality was *my* issue; I thought it was *all* of our issue. I thought you cared about the same causes that I do."

"I do," she says, her tone revealing the same frustration, impatience, and hurt I feel. "You know I do. We've been standing together for equality for years."

"Am I supposed to be grateful to you for that?" I blurt out without thinking.

She raises her hands in the air. "What is happening between us? I'm not asking for gratitude; I'm asking for your understanding, because today I am being pulled in the direction of important First Lady duties." Eleanor's eyes flash with anger.

In the passing seconds, I wonder, *What am I doing?* I can't allow the pressure I feel to impede our friendship. I collapse into one of the upholstered chairs and hold my face in my hands. "I am so sorry, Eleanor," I whisper, not able to even look at her. "I can't believe I barged in here today, all fight and fury, and spoke to you this way. You've been nothing but a friend and an ally for years."

Eleanor's shoulders relax, and she sits in the chair next to me. "I apologize, too, Mary. I certainly didn't mean to take out my frustration on you. It's just that I feel like I'm drowning in demands and pressure in my professional *and* personal lives." Her shoulders slump.

For a moment, I forget why I've even come. "What is it, Eleanor? What's going on with you?"

"Oh," she waves her hand, "it's nothing for you to fret about."

"I'm your friend and I can't help but be worried. Do you want to talk about it?"

She hesitates. "It's Franklin. The other day, out of the clear blue, he asked if I'd consider living together again as man and wife."

"Oh!" These are certainly not the words I expected to hear.

"It was such a shock," she continues, "and when I asked him what that would mean—aside from the obvious—he mentioned wanting me to stay home more and commit myself to our life together."

She peeks at me, waiting for my reaction. "My goodness. I can imagine your surprise," I say.

"It's a bizarre request, isn't it? Especially since he's never given me a hint of wanting something like this. Not since I found out about his affair. I suppose I should have been on the lookout for some sort of overture, given our changed circumstances. With his mother gone and his most trusted secretary ill lately, I think Franklin's been lonely, even though there are always women fluttering around him. He's a man who thrives on constant companionship, and I guess I became the prime candidate for the role, in these circumstances."

"So . . ."

She shakes her head. "I'm like an elephant, Mary. After listening to your experience forgiving your husband, I worked hard and chose to forgive Franklin. But I will never forget, and I will never go back to being the naive, trusting woman I was before his affair with Lucy. And in reality, Franklin doesn't want me back in his bed; Lucy is who he really wants." Her voice is so mournful. After all these years, she hasn't quite made peace with that, and my heart aches for the pain she still feels. "I didn't have the courage you had to walk away, Mary, but I do have the fortitude and presence of mind to stay true to who I am now. So"—she lifts her chin—"I declined Franklin's offer."

I squeeze her hand. This must have been overwhelming for her.

Suddenly she shakes her head. "Look at me," she says, as if she's just remembering why I'm here. "How could I prattle on about my personal matters when you came all the way to the White House to discuss something important?"

After hearing this, I don't want to be another burden. Maybe my situation *can* wait until tomorrow.

"Please, Mary," she says, sensing my hesitation. "I want to know. Whatever's important to you is important to me."

I nod. "I'm under investigation by the FBI for being a Communist."

"What?" Eleanor says with a gasp.

I continue, "I've been placed on a custodial detention list. I'm considered a potentially dangerous subversive, it seems."

She sputters for a moment, then says, "What are you talking about?"

"I probably should have told you this before."

"What? How long have you known?"

"I've known about the investigation for a few months. A couple of members of my staff at the NYA told me they'd been questioned by the FBI about me."

Eleanor squints as if she's trying to make sense of my words. "But why would they think you're dangerous?"

I shrug. "Because of meetings I've had with Communist and Socialist groups as part of my work. That's what they allege, anyway."

"Oh, Mary, they should have come and talked to me. You're no Communist or Socialist. You're a woman who will work with anyone who will help either Bethune-Cookman or the youth of this country."

"Thank God that's what everyone who was interviewed told them."

"Then perhaps the investigation is over. Maybe they got all the information they need to clear you and they've closed your file. So many of these so-called investigations have no basis in reality. They're just politically motivated. It's a damn witch hunt."

"For a few weeks, that's what I believed. But then yesterday, they came to speak with me."

Eleanor's eyes narrow. "The FBI came to your home?" Her voice is low. "Right here in Washington, D.C.?" When I nod, she stands as if she cannot sit. "No wonder you came to me today. Oh, Mary, I'm so sorry for my brusqueness with you. What did they say? Tell me everything." Eleanor is serious and intense now, and she begins pacing.

I begin with the moment the agents knocked at my town house door. Before the two white men dressed in dark suits identified themselves, I knew who they were and what their motives were.

Now that Russia is on the rise militarily, the fear of "fifth column"

Communists has taken hold of the American people. Alarm has spread throughout the country that America is being undermined from within. None of it makes sense, especially since Russia is among our allies in this war. But the most nonsensical piece is the idea that *I* could be on a list of dangerous Americans—or maybe even at the top of J. Edgar Hoover's infamous list.

"They asked about my connection to a list of organizations. I explained that my only affiliation with those groups was through their support of my college or community programs. I did my best to convince them that my *only* goal is the furtherance of racial equality."

"How long were they at your home?"

"For about an hour. But I didn't let them go until I explained that I had not one bone in my body nor thought in my mind about Communism. It is the antithesis of everything I believe, especially in its irreverence to the God I serve, Eleanor." My voice trembles as I speak. "How could anyone ever think that of me?"

Eleanor eases back down in the chair next to mine. "And that's everything?"

"Yes. I've been so worried, because I know the FBI plans to gather up everyone who's considered a danger to America. Who knows? I could find myself locked up somewhere!"

"I will never allow that to happen." She shakes her head. "Mary McLeod Bethune, a danger to America? How ridiculous! You are not going to be any such list. I will handle this." She pauses for a moment. "I wonder if Steve Woodburn is behind this."

"That's what I thought, but I believe it's actually that congressman from Texas."

"Oh, Martin Dies, the chairman of that committee investigating un-American activities. How can anyone take him seriously after he included Shirley Temple on the suspicious list a few years back? My goodness, she was only ten. And just like with Shirley Temple, no one will take him seriously about you."

"There's a big difference between me and Shirley Temple."

Eleanor gives me a long look and I know she understands. The color of Shirley's skin is enough to give her a pass, while my complexion makes me guilty of any crime someone wishes to accuse me of.

But Eleanor shakes her head. "The only real difference between you and Shirley Temple is your age. You are both Americans who love this country. And by the time I finish, everyone will understand that. Even if I have to speak to J. Edgar Hoover myself!"

CHAPTER 65

MARY

Washington, D.C.
February 18, 1943

It's been five months since my last visit, and during that time, there were so many days when I wondered if I'd ever return to the White House. Four months ago, I had another life-threatening attack, this time my asthma. I was compromised so severely, it was doubtful I'd ever reenter public life, let alone travel.

Only the dedication of my team of doctors, the tears and prayers of my son and grandson, and four months of actual, real rest fostered enough recovery for me to return on this day.

Tightening the fur collar around my neck, I take a few moments to study each detail of this beautiful building. Even though the temperature is biting, I don't feel cold. I only feel grateful. Perhaps it's my gratitude to be alive that warms me.

After a minute, I realize that Eleanor isn't coming to greet me. Not that I blame her. The burden of this war remains great, and Eleanor's presence on the world stage has been immense.

That little voice that's been poking at me over the last months nags again. *You've reached the end, Mary Jane. Your time in Washington has come to a close. Your friendship with Eleanor is over.*

Even though I'm able to ignore that voice on most days and I try to silence it now, it's hard to disregard. After all, the NYA has been defunded to the point of obsolescence, and the Federal Council has completely disbanded. I still have Bethune-Cookman and NCNW, but the truth is, my greatest professional accomplishments have come from my federal work.

So, if that time has ended, what place will I hold from this point forward? What and who will I be if I am not the First Lady of the Struggle?

After waving to Earl and the familiar faces of the other security guards, I make my way through the bustle of the White House hallways to Eleanor's quarters. I am barely inside the door of her sitting room when my friend leaps to her feet.

"Mary!" she exclaims, and races toward me. My grin is wide as she wraps me in a hug. "Can you forgive me for not greeting you at your cab? I was finishing a call."

"There is nothing to forgive," I say, releasing a deep breath at her reception.

I'm not surprised Eleanor is busy. What does astonish me is that she's found time to see me at all. While my life has been frozen, her life has moved on at lightning speed. Through her letters to me and newspaper accounts, I've been able to follow along with her successful trip to England, which included visits to the king and queen, the Churchills, and countless military bases; her ongoing national travel to raise awareness and support for women in the war effort; and many other crucial causes, especially equality.

With each of her trips and accomplishments, that little voice inside kept filling me with doubts, but as she leads me to the sofa, she seems just like herself. "Finally, we're able to get together. I'm so relieved you're healthy again."

"You've been a busy woman."

"Never too busy for my friends." She squeezes my hand. "You gave us quite the scare."

"I scared myself." I chuckle. "But I've had some time to rest, and I'm fully recovered."

Most of what I've said is true, though the coughing fits still come upon me often and my medication does not fully address that problem. However, I feel stronger than I have in a year.

"I hope you enjoyed those sweet treats I sent along from Mrs. Nesbitt," she says with a mischievous tone.

"I did. But honestly, what I appreciated most were your updates. Without you, I would have felt even more on the periphery of life."

"Oh, Mary, you don't know how relieved I am that you're well. So anything I did to speed that along was selfish. I needed my Mary back."

Her words make my heart sing.

We talk about the two Alberts—how they were attentive but strict taskmasters during my illness, especially over the Christmas holidays. Both my son and grandson were adamant about enforcing the doctor's orders that I not experience any stress. That meant not engaging with Eleanor's letters too much. It was hard not to ask the many follow-up questions I had, but I obeyed. We then discuss how Albert Jr. will be graduating from Morehouse in a few months and is thinking of enlisting. And I get updates about her family, particularly how her boys are faring in the war.

"I am so happy we were able to put all of that FBI nonsense behind us," she says.

"I was so grateful to receive your note. I can't imagine what you had to say or do to get the Justice Department to tell the FBI to end their formal investigation of me. Thank you so much, my friend."

As she pats my hand, I don't tell Eleanor that I suspect my file is not completely closed. Congressman Dies has continued his accusations against me. And whenever the FBI is asked about me, the answer continues to be that they cannot confirm or deny my status—which means that I am indeed still on their list.

"Now that you're back, are you willing and able to get to work? Because I've got a project for us," she says, her eyes shining.

If I were fifty pounds lighter and forty years younger, I would leap from my chair and dance a jig. Eleanor still sees us as a team.

"Are you kidding?" I say. "I've been waiting, especially after all that's happening—or not happening, I should say—with the NYA."

"I know," she says. "But as important as the NYA was, and all the work you did there, I have an idea for us that can be just as important." The pitch of her voice is high, which always happens when Eleanor is excited. "You remember when you put in motion Franklin's signing of that public law in 1939? That law that allowed for Air Corps training programs for Negroes, especially at colored colleges?"

"How could I forget?" I remember the day when Robert Weaver and Bill Hastie came to my hospital room and I tried to convince them of the significance of that law. Many colored colleges went on to use that law as a way to implement pilot training programs.

"I wasn't sure if you remembered. You've been the force behind so many laws and changes, it's possible to forget a few," she teases, making me feel as if no time at all has passed between us. "So, do you remember the 99th Pursuit Squadron at the Tuskegee Institute?"

I nod. "Yes, they were created right after Pearl Harbor. It was just one of our many training projects." While I will always look at the Tuskegee squadron as a success, like the other training projects it had its pitfalls.

The programs remain segregated, and the conditions at the Negro training sites are as poor as everywhere else in the military. Bill Hastie, as the aide to the secretary of war, has done all he can to improve the situation at Tuskegee, but to no avail. It's been frustrating, but I prefer to keep my focus on the fact that these programs allowed Negroes to be trained as pilots and that Tuskegee was one of the best.

"Well," Eleanor says, "I just received a letter from Tuskegee director Patterson informing me that no one will send the colored pilots into battle, even though they are ready and willing."

"What?" I thought she had good news for me. "We're at war! Why wouldn't the country want every able-bodied and well-trained man available?"

"Oh, Mary," Eleanor says, "we know why. Everything in this country is about race. Even during war."

"It's a shame, because those Tuskegee pilots are fully trained."

"They are beyond fully trained. They've been practicing and preparing for the better part of a year. These colored pilots may be the best-trained unit of pilots in America."

"And yet, because of the color of their skin . . ." I trail off.

"It's inexplicable to me and demoralizing to the men, but I believe we have a tool to change this . . ." Eleanor lets her words hang in the air. "Just a few months ago, Franklin signed a new executive order that allows colored men to register for the draft without *any* restrictions—including the Air Corps."

The opportunity here registers almost instantly. "So that executive order will get those young men out of Tuskegee and into the sky because the Air Corps can no longer ban them from flying based on race."

Eleanor gives me a toothy grin. "Exactly. But I think what we need to do first is draw attention to these Tuskegee pilots. If the country knows who these men are and the extensive nature of their training, then when people learn that their skills are not being utilized when they're needed the most, everyone in the country will clamor to get those young men into the air and in the war."

I feel a rush of energy and enthusiasm. Eleanor has filled me with purpose again. "I'd love to tackle this project with you."

She grins. "Even though the New Deal agencies have been eliminated and the Federal Council has dispersed, you and I can make this one big splash to show that transformation continues to be possible."

"I'd like nothing more."

Eleanor claps. "Perfect! So, fancy taking a trip with me to Tuskegee?"

"When should I pack my bag?"

CHAPTER 66

ELEANOR

Tuskegee, Alabama
March 12, 1943

We spill out of the car, laughing like two schoolgirls. The whole journey has been like this: unexpected humor and profound, serious exchanges in equal measure. *What a gift these two days of travel with Mary have been.* More than any marathon planning session in my White House sitting room or hastily grabbed conversations at the NCNW town house in between official engagements could ever be. We even managed to find levity in the chatter about *both* of us being Communists, a laughable proposition if ever there was one.

As I step onto the Tuskegee Institute campus, the air feels warm but refreshing. I crane my neck to glance at the sky. Not a single cloud.

"Clear enough day for you?" Mary asks as she sidles up to me. She knows just how important the weather is today.

"Clear as a bell, don't you think?" I reply, and we smile like naughty children. We are definitely up to a mischief of sorts, and I dressed for it in a sensible skirt and top and very sturdy oxford shoes. No fussy First Lady attire for me today.

After a lovely hour touring Tuskegee Institute, we are driven the short distance to the Tuskegee Army Air Field, where a much-beribboned white officer strides from an impressive white clapboard building to greet us.

"Mrs. Roosevelt, I apologize for my delay. We weren't expecting you for another thirty minutes," he says. "Ma'am, my name is Lieutenant Colonel Thompson, and it is my honor to escort you on the tour today."

I notice that he hasn't acknowledged Mary at my side. It's one thing to ignore Earl and my security detail—they're meant to be invisible—but Mary?

"Lieutenant Colonel Thompson, this is my friend Mrs. Mary McLeod Bethune. She serves in President Roosevelt's cabinet, among her many accomplishments."

Thompson's mouth forms an almost comical circle, but I would never be lighthearted with this man. And anyway, Mary and I are here on serious business, to accomplish something very specific. Something that's been long in coming.

I keep my eyes fixed on him until he greets Mary properly, and then we set off. I keep my pace slow to accommodate Mary—she claims to be fully healed, but I see the effect exertion has on her. Earl nearly bumps into us; he's used to my brisk clip.

The Tuskegee Army Air Field is a tidy if hastily assembled affair, and once we round the barracks, mess hall, and periphery of the airfields, we arrive in the central quadrangle to find rows of uniformed men. The sight of these sharply dressed, perfectly assembled colored pilots nearly moves me to tears. Glancing at Mary, I see that the same is true for her. I'm directed to the podium, where I give a brief but hopefully inspiring speech to these brave young men.

After I finish, I gesture to Mary. We purposely left Mary's talk off the formal agenda. Probably under orders, Thompson moves to intercede by trying to stand between Mary and the microphone. But I motion toward the podium, and Thompson steps back. When she speaks about the uplifting, crucial role these men have and will play—using that powerful, persuasive voice of hers—tears roll down my cheeks, and I don't wipe them away.

Afterward, Mary and I move through the crowd, shaking the hand of every single soldier. I imagine Thompson finds the sight of a white woman shaking a colored man's hand unnerving. As we reach the final row of cadets, Thompson—who has been behind us—says, "I'd be happy to give you a tour of our planes if you like."

"Actually, Lieutenant Colonel Thompson," I say, turning to face him, "I would like to meet the renowned chief flight instructor Charles Anderson and have *him* give us the tour of the fighter planes."

Thompson recoils as if I asked him the unthinkable. But I have no intention of allowing this man to show me the planes and describe the training when Chief Flight Instructor Anderson is nearby.

I've been yearning to meet the famous pilot, already well-known before the war as the first Negro to earn a commercial pilot's license. He was specifically recruited to develop the Tuskegee pilot training program. I also learned that this tenacious young man actually had to scrimp to buy his own airplane because no one would allow a Negro in his plane so he could be taught to fly.

"You want to meet Chief?"

"I want to meet Chief Flight Instructor Charles Anderson, if that's who you mean," I answer.

"I'll endeavor to locate him for you, ma'am," he replies, clearly unhappy with this assignment but unable to refuse the First Lady.

"Thompson sure didn't like that," Mary whispers to me.

I grin. "Sometimes it is wonderful to be the First Lady."

Mary grins back at me.

A few minutes later, an attractive, uniformed colored man strides toward us, with Thompson lagging behind, a petulant expression on his face. "Mrs. Roosevelt, it is an honor to meet you. I am Chief Flight Instructor Charles Anderson, and I understand you've requested to see me," he says, awkwardly bowing toward me and then Mary. "And it's an honor to meet you as well, Mrs. Bethune. My mother has followed your work her whole life."

Here is the respect Mary deserves. And I don't have to facilitate it; instead it's offered freely and sincerely.

"That's a lovely compliment, son. We've been following you as well and are very impressed," Mary says, taking the lead. "We thought you'd be the perfect person to guide us around the airfield and show us the planes."

"It would be a privilege," he says, his round, appealing face lighting up with a wide smile.

With Earl, his security guards, and Thompson in our wake, we walk the short distance to the hangar with Mr. Anderson. As we amble there, we pepper him with questions about the pilot training, and he describes the intense program in which the trainees study meteorology, instruments, and navigation in a ground school. Only those cadets who thrive are transferred to the airfield to begin learning on the planes themselves.

"What a rigorous plan of study," I interject.

"Thank you, ma'am. We want our pilots to be the absolute best in the sky. And we need them to be if they'll ever be given leave to fight," he answers, his face somber now.

Quietly, I reply, "We are very aware of the inequities happening here at the Tuskegee Army Air Field—both the disparate treatment of the cadets and the resistance to launching an air squadron. That is precisely why we are here today."

"You are not here for a tour?" Confused, he scans my face, then Mary's.

"Ostensibly we are. But there is much more to it, as you'll see," I answer, keeping my pace steady.

We arrive at the hangar, and Mr. Anderson gives us an expert description of the various airplanes, including the impressive P-51

Mustangs. As we pause at a JP-3 Piper airplane situated in the front, most exposed section of the airfield, I see that a line of photographers has formed, white and colored faces among them. They are all women, those stalwart journalist friends of Hick's who have been part of my inner circle and women-only weekly press conferences, and they are the only ones I would trust for this day. I could not allow Steve Woodburn to get wind of our plan through *his* media connections or this grand effort would be over before it began.

Although Mr. Anderson looks at me quizzically at the sight of the journalists, it is Thompson who pushes to the front of our group and calls out, "What are you all doing here? I demand you leave immediately. If you don't do so of your own volition, I will provide armed escorts." The rage I saw in his eyes earlier can be heard in his tone now, and I guess the fury he feels with me is misdirected at the press.

I walk toward him. "You'll do no such thing, Lieutenant Colonel Thompson. These members of the press are here at my invitation and that of Mrs. Bethune."

Thompson sputters, "You can't—safety risk."

"Oh, I cleared it with President Roosevelt before I came. So indeed I can," I say, although I've done no such thing.

Having effectively silenced Thompson, I turn to Mr. Anderson. "Actually, the reason I've invited the press to the Tuskegee Army Air Field today is because I thought they might like to record this historic occasion."

"What would that be, Mrs. Roosevelt?" Thompson seethes.

Instead of answering him, I speak to Mr. Anderson. "Chief Flight Instructor Anderson, I am hoping that you'll take me for a spin in this JP-3 Piper airplane. I'm no expert, but it sure seems like a perfect day for flying."

Mr. Anderson freezes. Thompson stops dead in his tracks.

Before Mr. Anderson can answer, Thompson interjects, "No white woman has ever flown with a colored pilot before, and I cannot allow that first time to happen with the First Lady. Not on my watch."

I turn toward this odious man and, not bothering to mask the anger in my voice, I say, "I don't believe I asked you for permission, and I don't think I need it. In any event, Chief Flight Instructor Anderson is one of the most talented and experienced pilots in the country. Chief Flight Instructor Anderson, what say you?"

CHAPTER 67

MARY

Tuskegee, Alabama
March 12, 1943

The shell-shocked pilot stumbles over his words as he answers Eleanor's question. "M-Mrs. Roosevelt, I can think of no greater honor."

Eleanor smiles at the group and then turns to the press. "Then it's settled."

Finally, she faces me, her voice quieter. "Are you sure you don't want to take a flight as well? Imagine what a glorious message that would send to the world."

"Oh, how I wish I could. But you know these old lungs can't handle the altitude," I say. "At least, not on a plane like that."

Eleanor knows this. It's the reason we took the train to Alabama. Even then, I wasn't able to control my coughing fits. Eleanor has seen me struggle with breathing and even walking. For the first time in my life, my cane is no longer for show alone. So she understands. But I understand her question as well. Not only would this be quite a flight, but imagine what a photograph us on that plane would make.

After giving me a nod of appreciation, Eleanor turns to Chief Flight Instructor Anderson. "All righty, then, it looks like it'll be just you and me up there."

"Yes, Mrs. Roosevelt," the chief flight instructor says, his tone filled with wonder.

Eleanor asks him, "Do you mind if the press gets a picture of the two of us in the plane after we suit up for the flight?"

"Of course not," he exclaims.

I watch as a gaggle of instructors descend to prepare Eleanor. The air is suddenly charged with motion and purpose. The crew layers on a tanker jacket and coveralls over her sensible skirt, and then a helmet and goggles on her head. And I wonder: Can I go up there? Imagine what we could demonstrate to the world about our partnership and humanity and equality and our friendship. We'd be showing—not telling—the world that we are sisters.

My thought is only fleeting. I'm having enough trouble breathing with my feet firmly on the ground. I'd ruin everything if I had one of my coughing spells up there. So I stand to the side and watch my friend, beaming with pride as I think about what she's about to do.

Once she's outfitted, Eleanor reaches for me, and we walk arm in arm alongside Mr. Anderson. The press follows us, but then, at the edge of the plane, Eleanor holds up her hand, directing everyone to stand a few feet away.

With Mr. Anderson between us, Eleanor whispers, "I think we should tell you the reason Mrs. Bethune and I are here today. We want to help get the Tuskegee pilots where they belong—up in the air and into battle."

His eyes volley between Eleanor and me. "All this is to advocate for us heading into active duty?" His tone is incredulous.

"Yes," I say, "and it is our honor to assist you in this struggle." I give the two a final nod and then back away as they climb into the cockpit.

The reporters rush to the plane, each angling for the perfect shot. From her seat, Eleanor calls out to them, "Afternoon, ladies! Thanks for coming to Tuskegee Institute! I'll be taking a flight with the immensely talented Chief Flight Instructor Anderson at the helm to prove something once and for all. If it's safe for the First Lady to fly with a colored pilot, then it is safe for these expertly trained colored pilots to fight in the war. Let's get these men in the air!"

There are gasps of astonishment as camera bulbs flash, and reporters scratch away on their notepads. Glancing to my left, I cover my mouth with my hand to hide my laughter at the sight of Lieutenant Colonel Thompson, standing with his arms crossed and his face crimson. I remember his words—*No white woman has ever flown with a colored pilot before.* Well, that is changing today.

As Mr. Anderson brings the engine to life, its roar drowns out all the noise of the airfield. Right as the plane begins to taxi, Eleanor turns to the window, and I grin widely and wave. But then, as the aircraft moves farther away, tears pool in the corners of my eyes. I am overcome with emotion. Yes, I am thankful for the opportunities that will come for these well-trained pilots and others who follow. But the gratitude that fills me is beyond that. In just minutes, I will watch my friend take an unprecedented flight—for both of us.

We have accomplished so much together, but seeing Eleanor's transformation has been life-changing for me as well. We met when Eleanor was a shy politician's wife who believed her calling was to empower young girls through education. But she has grown into a woman of the world. She has had serious conversations with heads of state and held court with kings and queens. She has brawled with congressional leaders and has generated a meaningful, honest relationship with millions of Americans who depend on her practical, empathetic advice. She inspires and consoles them, just as she has done for me. Her mission and reach are now global. It has been a joy and an honor to be at her side.

As the JP-3 Piper airplane climbs, I shield my eyes from the sun, and I am overcome with the strangest feeling. It's as if I'm sitting in that aircraft with Eleanor—I can hear the engine's rumble; I can feel the vibration of the seat as the plane rises higher and higher. I close my eyes and imagine that Eleanor and I are ascending into the cloudless azure sky—because I know that only together do we soar.

EPILOGUE

San Francisco, California
June 25, 1945

ELEANOR

I hear a cane tapping on the marble floor outside the private box at the San Francisco Opera House. The distinctive sound of Mary's walking stick I would know anywhere, not to mention that Earl wouldn't allow anyone but her to approach. Leaping up from my upholstered crimson chair, I ready myself to surprise my dearest friend on this most auspicious day—the vote for the Charter of the United Nations.

As the door to the box creaks open, the tip of her cane enters first. The sight of that distinctive walnut and silver walking stick takes me back to Franklin's funeral, only two and a half months ago.

That afternoon, the sight of Mary's warm, caring expression as she stood in line with the mourners shattered my composure. For days, thousands had lined up to pay their respects to the man who had been their deep-voiced companion through the hungriest, bleakest days of the Depression and through the most violent, anxiety-producing years of war. But, this being the capital, some of those thousands held views that opposed Franklin's and may have dabbed their eyes while simultaneously praying that they could now turn back the clock of integration.

In hushed tones, I told Earl that I needed to excuse myself, and I retired with Mary to a small adjoining chamber. "You came," I cried, falling into her arms. The suppressed tears came fast and hot.

"Of course." I could feel her body shudder with her own grief and sobs. "I got on the train as soon as I heard. I need to pay my respects to President Roosevelt, of course, but mostly I want to be here for my friend."

"I knew Franklin wasn't perfectly well, but he seemed healthy enough. I mean, he'd just come back from negotiating the landscape of postwar Europe at the Yalta Conference. And he was working on his speech for the opening of the United Nations." I choked the words out. "It seems impossible that he's gone."

"It does, doesn't it?" Mary said through her tears.

In her soft embrace, I surrendered to my emotions for the first time that somber day. Somehow, her words seemed to be the only ones displaying concern for me, and they showed her comprehension of the full nature of my loss. With Franklin's death, I grieved not only over my husband and political partner of four decades but also for the girl I had been, for the love squandered and the marriage destroyed.

After a few minutes, I calmed my breathing and stepped away from her. "I have something for you."

"I hardly think this is the time for gifts, Eleanor," Mary said.

But the silver handle of the present was already in my hand. I passed the walnut and silver walking stick to her and said, "It's not from me; it's from Franklin. He specifically asked me to give it to you. He once told me that the two of you were the only ones who could fully appreciate the swagger of a cane; he thought this one would suit you especially."

Mary turned the cane around in wonder. Her eyes glistening with tears, she said, "I'll cherish it always."

My friend's face finally appears in the velvet-draped box. Her look of complete amazement is a delight, and I am happy I chose to surprise her here.

"Eleanor!" she exclaims. "Is that really you?"

"It is!"

"I thought you couldn't come," she says as she races to my side—as fast as Mary can race, that is. We hold each other close. "I cannot believe you are actually here. I haven't seen you since the—the—" She falters, not wanting to say "funeral." This is the first time I've ever seen Mary at a loss for words.

"How could I miss this historic occasion? Even if I have to hide in the shadows. Today, the delegates vote on the United Nations charter. Imagine," I say, and I lower my voice, "everything we've worked for in terms of equal rights—on a global scale. And here you are at the center of it all, acting as a special consultant to the American delegates and expanding your influence as you expand your belief that racism is a world problem." My cheeks ache—my smile is that wide. "I'm so proud of you."

MARY

"I only wish you could have been here these past two months," I say as I think of my work advising the American delegation on the human rights portion of the UN charter. "Maybe together we could have secured more concessions. Strides were made, but I'd hoped for more."

"It was too soon," Eleanor says.

My heart clenches for her loss. "I can only imagine."

"Mary, I think you misunderstand. It wasn't too soon for me. It was too soon for the American people to see the widow of their beloved president out of mourning and back at work. The conference started less than two weeks after his death, after all."

"You don't think *you* needed the time to mourn? You really feel like you could have plunged into the conference?"

"I miss Franklin, but it's complicated, as you know well. Further complicated by the fact that he was with Lucy Mercer when he died."

There is no way for me to hide my shock. As she continues, Eleanor struggles to keep her voice even and matter-of-fact, but I hear the quivering beneath.

"I was shattered when I got the report. How could he have continued to see her after his promise? How could he have summoned her during his final days and not me?" Her voice cracks with emotion.

"Oh, Eleanor, I may be sorrier for that than anything else." When I touch the padded shoulder of her black dress, she faces me, and I add, "I'm at a loss for words, other than to remind you that you only harm yourself by holding on to this."

"That advice, which you gave me too many years ago to count, has been reverberating in my mind since I learned she was with him in Warm Springs. And I've decided the best way to forgive Franklin is to finish the work for peace and equality he began with the Atlantic Charter, the Dumbarton Oaks proposals, and the Yalta Agreement—work that culminates here at the UN." She lifts her chin and squares her shoulders when she adds, "By pursuing the principles we shared, I can honor his memory and the person he wanted to be while trying to forgive the flawed man he actually was."

How Eleanor has grown, I think, and tell her so. "Now who's proud?"

Just then, the Opera House speaker makes a sound, and we turn toward the stage. The soaring, voluminous space is awash in gold—from its huge chandelier to the enormous, shimmering curtains framing the stage. Flags representing the participating countries are lined up at the back of the stage, the colors of the world. And the pale blue ceiling, like the sky, floats above it all.

"Please take your seats. We are about to undertake the vote for the Charter of the United Nations," a voice announces over the loudspeaker.

I am filled with so many emotions for what I am about to witness. With this international organization, Negroes in America will become aligned with the darker races of this world, and I pray that the power of those numbers will lead to the independence and freedom we all seek.

As the delegates begin to occupy the seats below, I take in the beautiful sight: the rainbow of shades representing the fifty-one nations. Men in suits sitting next to men in the traditional Arab dress of white robes. Mixed in is a smattering of women wearing suits with padded shoulders and nipped-in waists and elegant hats.

Eleanor reaches toward me, and as I link my hand with hers, I glance down. Memories rush through me of the first time our hands were clasped together that day in the Mayflower Hotel. That forbidden act came as naturally then as it does now, and so it should be: Negro and white together.

When I glance up, Eleanor's eyes are on our intertwined hands, and I imagine she has the same thoughts. Smiling, Eleanor says, "This is your moment."

I squeeze her hand and insist, "No, my friend. This moment is ours together."

HISTORICAL NOTE

The friendship of Mary McLeod Bethune and Eleanor Roosevelt was not an easy one to bring out from the shadows of history and into the light. We anticipated that might be the case when we decided to write a fictional account of their very real friendship. After all, their friendship was, for all intents and purposes, forbidden, and even the First Lady of the United States was not above the Jim Crow laws that ruled the land and dictated that the races should not mingle. But it is a friendship with a far-reaching, essential legacy, one we felt compelled to share.

So we searched for the ties between Mary and Eleanor in a variety of ways, particularly since, despite the fact that there are numerous books on the Roosevelts and Eleanor herself, very little has been written about her friendship with Mary. We visited Bethune-Cookman University, exploring Mary's school and home. There, we learned that Mary, in the later years of their friendship, had a special room for Eleanor—reserved for her many visits to her friend—where the two women giggled like schoolgirls together. We met with Mary's great-granddaughter and reviewed the self-published biography written by Albert Bethune, Jr. about his grandmother. Using a microfiche that had lain in a dusty corner for over twenty-five years, we sourced documents from all over the country and pored through archives of all sorts in an effort to locate the letters between Eleanor and Mary, and those from each of them to others, about their shared endeavors. We studied newspaper articles and accounts of their whereabouts and interactions, finding the "colored" newspapers like the *Pittsburgh Courier* to be valuable resources.

Then we filled in the gaps. In the areas where the record about Mary and Eleanor's connection was spotty or unclear or altogether missing, we extrapolated from our understanding of their characters and our own experiences. As a Black woman and a white woman with a very close friendship and a desire to make positive change in the world, we've had honest, challenging conversations that we imagined Mary and Eleanor might have shared as well. And so we included them.

We also had to guess where Mary and Eleanor would have met to develop their relationship and work on projects—not an easy task in an era of segregation. We orchestrated teas and desserts and meals in restaurants real and fictional—like the Mayflower Hotel or Marino's—even though we weren't certain they actually visited them. Although we had no proof it ever occurred, we arranged for Mary to sleep over at Val-Kill Cottage; it seemed logical, given that Eleanor had indeed stayed over at Mary's house on the Bethune-Cookman campus on several occasions. But the most imagined encounters took place at the Tuskegee Air Field and in San Francisco during the meetings on the United Nations charter. While those events did indeed occur, Mary did not accompany Eleanor to the Tuskegee Air Field, and Eleanor did not go to San Francisco to surprise Mary. We felt strongly, however, that they were together in spirit on those momentous occasions, and depicted them as such.

Sometimes we elaborated on or extrapolated from the historical record in order to throw certain qualities and issues into bold relief. This is certainly the case with regard to the following: exchanges between Eleanor and Franklin on charged topics, as well as the timing of certain of those discussions; the precise manner and time frame in which Mary and Eleanor became involved in certain undertakings; the ongoing nature of Earl Miller's role in Eleanor's security team during her White House years; elements of Eleanor's interactions with Marion Dickerman and Nancy Cook; the creation of and interactions with the Steve Woodburn character, who came to epitomize a political outlook and belief system that Mary and Eleanor came up against; aspects of Eleanor's relationship with Hick, including conversations and feelings; and details about Franklin's physical condition, especially how Eleanor felt about certain aspects of his limitations. We tried to portray Franklin's mobility in a historically accurate manner—occasionally using words like "cripple" or depicting the worries around public awareness of his disability, even when these terms and views were off-putting to us as modern people and readers— because of the importance to the story.

We undertook this extrapolation and occasional alteration especially with respect to Mary's story, as it's lesser known and we wanted to highlight key aspects of it. For example, although we suggest at the beginning of the book that Mary already had her honorary doctorate, she actually didn't receive her Doctor of Humanities degree from Rollins College until 1949; she was the first African American to receive one from a white Southern college. Why did we do this? We wanted to highlight not only her accomplishments right from the start, but also her humility in not wanting them referenced.

Other date changes were made for different reasons, to ensure that readers understood aspects of Mary outside her interactions with Eleanor. As one example, we wanted to ensure Mary arrived in the first scene from a European whirlwind tour, so we utilized the 1927 date for the trip, although there are some accounts that have Mary in Europe in 1920. As another, because we wanted to highlight the work that Mary did for the city of Daytona Beach with the mayor Edward Armstrong, we moved forward the date of his mayorship to 1929. Also,

Mary did indeed see her students turned.away from the Whites Only beach in Daytona, and in response secured a beach and an entire beachside housing development for Negroes. Although this occurred later—the beach opened in 1945—we wanted to show Mary's capacity to effectuate change against all odds. And while Dovey Johnson (later Dovey Johnson Roundtree) never worked for Mary in Washington, D.C., she did work for Mary at the NYA before Mary tapped her to become one of the first Black women for the Women's Army Auxiliary Corps officers' training, and we wanted to draw attention to the support between these important historical women.

With respect to other clarifications, most people think of the "Black Cabinet" as Mary McLeod Bethune and the African American men who were part of Franklin Roosevelt's cabinet. But they were actually the second "Black Cabinet." In fact, there were a number of African American federal appointees in President Theodore Roosevelt's cabinet, some thirty years before, who supported one another through all of the racial challenges they faced in the federal government. One of those men coined the term "Black Cabinet," though many of the other men were offended by the term "Black." That "Black Cabinet" didn't last beyond President Theodore Roosevelt. When Mary McLeod Bethune organized the African American men working in the FDR administration, once again they were called the "Black Cabinet." While there's no evidence of a similar discussion about the name being offensive, it's hard to believe that such a conversation didn't take place, as the terms "colored" and "Negro" were preferred at the time. It would be several decades before "Black" was considered an acceptable description.

We'd also like to explain the proper name of Mary's college. When our story opens, we describe it as Bethune-Cookman University. In fact, the school underwent several name changes before that became its official name. On October 3, 1904, Mary opened the Daytona Literary and Industrial Training School for Negro Girls, and then, in 1923, the school merged with Cookman Institute, which was in Jacksonville,

Florida. The school was then known as Daytona-Cookman Collegiate Institute. Several years later, in 1931, the school became accredited as a junior college and the name was once again changed, this time to reflect the leadership of Mary. It became known as Bethune-Cookman College and achieved University status in 2007.

We also want to take the opportunity to share more about Mary's life, one we feel should be as well known as that of her dear friend Eleanor. In fact, when she died in 1955, the *Christian Century* said Mary's life should be taught in school so every child could be inspired by her accomplishments. Schools haven't quite fulfilled that goal, but Mary has received recognition in recent years—like a National Women's Hall of Fame induction; a postage stamp in her honor; and, most importantly, her statue representing Florida in the U.S. Capitol's National Statuary Hall—and we hope this novel introduces more people to her astonishing life.

Mary was unbelievably productive, even beyond the accomplishments in the pages of *The First Ladies.* Leading an HBCU should have been all-encompassing, but apparently Mary was so involved with her students that they called her Ma Bethune. She was also a prolific writer who submitted articles and pieces to many newspapers and periodicals, and had regular columns. Many more organizations than the two highlighted in our book—the National Association of Colored Women's Clubs and the National Council of Negro Women—benefited from Mary's leadership, including the Southeastern Federation of Colored Women's Clubs; the United Negro College Fund; and her sorority, Delta Sigma Theta Sorority Inc. The list of businesses that Mary originated and ran was numerous—McLeod Hospital, an insurance company, Bethune Beach, a funeral home—as were her investments, like the one in the *Pittsburgh Courier.* During World War II, Mary was also a consultant to the U.S. Secretary of War, helping to identify and select Negro female candidates to become officers.

As we mention in *The First Ladies,* during Mary's European trip, she saw black roses in the gardens in Switzerland. While we have no proof that she was able to grow them in Florida, we believe that if she could grow them, she would have—because these rare blooms became, for her, an important symbol of diversity and the acceptance of individuality. We do know that she began referring to her students as her Black Roses. And her statue in the United States Capitol features Mary holding a black rose.

A year before Mary passed away, she wrote a beautiful piece of literature—her *Last Will and Testament*. This writing is based on Mary's philosophy of how we should live and how we should live to serve. While she said these words were a legacy she was leaving to her people, they read like a love letter, almost like a poetic prayer to all of America.

This letter contains eleven "tenets," which Mary hoped would not only inspire but would teach and guide us. She was an educator to the very end. Her *Last Will and Testament* closes with:

> If I have a legacy to leave my people, it is my philosophy of living and serving. As I face tomorrow, I am content, for I think I have spent my life well. I pray now that my philosophy may be helpful to those who share my vision of a world of Peace, Progress, Brotherhood and Love.

We hope you will have the opportunity to read Mary's *Last Will and Testament* in its entirety. It will provide not only more insight into this incredible woman but an even greater understanding of Eleanor and Mary's friendship and what these women hoped to achieve.

MARIE BENEDICT'S
AUTHOR'S NOTE

The Personal Librarian changed my life. I am not referring *only* to the immense privilege of sharing the life and legacy of the magnificent, inimitable Belle da Costa Greene with readers everywhere, although, of course, that has been an incredible journey. What I mean is that I've been personally transformed by the tremendous honor of becoming partners, then friends, and then ultimately sisters with my cowriter, Victoria Christopher Murray, as we navigated the challenging racial landscape of Belle's world. We had difficult, honest, and sometimes awkward conversations about the similarities and differences in our experiences as a white and a Black woman in America, and we forged the sort of unique and rare bond that we wish everyone could have. Thus we decided that our next book would not only approximate our experience but invite readers to share in it as well.

What would that next book look like? How could we bring readers into this tricky, fraught space in a way that linked rather than divided them? Were we too ambitious in attempting something so challenging, no matter its importance?

This was the focus of much discussion between us as we launched *The Personal Librarian* into the world, and we had the great fortune of hearing readers' reactions to Belle's story and to *us*. When we realized that readers from all sorts of backgrounds longed for the same sorts of discussions Victoria and I had and for the kind of connection we shared, we knew we had to proceed.

But a question remained. Which women from the past could best embody our experience and fully draw readers into the pages of our next book? We turned this conundrum round and round. There is no shortage of astonishing historical women who have addressed the sorts of issues Victoria and I routinely discussed as we wrote *The Personal Librarian* (and, to be honest, that we talk and Zoom and text about every day). But when we uncovered the largely unknown, very close friendship with the much-beloved (and occasionally reviled, especially in her day) First Lady, diplomat, and activist Eleanor Roosevelt and one of the most important civil rights leaders, Black educators, and governmental officials of her time, Mary McLeod Bethune (known as the "First Lady of the Struggle"), we knew that we had found our women. *Two* First Ladies.

Hand in hand, Victoria and I walked alongside Mary and Eleanor as they first met at a ladies' luncheon, a Black and a white woman, one deeply entrenched in the fight for civil rights and one just beginning her life's work as an activist. We followed them as their friendship grew, despite the fact that they became close in a time of segregation and struggled to even find places where they could share a cup of tea. We held our breath as they sometimes stumbled and had to undertake difficult, uncomfortable conversations to get to the other side, to a place of real intimacy and honesty. And we rejoiced as—behind the scenes, often in the shadows—they joined hands and leapt over the man-made barrier between Black and white people to fight for equality, helping to forge the very foundations of the civil rights movement.

While neither Victoria nor I would ever dare to compare ourselves to the esteemed Mary and Eleanor, certainly there are parallels between the evolution of the world-changing friendship in *The First Ladies* and the arc of our own close relationship. Writing about these brave visionaries and the challenges they faced invited us to go deeper in our discussions about race, thereby strengthening our friendship and, for me at least, inspiring me to take an even stronger stance against racism in my writing and in my everyday life. Those discussions also helped inform Mary and Eleanor's courageous conversations in *The First Ladies*. More than anything, we hope that you, reader, will be energized by the historic friendship of Mary McLeod Bethune and Eleanor Roosevelt and link hands with Victoria and me as we walk this path together, becoming closer in understanding and working toward a more equitable future.

VICTORIA CHRISTOPHER MURRAY'S AUTHOR'S NOTE

When Marie and I began writing *The First Ladies*, I knew what to expect. Not only had Marie and I known each other for more than two years, we'd cowritten *The Personal Librarian*, a novel that opened up a space for me to speak about race with a white woman (or with anyone) in a way I never had before. And writing *The Personal Librarian* in the summer of 2020, when issues of race were erupting all around us, we had conversations where we were angry but mostly sad. We were able to find moments of laughter, but often we shared tears. There was no way to have deep discussions of race, sharing about the lack of opportunity and equality, the mask that Black Americans have to wear every day, and the daily microaggressions that are so real but sometimes are imagined, and not be changed. Marie and I drew so close that we truly became sisters.

I was excited as we began to think about and discuss *The First Ladies*. Mary McLeod Bethune was a childhood hero of mine. (What eight-year-old wouldn't love a woman who had her own college? That meant that one day, I could have my own college, too!) And of course I knew about Eleanor Roosevelt, the outspoken First Lady who believed in equality for all citizens. What I didn't know about was the friendship between the two, so I was looking forward to exploring their bond—what drew them together and propelled their lifelong alliance.

Marie and I began working on the novel, and like I said, I knew what to expect.

Except, I did not.

Once again, writing a book with Marie was filled with so many aha! moments, so many new life lessons. As we began this second leg of our writing journey together, we were still touring and meeting with fans of *The Personal Librarian*. In every city, readers told us how touched they were by Belle da Costa Greene's story, but they were just as affected by our collaboration. Readers asked us all kinds of questions about how we came together, how we worked together. And most importantly, was it really possible to have this kind of close relationship with someone of a different race? Was it really possible for a Black woman and a white woman to have these deep, sometimes hard conversations that we described and still come away as sisters?

It was amazing to hear these same questions from Black and white readers. But what was even more inspiring was to see and hear the hunger in readers to have these kinds of conversations. "We want what you two have" were words we heard often.

All of this was in our minds when Marie and I sat down to write *The First Ladies*. We had done our research and knew the facts about this little-known but impactful friendship. However, now, because of the readers we'd met, we were even more motivated to capture the spirit of their bond. What were the emotional beats of their alliance? What did they talk about in private? How did they discuss race?

We wanted to portray Eleanor and Mary's interactions in a very real way and show how friendship would impact their discussions—how each felt safe to speak her mind, even though many of the conversations were challenging and often hurtful. Interestingly, these discussions in the book were some of the easiest parts to write because of the long talks Marie and I have had and continue to have.

I didn't think it was possible, but walking alongside Eleanor and Mary, Marie and I deepened our friendship. We were moved to talk about race and our beliefs more *personally* than ever before. In the past, our discussions often felt "global"; we were talking about *other* people. But with this book, we talked more about *us*. We spoke more about our individual thoughts and beliefs. Several times Marie and I were faced with situations where the two of us saw the same circumstances through completely different lenses. It made us confront our own differences, which was shocking but gave us both new understanding. I came to realize how Eleanor and Mary's lifelong friendship was in part sustained by continually pushing themselves to have these challenging, often eye-opening discussions.

Once again, at the end, we had a novel, but what I gleaned from this experience was so much bigger than a finished book. As we traveled through the pages of this novel, I began to understand the strength of Eleanor and Mary's friendship. At the core of any relationship is trust, and Eleanor and Mary had that. They trusted each other and felt free to share, to laugh, to cry . . . and sometimes even to get annoyed with each other. They were safe in each other's space—just like Marie and me.

My hope is that this story of Eleanor and Mary will provide everyone who is seeking this kind of friendship a safe place to begin. Eleanor and Mary started out as strangers, and Marie had no idea who I was when she first reached out to me. But both of these friendships were built through the willingness to talk, to listen, and to grow. This has been the greatest gift for me, and I hope that, through these pages, Marie and I can pass this gift to you.

MARIE BENEDICT'S ACKNOWLEDGMENTS

Envisioning the singular friendship of Mary McLeod Bethune and Eleanor Roosevelt was a rare, special, and challenging gift, one we hope touches the hearts and minds of our readers. It is an undertaking only possible with my partner-sister Victoria Christopher Murray at my side every step of the way, and I will be forever grateful for her generosity of spirit, brilliance, trust, and kindness.

My wondrous and ever-insightful agent, Laura Dail, helped shepherd this book into the world, and I am indebted to her unflagging support, as well as that of Katie Gisondi, who handles our translation rights. Immense thanks are also due to Kate Seaver, our lovely editor and executive editor for Berkley, who believed in the importance of Mary and Eleanor's friendship from the beginning and encouraged us to persevere in uncovering their crucial story.

We are so appreciative to *so many* incredible people at Berkley and Penguin Random House: the former CEO of Penguin Random House US, Madeline McIntosh; the president of Penguin Publishing Group, Allison Dobson; the president of Putnam, Dutton, and Berkley, Ivan Held; the senior vice president and publisher of Dutton and Berkley, Christine Ball; the vice president and editor in chief at Berkley, Claire

Zion; the vice president, deputy publisher, and director of marketing at Berkley, Jeanne-Marie Hudson; the vice president and publicity director at Berkley, Craig Burke; the senior vice president and executive creative director at Berkley, Anthony Ramondo; the senior designer for Berkley Art, Vikki Chu; the deputy director of marketing at Berkley, Jin Yu; marketing assistant at Berkley, Hillary Tacuri; marketing assistant at Berkley, Natalie Sellers; publicity manager at Berkley, Lauren Burnstein; publicity manager at Berkley, Danielle Keir; associate publicist at Berkley, Dache' Rogers; executive managing editor at Berkley, Christine Legon; associate director of art and design for PPG Interior Design, Kristin del Rosario; senior production manager for PPG, Joi Walker; associate director of production editorial for PPG, Michelle Kasper; production editor at Berkley, Lindsey Tulloch; and editorial assistant at Berkley, Amanda Maurer. We are also immensely grateful to senior vice president and group sales director Lauren Monaco, director of imprint sales Jen Trzaska, and the amazing Penguin Publishing Group sales team.

So many supportive family members and friends have advocated for this book and my mission in general, but it is Jim, Jack, and Ben who deserve the most thanks. Only with their championship, inspiration, and understanding would this novel be possible.

But we know that it is the readers, librarians, and booksellers who deserve our *utmost* appreciation.

VICTORIA CHRISTOPHER MURRAY'S ACKNOWLEDGMENTS

From the moment we began collaborating on *The Personal Librarian*, I knew I'd want to write another book with Marie Benedict, who, throughout this process, became more than just my friend; she became my sister. Marie has not only introduced me to but taught me about this genre of historical fiction that I now love so much. So my first words of gratitude must go to her. Thank you, Marie, for all of this!

I am surrounded by the best, starting with my agent, Liza Dawson, who for the last twelve years has guided my literary career. Thank you for seeing a vision for me beyond what I could have ever imagined.

We would have never been able to bring you Eleanor and Mary's story without our amazing executive editor, Kate Seaver. How many times did you read this manuscript? You never stop believing. Thank you for challenging us and for loving Eleanor and Mary as much as we do.

There is not enough gratitude in the world for the phenomenal team that we work with at Berkley and Penguin Random House. First, to the former CEO of Penguin Random House US, Madeline McIntosh (thank you for coming out to meet us!); the president of Penguin Publishing Group, Allison Dobson; the president of Putnam, Dutton, and Berkley,

Ivan Held; the senior vice president and publisher for Dutton, Putnam, and Berkley, Christine Ball; the editor in chief of Penguin and Berkley, Claire Zion; the vice president, associate publisher, and director of marketing of Berkley, Jeanne-Marie Hudson; the vice president and publicity director at Penguin Group, Craig Burke; the senior vice president and executive creative director at Penguin Random House, Anthony Ramondo; the senior designer for Berkley Art, Vikki Chu; deputy director of marketing at Berkley, Jin Yu; Christine Legon, executive managing editor for Berkley; senior publicist at Penguin Random House, Lauren Burnstein; publicity assistant at Berkley, Dache' Rogers; Berkley publicity manager Danielle Keir; Kristin del Rosario, associate director of art and design for PPG Interior Design; Lindsey Tulloch, production editor; Joi Walker, senior production manager; marketing assistant at Penguin Random House, Natalie Sellers; Hillary Tacuri, Berkley marketing assistant; associate directior of production editorial at Penguin Group, Michelle Kasper; and Berkley editorial assistant Amanda Maurer.

Then there are all the extraordinary people who make the magic happen in sales: the SVP and group sales director, Lauren Monaco; director of imprint sales, Jen Trzaska; and the entire Penguin Publishing Group sales team.

What can I say about everyone at Bethune-Cookman University who opened their doors and shared their knowledge of Mary with me? First, thank you to Dr. Lawrence Drake II, the interim president of Bethune-Cookman University, for suggesting that I visit the university and for making all the introductions. Tasha T. Lucas, the Dean of Libraries—the time you spent showing me around the university and Mary's home meant everything. So many of our discussions are inside this book. And finally to Mary McLeod Bethune's great granddaughter, Mrs. Patricia Bethune Pettus. Your insights were invaluable and your love for your great-grandmother shone through. Thank you to everyone at BCU.

Finally, I want to thank all of YOU who are outside the walls of our publishing house and agents' offices. Because without your never-ending support, Marie and I wouldn't be here. So thank you to the booksellers and the librarians who encourage people to read our novels and cheer us on from afar. Thank you to the many book clubs who gather to discuss our novels and these women who, we hope, are no longer lost in the folds of history. And to all the readers across the country who have embraced these stories, I wish I could thank each one of you personally. It is because of you that we do what we do.

The

FIRST
LADIES

Marie Benedict

AND

Victoria Christopher Murray

READERS GUIDE

DISCUSSION QUESTIONS

1. First Lady Eleanor Roosevelt is a well-known historical figure in America, but were you familiar with civil rights activist Mary McLeod Bethune before reading this book? Having finished *The First Ladies*, what are your views on her and her role in history? How might you rewrite her back into the narrative?

2. Eleanor and Mary were both so accomplished in their professional lives. What personality traits do you think helped them achieve this success?

3. Eleanor and Mary came from very different family backgrounds. How did their families and early experiences inform the women they became and the roles they chose to play in their communities?

4. At the outset of the book, Mary and Eleanor handle the women at the club luncheon very differently. How would you have reacted?

5. Eleanor and Mary became close friends at a time when Black and white women were not often publicly friends. Why do you think they became such close friends? What inspired each of them to pursue the friendship? What interests and personality attributes drew them together?

6. Through the course of their friendship, Mary and Eleanor had challenging conversations about race, and they faced public and private opposition to their friendship. Why do you think Mary and Eleanor were able to have these difficult conversations and remain friends? How did they combat both the public and private opposition to their alliance?

7. How did Eleanor and Mary influence each other's lives? What did they learn from each other? How did they help each other achieve their dreams and goals?

8. How did Mary and Eleanor's friendship change over the course of the book? What factors influenced this transformation?

9. Eleanor and Mary both had husbands who were unfaithful to them. Each woman responded differently to her husband's infidelity. What life circumstances informed the decisions they made? What did you think of their choices?

10. Mary and Eleanor were continually pushing boundaries, challenging the status quo, and working together to bring about policy change. How did they use the media to help them? What did you think were the most effective ways they advocated for equality?

11. Sara Delano Roosevelt, Eleanor's mother-in-law, could be very critical of Eleanor, but she also supported Eleanor and Mary at crucial moments. What motivated her actions and opinions?

12. What did you think of Franklin Delano Roosevelt? In some instances, he was a great supporter Eleanor and Mary's work, but at other times, he refused to help them for political reasons. How did you feel about his decisions at various points in the book?

13. What did Mary's and Eleanor's relationships with their children and grandchildren illustrate about their characters and motivations?

14. What did you think about the way Mary addressed racism in the book? For example, her encounter with the woman in the clothing store or with the train conductor. How did her reaction to her grandson's terrible treatment at the beach strike you?

15. *The First Ladies* offers an up-close look at United States politics in the 1920s, '30s, and '40s. Do you feel like there are any parallels to US politics today? What has changed, and what felt familiar? Were you surprised by any of the depictions?

Photo by Anthony Musmanno

Marie Benedict is a lawyer with more than ten years of experience as a litigator. A graduate of Boston College and Boston University School of Law, she is the *New York Times* and *USA Today* bestselling author of *The Mitford Affair, Her Hidden Genius, The Mystery of Mrs. Christie, Lady Clementine, The Only Woman in the Room, Carnegie's Maid,* and *The Other Einstein.* All have been translated into multiple languages. She lives in Pittsburgh with her family.

VISIT MARIE BENEDICT ONLINE

AuthorMarieBenedict.com
⬤ AuthorMarieBenedict
⬤ AuthorMarieBenedict

Photo by Jason Frost Photography 2020

Victoria Christopher Murray is a *New York Times* and *USA Today* bestselling author with more than one million books in print. She has written more than thirty novels, including *Stand Your Ground,* a NAACP Image Award winner for Outstanding Literary Work (Fiction) and a *Library Journal* Best Book of the Year. She holds an MBA from the NYU Stern School of Business.

VISIT VICTORIA CHRISTOPHER MURRAY ONLINE

VictoriaChristopherMurray.com
⬤ VictoriaCMurray
⬤ VictoriaChristopherMurray
⬤ VictoriaECM